Edward Everett Hale, Lucretia Peabody Hale

The New Harry and Lucy

A Story of Boston in the Summer of 1891

Edward Everett Hale, Lucretia Peabody Hale

The New Harry and Lucy
A Story of Boston in the Summer of 1891

ISBN/EAN: 9783743401327

Manufactured in Europe, USA, Canada, Australia, Japa

Cover: Foto ©Andreas Hilbeck / pixelio.de

Manufactured and distributed by brebook publishing software (www.brebook.com)

Edward Everett Hale, Lucretia Peabody Hale

The New Harry and Lucy

THE

NEW HARRY AND LUCY

*A STORY OF BOSTON IN THE
SUMMER OF 1891*

BY

EDWARD E. HALE

AND

LUCRETIA P. HALE

BOSTON
ROBERTS BROTHERS
1892

𝔘niversity 𝔓ress:

JOHN WILSON AND SON, CAMBRIDGE.

PREFACE.

THE patent laws of the United States and of most other countries require that a person who offers an invention as new to the examiners in the Patent Office shall state first what he does not claim and then what he does claim. That is, the inventor is made to say : "I do not claim the invention of carrying passengers by steam ; that invention has been made already. I do claim that I have made such or such a change in the application of steam-power."

As we submit this book for the approval of the examining committee of that body of a million persons, more or less, who read books in America, it is our duty to make a similar announcement. It is perhaps called a *caveat*. First, then, as to what we do not claim. We do not claim that the title "Harry and Lucy" is new. Although most of the present generation have forgotten the fact, nevertheless it is true, as the bewildered parson said, that Miss Edgeworth used the name "Harry

and Lucy" as the title of one of her more successful books for children. This book began "Harry
was brother to Lucy, and Lucy was sister to
Harry;" and it described their training, apart
and together, until, at the end of it, they were
both well up in the methods then employed in
the steam-engine. Neither do we claim as our
own the union of two persons named "Sandford"
and "Merton" in the same book. That device
had already been attempted by an author named
Thomas Day, a friend, if anybody cares, of this
same Miss Edgeworth. Her father had undoubtedly conferred with Thomas Day on the subject
of "Sandford and Merton," and certain quotations
from the original "Sandford and Merton" will
be found in the original "Harry and Lucy."
From the ideas of Miss Edgeworth and Thomas
Day the authors of this book have profited, but
they disclaim any wish to include them under
the copyright of this volume, or to assume credit
for them in any other form. What we

Claim

is that, with the facility of a promptly printed
weekly newspaper, we have been able, in this story,
to relate the experiences of the hero and the heroine,
as those experiences passed. We have had the
advantage, which most novelists do not have, of
letting the plan of the book, so far as there is any,

develop itself from week to week, almost from hour to hour. The novelist is generally embarrassed because he knows at the beginning of his story how it is going to turn out. We did not suffer under such embarrassment, because when we began this story we did not know but that Boston might be burned up, and every Harry and Lucy in it, before the summer was over. Our hero and heroine, therefore, go on their way unconsciously from week to week. They record their own experiences, and the reader is therefore as much at a loss as they are themselves, as to the goal to which those experiences shall lead them.

We venture the farther remark, and we hope it does not savor of vanity, that whatever the reception which the critics of to-day may give to this book, it is a book of that class which, as Abraham Lincoln once said, " people who like that sort of book will read with satisfaction " two hundred years hence, if by good fortune a copy be preserved in the public library. The critical student of Anne Hutchinson or Thomas Dudley or John Winthrop to-day would be delighted if some boy or girl of 1635, 1636, and 1637 had condescended to leave for us any such statement of the methods of daily life in the peninsular then known as " Lost Town." To the young, it may be said that this is the Boston of to-day.

To the dull reader, supposing that there were such who bought books with the imprint of our publishers, it may be added that the several chapters of this book appeared in successive numbers of the BOSTON COMMONWEALTH, within a few days of the dates which appear in the several chapters. The book, therefore, is really a contemporaneous picture of the life of Boston in the summer and autumn of 1891.

EDWARD E. HALE.
LUCRETIA P. HALE.

ROXBURY, MASS.
Feb. 13, 1892.

NEW HARRY AND LUCY.

CHAPTER FIRST.

I.

HARRY TO HIS MOTHER.

BOSTON, June 2, 1891.

MY DEAR MOTHER, — When I wrote you my hasty cards last Sunday and the week before, I told you that there was no moment for writing. The fat was in the fire indeed; and I assure you that I have had to hop about, or to fly around, as you never saw a sausage in your frying-pan.

The first intimation of a change at Leeds came to us on Saturday morning, a week ago. Our Mr. Coddington came back from New York, where there had been a great meeting of the corporation. I do not think he had been snubbed, and yet I do not think he had had exactly his own way; but it was none of my business to ask. He sent for us at once, — me and Mr. Clarke, — and said that, though he did not know anything about it and must not tell any secrets, it was quite possible that the whole of the treasurer's office might be moved from Leeds to Boston. You see it is quite possible that Mr. Coddington himself will be chosen vice-president of the company, instead of being treasurer. In that case, there is a Boston man, whose name I must not mention to you, who will be chosen treasurer, and he will want to have the office in Boston, instead of having it at Leeds. This means that the whole kit of us — chief clerks, second clerks, little clerks, cashiers, typewriters, and stenographers, down to Mike who blacks the stove — will all have to move to Boston. And we shall have to move in pretty short metre too ; for all this is to be determined at the great stockholders' meeting, which will take place sometime as the summer goes by, I do not know just when.

Of course at the last moment they may tip out our whole crowd with proxies ; but I do not think they will. I have heard that proxy talk for a good many years, and have come to be confident.

So what this means to you and me is that I have been sent down here to see at what place the new man, whom I must not name, would like to have the office ; and to inquire, for the benefit of the others, about hiring rooms and houses, and how we are all to live. You will not be surprised to know that, on the whole, all the men like to go to Boston. We do not know anything about Boston in the office ; but we all pretend to, and there is hardly one of us who has not an old friend or a cousin here. I cannot help thinking myself that it will make my letters to you more interesting. You ought by this time to know every caterpillar on the sidewalk at Leeds, for I am sure I have written them all up for your benefit. ·

But this is simply to tell you that I am here. I do not call it a letter. I will try to write you a letter, however, before I go away.

II.

HIS MOTHER TO HARRY.

ATHERTON, June 4.

MY DEAR BOY, — It is wonderful that you should be in Boston. Do not forget your father's cousin, old Miss Tryphena Dexter. I have no idea where she lives; but she goes to Dr. Gordon's church, or did go there. It will please her more than I can tell for you to go and see her.

Thank you for writing never so little.

Your poor old MOTHER.

III.

HARRY TO HIS MOTHER.

BOSTON, June 10, 1891.

MY DEAR MOTHER, — I wrote you with a beastly pen, and ink that I had made myself by pouring water into an inkstand, a short letter, which I am afraid you could not read. Since I wrote that, I have seen some very good-natured people who print a newspaper here. They have agreed, for a consideration, to put all my letters to you in this nice type in which you will read this, — so that I shall not have to give you the new spectacles which I promised you. You must not be troubled about the letters being in print. I never tell you any lies, and nobody will know who it is. I do not see why anybody else should take the trouble to read the letters; but if they do they may, as far as I am concerned, and I do not think it will hurt them.

If the newspaper people are satisfied, that is all you and I need care for.

Dear mother, you know how I hate to write, and

by doing this I get the great advantage that I need write only to you, and do not have to get up a lot of scrub side-letters to send to my other correspondents. For all I have to do is to fold up one of these newspapers, and send it to Jerry, or to Mr. Wilder, or to Kansas City, and the thing is done. I am sure I would rather pay five cents for a good printed copy of my letter and a cent for postage than write another letter any day. This will show you that I feel prosperous, and that I am happy.

Now, as I said, I have a chance to tell you something about Boston. Who was it — you used to read me the verses — that said, when he went to Rome, he thought Rome was going to be the same place as his own village made bigger? I believe it was thought best to laugh at this old sachem, whoever he was; but I am rather in the mood to think that Boston is only Leeds under a magnifying-glass. Anyway, I could have sworn that the piece of steak they put on my plate this morning was the same piece I ate at Mrs. Williams's the morning I came away, if only I had not inwardly digested that beforehand. I wish I knew whether these funny oval bits of steak which they give you at such places were made of horse or ox; but I don't know.

I have been inquiring a good deal about boarding-places; but I will not bother you with all that. First of all, I desire to tell you about my visit to your old friend; only it turned out that she had hardly seen you, and was not your old friend at all. I went to Dr. Gordon the evening that I got your note. He was very civil and nice, but knew nothing about it. He looked on his indexes and in his visiting-list, and it was clear that he had never heard of this Tryphena Dexter. Indeed, as he said, Tryphena was not a name to forget. But then he said there was another

Dr. Gordon, and I went to him, a nice, cheerful man, whom I know I shall like; and I am rather glad that you gave me the introduction to both of them, for they were very cordial, and I felt as if I had made two friends in Boston. The new Dr. Gordon knew all about Tryphena Dexter, although she does not go to his church, and has not been there for twenty years. But she has near friends in a church which took off some members of their church when it was founded. So he sent me to one of their deacons, and he gave me Tryphena Dexter's address; and the next afternoon I went there.

I do not know how you thought she was living, or how anybody in Atherton thinks she is living, or whether anybody in Atherton cares anything about her. And I do not mean to say that the old lady is not very comfortable where she is; but I confess, as I went up three flights of stairs to find her, I hoped that her knees and legs were better than mine. However, when I came there, she was, as you say, immensely pleased to see me, and I now feel as if I had six friends in Boston. First, our treasurer, who is to be here; second, Mr. Henry Waldron Curtis, whose rooms we are or are not to occupy; third, Mr. Goodrich, the editor of "The Commonwealth;" fourth, Dr. Gordon No. 1; fifth, Dr. Gordon No. 2; and this makes six for Miss Tryphena Dexter. She is wise beyond account, she is very sententious, and I am quite clear that an occasional visit to her will give me a new view of life.

To tell you the truth, when you gave me her name, I supposed I was going to see one of the A 1 Boston ladies, who do not know of the existence of anything five miles out of this town; and the reason I followed her up so closely was that I thought she could tell me of some quiet place where they would like to have me come and board. But it is quite a different affair. I found a nice old lady, — for lady she is, — who is living along, I fancy, on some very small quarterly dividends of some stocks which have not panned out as well as could be wished, who is on the books of some needlewomen's society or other, and still · has eyesight enough to do firstrate needle-work, and earns a few dollars a week by doing so. She is what you and I would call very poor; but she does not think she is. Her position is so entirely better than that of the people around her that she considers herself to be quite a Lady Bountiful to them.

Fortunately for me, she was not at all deaf. You know I hate deaf people. I always think that they hear when they want to, and don't hear when they don't want to, and I am by no means sure that I am not right. But fortunately she was not deaf at all. It took me a good while to explain who I was and why I was here. But then she knew all about father and you, — though she did not seem to have a very distinct personal recollection of you, and I rather think her last memory of you was when you were held in your father's arms the day you were christened. All the same, she told me more genealogy than I have heard since I was born, and begged me to come again.

Of all this I must wait to tell you till I come home — only that she is funny beyond words. Her pride about Boston is such as I had not dreamed of. I should have thought she was a Champernoon and an Otis and a Winthrop all rolled into one. I do not know whether she thought it would wound me or not, but, with the greatest asperity, she said once or twice, "Country folks is fools." I hope that I rated as one born in cities from having lived in Leeds for the last two years. Certainly she had not any condescension toward me. On the other hand I thought she was rather flattered to have a fine young gentleman " waiting on her," as she said.

She is a sort of magistrate, I should think, of the whole court, which is a little narrow crack, of houses five stories high, where the sun never comes in. I could tell you the gossip of fifty or sixty families there, who, according to her, come up to be shrived and brought out of their scrapes. So you need not be afraid, my dear mother, that if I should be picked up by the police in the night, drunk in the gutter, or if should be suspected of stealing a pocket handkerchief at Hovey's, I should be found friendless in this great city. For my dear Miss Tryphena will appear, either at the police station or at the municipal court, and will pull me through. She was eager that I should understand how experienced she was in all city ways. The only mistake she confessed to was going up to the sixth story at Jordan and Marsh's in the "refrigerator," when she should have known that the stockings she wanted to buy were at the first story or the second. She was a little anxious to know what church I should attend, and offered me a seat with her. And when I told her that William was going to take me round to hear Mr. Haynes on Sunday morning, she expressed herself grimly as if only partly satisfied.

Mr. Haynes, you see, was in Tremont Temple, which is, I believe, the largest congregation in Boston, and he is now in the People's Church, which is only not so large, so that the fame of both these branches of the vine had come to Miss Tryphena's ears.

Briefly, my dear mother, I love her and she loves me, and I am very much obliged to you for making me go there.

Now let me tell you something that is even more interesting. It was clear enough yesterday that I was of no use to the firm, and I had the afternoon for myself. The day was as beautiful as a June day can be, and, at William's suggestion, I took it for a country spree. As far as I can see, Boston people have really a better command of country life, I will not say than you have in Atherton, but certainly than we had in Leeds. The country around Leeds is just as beautiful as the country around here, but at Leeds we do not have a train going somewhere every five minutes, or if there is no train, a steamboat. Anyway, I was told to go to Columbus Avenue, and take my ticket to Wellesley, and then to follow my hand, or, as it says in Rollo, do as the rest do. I hunted up George Car- ruthers, and made him go with me, but he did not know any more about the place than I did. Wellesley is, I should think, fifteen miles from Boston. When we left the cars, there was a bevy of girls, twenty or thirty I should think, who were on their way to Wellesley College; but with that, of course, we had nothing to do. I could not have got in if I had been a girl, because I could not pass the examinations; and I was not a girl. But the barge which carries girls to the college goes on, for any loafers like us, who want to see the Hunnewell grounds.

Now please to understand what the Hunnewell grounds are. This Mr. Hunnewell seems to be a friendly gentleman who wants to be of use to all the world. Anyway, he has laid out the most magnificent place I ever heard of or dreamed of, so far as I can see for the benefit of all mankind. There was a pretty porter's lodge at the entrance, but I saw no porter nor anybody else to hinder admission. I was told by a friendly man whom I met that anybody might go in and walk about and enjoy everything here, but that people might not carry in lunch baskets. I suppose Mr. Hunnewell has the same horror of orange peel and papers in his woods that I have of seeing the same things anywhere when I am out in the wilderness.

First of all, we came to the azalea tent. I never dreamed of such beauty of color, and was all the time wishing that you were there, you know so much more about these things than I do, and you would have known how to dilate with the right emotion. There were seats in the tent for anybody to sit in, and there were all sorts and conditions of men, nice little children, and one old fellow in a white necktie, who was, I thought, a doctor of divinity. Outside the tent were great tufts of native azaleas — or rather, azaleas which will grow in the open air. George said some of them were from the Himalayas, and I dare say they were. It occurs to me now that you may have seen a part of this collection when you went on to Philadelphia, for this very gentleman was at the pains to establish an azalea and rhododendron exhibition at the time of the Centennial.

Outside the tent we walked and walked. We came to an Italian garden, where they have those queer trimmed trees that you see pictures of in the books and that you read about in the old English novels. Below this is a great pond, which I believe is dignified by the name of Waban Lake, and on the other side we could see the girls' college, with their boats. In another place there is a rhododendron house, with as large variety of color and blossom as there is among the azaleas. And I am not sure but I was most pleased of all with the wealth of native wild flowers, — such things as I have read about in Gray and as I have heard you talk about, but as I never saw before. Don't you remember how you tried to make me find the elegant lady's slipper, the white and pink one, up in Vermont, and that I could not find it ? Here they were growing just as if they were at home.

In short, dear mother, it is a place that would drive you nearly crazy, so perhaps it is as well that you did not go. But I could not help thinking what a good fad it is for a man to have! One man has boats, one man has horses, and here is somebody who is willing to lay out two or three hundred acres — I do not know how many — in the most beautiful fashion, and just throw them open for the world to enjoy, so long as the world will enjoy them without doing them any harm. That is what your parson would call the twentieth century, I am sure.

As we came back another thing turned up which makes me more sure that Boston must be a comfortable place to live in than anything I had seen. The train stopped at a place called Riverside and took on a car that was waiting there. We had not good seats, so we went back. There were sixty or eighty people, some with great bunches of wild flowers, and all with some token that they had been in the country. George fell into talk with a. lady whom he knew, and it turned up that they had all been up to Riverside, where I had noticed great fleets of boats on both sides of the bridge, and these boats are for anybody who chooses to use them " to the extent of sixpence."

So, if you can get an afternoon off, you can ride up to Riverside in twenty minutes, hire a canoe or a boat or anything else you want, and go paddling or rowing up or down this pretty river. Judging from what we saw, plenty of people have found this out and availed themselves of it. One of the ladies said that the Waltham people do the same thing. That is the place where they make the watches. There are boat-houses there, and they come up the river, as people from Riverside go down.

Now all this is different, of course, from harnessing up the horse and riding over to Cat Head or to Purgatory, as we do at home. But it has its advantages, as you see. You make as big a party as you want, or as small. You go off at a minute's notice, and these people have to keep the boats waiting for you all the time. You do not find that the last rain has filled them full of water, you do not have to sponge them, and you do not have to go up to Mrs. Edwards's for the oars.

I must leave till my next letter the account of my boarding-place, which is on the whole so comfortable that I think I shall tell Mrs. Metcalf that I will engage rooms for the winter if we come. She is glad to know what the chances are, for at this season all her boarders go off into the country, and she, poor soul, is left lamenting; and even a half chance at a "regular" in the autumn is better than nothing. I have hardly made any acquaintance with the people who are there. Now I will only say that it seems to be a decent place, and that, if I have tolerable luck, I shall not be uncomfortable. You know perfectly well that I shall never be as comfortable anywhere as I am at home.

What will interest you more is to know about my experience at the People's Church. I had seen it as I passed by, but I need not say I was an entire stranger there. It stands just in the middle of Boston, though the Boston people do not know this; they think it is a good deal out of the way. But it is really on the corner of two of the principal streets, by which I mean the streets that most people pass through. It was built a few years ago by a sort of general contribution among the Methodists, that they might have a church for everybody to go to, — such people as me, for instance, — and it seems to me that I shall rather like it. This corner that I tell you of, of the two great streets, is interesting in a way. On one corner is a Presbyterian church. They told me it was Dr. Dunn's, — he is the famous Committee of One Hundred man, — but there is another name on the sign; for we have signs on the churches here, so that people need not hear a Baptist minister by mistake when they think they are hearing a Universalist. On another corner is our People's Church. On another is a great building going up for the Youth's Companion; so you can tell Tom that I can get him his numbers very early as I come out of church. It seems to me there ought to be a public building on the other corner, but if there is I have forgotten it. When you get into the church, it does not look like any church that I was ever in before; the seats are in semicircles, and rise exactly as they do at the theatre, and there is one great gallery. The windows are of stained glass, but the place is not inconveniently dark. There is a great large platform so that the speaker could walk about as much as he wanted to. But Mr. Haynes is not much that kind, and did not do a great deal in that way. I took some notes of the sermon, which perhaps I will write out for you some day, but just now I will only say that the whole thing was cheerful, everybody was cordial, and I was very glad I was there.

In the afternoon Carruthers had had enough church-going. But I went to hear the new Bishop. You know you always said we should not go to church to hear preaching, but to worship God. I was not punished, however. Mr. Brooks did not preach, but a nice, manly fellow named Roberts did. I should be glad to see and hear more of him. The church is all you said.

On the whole, dear mother, I am quite clear that I shall not find the time hang heavy in Boston. I do not want you to feel that I am in the midst of lions and tigers, or serpents and scorpions. The people are

very much like the people that you and I are used to.
They do put their heads forward in the streets a little
more than I think is good for them. They are all in
a terrible hurry for fear they should miss their trains.
There is a slight expression of anxiety on their faces
when you stop them to ask the way, as if they were
afraid they might lose some important appointment.
But these are mere tricks of manner, and I shall soon
get used to them. On the other hand, they are perfectly cordial to strangers, they are entirely satisfied
with the place they live in, and if they resent a little
the intimation that there is any other place in the
world, that is much the same as you find anywhere.
I know a man in Leeds who is sure that Leeds is the
hub of the universe, and I think you may recollect
one or two of our neighbors who think the same thing
of Atherton.

CHAPTER SECOND.

IV.

LUCY TO KATE.

Boston, June 20, 1891.

My dear Kate, — I do not see how you could have expected any letter from me before now, as you sent me no mention of your whereabouts, and you gave me no address; you only told me you were not going to stay at Denver.   However, I will confess that I have not had a minute's time to write.   How could I find it, in my first week in Boston ?   So I contented myself with sending you that message by Caroline, trusting that she will have told you how we all met at the Graduating Exercises, and how she carried me all over the Technology Building.   But that was on Tuesday, and, my dear, on Thursday I was to present myself for "registration" and the entrance examinations for the University!   So you can imagine that I did not really have my senses, that day, nor the next, nor all that week, indeed.

And perhaps Carrie told you how I was staying at Aunt Martha's, and how kind they all are to me. You know she is not really my aunt, but an old friend of my mother's; and they are so hospitable, and would like to have me stay on with them next winter and all through my University work, so they say. But my family don't like the idea, and I don't, of my being dependent upon them.   Besides, they always have their house full anyhow, and perhaps Jane comes on from the West next winter, with all her

children; but they all say they would find room for me.
There is so much going on in the house, however,
that it is quite bewildering, — everybody says this is
the Boston way, — and I am afraid I should not easily
find time for study, so I resist all entreaties to stay.
But it has been very good here for these few weeks;
only I am sure it is not a picture of *my* Boston as
it is to be.

I hope it is not! It is all quite too confusing. Yes,
Graduating Exercises at the Technology Tuesday af-
ternoon, and Boston University Graduating Exercises
Wednesday afternoon, my examinations Thursday.

I ought to go back and talk more about Tuesday.
I got in late, but succeeded in joining Carrie and the
others; and how we talked over last summer, and
of how little we expected then all to meet here in
Boston! But I determined to write you about a
lovely dress a girl had on, who sat near me, because
she reminded me of you; and it was so sweet, the
dress, a lilac, soft material, that would be so becoming to you, — some kind of woollen; I wished I could
ask her for a pattern! Plaited ruffles up from the
waist, and round the neck; and such a pretty hat!
and fan with lilac flowers on it; gray gloves fitting
perfect! Can't you see her?

Aunt Martha wanted me to go that afternoon to
the Tremont Temple to see the exhibition of the
Blind Institution. It was so touching and lovely
as she told about it, — and the chance to see Helen
Keller! Just think of her describing scenes in
geography, and of her wondering "what Romulus
would say if he came back to Rome to-day!" Well,
one can't do all things; and this would always be the
way if I stayed on in this house, I should have so
many things distracting me I should be in a flutter
of excitement as to which I ought to do. You see

I can't help going over the pros and cons with you; for, besides my examinations, what I came up to Boston for was to plan out my next winter's life, — a very sober one, as I laid it out on a very economical plan; but I won't discuss it now.

Wednesday afternoon, the Graduating Exercises of "my" Boston University; and what do you think, that evening Cousin Rupert insisted upon my going with him to the theatre! In the midst of it all, with my examinations hanging over me for the next day!

I had planned doing a little studying that evening in a little room that opens out of the library here, so quiet, and where Aunt Martha said I might have my books all to myself.

Of course, it was foolish to think I could do anything more with my preparation for the next day's work; but I did want to look at my Algebra, and I thought it would calm me to read a little Cicero!

But Aunt Martha and all of them insisted I had better join the theatre party; and oh, it was lovely, — Shakspeare, my dear! — "Love's Labor Lost;" and Cousin Rupert had so much to tell about its being one of Shakspeare's earliest plays, and how you could trace the characters that appear afterward in later plays, more complete; and it all seemed very instructive, and Miss Rehan was lovely, and Rosaline! Somehow, they did take me out of my day's experiences, and of my to-morrow's fears!

You see it had been rather a day! I started o t by myself at noon, and among other things mean to go into Houghton & Mifflin's, on Park Street, for a book. But the family here have so laughed at my mistake, for the street-car took me on, a street too far, and I got out at Houghton & Dutton's, — where they do sell books, but everything else too! I saw I had made some kind of mistake, and I was bewil-

"Happily, here is a policeman, to whom I now venture to trust myself."

PAGE 17.

dered by all the elevators, and the shop in itself as large as a city! So I tried to compose myself by getting a lunch in the upper story, coming down to buy some ruching and note-paper, and to find that they had not my book, and that I had only just time to get over to the Tremont Temple and the Graduation Exercises.

I must confess here that I am often terribly giddy at the crowds at the street crossings, and there is a fearful place at this corner of School Street. Happily, here is a policeman, to whom I now venture to trust myself, and who helps one across in safety. They do say that sometimes you do not see him, and that he has probably been killed in a collision the day before; but this may be an exaggeration, and I don't quite believe it.

Meanwhile, Wednesday afternoon, mamma appeared. She came down to the meeting of her beloved Society for Encouraging Studies at Home, to which I owe so much, for she learned there how important all such education is for women. So while I was struggling with my examinations, she was trying to calm her mind by listening to the interesting papers that were read there; and I do think that she was much encouraged in letting me go on and take an university course, by what Mrs. Richards said so forcibly as to the importance of a thorough education for a woman, and how much she could learn away from home that she could carry back to help in elevating her home.

I have mailed to you the pamphlet, "Ad Sollemnia Academica," to show you how interesting the exercises were of the graduates of the Boston University, and have marked for you what seemed to me most interesting. "Solemn," indeed, they all seemed to me, when I felt that this was indeed the "commence-

ment " of my university work, and all through my
racketty gay life since, some of the solemn words I
heard then hang over me, and seem to consecrate my
next year's life.

For a " racketty " life you will think I have had this
week, ending off in yesterday's Class Day at Cambridge; and beginning with " Float Day " at Wellesley!
You can imagine how the time is filled up, and how
my head is turned, — I, who never was out of Vermont
before, and had never been nearer a theatre than
Barnum's circus, on occasional hot days in summer, —
imagine me, going to see "Niobe " one night, "Monte
Cristo " with Salvini another, and evening concerts
at the Music Hall! Cousin Rupert insisted upon my
doing all these things, as the family here are all going
away next week, and he declares that I shall be left to
absolute solitude. He insists that there will not be
another human being remaining in Boston; you will
have opportunity to see if this is true, from my letters! Besides these evening excitements, the days
have been filled in.

Yes, my dear, I have been to the Cat show, mainly
on your account. Of course you would go if you were
here, and you remember that I admire cats seen in
the distance, though I do not love them crawling all
over me as you do! Now there was no danger of their
coming out of their cages, and I could venture. The
weather has been very trying for these poor beasts,
as well as for the humans; so, as I went in the middle
of a warm day, I found them very torpid. The
"Wideawakest" of all usually, as I was told (pronounced to me as if Italian, "Veedavarkest ") was the
"longest cat;" but even he was fast asleep, with his
head bent under his front paws. Still, the show is interesting, with two handsome, tawny-yellow cats, a
splendid Angora, and other choice specimens. I fell in

love with a fluffy, brown-feathered owl, whose expression was so wise that I don't wonder that Minerva should choose him for a constant companion; this owl is one of a "happy family," living with an excellent cat and other choice companions. The little monkey is ever interesting.

I wanted to give a seriousness to the week by going to the oration in honor of June 17, and I felt that I ought to go out to Bunker Hill that day of all days. But the family here insisted there would be too much of a crowd, and we must all go down the harbor in their yacht.

And such lovely drives have been interspersed. The surroundings of Boston are so much a part of Boston that I do think I am fortunate in seeing it all for the first time in June, as you see I do now. Just the drive to the Chestnut Hill Reservoir is perfect, and Saturday morning we had the beautiful view from the "Arboretum" when we slowly went up through the trees to a point where we could look off and see the water.

I am always complaining here, that we can't see more of the sea or even the harbor. You would never imagine that Boston is a sea-port, and I am disappointed that there is no place where I can go to see the great ships going out and coming in! The family all laugh at me for this desire of mine, and they are very good in taking me on drives to places where we can see the rare and distant view of the harbor.

As we drive luxuriously, I am constantly fancying how I shall, through the summer, go off by myself in a more simple manner, in open street cars, to all the lovely parks that are open to everybody. But Aunt Martha is very much afraid I shall come to grief by myself, and is giving me all kinds of warnings. The street cars are indeed very bewildering, and I must acknowledge that I have a facility for making mistakes.

I must tell the history of one of my last week's muddles, though it is a terrible confession. We were to go to lunch at Chestnut Hill, with a friend of Aunt Martha's, — my cousin Maria and I. She wanted to go down town first, and so would take the steam train at the station on Albany Street, and I was to meet her at the Columbus Avenue station farther up town. Cousin Rupert went with me to this station, and explained just what train I must take, telling me that I must be all ready for it on the platform as I should have to hurry into it, and he had to leave me.

He got the ticket-man to tell me just which train it would be, and he left me. The trains came whizzing along in either direction, stopping and going on, and I suppose I got bewildered, though I am very sure I took the "second" train as I was told. But I soon found out, after hurrying into the car and the train getting off, that the next stopping place was Newton, and that I was on the wrong track, as Chestnut Hill is off on a branch!

I asked all sorts of questions, and everybody got interested in me, and they all say now I kept my head pretty well; for when I found I really had missed the lunch at Chestnut Hill, with no hope of reaching it in time, I inquired about Auburndale, and found I could go on and be left there.

It did not happen to be their Commencement Day at Lasell, which came off a week ago, but there was Annie Davis on the platform, and she took me down to the Riverside, where was a canoe, and a friend of hers who took us out on the river, and then we had lunch, and then, only think of it! they drove me over to Chestnut Hill, where I had to apologize for my stupidity — a lovely place — and I am afraid they will never invite me again; how should they, when I had seemed so rude and impolite ?

But this letter must go, though I have not yet said a word to you about my future plans. I can only say, as if I were writing a serial novel : To be continued.

From yours,

LUCY.

CHAPTER THIRD.

V.

HARRY TO HIS MOTHER.

Boston, June 21, 1891.

My dear Mother, — It was very shabby in me to send you nothing but a postal-card last Sunday, after all my grand talk about long letters. But I am sorry to say these "Commonwealth" people have found up another person whose letters they are going to print, and they think they can only have mine once a fortnight; so that on the week between you will have to be satisfied with letters of the old sort. Naturally I shall write more now, and it may be that you will get all you can read. Who this other person is I do not know; but I see by the paper that she is a woman. It is cheaper for me to send you all the papers as I do, clubbing them with your beloved "Harper," than it would be for me to mail my separate copies; so you will have to read the woman's letters as well as mine. If you do not want to read them, you can use them to clean the flat-irons, or in winter to kindle the stove fire, or for both. I have already found it an immense convenience to be able to send my letters to the boys without writing them again. This is all by way of apology.

I am surprised that the Company keeps me here so long. It shows we are prosperous, does it not, that my salary should go on all the same as if I were sweating myself to death, with the thermometer at 150, in that old office at Leeds? If they don't care,

I don't care; and I hope I may be of some use to somebody, as you will see.

Of course I understand Boston better than the people do who have lived here fifty years. I am very much pleased to see that one of my remarks has been copied in the "Transcript," which is the paper that everybody reads and swears by. If you understood Boston as well as I do, you would know that the greatest occasion of the year is Class Day. The battle of Bunker Hill is a very great day. If you care anything about it, it is St. Botolph's Day, — the saint's-day of the man who gave the English Boston his name; but I believe nobody in the world knows this excepting me and the man who told me. I observed that there were no special ceremonies in the Catholic churches, and they will not know it themselves till they read this letter in "The Commonwealth." All the same, the forefathers, without knowing it, fought their battle on St. Botolph's Day, and so all parties in Boston had a holiday. For my part, I went fishing, and do not know what happened in town; but over in Charlestown they have a very funny celebration, which is a sort of carnival.

But I spoke of that merely by accident, because, though in the newspapers they pretend it is a great day, they do not really care anything about it at all. What they do care about is Class Day, which comes somewhere in the middle of June ; and to that all the young people go who can go. Now that there are two or three thousand students at Cambridge, it is pretty clear that, by hook or by crook, you can get tickets to something ; and if you have not any tickets, you can "run your face," — which is very much what I did, quite sure that something would happen to me before the day was done. Observe that Class Day this year came day before yesterday. There is some order of the planets, I do not know what, which settles it, and I think it always comes on Friday.

I suppose grand people go in carriages, but for my part the electric cars are generally good enough for me, and I have now learned how to take them. The rule they give to all strangers in Boston, who wish to learn their way, is to find out in what direction the place is, and then to take a street-car which goes the other way. This works generally very well, particularly because nobody knows how much he has gone astray, or if he does know, takes care not to tell. But since I have been here I have been in good hands, so that I believe I have made no mistake. George went with me, as I like to have him, and he made it, or they made it, some sort of a holiday at the bank, so that he might go.

· Cambridge is a pretty place, all overgrown with elm trees, and on Class Day it had the advantage of being more than reasonably cool. When I was there before it was so hot that the shoes were almost burnt off my feet, and the fellows say it can be awfully dusty. Carruthers says that the joke used to be that the people started a college there because nobody had taken up the land for farming, it being too sandy to grow even trees. Somehow or other, they have got some trees growing since, and the college grounds are very pretty. But Class Day involves a great deal more than the college grounds, for you might say that almost every large house which has a large garden around it had been retained by some of the fellows for the purposes of a spread. This year there are so many spreads that they began the night before, but that, I think, is an innovation.

We meant to do the thing brown, and we went bravely to the morning exercises. I say this, because the young people, in their dancing shoes and gay

dresses, are a little apt to reserve themselves for
the dancing of the afternoon, and not to come to
hear orations and poems. But in truth the whole
thing began with an oration and a poem, from which,
by a gradual evolution, has come the dancing, which
is now considered by some people the more important
of the two. Carruthers was as good as gold, as he
always is. We had no tickets to Sanders, as the
place is called, but we waited on the outside for the
procession. The procession means the whole senior
class, — in this case more than three hundred, — all in
swallow-tailed coats and new silk hats which looked
as if they had never been worn before. There was a
band, and they marched round the college yard and so
went into Memorial Hall, we tagging after them as
little boys do after a company of soldiers.

However, when we arrived at Memorial Hall, the
moment they had got in the door was shut in our
faces. We laughed, as did a company of other people
who were shut out in the same fashion. It was explained, however, that the door would be opened as
soon as the prayer was done. This was edifying to
me, because it showed how sacred and secret they
were, — that we were not good enough to pray with the
others or for them. However, this all proved to be a
mistake ; for when we came in the theatre, after all,
the prayer had not begun, and we prayed as well as
the rest.

You go in first to what is, I suppose, the proper
Memorial Hall. I did not stop to look at it then, because we were rushing to get the best seats. But in
fact there are tablets all around it, which tell the
names of the boys who died in the War. You know I
always say I am one of the children of the public, and
the powers which take care of them took care of me.
For somebody or other had a headache at the last

moment, and did not use her tickets, just in front of
the speakers. As we hustled in, Carruthers spoke to
one of the professors, who seemed to be in much the
same fix as we were, and he very kindly led us right
round to the place as if he knew all about it, so that
we were as well off as if we were the king and queen.
I observed that the real king and queen, President
Eliot and his wife, sat exactly in the middle, in front
of the speakers.

As I say, after we were well in, one of the professors came forward and offered prayer, and there was
music by a band who were in a gallery high up over
the platform, and then the speaking began. I thought
it more than fairly good. There was a great deal of
fun, which of course the class understood more than
anybody else did. The poem was in a good helter-
skelter, go-as-you-please sort of metre. The ivy oration was capitally well delivered, with hits right and
left, some at the government, some at the class, some
at the other classes, and most of all at Yale, which were
taken goodnaturedly, and by a good, quick audience.
It is always funny to see how the elect applaud first,
and then a second set of people, who have to think out
what the humor means, applaud afterwards. This was
so with this audience, just as much as with any other.

When I came out Carruthers introduced me to one
of his friends who is of this very graduating class, and
he took us around to his room, and here there was a
sandwich and a cup of coffee, and it made, I may as
well say once for all, a convenient resting-place in the
business of the day. This was not what is called a
spread precisely, but was a comfortable little lunch
for anybody who comes or goes, and such little lunches
materially facilitate, as you can understand, the business of, what is, on the whole, an open-air party.

After we had thus got a little ready for possible

fatigue, we three went round to the gymnasium. This is a handsome building, which one of the young men built, a few years ago, just after he graduated, and gave to the college.

When we came there the band was playing and people were already waltzing. But seated all around were nice-looking people, old and young, eating ice-creams and salads and other such things. And this, by the way, was going on at sixty or eighty places in different parts of Cambridge through the day, only you will understand that this meeting at the gymnasium was one of the largest of these.

Of course, if anybody felt an entire stranger on going, I did. But it is a free-and-easy place. I should think all the Cambridge ladies felt themselves rather bound to be hostesses there; indeed I do not know but what some of them were asked to be so by the gentlemen who gave out the invitations. Anyway, Carruthers and his friend introduced me to one or two nice girls. Carruthers's sister was one, a Miss Osborne was one, and a Miss Sanborn or Sanford was one; and I waltzed, — I dare not say as well as the best of them, but still I hope I did not disgrace Miss Lightfoot's teaching. I recollected the old rule that, whatever else was certain, it was absolutely certain that nobody was looking at me, and so I did not find myself frightened even in the midst of the grandees of the land. Carruthers pointed out some people whom I was glad to see. Howells was there, and his daughter was there, who wrote that nice little story in the Bazar that I sent you. A good many of the college professors were there. I saw Mr. McKenzie, whose son, by the way, was the chorister of the day. In short, it was really a very pretty party.

But it will never do for me to undertake to tell you of all the pretty girls I saw, nor how their hats were

trimmed. You must look in the Bazar or in Madame
Demorest, and guess it out as well as you can. Their
descriptions in general will be much better than mine
in particular. I went back from here for a little rest
and to one or two smaller spreads, which Carruthers
or his friend, or some of his friends invited me to.
And at half-past four, by great good luck, I found myself the possessor of a ticket to see the dancing around
the tree. This is what you and I have heard of, and
it is a very amusing business. It used to be a simple
frolic of a lot of seniors, holding hand in hand and
dancing around what was called Liberty Tree, I think.
But year by year it has grown more and more of a
ceremony, so that now a great theatre, you might call
it, is built up around the tree, as if it were a circus,
and all this is fenced in and kept by policemen that
nobody may get in who has no right there ; and as I
say, tickets are given for the seats, so that you know
in advance about where you will sit, and are sure of a
place.

Please observe that all day it had been cloudy, and
everybody had said, "What a pity!" and there was
great terror lest it should rain in the afternoon, because the newspapers had said "Showers." In point
of fact, it did not rain, but a stiff, sharp east fog came
in, with threat of rain all the time. In view of this,
awnings had been stretched above the seats, and nobody
would have got wet if it had rained.

The senior class, meanwhile, have retired to places
known to them, have taken off their dress-coats and
hats of which I told you, and have come in in the
most absurd costumes you can conceive. They are
dressed ostentatiously for frolic, some in real athletic
dresses, some in absurd dresses, — the great object, as
you will see, being to be ready to climb the tree-trunk
for the flowers which are nailed, oh, ever so high.

They marched round and sat down, and the other classes stood around them in a fixed order. They sang and they cheered the different officers of the college whom they like. They cheer the different classes, and so on, till, at a given signal, there is a regular dance in circles around the tree, and then a rush made at the tree, to secure as trophies the bunches of flowers which have been put in a ring high up, as I say, above the heads of everybody.

Now this Liberty Tree, if that is its name, is a large elm, more than a hundred years old; and you know one does not climb a tree like that by putting his arms around it, and "shinning" up, as we used to say. The only ladders, however, are ladders of living men; so that you see a group of fellows advance, close-shouldered, to the tree; you see two other fellows, lighter than they, run up on them and stand on their shoulders, and a third, the lightest of all, run up on them just as you have seen clowns do at a circus, and if he gets up he is able to handle the flowers. But meanwhile another group is hauling away upon the six lower fellows in this pyramid, and trying to pull them from their station, so that the climber shall be disconcerted as he gets up; and you can imagine what fun takes place. It is for this contest that they are dressed as they are. In some cases it did not make much difference how they were dressed, for they came out as naked above the waist as the day they were born. But in our recent enthusiasm for athletics we do not care a great deal about that. And the people who could see a boat's crew strip to the waist when the seniors row against the juniors need not be distressed if they happen to see a man's shirt ripped open so that the color of his skin is visible. Of course there was great cheering, laughing, waving of handkerchiefs, and the rest; and

after all this, the last flower is pulled down. Everybody has some of the flowers; everybody presents
them to the particular lady who has witnessed his
struggles with most interest from the tournament
seats, and they give something to talk about in the
evening's dancing.

I have written all this at length, because I told
the girls that they should hear all about Class Day
from me and should know what to wear [if they come
down next year. It is a first-rate frolic, and I know
they will like to come.

But now I must tell you about to-day. You must
not think Sundays are dissipated, but I will own they
are very different from any Sundays I have known
about before. Our minister, Mr. Haynes, preached
about tenement-houses, and I wish you could have
heard the sermon. I have not seen much of them
here, but I can understand what I read in your " Lend
a Hand " last summer, that there is no solution of the
tenement-house problem; that the only solution is to .
be done with them and not to have any more of them.
I thought so all the more after I had heard Mr. Haynes.
I really want you to spend Sunday with me some time,
after we get established, — Mrs. Metcalf will have a
room for you any day. I want you to come, if it is
only to hear him, and the first-rate singing that we
have at our church. But I will tell you more about
that another time.

In the afternoon I went down with Carruthers to
see and hear the Salvation Army. Ever since we
read Booth's book, it has seemed to me absurd to
have such people right under our lee, as the sailors
say, and to know nothing about them. I knew there
were " posts," as they say, here. You see the signs
and flags on different buildings, and last Sunday I
fell afoul of one of their speakers on the Common.

Carruthers said we should have to pay to go in, and I had my ten cents ready ; but it was no such thing, though he says he has paid before. It was at the top of a big building in Washington Street, over a market ; I saw the sign Friday, and I made Carruthers go there to-day.

He had made fun about paying to go in ; but I told him I liked that way, — to pay as you go. Anyway, I know that these people are poor people, and that there would be no thousand-dollar boxes or pews. Do you not remember what that New York man told us, — that his box at church cost him more 'than his pew at the opera ? but here there was neither pew nor contribution.

It was a great square hall, not high, but high enough, with windows on two sides. The front was partitioned off, and it turned out afterward that the officers and their wives and children lived there. I liked that ; it seemed business-like, and as if they were not ashamed of their business. Across the hall were lines of wooden chairs, and the whole front was taken up by a long platform, as if there was to be an exhibition at an academy. This was divided like any other stage from our part. There were two or three flags, long pennons of red, white, and blue, and blue and white stars, and an archway with the motto, " Holiness to the Lord." On this platform were the officers and people with horns and other military instruments. They were in some sort of simple uniform, — that is, the men were ; the women, I think, had only flat poke bonnets on. On one side there was a man with a big drum.

Now I have told you all the things that made it different from any common conference meeting, unless perhaps it was the looks of the people. The hall was one-third full, perhaps. There were a few chil-

dren, and they seemed to be amused and interested
as they would not be at a common meeting. They
talked a little, — not much, — and nobody minded.
People came in, just as we did, and went out, just as
they chose, without inquiring about times and sea-
sons. The speaking and singing went on all the time,
quiet and loud, good and bad, much as it is in all
meetings. The captain's wife read from one of the
epistles, and started two or three hymns, which all
the people joined in singing. Think of the simplicity
of a service where some one says, " Here are a few
more copies of 'The War-Cry.' Does no one want
them?" Then a "lady-captain" takes them down,
and sells them at five cents each, and then all sing
the hymn which is in the. paper, say on page four.

Dear mother, you would not have been shocked in
the least by the ways of these nice people. I think
you would have liked it, as I certainly did. As for
drums and cornets, I do not know why they are not
as much like harps and psalteries as are the trumpet-
stops of organs. I believe the bit of ritual I liked
best was a hole in the elbow of the shirt-sleeve of one
of the [speakers. People will not think a church too
toney where the robes of ceremony have holes in the
elbows.

Carruthers went off when we came out, and I went
up on the Common alone. It is an old story to him,
but it never tires me ; and in a fortnight that I have
been here, I have not yet seen a Boston man who had
seen it. I mean the crowd for the music, Sunday
afternoon. The sky was overcast, so there was no
hot sun. The trees are just perfect, and the grass.
And here were — well forty thousand people is a
small guess — walking about, lying on the grass, or
standing tight crowded near the music-stand. On
the stand a band, and a good band, playing, and play-

ing well. That is another good piece of "Twentieth Century," is n't it ?

One of the first things I noticed was a little shaver with a board on a stick as high as he was. He had pulled it out of the ground, and was trying to set it up again in another place. I looked on the side of it to see what he had got, and read " Keep off the grass." He had taken the policing of the grass wholly into his own hands.

In fact, this "Keep off the grass" is only for week-days. Sundays we do as we choose. It is just as you and the boys might go down in the afternoon and sit or lie under the maples in the cow pasture. And so, as I say, some people were lying, some walking, some playing, and some standing still. The music was the central attraction; but there were lots of people who had no care for that, and were only mak-ing the best of the open air.

It is very queer to find yourself among so many people, and not to see one you ever saw before. I was really glad to meet the man who runs the ele-vator at our new office. He remembered me, as his business required; for elevator men are like kings and hotel-keepers in that business. Like them, too, I believe they often remember wrong. And you can understand that I was really glad as I walked by the Frog Pond, throwing bits of bark and chips to a dog who was swimming, to find our dear old Miss Tryphena Dexter sitting on one of the benches. I asked if I might sit by her a little, and she readily assented, drawing up the folds of her nice Sunday black silk, that I might have my fair share of the seat.

No, she said, she was not listening to the music. That was for them Germans and other foreigners, and was a part of their method of taking away our free-

dom and overthrowing our institutions. And why
people permitted it, and why they did not send them
all back to England where they came from, she did
not know. There was a time once, she said, when
King George's men were sent back faster than they
came; and here she nodded with approval at the
column on the hill which celebrates the heroes of
the Civil War.

But I found afterward that this was no blunder
of hers. To her the hill still represents the English
fort which was there in her girlhood. In fact, she
told me that she had danced round the Wishing
Stone backward in earlier times, and that "they"
had afterward blasted it to make the stone curb
around the pond.

"They" is a sort of evil spirit who represents all
the powers of darkness, and is therefore spoken of in
the plural number by Miss Tryphena. "They" have
changed the line of the horse-cars, or "They" sung
the hymn to the wrong tune, or "They" brought
milk that was sour. I could see that she disapproved
of my throwing chips to the little dog; so I desisted.
But she was, on the other hand, pleased when I gave
him a cracker. "I tell them," she said, "that we
don't know what we should do if we had four legs.
Mebbe we might bark and bite too. There's no saying what nature will do when we are not converted."
And she explained to me that we might feed the most
benighted on the Sabbath, even though they had
many legs. But chips, which tempted them to do
their labor and work on the Sabbath, seemed to her
doubtful. "Anyway, my child," she said, "it is well
to shun the very appearance of evil."

She had made it her habit to sit half an hour on
the Common, by the Frog Pond or not, as the seats
might offer, ever since there were seats. A cele-

brated English preacher, quite the Parker or Farrar
of his day, had preached for Dr. Sharp, on the text,
"Consider the lilies." And Miss Tryphena had been
struck to the heart, she said, that she did not consider
them enough. So, as she walked home that afternoon, — this was all centuries ago, — she had sat
down to consider them. "My dear, there was n't any
lilies. There never was a lily on the Common, unless
one of them lazy messenger boys dropped one when
he was carrying of it to some wedding, and he was
sitting and reading a novel, and some of them Hun-
garian children ketched his blue box and run. But
the Scripture is not to be literally read. Dr. Sharp
taught me that, long before this Dr. Primrose
preached about them. And so I sat and considered
the dandelions and the buttercups and the red and
white clover. There was always plenty of them before they got the mowers going, — what you call
lawn-cutters. Now these children don't consider
either of them, because they don't know 'em; and
they would not consider them either, if they did.

"But I got in the way of it then, and I never shall
give it up when it 's as pleasant as to-day, — not if
twenty million of them Bohemians and Moabites, as
I call 'em, invaded the Common with their trumpets
and their shawms. Only if there was any such thing
as law, as there was when we had Governor Lincoln
and his body-guard, they would all go back where '
they came from in double-quick time."

I tried to get her on some personal reminiscences of
Governor Lincoln and his body-guard. But they were
vague, and consisted mostly of accounts of different
"elections" when she had bought candy here, and
looked in at a sort of camera obscura in the shape of
a temple of a certain nereid in which she pointed a
quill pen at Lafayette. She had seen some Indians

dance here — or said she had. I thought her mind was wandering. But no. They were Western Indians — one was named Black-Hawk — who were brought here after some triumph of our gallant army. Then she told of the first rush of water up the fountain, the day when the water was introduced into Boston. She was fairly poetical as she described the rush of the great column.

"Oh, then they let it play," she said, "high, high, high, high above the trees. And it can play so. And it will when them foreigners has gone back to their temples and cathedrals and mud cabins and pigs again. But, my dear, it is time for me to get supper. I only give one hour for consideration."

But I would not let her bid me good-bye. I gave her my arm, and by such routes as she approved, I led her down the hill. On the way, we passed a group who were listening to somebody expounding the Bible. Here she stopped for a moment, enough to satisfy herself that the doctrine was correct.

"I was afraid," she said, "that some of them Sabellians or Sub-Lapsarians has got in here. But this man is all right. I have heard him before. You know how they tried to take from us the sacred privilege of hearing the Word on the Common. Why, even Mr. Whitfield could preach on the Common, when he could not preach in the churches. But their triumph was not long. Our dear Mr. Davis, he was haled before magistrates and kings, and he was true to the last. He went to prison, and he sung hymns there, and the prisoners heard him, and since then the word has been proclaimed here and with power."

We saw another group to which she led. But I knew that the speaker was laying down some rather advanced doctrines on the circulating medium, the silver and paper question, and I advised her to keep on the long path. We came out safely to the street, and fortunately the "spinner," or electric car, she needed, appeared. It was badly crowded; but I saw one seat for her, and she mounted. For myself I ran forward to stand on the platform. The man started, I believe, at the same moment. Anyway, something seemed to wrench my arm and something must have hit my head. I fell on the ground. I recollect thinking that the wheel would pass over me. And then I remember nothing more.

[NOTE BY THE EDITORS OF THE COMMONWEALTH. — This young man does not seem to understand the demands made on a weekly journal which is the organ of 116 literary and scientific Societies. He has been tempted to exceed the limit of space which we allow him. For our part, we protect our readers by making him stop where he should have stopped.]

CHAPTER FOURTH.

VI.

LUCY TO KATE.

BOSTON, June 26, 1891.

MY DEAR KATE, — I am still having such hurried days in this busy Boston that I hardly know how I can ever finish a letter to you; but as I have a few quiet moments, I will begin a letter "between the drops," as it were, although I have not yet heard of your receiving my last letter. I had supposed that this was to be a quiet week, for "my family," as I call them, went away Tuesday, and I supposed I should enter upon that "solitude," that Cousin Rupert has promised me in my summer in Boston.

For a summer in Boston it is to be. Everybody has consented, and I am quite happy. My own plans are not exactly to be carried out, it is true, for I have ventured to have plans of my own for the first time in my life, and some of them are to be allowed. For instance, I am going to begin on some "work," actually, such as we used to talk about that last summer, in our dreams of idleness on the "mountain side" in dear Vermont. I am afraid you will think it sounds like an idle kind of work, from its name, for I am really going to "try" and teach in one of the Vacation Schools for the Boston children. I want to begin on something, and I do want to earn a little bit of money. And Anna Davis has told me about these schools, how they have been going on for some years.

She says she was here one of the very first summers, when the whole thing was to be tried for an experiment, and they did not know how many tables would be needed, or how many rooms, for nobody knew how many scholars there would be. Of course, there were a great many sceptical people who laughed at the idea of any children coming to school voluntarily. "Of course, they would stay away, if they were not obliged to go to school, and in summer too, when they might be playing out of doors and having a good time." These wise people did not realize how many children there are in Boston who have only the street sidewalks for "out-of-doors" to play in, and oh, such narrow streets, if you could but see them. So Anna tells me that the very first summer that the Vacation Schools were opened at the South End, she went to the school building granted for their use for the summer months, and she had many misgivings, expecting to find only a group of teachers and committees on the school-steps; but as she approached, she found a crowd before the doors, and there were three hundred children waiting admittance. Well, you have heard how successful they have been since, and how many interesting things are taught there, all kinds of occupations, and children are very ready to learn that "to do something" is as good fun as any kind of play. —

Anna Davis came in to interrupt my letter; but we went on in our talk with a little of the same subject. She was amused at seeing on my table an old copy of "Harry and Lucy" that I found in the library here. I always have suspected that my mother named me after this celebrated old-fashioned "Lucy" of Miss Edgeworth. So I have been again looking up her history, and have been wondering if my character had been formed on the "Harry and Lucy" plan,

and spite of much that Anna and I find to laugh
at in this very instructive work, that the children of
the present day would turn up their noses at — in
spite of this — our mothers and fathers did well to
teach us to love to be occupied with "something."

Listen to this description of the father and mother :
they "took care that Harry and Lucy should neither
be made to dislike knowledge by having tiresome, long
talks, nor rendered idle and unable to command their
attention, by having too much amusement. Spoiled
children are never happy. Between breakfast and dinner they ask a hundred times, ' What o'clock is it ? '
Or they *must* have somebody to amuse them, or some
new toys," etc. Harry and Lucy were not like these.
"They loved reading, found continually a number of
employments and of objects which entertained and
interested them. . . . If any extraordinary amusement
was given to them, such, for instance, as their seeing
an elephant, they enjoyed it as much as possible ; but
in general Harry and Lucy felt that they wanted nothing beyond their common, everyday occupations. Besides these, there was always something going on in
the house," etc.

This is so much a picture of the way in which I was
brought up that I do hope you will forgive my sending it to you ; but you don't know how much I have
spared you and left out. And if my letter takes an
instructive strain, you must remember I am in Boston, and it is Commencement week. When you hear
the list of all the places I have been to, you will only
wonder that I have not put more orations and disqui-
sitions into my letter. Twice to Cambridge since
Class Day ! Yes, indeed ; for Aunt Martha took me
Monday afternoon to the lovely Harvard Annex Day.
So tempting and lovely the beautiful house stands,
like a real family home, only so largely hospitable to

so many "daughters." As I sat in my little corner, with my ice cream and cake, near the end of it all, I could look out on such famous people. Maria could tell me all their names, and I can now put their faces along with their names, in my memory and my gratitude.

But I must not stop over this, for we hurried away, and I came into town to go with Anna Davis to the banquet at the New England Conservatory of Music. Don't you think I am fortunate? — for she seems to know everybody that Aunt Martha and "the family" here do not know. And I met at this "reunion" so many unexpected friends, and have made so many plans for the next few weeks.

But to go on with my journal. Tuesday was terribly crowded, "the family" going off in the morning, and perhaps I may as well tell you now what is going to happen to me. It is the result of a deep-laid plot of Aunt Martha's. She has insisted upon my staying on, in this large deserted house, which they leave this week for a summer at Bar Harbor. The house is not utterly deserted, for a delightful old housekeeper stays all summer, with her son, whose principal business will be to keep off the burglars. She will give me my breakfast and late dinner, and I may get my luncheon elsewhere, or at home if I prefer. It all seems quite too magnificent an arrangement for me, but Aunt Martha says that "Hetty" (her real name is Mehitable) will anyhow provide for herself and her family, — she is to have a dressmaker daughter stay with her, — and she may as well provide for me too. So I am to keep the dear little bedroom I have been occupying here, while much of the rest of the house is to be shut up. Only, for my very, very own, I am to have the little room off the library, where I can study and scribble as much as I please, as I am doing now, and which makes it so tempting to linger along over these letters to you. And I can go into the library as much as I please. My hours at the Vacation School will be in the morning, so imagine my afternoons here. Only I do not yet begin on those quiet afternoons. Cousin Rupert and his father stayed on for Commencement, so that is how I happened to go to Cambridge that day — only there is more to tell first.

I do not get a letter from you, and I am very sure that your first letter in answer to mine will be full of questions and wonderings about "Cousin" Rupert, and with justice, since he is not really my cousin. So let me calm your anticipated fears. I think I can venture to tell you something — since you are so far away, and it will not be likely to get into the newspapers, which, by the way, I never find time to read here — something I will confide to you, though it is a profound secret. It was quite early in the business, I think the very night I arrived, that "Cousin" Rupert told me that he is engaged to a young lady "out West," but that it was all kept secret for the present (I believe his mother knows about it); and I did n't quite understand the reason for its being secret, but I think the young lady wishes it; so if you meet her anywhere "out West" don't you mention it to her! I only speak of it to you, lest you should think "Cousin" Rupert too devoted to me. But in all these expeditions, the family have gone round with me, only he has been the one to explain things.

It was his father, however, who took me about Commencement Day, and I really saw Cambridge for the first time, because it was such a brilliant, glorious day, and Class Day there was such a deplorable rain in the evening. If you could have seen my white muslin skirt after it was all through — through with that, I fear. But mine was no worse than anybody's else; and

during the dancing time our dresses were really very
respectable. I have cut you off short in my description of that wonderful Monday, but I shall return to
it when those leisure days come in which I am to have
plenty of time to write.

This goes in "scrabbles" between many goings and
comings; but I must tell you how it was not Cousin
Rupert, but his father, who went with me into some
of the college buildings, and he showed me the room
where my father lived most of his college days, and
we met many of his old friends, and the whole place
is so charming, with the old buildings and new ones,
and the college green. It does look fascinating, and I
should think they would all wish it was really the
"Commencement" — the graduating class, I mean.

But I must tell you about the day before. Aunt
Martha, and Maria, and the rest, all off at an early
hour. It was a dreadful piece of business for them,
as they usually breakfast so late, and Maria did not
look half awake as I bade her good-by. Meanwhile,
I had written a letter home, and after they left I set
off by myself, and it did seem pleasant to be doing
what I liked all by myself, which was to go to see the
Normal Art School exhibition, not far from us here,
in a hall in one of the school buildings. And here I
met Anna Davis, and she introduced to me some of her
teacher friends, and we went all round the building to
see the different rooms, besides the exhibition itself,
which was very interesting. It made me a little envious of other girls' advantages, as I wished I might
have had just such a training. Then with one or two
friends we went down town to lunch, interspersing
first a visit to the Flower and Fruit Show at Horticultural Hall. Oh, the exquisite roses! I never saw anything like them before, — great, full-blown white and
red roses, so gorgeous! We had to run away from the

strawberries; they were too tempting, and reminded us
of luncheon. I sat thinking of all those glorious
flowers, and then of our beautiful mountain laurel all
in blossom at home, and then of the children here in
town, not seeing any of it, and going to school because
the school-rooms were the airiest places they could go
to; and I could not help speaking about it, when one
of Anna's friends exclaimed: "But, oh, you must go
down with us, this very afternoon to the Flower Mission at the North End, and you will see that the
children in Boston not only see, but give away
flowers."

So then she went on to tell us how there was to be
a meeting of this mission at one of the school buildings that afternoon, and we all went to it, and heard
the report of all their work. They call it the Children's Flower Work Mission, for it is the children
who carry it on. There are fifty girls from the North
End schools who distribute the flowers in bands of
ten; these they call "the Advance Guard." Then
there are fifty friends in the towns along the Boston
and Lowell railroad, who are called "the Relief
Guard." I wish you could have heard the account of
all the work they have done. They carry bunches of
flowers to old people and sick people, and to the public
institutions and the Copp's Hill burial-ground, and
6,052 bunches of flowers were distributed last year.
Now, please multiply the pleasure that these six thousand gave to those who received them in their stifling
rooms, by the pleasure of the six thousand girls who
carried them about, and it will give you some idea of
what these missions are doing. I am promised some
flowers to take myself some day — and here, let me
tell you of a little adventure!

Later. I left off at an adventure, but you may not
think it so very exciting, and I shall have to begin by

a long story. My mother left as a parting injunction, that I should hunt up an old "retainer of the family" as I call her, whom nobody has séen or heard from these years and years. But we have only known that she lived somewhere at the North End, a very worthy person, named Miss Dexter, with a very odd first name. I happened to think about her as we came away from the Flower Mission the other day, for we passed the street where she is supposed to live. So a day or two ago I made Anna go down in that region again with me, and we found the narrow street and passed into a little court, such as they have in Boston, with crowds of children on the door-steps, though it was not one of the hottest days ; but you did not wonder that they wanted to be out of their houses.

Well, they all of them seemed to know where Miss Dexter lived, and a little girl went along with us to show us the house and upstairs. For, my dear, we had to mount three flights of stairs, that seemed to grow narrower and narrower the higher we went, or, perhaps, it was because I grew more and more frightened. At last we reached the door, but we found it locked. The little girl supposed "she" must be out, and as we pounded with the ends of our parasols and could not make anybody answer, we came to the same conclusion. The little girl said Miss Dexter was apt to go out in the afternoon, if it did not rain and if she had not been out in the morning, and she declared she was not deaf. I was a little afraid she might be in a fit, and that one ought to get in somehow to see to her, but the little girl declared she was not likely to lock the door in the daytime, if she were in ; so we reluctantly turned away ; for I am sure I do not know when I can ever find my way there again. But Anna Davis says she is willing to go again with me. So I stuck a great bunch of laurel into the door-handle and left. I did not have any card or pencil with me to write anything, and I don't suppose she would have understood who it was, if I had left a card. So we came down the dark stairs and into the court again.

But here was the adventure. On the very lower stairs, which happened to be particularly dark, we passed a young man hurrying by us. As he made room for us to pass, a door opened at the foot of the stairs, and flung a little light into the darkness. For some reason I turned back, and for some reason he turned back to look, and I am almost sure. that he was one of my partners Class Day, at Cambridge. I could not tell very well, for his face was bandaged up, and he really did look different; only I felt sure he was the same. One of Cousin Rupert's friends introduced him to me, — my Class Day partner, I mean; but I did not understand his name, and Cousin Rupert declared afterward that he did n't know him, and never saw him nor heard of him, and that Dick ought to have asked his permission before introducing a strange fellow to his cousin. But I found the "strange fellow" very agreeable in the little time I saw him and talked with him. We discovered that he was as much of a stranger in Boston as I am; but I got the idea he was going off again, so I can't really quite believe that it was he. For I felt so confused after turning round to stare at him that I hurried Anna away as fast as we could go down, through the court into the street; and happily we could find the street-car very soon.

Anna declares that my partner looked very "rowdy" with his bandage on; and she declares he cannot be any of Cousin Rupert's friends' friends, as doubtless he had just come from a street fight. But anyhow, he looked like a gentleman, even with his bandage on; and I am pretty sure she really thinks so too, only she wants to bother me; and I have felt some compunctions, and as if I ought to have stopped and asked what had happened to him; because if he is a stranger in town, we might have given him some help.

But what was he doing in that out-of-the-way court and that tenement house? Anna has quite upset me by suggesting that he, too, may be asking what I was doing there. She also is very sure that she saw him looking after us, as we got into the West End car.

Your letter has come at last, but you have not yet received my first one to you; but Cousin Rupert took care of that, and said he would see that it reached you; and he has arranged for some one to call every day for my letters to you and to everybody, — somebody who will see they are mailed properly. You hope, in your letter, that I will write you some description of Boston, and the streets and the Common, etc., and I have not sent you a word of description.

I am still much bewildered at the crowds in the streets, and wonder if the time is really going to come when "everybody" is out of town. One place is particularly dreaded by me, and that is the crossing over Park Square. There seems to be no reason for calling it a square; for four or five streets all come in at angles, the Common and Public Garden form an angle on one side, and electric cars and horse-cars of every description and color come crossing each other on all these streets. They do say that as many as two women a week are knocked down here by carts or cars and carried to the hospital, and many of them die. This may be an exaggeration. I am most afraid of the wild horses careering about here as I struggle to cross to a middle point where there is an electric lamp and a place of refuge, — not such wild

horses and mustangs as you are seeing in your Western wanderings, only extra car-horses that stand about
at this corner, to drag any horse-cars that come along
up a slope that there is supposed to be here. I have
failed to see that there is any ascent, having been
brought up on the side of Astney Mountain in Vermont. But I am always glad to see an extra horse
come to help pull on the crowded cars any time; only
I am very much afraid of them, and fear that one day
I may be one of the women carried to the hospital.

A delightful plan of Aunt Martha's has just been
carried into effect. She was a little worried that I
should be in the house alone, as she calls it, even
with the staid housekeeper. "Suppose anybody
wants to come and see you," she said before she left.
"I do not think it would be quite proper to receive
company alone." I insisted I should have no "company" and no time to receive; but she has been
writing notes, and arranging that Anna Davis shall
come and stay here with me. Anna is many years
older than I, with experience in Boston; and Aunt
Martha evidently thinks she will tame my wild aspi-
rations with her sober wisdom. So she has just come,
and is established in Maria's pretty room, and we are
very happy. She is a very busy person, so we may
not be together so very much; but we shall have our
evenings together, and can make such pleasant plans
for excursions about town. Anna points out that
if my friend of Class Day should turn up to call some
day with his bandaged head, she can receive him with
all propriety; but I tell her, as I have told Aunt
Martha, that I shall not "receive."

We went Saturday last to the school festival at the
Mechanics Building, where over three thousand graduates from the Boston public schools assembled for a
reception. It was a beautiful occasion. I was so

glad to see this famous large building, of which I
have heard so much, — and all crowded, my dear, —
and bands of music, with processions of the children ;
and each one of them, as all passed over the platform,
received a beautiful bunch of flowers. Every girl in
Boston must have been in that crowded hall. The
Mayor spoke to the children, and after the giving
of the flowers, every child had a mug of ice-cream
and a box of cake ; and after that came dancing in the
large hall ; and it was all such a pretty, merry sight !
It was a lovely occasion, and we were very fortunate
to have tickets.

I have not told how I have enjoyed the Sunday here.
Anna and I went first to the Arlington Street Church,
but it was closed ; so we went to the Second Church,
where we came in upon an exquisite choral service,
and heard a beautiful and most helpful sermon from
Mr. Horton. I can't venture to tell you how full
of poetry and strength the sermon was, about the
" lions " in one's path, " social lions," even " religious
lions."

Some of the churches will close for the summer ;
but we are promised good preaching in many that
will be open. We had a lovely walk through the
Garden, as we left the church, along the gay flower-
borders, and sitting a while on the inviting seats.
This letter will have to hurry away without my telling you of the delights of the Common and Garden.

CHAPTER FIFTH.

VII.

HARRY TO HIS MOTHER.

North Ness, R. I., July 5, 1891.

My dear Mother, — You will wonder to know why I am here; but I will tell you before I have done, if these newspaper men do not cut off the end, as they did the last time. Indeed, I was so sorry, not to say angry. I sent you the card as soon as I knew; but I did not get their old paper for a day or two. Our newsman is a fool, and he did not have enough; and it was not till I met Carruthers in the street, and he said he thought I was dead, that I was alarmed about you.

Really, if it had been at all bad, they would have telegraphed you from the hospital, or they say they would. But as they did not know who I was, how they would know where to telegraph I do not know. You see, the first thing I knew was Monday morning when the man next me — I was in 27 and he was in 28 — had his breakfast. He had only one arm, and was awkward with the other, and knocked down his coffee-cup. That made a smash, and they came in between his bed and mine, and that made a row. They pushed my bed one side, and so I woke up. Then I made a row, and asked where I was. And they said I was all right, but I must not talk till the doctor came. I said who was the doctor; and then I found out that I was in the hospital. I was for getting up; but I could not see my clothes, and the "sense of the meeting" was that I should stay in bed. If I had got up, I should have had to go about town in the nightgown they had put on me. That would have excited surprise, and I might have been put in the newspapers. So I compromised; I said if they would let me wash myself, and bring me some breakfast, I would not spill it, and I would wait till the doctor came. I said they might bring beefsteak and omelette. They laughed and went off, and true enough the beefsteak and omelette came.

Then they brought me the "News," a jolly little paper we have which only costs one cent, and I read that through. Then a fellow lent me a novel, all blood and thunder, and I got tired to death of the bed and the nightgown and the novel; and then the doctor came. He took off a bandage they had put round my head, and he looked at my tongue, felt of my pulse, and asked a lot of questions. And then he said there was nothing the matter, but that it was very remarkable.

I told him that was just what I had told the nurse. Then the nurse asked what she should do. By this time I think the doctor was tired of us both, and he laughed and told her to bring me my clothes. And she did. There was a screen up so I could dress myself with decorum; and I bade them all good-by, and said I was much obliged to them, — which, in a way, was true. I got the doctor to tell me what had happened.

You see, a great thundering wire had come slamming down, and hit me on the head, — or hat. They say if it were a horse, it would have killed him, because he has no hat. It is not really a thundering wire, but a lightning wire, because it is as full of electricity as they can make it. Well, this one broke or something, and came slamming down. "Fortu-

nately," the doctor said, "it did not strike the
horses." By which he meant, I suppose, that it
did strike me. All the good fortune that I see in
that is, that Mrs. Metcalf was in for my breakfast;
for nobody offered me any bill at the hospital, and
I offered nobody any money.

They did say I had better have a bandage on my
forehead; for there was a visible cut there, and I
believe some blood had flowed from it. So an attendant, a sort of Bob Sawyer, put on this bandage in an
ante-room there was, and I went into the office of the
whole, and bade the regular "Top-Sawyer" good-by.
They made me count my money, which had all been
saved for me; and I gave them a regular receipt for
that and the office keys and my knife and all my
things.

I tell you I made tracks for the office. But when
I came there, nobody seemed to have missed me.
There were a lot of paper-hangers and grainers and
whitewashmen, making things generally uncomfortable. I rather think everybody had been late after
Sunday, and that they all thought I had been early
and stepped out. I did take care to go round before
night to Miss Tryphena's to tell her that I was all
right. But I did not find her at home. Then I wrote
all this at length to you. And those COMMONWEALTH
people just cut off all the end of it, so I was awfully
frightened when I came to read their old paper; for
I knew how it would startle you. And when I went
to blow them up, they took the other tack and blew
me up for being too long. And when I asked for the
end of my letter, they said they supposed it was in
the waste basket; perhaps the boy had kindled the
engine fire with it. Anyway, I had to come home
and to send you the postal, which I hope you received.

I told you I would write a journal. But it is as old

John Adams says, when you are doing anything worth doing you have no time to write your journal, and when you write a journal, therefore, it is clear that there is nothing worth putting down. I remember that Robinson Crusoe said that when he wrote his diary he found he put into it many things which he thought important at the time, which afterward did not seem necessary. You know he was short of ink, and could find no nut-galls on his island, nothing but water-melons and turtles. Anyway, I will not try to distinguish Tuesday from Wednesday now, nor tell what my new chief did and did not determine about the color of the office walls and the gas-burners. I shall skip to the great event of Friday.

. . . .

Only think of it! I came within one of coming up to see you at Atherton. But even if I had been willing to spend the money — as indeed I was, dear Mother — I should have had to turn right round to come back again, as soon as old Segar could water his horses so as to go back by the night train. You see the whitewashers got in with their scaffolds at last into the new offices, and even the new treasurer could not pretend that there was anything for us to do. His name is still a secret, and I am afraid that if I told you, some of the wrong people might get THE COMMONWEALTH. This gave me Friday for a clear day out, for we were told that we need none of us come till Saturday. I hardly knew what I should do in that desert; but as dear Aunt Joey says, " it was well ordered," as we shall see. I went round with George Thursday night to the " Pop." This is short for the Popular Concerts in the Music Hall. No, it is not one of the organ concerts you used to go to when you were here. They took down that organ, because it was the largest in America, I believe, and packed it up in a burying-ground. This gave them more room, so they now fill that great hall with nice little tables, with chairs round them; and you go in and sit at a table, and may drink anything you choose from water as far as lager, but no farther. You need n't drink anything; but you can eat ice-cream or whatever you want to eat, if they have it. I should not ask for buffalo hump. I enclose the little programme, and you will see that the music is really very good. It is a nice place to spend an evening. What you mean by "popular" is that the music is not Bach or Beethoven, or even Wagner; but something more light and jolly. The orchestra is made up of some of the best musicians in town.

Well, here it was that George's friend, who was so good to us at Class Day, proposed that we should go to New London the next day and see Harvard beat Yale. I did not think Harvard would beat Yale; but all the same I said I would go gladly. And we went.

We came down on a special train from Boston. We had to start at 7.30 in the morning and were to come back in the afternoon. As we came over the new bridge at New London, we could see a swarm of tugs and small boats hovering around to watch the race. It was a perfectly lovely day. We had deliberated a good deal as to the best way of seeing everything, — whether to follow the boats on a tug or to take the observation train which goes on the railroad line parallel to the course. But it happened by good luck that as we came into the station a friend of Carruthers gave him two tickets for a good car on the train. You see the train runs along the shore, so you keep nearly even with the boats. We got on board and found ourselves with a lot of Harvard fellows. Two of them had made up a lot of awfully funny songs, and sang them at intervals, some of them with "gags" selected

" Harvard gained from the very beginning." — Page 55

for the occasion. The observation train, as they call it, is a lot of common freight cars with board seats put on, rising above each other, so that you sit just as you might at the circus and ride sideways. They are covered with bunting and make quite a fine show. There were fellows from both colleges on board; but we were in car 22 with a great lot of Harvard men.

Generally, the race begins way up the river, and the boats come down with the stream. But this time it began at Winthrop Point, where is usually the finish. The start is just above the new bridge, if you recollect when we crossed it last year. They were very punctual, starting at three minutes after eleven. The man says, "Are you ready, gentlemen?" waits a minute, and then says, "Go!" and they start; but of course we could not hear this. From the very first, Harvard went right to the front. We could tell which was which by the blades of the oars, Harvard's being red, and Yale's blue. The men are stripped to the skin, so you cannot tell them by the university colors; but I suppose the time will come when they will go into such contests like the old Picts, in two colors. If you care to know, the Harvard boat was cedar, and the Yale boat was paper. Harvard gained from the very beginning. Still, I think it was supposed at first that this was by a special spurt, and that Yale would overtake her; but she never did. In two miles Harvard was seven lengths ahead, and, practically, as great an advantage as this at that point means that a boat is going to win. Harvard had the east track, which is called the eel-grass track, but that did not seem to make any difference.

Now, in the observation car, you keep abreast of them all the time. But you can see how exciting it is when you pass into a cut on the road, where you cannot see the boats, so there is great yelling when you come out of the cut into the open air again. At the finish Harvard was thirteen lengths ahead. This was just opposite the Harvard quarters where the men had stayed while they practised. The Harvard boat-house was below, the Yale and Columbia farther up the river. You can guess if there was not terrific cheering on our car when the victory came. And when there was a chance for singing, our poets had some fit lines for the triumph.

The crew went at once to their quarters, so that we saw no more of them then. We went back to town on the observation train. But in the afternoon we saw all the crew at the Pequot House. Here was a procession and great congratulations. But we could not stay for the evening jollification, and came home on the eight o'clock train. I asked everybody why one of the two colleges did not row against Cornell, seeing that boat seems to make better time than anybody. But the question was not popular, and I did not push it too far. Certainly, I got no answer.

. . . .

Here I was interrupted, and I finish this letter at the office. The whitewash men have gone. And now I have so much to tell that I shall tell nothing. Certainly, as that Frenchman said, Boston is the most entertaining place in summer. In winter, I am afraid, it is more stupid. You know they say that there is not one of the real *Bostonese* who knows there is anything beyond Watertown. That is the town next Cambridge. They built a road there in the first years of the colony, and the builders reported that there would never be any need of its going any further.

The Frenchman reminds me of my Russian, whose name is Gabriel Vostikoff. He seems to think that I shall know that this is a very great name. Perhaps

you and father do. But really I never heard of it
before. Anyway, here he is, — and I met him in a
street car, which is a sort of a club-house. I bowed
to him, because he moved into the middle of the seat
and let me sit down. This showed he was a gentleman. A blackguard keeps the end of the seat and
makes you crowd by him. I am sorry to say that
most women do the same thing. I bowed to him and
thanked him. He then took out a writing tablet, and
in an exquisite hand wrote, "Canst thou inform me
which road I shall go to find the Bureau of the Post?"
So I told him. But he shook his head, and gave me
the tablet and pencil for me to write my answer. Of
course, I supposed that "he was deaf and was dumb,"
as our old story used to say. But no such thing. We
are great friends now. I had him up at the office to
direct some circulars, and everybody likes him and
his good-natured ways, and his exquisite handwriting.
What a passport into civilized life that is, to be
sure.

It seems that he was a student somewhere in
Russia, and he fell in with an old French review,
where there was a very rosy account of Cornell University. It told how it was a school for all, if only
they wanted to learn, and especially how you got
through for nothing by dint of working with your
hands half the day, so that you could work with your
head the other half. So the good fellow started, and
got some money together to come to Cornell. Little
enough it was, too. He got to Hamburg, and then
had the wit to earn his passage on a tramp steamer
somehow, so that he landed here with a lot of German
coin, which may be worth six dollars.

Then comes the droll thing which made me think
he was deaf and dumb. He had learned English so
that he might be ready to come. You know how

good they are at languages. But he had learned by
some double-refined improved patent system, so that
when he spoke it nobody understood him, and when
they spoke to him he did not understand them. I
wish I could write down for you how queer it is, and
how senseless when he speaks. But he had his gram-
mar and his spelling and his handwriting quite right.
So that, by taking a deaf and dumb man's methods
he comes out first rate. And he is so jolly and good-
natured that everybody likes him. He and I are
going at this moment down to "The White Squadron."
That is the United States fleet which is now in the
harbor. Our company has a contract for supplying
Jack with all his clothes-pins, and I am to see one of
the officers about it, if I can find him.

. . . .

P. S. As you see, this letter is a thing of shreds
and patches. I had hardly written the within, when
my Russian bear, as we call him, came in, and I took
him off to lunch. We do this when we can, for we are
afraid he will starve before our eyes, so eager is he to
save up the money for his journey to Cornell. What
a shame it is that so many fellows, who have all the
chances to go to college, do nothing when they are
there, while so fine a fellow as he is, finds his wheels
blocked all the time when he wants really to go to
work.

Well! little, enough I thought when I was writing
before what would happen before I was done. I took
him to a little place I have found, where the coffee is
good ·and the bread good enough, (though not like
yours, dear mother), and where on clam-chowder days
they know how to make that. And I gave him his
lessons in pronunciation, — that he must not say
"co-ug," but "koff," when he was talking about a
sudden ejaculation of breath from the lungs, and so

on. I took care that he should have enough nitrogen and phosphorus and carbon tucked into him to keep the furnace a-going, and then I brought him back to the office.

We understood well enough that it was half a show day and half a day of instruction. Still if I could get a chance for business, I was to try to see somebody who had some authority and who knew something at the same time. You see our contract provides that their clothes-pins are to be made of cherry wood. A wise Providence only knows why. Anybody who knows anything about clothes-pins knows that when they are made of walnut they are just as good as the cherry ones. Why the contract says cherry, nobody can guess.

I did not really suppose that Admiral Walker knew or cared. But it was supposed that if I kept my eyes open and used my advantages, I might have a chance to find out, and that, in an informal and unofficial conversation, I might do what we had not been able to do in correspondence with the Department. They only respectfully refer our letters from one bureau to another and we never get any answer. For this enterprise the new treasurer gave me a general letter of introduction to Admiral Walker or any officer on the squadron. It was written in our handsomest style and put up in the Company's envelope. I asked if I might take the Bear with me, and they said certainly, and we started.

We went to Long Wharf, — the historical Long Wharf. It is very different now from what it was when it was so very Long, for the land has encroached on it so that half of it is not a wharf at all. I was tempted by Satan to take the Bear and show him T wharf, and I explained to him, what he did not in the least understand, that it is named T from its shape. [Memorandum: the Governor's aids took a distinguished historian down there a few years ago, and told him it was named T because the tea was thrown over there. Really that was at a wholly different place.] Then we crossed over and I tell you all the boatmen went for us.

After a minute I took a sailboat which I liked and I let two other fellows go with us. Of course they were to pay their half. But thence came all our woe. Just as the man was ready and we were going down the steps, a larger party came along, and their boat, a private boat, ran up, with two or three gentlemanly looking oarsmen. I told my boatman to wait, and we stood back to let their people pass. Of course I supposed they were all strangers. But at once I recognized that pretty girl I told you I danced with at Memorial Hall.

We had a sail, as I said, and they rowed. But they rowed well, — used to it, as half those Harvard men are, so that they got to the Newark just as soon as we did. Once more I told my boatman to wait for them, and he did so. This time my pretty partner recognized me, and she bowed to me very nicely as she went up the great high ladder which takes you up the ship's side. At the top and at the bottom there are fine looking sailors to make it as easy as they can. I was well pleased to think that I had so good an opportunity to speak with her again as this would give me. But I must tell all this story as shortly as I can, or they will cut off the end of it and that is the only part which is essential. For there is many a slip between cup and lip. Two ladies went up after her, and as the last one came near the top, she started about something and dropped one of her wraps, which came floating down above us. One of these other men, a clumsy fellow, tried to catch it. I believe he did catch it, but he caught his foot in a thwart and went over heavily himself. He grabbed as he went at our boatman who was taking in his mast, — I do not know why, — and was using both his hands. Both of them fell together, the boat was already a little keeled over, and in a minute she took in a great wave of water, and all of us were ducked into —

CHAPTER SIXTH.

VIII.

LUCY TO KATE.

Boston, July 17, 1891.

My DEAR KATE, — I suppose you will hardly believe that my life is still of the "rackety" sort, and if it is going to be more so next winter, I do not quite see how my poor little head will stand it. I have not yet had a chance to begin on "regular hours of study," which I had planned out, at least for the summer days. I do have now my work in the morning, — for "work" it is, as I shall show; and I will begin with it the first thing, lest it should be crowded out by the history of afternoon experiences.

I wish I could give you a picture of that first day at the Vacation School, and the crowds of children who "come to school because. they want to." There were between two and three hundred, of various ages and sizes, boys and girls. I quite wished I could have the little things who crowded into the Kindergarten, but I do not know that they were more interesting than the rough boys over twelve years of age, because you wondered at seeing them there, and these were to fall to my share. The Kindergarten teacher, with fifty children to attend to, must have something of an experience with them; but not greater than mine, you can believe, to find myself standing up opposite twenty or thirty boys, great fellows at least twelve or thirteen years old, evidently coming for fun rather than for "instruction." A terror came over me at the remembrance of some of the experiences in these

schools in earlier years that I had been told of, when
it was necessary to have policemen in the building
to keep down these struggling spirits. But this year
they were going to do without a policeman. What a
dreadful thing it would be if they should get the better
of me, and a policeman should have to be called in!

But I looked round on the bright, jolly faces, and
the very terror of the policeman gave me courage.
What a pity, I seemed to say to myself, that these
gay boys should grow up with the idea that only the
policeman's club could keep them right. They are not
criminals or convicts; they are boys that like to have
a good time. So I found myself telling them how I
had come to Boston for the first time, and how I had
not yet seen all the wonderful public buildings, and
how they would have to teach me where to go and
what to see. And I went on by telling them how, a
day or two before, I had walked out through the park
that lies beyond Commonwealth Avenue, and I had
to stop and tell them who Lief Ericson was and how
his statue looks up through the park, and how I
wonder if he does not want sometimes to turn the
other way and look down the avenue of beautiful
houses on either side, — because they had all grown
up since his time, — with its brick sidewalks and easy
driveway; while, as he looks out now he sees the
trees and flowers, sweet as perhaps he saw when he
first landed here. At least there might then have
been the wild roses in bloom, such as I have seen
there — that is, if it were in the season, — and I said
we would try and find out if it were. And I asked
them if they knew what flowers there were in that
park, and most of them had never been there and did
not know there was such a statue as Lief Ericson's,
nor had heard his name, though they had seen George
Washington in the Public Garden.

I may as well go on and tell you how I told them about my walking further some days before, through the park to the new bridge to Cambridge, — such a lovely walk as it is, perhaps the most beautiful one can take here, — and how I had also seen a map of old Boston. It was one that Dr. F. showed to me which gave a picture of how Boston looked on the day of the battle of Lexington; no bridges but one across the Charles River (and I set them to counting how many there are now), and this one bridge very much in the place of the new Harvard Bridge one walks across to Cambridge. It was to this bridge that "our" men went on that day of the battle of Lexington, and they took away the boards from off the bridge, so that the British need not follow them out of Boston. But they left the boards in a pile so near the bridge that the British could put them back again, which they did, and marched over on their way to Lexington. I don't believe I told it as connectedly as this even, for I let them ask questions and stop me to give their views, and they were very sure they should not have been so stupid as to leave the boards. But I do not have to draw upon my own resources in this way all the time, for there are so many delightful occupations, and teachers arranged for the different hours, that we can fill up the time with great variety.

The boys enjoy the drawing and clay-modelling and whittling and cane-seating, and I can't yet tell you all of the varieties of work. You see it is, as I wrote you, all on the "Harry and Lucy" principle. The scholars are not kept studying all the time, but they are led to be interested in things, and to do something themselves with their hands with things. Harry and Lucy in the old book were taken by their parents to see a brick kiln, and Harry immediately wanted to make bricks himself, and his father let him try. So here, the boys can carry out the Yankee love of whittling, or cultivate it if they are not real Yankees themselves, and they are encouraged to make something. Harry did not succeed very well with his bricks, but just his failures taught him something. One of " my " boys has got hold of some of " Hetty's " favorite old-fashioned chairs that I sent from the house here, and he is very proud of putting in new seats.

At Denison's, a store on Franklin Street where I have been, they have most bewitching things made of tissue and *crêpe* paper, of every possible shade and color. There are baskets *crocheted* of tissue paper and twisted like ropes, lamp-shades ornamented in all sorts of ways, and paper-dolls' dresses that are perfectly fascinating. They have kindly asked some of the teachers to come and examine all these things, that they may teach the children. I think of sending some of the things home, the work is so inviting, and they would like it, I know, at the Sewing Circle, when they are making up things for a sale in the autumn. Just think, they had even a trimmed hat all made of tissue paper, very ingenious and pretty, but I fear not very useful in a shower; perhaps, however, it will do for a fair. I should like indeed to tell the children at home about the numerous things they might learn here; there are countless things to be done in the way of paper-folding, boats and boxes to be made, and very good work is done by the girls in sewing.

But I must tell you how fast my afternoons fill in. Last week I tried to devote them to excursions that might rest me from my morning's work, and you can't think what entertaining things turned up. I must reserve for the very last the most exciting of all, and

our visit last week to the White Squadron. I want
to tell all the other things first, lest they should be
forgotten; and there hangs a tale to it, that I must
leave for the end of my letter. It was not my first
glimpse of the White Squadron, because the day
before Anna and I made such a lovely excursion to
Revere Beach.

I have written you how I pine always to see the
harbor and the beach and the great sea, and how disappointed I was in the beginning that I could not sit
on a bench on the Common and see the great sea come
in from there. So Anna agreed to go over with me
to Revere Beach, where she had never been, and
where she was very sure we could see the real tide
coming in. We looked up the advertisements in the
papers, and found a new way of going through East
Boston to Winthrop Junction in the regular horse-
cars — five-cent fare — and from Winthrop Junction
to Revere Beach on the electric cars, a new line, for
five cents more, advertised as the cheapest and pleasantest way to Revere.

We took an East Boston car at the corner of Ches-
ter Park and Tremont Street and went down through
Hanover Street to the East Boston ferry, which means
going straight through Boston from the South End to
the very end of the North End. Crowds are still in
the streets, but even I could believe that they were not
the real Boston. Anna said they all looked as if they
came from " Way Back " somewhere. All the shopping streets, Temple Place and Winter Street, were
by no means deserted, but were full of people. Then
down at the end of Hanover Street, they all looked so
foreign, Italians and Jews, women bare-headed with
large ear-rings, and oh, such care-worn faces. They
all seemed full of business, the women looking at the
gay bedquilts and calicoes hanging from the shop-win-

dows, and the men busy too, the corners of the streets crowded with stands for bananas and neck-ties. We saw a party of immigrants just landed, who looked bewildered enough.

Then, as we crossed the ferry, we had an admirable view of the White Squadron. We passed down beside the " Yorktown " and could really see the officers and sailors walking and lounging about. I must say they looked bored to death. Tugs were taking visitors over to the different vessels. I supposed then that this would be my only view of the whole fleet. I little knew how I was to be taken out myself on just such a little boat as we saw — but I will not anticipate, as Harriet Byron says.

At East Boston we changed to a Winthrop Junction car, passing through deserted streets, and at last we came in sight of the sea, and a real view of the harbor. At the Junction we found the electric cars, and then such an enchanting ride across the salt marshes, with the sea on either side, whizzing across a narrow bridge, then down a steep hill; and I really trembled with terror, it all looked so dangerous, and it seemed as if we were skimming through the air. And then we were on the beach, and far away the tide was coming up, on the long stretch of gray sand that invited us, and we came down to meet the water and scamper away from it as the children did. If we had been earlier we should have stood there in silent wonder, or have thought of our Tennyson and all the wonderful descriptions of tide and sand. But the beach was crowded. Women had brought out their children to breathe the salt air, and the children were digging in the sand, or perhaps they were begging their mothers to buy them pop-corn, and there was the tin-type man and the goat-cart filled with children, and everybody enjoying everything. How Anna and I wished we might make a picture of some of the lovely groups.

We stayed longer than we meant, for some of the children told us we ought to wait for the "gospel carriage." Pretty soon it came along, with "Gospel Carriage" written on it. It was occupied by half a dozen men and women, with a small organ used also as a pulpit. A hymn was sung which attracted a crowd, and then a short discourse was given. I can tell you there was something quite exciting about it, with the background of the tide coming up the long beach, and the crowds of children looking up with wonder from their different amusements. The wagon is hired by the city missionaries and goes wherever they think a little good can be done. In the evening they go to the Common or the North End or West End.

We came home the same way, having had a delightful afternoon, returning into the golden glow of a sunset that lighted up the ships in the harbor, as we crossed again in the ferry-boat.

I thought of these children in the sand the other day, when I went to a lovely place that has been fitted up for a girls' gymnasium. It is also a playground for girls, and one of the most enticing places you can imagine. It is a little park on the Charles River Embankment. And sometime or other, this embankment is to be carried all along the shore of Charles River, on Charles Street and Beacon Street. Nowadays, as you come into Boston from Cambridge over the bridge, you see on the curving shore of the river the stately row of houses on Beacon Street. But I must say the view is not impressive, for you see only the back doors of these houses; and I ventured once to suggest to Aunt Martha that I thought it would be an improvement to turn all the Beacon Street houses round, so that they could face on the river. She was very much shocked at the idea of back doors on Beacon Street; but I think they will have to ornament the backs of these houses, whenever this embankment is finished; for it will make a charming riverside to look out upon. Meanwhile, enterprising Boston is taking advantage of an open place on Charles Street for this gymnasium for the girls.

We went into the enclosure under a projecting roof, and such a happy party we found within. Here were some beds of sand, in which a crowd of little children were allowed to play and make whatever they chose, sand-pies or lofty towers, — for one girl had formed what looked like towers of Babel, a row of them, each one just like its next neighbor, — and all sorts of fanciful things. They were having such good fun with their pails and spades, like the children on the beach, and they delighted in talking to us, and telling us about their mud-pies. It was really hard to leave them, and go on to see the gymnasium, but we found this equally charming.

Here were tilting-bridges and balance-swings, inclined parallels, climbing-ropes, and ladders. Let me tell you about these "inclined parallels;" they are like two bannister-rails a foot or so apart. A girl goes up the ladder, or climbs up one of the ropes, and then slides down the parallels. Just think of the fun! I used to think it was the greatest bliss in life to get a chance to imitate my older brothers, and slide down the bannisters of our staircase when I was a child. But it was a forbidden joy, because it was so dangerous, and because I was a girl. Was it a part of its charms that it was forbidden? You see the advantages of being born into the present generation. Here the girls are not only permitted but invited to slide down the staircase, only under the name of "inclined parallels," and the children are encouraged to make sand-pies! We went up to the room for the Kindergarten, which looks out on one side upon the river, and the other way you can look down upon the playgrounds and see the mothers looking on, in the grassy enclosure.

In the Kindergarten were occupations for the children, stringing beads, weaving papers, picture-books, etc. And down in the enclosure with its pretty hedges of shrubs and roses, the children were busy with pretty Kindergarten work, with card-board designs, that they mark out with colored worsteds, all under kindly direction. They have had lovely donations of roses, so that there is everything to make them enjoy the idea of a real summer, such as you would not imagine in a city's crowded streets.

The working-girls are to come later in the afternoon, and it must be as much of a delight for them as for the children. The gymnasium is admirably fitted up, the apparatus suggested by Dr. Sargent of Harvard. I could n't help trying myself the "Giant Step" that we used to have in our gymnasium at Astney, when four ropes are attached to a pole with rings at the ends, the rings a little higher than the girls' heads. Four girls reach up to the rings, and holding on to them they run about the pole. When they lift their feet from the ground they are carried along by the momentum, round and round with a delightful motion, which must be helped from time to time by a little touch of the ground with one foot, and again on they go. The motion seems so like flying and is so charming that if Professor Langley can invent a method of flying for the human race that is equal to it, I hope he will succeed.

The tilting-bridges are much like foot-bridges over small streams. They have close fences on either side, and are suspended in the middle. A party of

girls get on the bridge and stamp up and down, the
girls on one side stamping more than the others. Up
and down they go, or, like an old-fashioned tilt, they
see-saw up and down, with a friend at each end to
start them. I hope to have the privilege of going
in for fun and exercise after I am really at work, so
that I can feel that I deserve it.

But I am writing too much without leaving space
to tell you of my excitement of last week in really
going out to see the White Squadron. Anna Davis
with some friends had an invitation to go out to one
of the vessels to see the shooting in the harbor the
other afternoon, and they were kind enough to ask
me to go too. I had to hurry off after my morning's
class, and met them at the Parker House. Here
were some young men who were going to row us out
from one of the wharves, among them Mr. Brand and
Mr. Jones, Harvard men, who were my partners on
Class Day. I have happened to meet Mr. Brand
since, and we all seemed to know each other after
lunching together, and went down through the bewildering streets to a real wharf, and looked out
upon the exciting, mixed-up scene. I was frightened
to death at being got down into the boat, but I succeeded in not disgracing myself by tumbling in between the wharf and the boat. But just as we were
getting off, I looked back at a sailboat that seemed in
our way, waiting for a party just coming down the
steps to go on board, and among them was my unknown friend of Class Day.

He seemed to have the direction of the party, for
he motioned to the boatmen to keep out of our way,
and we passed on; but his sailboat was near us all the
way out to our ship. There was plenty to attract my
attention, — all those little boats bobbing about, the
row of great ships beyond, and every kind of steam tug

and excursion steamer, whistling and puffing about us; but the sailboat kept along near us, and we saw it must be aiming for the same ship to which we were bound. For it appeared that Mr. Brand had met this same young man at Cambridge, Class Day, and he regretted much that he had not "caught his name" there, as he had been wanting to hunt him up since; for he understood then that he was a stranger in Boston, and that he had come to join some large firm just established in Boston; and he would like to do something for him if he could. So we bobbed in and out among the boats, but we kept well ahead with our oarsmen, for their sails did not seem to help them much; and I had no chance to bow to him till I happened to turn round on the very steps of the high ladder going up the ship's side. I looked off over the side of the ship the minute I reached the landing-place, the sailors making it all very easy, and then I saw such a confusing scene.

One of the ladies of our party — I am happy to say I did n't know anything about her — let her shawl fall into the water. It was very clumsy of her, because we had so much help from the sailors going up. One of the men in the sailboat reached out for the shawl and got it, but somehow caught his foot in something and went over the side of the boat. I believe they were taking in the mast, and the boatman, as he went down, seized hold of one of the other men; they both fell together, and then the boat turned over. I hardly dared to look to see what happened next, but the ship's sailors somehow went to the rescue, and Mr. Brand tried to help, and everybody said everything was all right, and more boats were coming up, and more people mounting the ladder, and we were hurried away, and I waited full of anxiety till Mr. Brand appeared, but without our Class Day friend. He did not have much to tell except that he saw that the boat got righted, and that our friend was on board the boat all right; but he believed they were going back, or somewhere else. He had to hurry up the ladder himself or he should lose his own chance.

I felt dreadfully about it, and I made **Mr. Brand** go back with me to look off in that direction; but somehow we had swerved round, or I had lost my bearings, for I could see nothing of the sailboat. Mr. Brand tried to quiet me, and declared they were all out of danger. But I silently agreed with him when he declared that he was disappointed that he had lost the chance of talking with him all the afternoon and evening and making his acquaintance. I did have time to see that he no longer wore any bandage, and he looked very handsome and manly as he stood giving his directions to the men. I feel so provoked that it was one of our party who dropped the shawl. You can't think (can you?) that he imagines that it was my shawl, and that I was so foolish as to drop it, when I never take a shawl with me? I am leaving no space to tell you of the grand show of the afternoon, which indeed was fine. Such a contrast, all this warlike, magnificent show, to the promise of peace we had pictured to us at the grand Fourth of July oration. For I have not told you how Anna Davis and I did succeed in going to the Boston Theatre to hear Mr. Quincy, and his oration was splendid. And when I saw all this brilliant show on the water that afternoon, I thought to myself, perhaps that is the way it is to be; we shall have all this firing of guns, and smoke of cannon and great war-ships just for the show, and we shall go out to see it peacefully, because there is "war no more."

CHAPTER SEVENTH.

IX.

HARRY TO HIS MOTHER.

North Ness, R. I., July 20, 1891.

My dear Mother, — I write this in the old Narragansett country, within a mile of the old Indian fort where your grandmother's grandfather was killed in the attack, as it says on the old matchlock over the dining-room door. You might mention it at the next meeting of the Indian Association of Windham County ; and you might add that there are not so many people in the Narragansett country proper as there were then. I mean that east and west of here is a strip of woods and ponds which is only fit for little farms, and from which the people have moved to factories and to the West.

I felt badly when I got The Commonwealth, because I was afraid again that you might be anxious. They cut off the letter in that short metre way, just as I was swimming in the bay by the side of one of the white ships. But I said to myself : " Surely mother is not a fool — and she will know that if I was drowned I could not have written that letter." If I had seen it sooner I would have written at once. As it was, the firm sent me up into New Brunswick, to inquire about our contract for wild cherry, and I never saw the letter till Saturday night. I got into town Saturday morning, and the newsman tried to sell me The Commonwealth with the woman's letter. But

I will not read her letters. I should only be out five
cents if I bought it and I had rather save that for
Christmas presents.

So I begin by saying that I was not drowned, but
was badly wet. So was the polar bear, and so, I am
glad to say, was the stupid land-lubber whose clumsi-
ness caused the accident. We all scrambled up from
the bottom as quick as we could, and there were only
too many to help. But I was at the stern of our boat
and I got in first. She never really capsized, though
she took in a hogshead of water. I pulled myself in,
and had nobody to thank, but I was thankful for the
memories of old days when we used to go swimming
in Gogmagog, and the first fellow got into the boat
that way and wiped himself on the shirts of the
others. Then I hauled the others in, with, I say,
profuse offers of help all round. The officer in command up above us sent down a young fellow, who was
perhaps a midship*mite,* to ask us to come on board,
and to offer the hospitalities of the engine-room to
dry ourselves. But I was not going to show myself
in that ducked-dog condition to all those ladies. So I
thanked the little man, and told our boatman, who
had kept tolerably good-natured in all this nonsense,
to get away from the ladder as quick as he could, and
we began to bail out ; fortunately he had a couple of
pails. Then in our ducked-dog condition we went
back to the wharf in Boston, not in such good spirits
as we started in, I can assure you. To you I will say
privately that I looked over my shoulder to see my
little parcel of clothes-pins floating off on top of a wave.
I was not going to claim any connection with them,
and I suppose they are in Palos or the island of
Hawaii before now.

Dear mother, do not mind where these people stop
the letters. Recollect that if I am dead or unconscious,

I will certainly telegraph you, and you must not give yourself any anxiety because the letter does not happen to be signed by my name.

You will not understand why I should be in the Narragansett country. All Carruthers's people come down here in summer. They have a nice place, in full sight of the sea, though it is a couple of miles off. And "sea" here means the Atlantic Ocean; for there is a little stretch, as you have perhaps never observed, between the eastern end of Long Island and Narragansett Bay, where nothing but Block Island breaks the sight and force of the Atlantic Ocean. So Carruthers made me come down here on the one o'clock train Saturday, and I have been spending Sunday here. I shall have a great deal to tell you about the place, for Mrs. Carruthers, who is very nice, has made me promise to come down again. But now I have only spent Sunday here, and I foresee that this letter will be so long that I had better not go into accounts of the Narragansett country, or of my sea-bathing, or of the people who come down to the beach, or of our experiences with ray's eggs, or of the museum that I have made of sea-urchins and other wonders for Florence. I have been writing this with a pencil, while we were waiting for the train to come. It is announced that it is now in sight, which means four miles off, and I will finish this letter at the office.

. . . .

If the engine had not come, I should have told you that this is the way that most of the Boston people live whom I see the most. It is all nonsense to say that Boston is all out of town, for, as I told you, on Sundays the Common is as full as any beehive is, and I should think, from what I see in the streets, that there are just as many people in Boston in the daytime as there ever were. But the railroad people

would tell you that a great many more people go out
of town in the last hours of the day than come in, and
on the other hand you have only to come in on a
morning train to see that a great many more people
come in than go out. This means that Boston is a
day-time city in summer; and that accounts for a
great many queer things. The Boston men say, for
instance, that they do not recognize nearly as many
people in the streets as they do in winter. And even
supposing that you live, as I and all our clerks here
live through the week, the chances are that you go
out of town on Saturday, spend your Sunday, and come
in, perhaps a little late, on Monday morning. They
made no fuss at the office about my being late, and, as
I said once before, I believe everybody was so late
himself that he supposed that I had been very early
and had gone out upon some errand. I did not give
myself away.

You must not feel sad about it, but I am getting in
love with the freedom of this sort of life, and I shall
be as bad a cockney as any of them are before long.
Perhaps I shall be rather more so. I heard old Mr.
Champernoon say the other day — he is one of our
directors, a man who likes to draw his money from
our investment, and takes the privilege of coming
around and talking for an hour in the office every
morning, while he does not understand so much of
the business as any fly that crawls on the window —
I say I heard old Mr. Champernoon say that you
could distinguish between the two lines of rich men
in Boston, — those who were brought up in the country and those who were not. He said the country
boys never went into ornamental farming; that they
had had enough of "laying stone wall" to serve them
for their life. He said it was only the Boston boy,
who had grown up without knowing the difference

between a cow and a sheep, who took, in later life, to
the elegancies of agriculture. I do not know whether
this is true. But I do know that already, after being
here a month, I have got into the stream so far that I
like to feel at the beginning of the week, on the one
hand, that before the week is over I shall have been
in Maine or Rhode Island or the Berkshire mountains, and, on the other hand, that I am ignorant to
which of these I shall go. You see I do not feel as
if I lived in Boston; I feel as if I lived in a circle of
two or three hundred miles radius, of which Boston is
the centre.

And I wholly understand, though I have been here
so short a time, the feeling that the whole belongs to
me, or, if you please, that I belong to it. I see entirely why cockneys are cockneys, and I can see why
men of letters and poets come to get the sort of enthusiasm about streets and buildings that you and I
have for ponds and woods and hills. Miss Carruthers,
where I was staying yesterday, — she is a very nice
girl, — showed me half a dozen pretty poems of this
Miss Levy, the Jewish girl who died of a broken
heart, about this very thing.

> " The human tale of love and hate,
> The city pageant, early and late,
> Unfolds itself, rolls by, to be
> A pleasure deep and delicate.
> An omnibus suffices me."

When you come down to make me your winter visit I
shall make you understand this.

For the present, however, — you see I am writing
this at the office on Wednesday, — I am no longer a
cockney. How long my change of life will last I do
not know, but when I came home on Monday, poor
Mrs. Metcalf came to me in a good deal of trouble; I
think she had been crying. It proved that all her

boarders had deserted her, excepting me. Some had acted in good faith and some in bad faith, but there she was, with that big house and I do not know how many servants, and I was the only person to whom she was bound — and bound she was — to keep me in fishballs and pork and coffee and bread and butter and whatever I might choose to have at night. She wanted to know if I could, without inconvenience, make some other arrangement for the next six weeks, and at the same time if she might rely on me in September. You know I have come to like her, — whether you know it or not, I have come to like her, this hard-fortuned woman, very much; and although it was rather a nuisance to be told that my permanent arrangement, of which I believe I bragged to you, had broken down in a month, I of course said I would do what she wanted me to.

"Too convincing, dangerously dear,
In woman's eye the inexorable tear,"

whether it be the tear of a pretty girl of nineteen, or of the keeper of a boarding-house who has passed her forty-fifth year. What I did will amuse you. I had an errand to Cambridge, about an order they have or have not given us there, and I went out there. As I went out, there were some people in the street-car who were evidently going to the Summer School. The Summer School is something I had heard of before, but I did not know what it was. It seems that they have run the long vacation business to death at Harvard. It seems that some of the professors and teachers, at least, want to do something in their four empty months, and they have fallen back to the law of the instrument and opened what they call a Summer School. You can go there and study with all the college advantages and all the other things, and

though I believe they do not give you a degree of
Doctor of Laws at the end of the summer, you have a
sort of feeling that you have studied with the best
men there are, and with a good many of the Cambridge advantages. Now I do not think I shall study
much this summer, though I might, for all the business our "shebang" is doing or is likely to do. But,
anyway, the thought struck me that, as I was to be
turned loose, I might as well enter as a student in the
Summer School for something. At any rate I should
find boarding-house keepers in Cambridge who did not
shut up at forty-eight hours' warning, while I should
be quite as near my business as I was at Mrs. Metcalf's. So I have taken a room, exactly as if I were a
sophomore or a junior, at Mrs. Gorham's house, and
now you will please to regard me as a member of the
University. You had better regard me so, for nobody
else will. I am not a member of the University any
more than you are. My name will appear upon none
of its catalogues, for they are quite too grand for that.
But all the same I can say, when I am ninety years
old, "When I was a student at Cambridge," and
people will think that I am a Doctor of Laws.

After I had got through with the man, who, as it
proved, had not given us any order at all (but may,
perhaps), I went down to the office of the secretary,
or whatever he is called, to see on what terms I could
enter the Summer School. It is a free-and-easy, go-as-
you-please sort of institution ; in fact, it is not an institution in any proper sense of the word. But I
found out that, within hours that were convenient to
me, I could fall in with a French class, which will
anyway improve my conversation from the Stratford-
atte-Bowe idiom in which I have talked till now ; and
possibly I may enter also for botany, or for something
else of which I know nothing, and should like to

know something. Of this I will tell you in another letter.

I came in on the electric car. The electric system runs perhaps more smoothly at Cambridge than anywhere else, principally for the reason that on the long bridge no one stops the car, unless indeed it overtakes him. They get one good run at their full speed. I got off as we came into town, because I wanted to see the open-air gymnasium, which I had never seen. It is really first-rate, and I shall take a great deal of satisfaction in it; for I can leave the office early and take as much exercise there as I want on my way out. Of course, some of these melting days a person does not want to use the machinery of a gymnasium. But, generally speaking, we get an east wind in the afternoon, and between five and seven o'clock it is not melting weather. Anyway, here is a charming place to sit and see the water and the ships and the fellows exercising. There is a gymnasium for girls under cover. That is not so big as the gymnasium for men, I believe. There is somebody who directs you if you want; but I never wanted to be directed in a gymnasium. I always take up the plan of going as you please.

Dear mother, I knew it would please you, and it brought back the memory of old Wednesday evenings at Atherton, if I would go to the weekly prayer-meeting. I happened to see a sign, as I passed a church vestry, that this was the evening of the meeting, and I went in. But I cannot give you a very encouraging account of what happened. I was there, and, as our old story used to say, "a little girl was there." Then a young man and his sweetheart or sister came in, and we were all. I said to him, "It is a hot day." He said, " Yes, it is a hot day." Then the girl who was with him asked him if he worked there. He said he

6

did not work there regularly, but sometimes when they wanted somebody to do something he came round and lent a hand. Then the little girl went to the door and went out. Then the other two went to the door and went out. Then I went out. But I will hope, dear mother, that we were all better for having rested ourselves for fifteen minutes in a place where, at least, we might have had some serious associations.

For me, after this failure, I walked on, and having picked up my supper at the Providence Station eating-room, where I am rather fond of going, I spent my evening in the Public Library reading-room. Now you may say what you choose, this is a luxury of city life. I could not have had it unless I were in a place where there were hundreds of thousands of people together. Those people, or the leaders of those people, have provided for me a resource which no gentleman in this country, I do not care what his income is, has at his command. I can go in there, and I can call for and can read any one of two or three hundred of the best periodicals in the world. Or I have, waiting for me, the book which I have said in the course of the day I should want to read in the evening. Just at this moment, something that Carruthers had said about a yacht voyage in the Mediterranean had made me stop in the afternoon and order that Freeman's "Sicily" should be reserved for me. I found that, therefore, lying on the attendant's desk, and I spent the evening in turning it over. Sometime I will tell you some of the things I found in it. I also looked at Life, and Punch, and the London Spectator, and the French *Revue des Deux Mondes*. It never seems to me to be hot in the Public Library; at least, I have never found it so; and there I sat, with say a hundred other young fellows, who had heads on their shoulders and wanted to use this opportunity. There

were half as many women, perhaps, in the smaller
room on the other side of the hall. They are at work
now on a new building, and before the century is over
I suppose they will move in there; but this is good
enough for me.

I ought to tell you about the fortunes of my Russian friend. The night before I met him he had
spent at the Hawkins Street Lodge for Wayfarers.
This is the place where, if you recollect, Howells's boy
went, and sawed wood for an hour to pay for his
supper and lodging and breakfast. I fancy the Russian Bear had often enough at home done three times
as much work as that for half as much pay. Anyway,
he did not grumble either about the breakfast or the
supper or the lodging. But they won't let a fellow do
that every night. If they did I am disposed to think
they would be overrun. You must be palpably thrown
out of a home, and must not be sponging on the ad-
ministration. Still they say that thing earned money
for the city, and that the city treasurer fainted away
when somebody brought him in some money which he
did not expect, and said it was earned in Hawkins
Street, and was the surplus of what they had sold
their wood for after it was sawed, over what it cost
them to buy it. I did not want to have the Bear go
back to Hawkins Street after I had made his acquaintance, and Carruthers and I, and one or two of the
other young fellows, interested ourselves in seeing
that he should get something to do somewhere. Now
do you know it proves, though he does say "Bridget"
where he should say "bright," — so that he is not in
the least understood when he speaks to anybody, —
that he writes the best hand, literally, that you ever
saw in the world. You see this is because he learned
to write Russian and then had to write English as a
separate accomplishment. He therefore excels in this

thing, as we very often excel in our accomplishments, while we let our every-day duties run in an every-day sort of a way. With the Bear, writing is an elegant accomplishment, and when he makes a letter A he thinks of the letter A, and does it with all his heart and soul and mind and strength. Now I had my eyes open and it proved that, after a few days, it was necessary for us to send off to the stockholders, and indeed to a lot of other people, some thousands of circulars. We have not yet got all the clerical force moved here from Leeds. I am sure I did not want to direct those circulars, and I explained to the chief here that we had not force enough for it, and got him to say that I might employ anybody I chose. So I put the Bear on the circulars; and now people all over the country are receiving these marvellous specimens of handwriting; and, what is more to the point, the Bear is receiving five dollars a week for directing them, and Hawkins Street has one person less. Whether I shall ever teach him to say "thought" and not to say "tho-ugt," or to say "where" and not to say "whee-ree," I do not know. Thus far he uses the little tablet, and writes his very funny English upon it in his very perfect hand, and we write our answers. I believe, after all, we shall send him up to New Padua, or some of the normal schools, where I dare say they will find something for him to do.

Now I will go back to my outing in the Narragansett country, and then tell of last night's dissipation, if these parsimonious people will give me what they call lines enough. Saturday afternoon, we had a splendid sea-bath at North Ness just before we dined, having dinner put late on purpose. I had been in the sea before, for I can go out for five cents to South Boston and swim in the sea at a public bathing-house; and when the tide is right I do this three or four

times a week. But that is nothing to the joy of swimming through these ocean breakers and lying on what
I am tempted to call the fresh salt water. The feeling
that there is nothing between you and the West Indies
has perhaps something to do with it; the infinite power
and kindness of nature has a great deal more to do
with it. Carruthers had to warn me that I was staying in the water too long. Then the exhilaration and
joy of life, after it is over, is something which does
not come too often to a man. The only thing to compare to it is the joy in riding on a fine horse, when you
love him and he loves you. Then Sunday we had a
pleasant, homelike service, where three or four of the
neighbors' families came in. Mr. Carruthers himself
led the prayers, we read the Psalms alternately with
him, he read the Scripture, and then read something
which served for a sermon, which he had found in
Littell's Living Age, — a very nice, homelike service it
was. And in the afternoon we all went, — dear mother,
you would have said it was to Central America, — into
a great grove of rhododendrons. I did not know that
there was any thing so tropical in New England. No,
you must not tell me about laurel; I know all about
laurel. Here you go into great covered ways of this
magnificent tropical plant. Don't you know, I tried
to describe to you Mr. Hunnewell's, out at his place.
But here is a grove of rhododendrons as big as his whole
place is altogether. The trees of it, for they are trees,
grow twenty and thirty feet high, and for what I know,
more. This has been a particularly favorable winter
for it, so that you see the great burning bushes of it,
crowded with clumps of blossoms; and when you think
you have seen the very best you stumble on another
opening where they are in other tints and even more
luxuriant. At first I had a feeling that I was walking
through avenues of it, as if it only grew by the side

of the wood-paths. But soon enough I found that here is one great tangle of hundreds of acres of it, only it is impervious in most places, and we can only go where the foot of man and the hand of man have gone before. Some of us had gone in boats, some had gone in wagons; it was a sort of ceremony to visit the rhododendron grove with the nicest people who could be brought together, and this was the great pageant of the year. I put up three or four heads in a box and sent them to you by Uncle Sam's kindness. You knew they came from me, but you wondered if such things grew on Boston Common.

Now for my dissipation. I am not so much of a cockney yet but that I could see the humor of it. Understand, then, that this dear, nice gentleman, of whom I spoke as being the director who likes to look in at the office, is, for his sins, spending the summer in Boston. He says forty years ago everybody in his social condition did so, or almost everybody. But now you may go through Marlboro Street or Beacon Street, and three houses out of four are actually boarded up, so that burglars may not be tempted to go in; and if a policeman meets a man at three o'clock in the morning, with a carpet-bag in his hand, he arrests him because he knows he is a burglar. But my Mr. Champernoon is waiting for the arrival of some members of his family from England, so his house is open still. He talks about it a great deal, as you or I might talk of having a floating-house in the middle of the Atlantic Ocean, as if it were an entire surprise to him to find that Boston is habitable in July. What really has an element of humor in it is that last night Mr. and Mrs. Champernoon had to give a party. I believe they really approached the occasion wondering whether the roof would not fall in upon their heads, so utterly impossible did it seem to carry it through.

But there had arrived from the South some very grand people who were classmates of his in college, and who, with that droll Southern ignorance of the North, coming on to see their old friends, had come of course to Boston, supposing that they should find their old friends there. Mr. Rutledge had called on Mr. Champernoon. Mr. Champernoon could not say that he was at the Adirondacks or at Nahant or at Bar Harbor, because he was not. And Mrs. Champernoon had been over to the Brunswick to see Mrs. Rutledge and the young ladies and nieces and all the rest. And then, sweet dear soul, she thought she must give an evening party for them, though, as I say, the thing seemed as impossible as for her to make the State House waltz with Faneuil Hall. To this evening party I was bidden, a little on the principle of the parable. That is to say, Mr. and Mrs. Champernoon had sent personal notes to all their friends who lived within ten miles of Boston, entreating them to come in. And why indeed should they not come in, as easily as Boston people go out in the winter to Arlington, to Watertown, to Brookline, or to Milton, when there are parties there?

But I think Mr. Champernoon was enough a man of the world to know that the Rutledges would never know whom they met, if his rooms were only filled with somebody. He certainly judged rightly when he thought I should not be disinclined to see a handsome Boston house lighted up for an evening party, to hear good music between whiles, and would even condescend to eat a nice piece of salmon, though oysters were not in season. He knows Carruthers well, and of course he had seen me in the office. So he came up to me and asked me if I would not come, in a perfectly informal way, to his house, to meet some gentlemen and ladies from the South; and I gladly

accepted.   I went with Carruthers, and Carruthers explained to me that we went a good deal earlier than
we should have gone if it were winter.   When I entered the room, it seemed to me probable that Carruthers would be the only person in it whom I had ever
seen before, excepting my host.   I certainly did not
suppose that Mr. Champernoon meant to let me with-
draw into a private room and discuss with him the
materials for clothes-pins, or the possibilities of making a market for them in the Antarctic Ocean.   However, I went in for luck, as I always do, and my luck
in no sort failed me.   Who should be the very first
person I saw, but the Miss Osborne with whom I
danced at Class Day, and her brother.   Of course they
knew I was a stranger, and the brother, in particular,
took care that I should not feel alone.

As for Mrs. Champernoon, she is a trump.   The moment she heard my name she insisted upon it that she
must have known my grandfather or his grand-nephew
or somebody, and I really expected to hear her say
that she went to Miss Beecher's school with you
at Hartford.   For, to tell you the truth, dear Mother,
I have heard that said so often in the last year that I
begin to think the school must have numbered five
thousand. people.   As to the Southern ladies, I was
presented to one or two of the younger of them, and
found them very good fun.   They were bright and
wide-awake, and just as much amused and surprised at
things which they had seen between Washington and
Boston as I should be if I were in a rice plantation or
saw a cotton-gin running.   We kept well clear of politics, and I believe they thought I should vote for Jeff
Davis and Grover Cleveland, if they were put up on
the same ticket at the next election.   There was a
well-nigh perfect band of half a dozen instruments, in
a balcony at the head of the finest stairease that you

ever saw. There were fifty pictures in the house which would have made the fortune of any exhibition of pictures in any city. There were so few people that the rooms were not crowded, and there was no reason why I and Miss Osborne, or I and Miss Rutledge, should not walk around and look at pictures as much as we wanted to. For one, I was not ashamed to be seen studying Corot or Meissonier with somebody who knew a great deal more about them than I did, as Miss Osborne did. I rather think she paints a little herself.

From the way in which little knots of people were glued to each other, I could guess that most of the people in that house were quite as much strangers as I was. But I could also see that dear Mrs. Champernoon's spirits rose as the evening ground itself along from nine to ten o'clock. As I was passing her with Miss Osborne, Mrs. Champernoon beckoned her, and asked if she did not think it would do to have some dancing. She said she had not really thought of it, there would be so few people; but there was the music and there was the floor. Of course, we young people did not object to that, and very soon the band was playing some lively music, and half a dozen couples of us were waltzing. Miss Osborne dances very well, and after a minute she told me to leave her and ask Miss Sarah Rutledge to take a turn, which I did. So that really the Champernoon party turned out a great deal better than they or anybody else expected. The thing to say was how interesting it was to have a dance in the middle of July; how beautiful the house was, which was easy enough to say; and how fortunate it was that one found one's self in Boston on the twenty-first of July, as if the only probable place to be were the middle of Greenland or a punt in the harbor of Sitka. By and by, "the eatables and drinkables" were on the table, and we were all as bold

as Diggory.   For my part, I have not been displeased
with my initiation into high fashionable society in
Boston.

Now, my dear mother, I have made this letter short
enough to please the printers, and so I have not told
you half I have to say.   What you will care for most
is that I am very well and am not yet tired of Boston.
I really hope that in my next letter I may have something to say.   Give my love to the children and to
Florence.   I was sorry she was not there last night;
we might have waltzed together all the evening, and
nobody would have known it was a brother and
sister dancing together.

.   .   .   .

P. S. — Did you see that they put in some pictures,
which they called illustrations of my letters ?   You
never can tell who is snapping a camera on you now,
wherever you go.   There would have been a picture
of me at the prayer-meeting, and another picture of
me at the party waltzing with Miss Rutledge, if those
fellows had yet learned how to take photographs by
such light as we had at the chapel or in Mrs. Champernoon's house.   I beg to say to you that I am not
responsible for these pictures, and I made such a row
when the fellows laughed about my being bald in the
back of my head, because they said I was the person
represented in the picture, that this time there will
not be any picture.   At least, so they promised me in
the newspaper office.   How soon they will change
their minds they know themselves; but I am sure I
do not know.

Truly yours,

HARRY.

CHAPTER EIGHTH.

X.

LUCY TO KATE.

Boston, July 28, 1891.

My DEAR KATE, — Such a really "country" morning as I have been having! You would imagine I
was actually in Astney and that I had wandered off
away into the fields. Only I was, indeed, more alone
by myself than I am apt to be at home in the summer.
The park into which Commonwealth Avenue passes,
— the green fields over which Leif Ericson looks, — is
not far away from the house here.

It was a holiday morning and I actually took a book
out with me; for I have had this plan ever since I
have been here, only the days have hurried by in so
busy a way that I have had no chance. Only think of
it! Those hours of study that I planned in the summer months of "solitude" in Boston! I have not
found them yet. I have not even found time to look
up the books for them, nor time to "establish" myself
at the Public Library, nor to arrange having a card of
permission for taking out books there.

So it was not a book of study that I took with me.
It was to be a time of real rest; for I was having a
Saturday. I was enchanted with the place I found;
such lovely walks in the midst of all sorts of wild
flowers that I wanted to botanize directly. There was
that Astragalus, don't you remember, that you and I
" did " last year in Vermont with our Gray's Botany?
Then besides such lovely wild roses, some daisies still

lingering, and wild morning-glories. Besides them, delightful, old-fashioned garden flowers, tiger lilies, magnificent groups of them that you would like to paint, shepherd's purse, gay marigolds, all hidden in masses of wild-looking shrubs, and not laid out with a tiresome regularity, but in the greatest luxuriance and confusion. Then there were such delightful seats, that looked so inviting and comfortable, not like the stiff iron seats usually in public places, as if they were meant for an unruly multitude, but as if for you and me or just one or two of us. I did sit there all the morning and listened to the birds singing all round me, and part of the time watching the ducks swimming about in a little lake close by. And, yes, I did read a little; and something that I read, set me thinking.

Laurence Oliphant says that the best part of everything is the anticipation. He went into a life of adventure, rushing from one exciting thing to another, so that you would think he would never have found time for anticipation, especially as with him the event always came so suddenly. It must have been always, indeed, a part of the anticipation, it came so quickly. I think, perhaps, that he is partly right. If what happens comes out to "meet our anticipations," as we say, it just doubles all we had fancied, and we enjoy it all over twice. We go back to our happy anticipation and have the two-fold pleasure, thinking : " Ah, it is just all I fancied it would be." Now this life here is quite different from what I fancied it. Still it has some of that very charm that made me long for it, and so ˙I really am having a double enjoyment in the anticipation and its following, like the image and the reflection in the water, only the reflection has come first.

.   .   .   .

I began a week ago, and many things have happened
since, of my kind of happenings, such as I think you
will be interested in, especially as you want to know
more about my mysterious Class Day acquaintance,
who, you write, " seems to be always tumbling into
adventures." He still remains in the rank of ac-
quaintances, though I have seen him since and have
learned his name, — which belongs to another chapter
of my history. Only don't expect too much ; for I
have not yet spoken to him. I think he is to remain
ever an inaccessible myth, for I seem to see him only
in the distance, as if on the stage, and I in one of the
boxes.

To begin, I must tell you about our Boston evenings. Anna and I have taken up a delightful fashion
of sitting on the door-steps here, just as if we were at
home at Astney, only instead of neighbors dropping
in to talk to us, as they always did there, we look out
upon the silent street, with its electric lights, and an
occasional policeman turning up round the corner.
Anna's brother and his wife are here from the West,
and are at the Vendôme, and they come almost every
evening. Sometimes we all go off somewhere, — one
evening to the "Last Days of Pompeii"! Yes, we really
all went in a gay party. Then one evening we took
a West End car and went all round the town and its
lighted streets, a trip that took us about one hour
and a half, and for five cents apiece, — on the same
car all the time. It was a splendid lesson in geography for me.

We took the car away up on Washington Street,
went on through Temple Place, where we saw no
" temple," into Tremont Street to Scollay Square,
where I have been before, to see the statue of John
Winthrop that stands in the middle of a cobweb of
streets, out of which we threaded our way into

streets still narrower, to another of these "squares," where stands the Revere House. Then on, turning right angles, almost jostling other lines of horse-cars, into Charles Street, that interests me, as there is the gymnasium I wrote you of, and I may decide to live there next winter. Then unexpectedly we turned up between the Common and the lovely Public Garden, shooting away from the latter into unknown regions again, when I found myself at the very place where we had taken the car. It was a most interesting tour all round the town, in the open car where I could see everything. Such crowds of people as we went through, getting some slight idea of the shape of the town ; and I have repeated it since by daylight in the afternoon, all by myself.

But we do enjoy our door-step evenings, taking our cushions to sit upon and wraps, for some of the evenings have been cool, and such delightful chats as we have there ! And we have not lacked visitors ; for sundry friends know where to find us, and we have some charming door-step parties. And one evening Mr. Brand brought his sister Rosamond. They live at Arlington, but there was a late train out they could take, so they planned this evening call. They have been very kind to me and have invited me to spend an . afternoon and night there. We had told Mr. Brand about our quiet evenings and solitary street, so we were all very much surprised when, as the evening passed on, we could see a house below us on the opposite side lighted up, and an awning in front of the door. Then carriages appeared, one after another, full of guests who were ushered in, and there was a band of music and every sign of a gay party.

Mr. Brand and his sister laughed at our idea of solitude which we had promised them, and we went down to enjoy the music. As we walked up and down on the walk in the middle of the street, we could look into the brilliantly lighted rooms, and were much amused at watching the figures moving about, and listening to the Babel of voices and the strains of music that overpowered all.

Suddenly Mr. Brand exclaimed, " There is our mysterious friend whom we did *not* see drown the other day." And at the same moment the very person, my Class Day partner, appeared talking to a young lady, whom Mr. Brand knew, a Miss Osborne, very pretty, with a lovely white gauze dress and a bunch of wild roses in front. Of course I hurried Mr. Brand away ; for I thought it would seem so horrid if we were seen spying into our neighbors' houses in that way. But Mr. Brand said if he had only known the name of the mysterious stranger, he would have gone across and spoken to him and Miss Osborne. I am thankful he did not, but I was really quite relieved to see that our unknown was indeed alive; for I have been very anxious about him.

All this took place some days before my discovering his name, which came as the result of a visit I have been wanting to make upon Miss Dexter, whom, you may remember, I tried to find some time ago. But I have been too busy to take an afternoon for it. My mornings do tire me ; I have to give so much attention to my class of boys, and they require so much watchfulness. They are just as full of mischief as they can be ; they want to be " carrying on " all the time ; and I like to have them lively, as I hate the idea of oppressing them and keeping them under, in their summer days.

I must tell you one of their jokes that I did not get at for a long time. I noticed that when one of the boys had been speaking to me by name, one of the others would shout out, "Jamaica Plain to the Depots,"

or something about the Jamaica Plain cars. I could
not make out what they meant by it, and supposed
they thought I lived at Jamaica Plain. But one day,
when a very small boy had been calling out, in a very
squeaky but stentorian voice, my name, " Miss Sandford," in a way that might be heard through the
whole building, half a dozen boys began, " Best puri-
fied Jamaica Ginger ! " " Good for families ! " " Sold
in bottles by the dozen ! " " No family should be without it ! " " Sandford's Jamaica Ginger ! " shouted another, and then it all came over me that it was my
name they were joking about, and I could not help
joining in the laugh. Did you ever know anything
so absurd ?

After the racket had died off a little, I stood up in
front of the platform and said, " Now, boys, you seem
to think that it is a very good joke ; so we will have
it every day, regularly at one o'clock, after the arithmetic lesson. I am a little tired of hearing it quite
as often as we have been having it, and I think once a
morning will do. But any boy that wants it oftener
can hold up his hand." Each boy grinned upon his
neighbor to see who was holding up his hand, but not
a hand was raised. The next day after the arithmetic
lesson — which I have not yet described to you — I
said, " Now we will have the Sandford joke, if there 's
anybody here who is not tired of it." But they looked
a little ashamed, and I have heard no more of it since.

In general, I get on very well ; but it does tax all
my strength, and makes me inclined to be lazy in the
afternoon, especially if we have a hot, muggy day, as
frequently happens. But one afternoon this week,
when there was an east wind, I walked all the way
down to the home of Miss Dexter. The Flower Mission had made its visit at school that morning, and
this always rejoices the children. Two young ladies

came to the school with large baskets of flowers. It happened that they came late, and many of the children were in the yard and crowded round pulling each other away in their eagerness. Even my older boys were glad of their share, and wanted me to put a pink or else a yellow daisy in their button-holes in the proper style. I took away a little bunch for my friend at the North End ; but I found she did not care much for flowers, and said she would take them down to a sick woman below. She said she had not anything suitable to put them in, and she never wanted to keep anything for them, it was such a trouble to wash up anything extra. She did take a marigold and stick it in her looking-glass ; it seemed to touch a chord somewhere.

For I found Miss Dexter at home and managed at last to make her understand who I was. She did not remember much about my mother, for which I was very sorry, as I wanted to hear about her youthful days. But she had many stories to tell of my aunt who was many years older. It was she who told me about Mr. Merton, who had been to see her, though she was forgetful of names, she said, and " mebbe she had n't it right." But she looked up a note he had brought from his mother, and there the name was fairly written out, — for fortunately she had sent a number of notes to Miss Dexter, — and the name is Merton. " I knew it began with an ' M, ' " said Miss Dexter, " but it might have been Milton or Morton, I am so forgetful of names." It was lucky I went early ; for I stayed a long time talking. I asked her if she did not want to get out of town in the summer, vaguely thinking I might find some kindly home for her in a farmhouse in the country for a few weeks — she seemed so shut in, in the midst of the brick walls. " Where it would be more quiet and cool," I suggested.

7

But she broke out in great indignation. Evidently she felt that I did not appreciate the advantages of Boston. She declared it to be the coolest place that could be found. All the Southerners, she said, came up to Boston to get cool; and when she was young nobody thought of leaving Boston, unless they had houses in the neighborhood where they could come in often. And as for the quiet of the country, it made her feel lonesome. And, besides, the cocks and the hens made such a crowing and a cackling that it woke her up early in the morning, and she could n't get to sleep again. She liked the winter better anyhow, because the days were shorter, and she could go out to the lectures in the evening. There were the Lowell lectures, to which she goes, I found, because she does not have to pay.

My interest woke up in these, and I asked about the subjects last winter, and wondered which she was most interested in, and supposed they would be those with the stereopticon. But no, that tired her eyes, she said, and she had to shut them while the pictures were going on; but, she said, it was a warm place to go to, and it was economical, as she could let her stove go out and could save in lamp oil, because she does not use the gas! Still she seems to be something of a reader, and had some well-worn books about and a pile of Christian Registers. Yet she said she had never taken a card at the Public Library. She supposed it would be a great deal of trouble to get one, and quite likely the books she wanted would be out.

Indeed, she seemed to me a sort of fossil specimen of a former date that does not care to attach itself to our present mode of life, and will not accept even its advantages and progress. It was delightful to hear her talk of the older time, of Brattle Street Church where she used to go, and of the steps that still lead to the place where it stood. I believe she thinks there is no other preaching equal to what she heard there and which she can hear no longer, now that the church is moved so far away and is not what it used to be, when the cannon-ball was still in its walls which Putnam's men fired there. I could not persuade her to say she would go to see the hollyhocks exhibited free last Saturday at Horticultural Hall. She told me much about Harry Merton and his family. His mother must be a lovely woman from her notes ; for Miss Dexter would read them all to me, though I felt she ought not.

I must hurry on in this long letter to tell you of another expedition to see the sea that Anna and I . accomplished. We went on a voyage of discovery to City Point, taking a car at Park Square and going through some miserable parts of the town on Albany Street and Harrison Avenue, perhaps more squalid even than the narrow streets of the North End. Anna and I are always struck by the contrasts of things, in leaving the large airy houses on Commonwealth Avenue and Beacon Street, all deserted now and boarded up for fear some stray intruder should venture in, and then finding, at the other end of the town, the close tenement houses swarming with men, women, and children, with scarcely even air to breathe. It seems as if it were all very unequal in an American country, and as if they ought to be allowed to go and breathe for a while in the large, unoccupied palaces at the other end of the town.

And then I remember the wide, unoccupied land around our little town of Astney at home and the deserted farmhouses ; and I can't but think that it is partly these people's fault that they are living here in these " stived " up places, and that they might go out into the country — many of them — if

they chose, and that if they went into the palaces for
a while, they would leave them perhaps as squalid as
their tenements are.   And as our open horse-car bore
us along, away from the close streets into the wide
thoroughfares, we praised the owners of the up-town
palaces, who are doing so much to purify these close
streets and give to their crowded inhabitants a chance
at fresh air.

Soon we began to have pretty views of the ocean,
as we turned corners here and there; and the car was
filled with women who were taking their children for
a breath of the sea.   When the conductor at last said,
"City Point," we alighted and followed the crowd
that went towards the Pier.   This extends far out
into the deep sea.   I heard a man say it was 3,580
feet long; it is wide enough for a dozen people to walk
abreast.   Hundreds of men, women, and children were
walking up and down, — such a blessing as the place
must be to them!   Several mothers had brought their
sewing along, and did their mending while they held
the ever-present baby in their laps and the children
ran up and down.   There are benches all along on
either side, and the Pier is partly covered, which
must be very nice when it rains.   Then there are
hundreds of electric lights and lamps, and it must be
lovely to walk there in the evening.   Here and there
girls were sitting reading, or with their embroidery.

And then the view was lovely.   All around were
hundreds of little yachts, and it was very entertaining
to watch their changing motions.   Just opposite the
Pier is Fort Independence on one side and on the
other Thompson's Island.   I believe there is an
Orphan Boys' Home there.   In the distance we could
see Deer Island, the terror of the boys, and its buildings look quite like some feudal castle.   I am sorry
to say that some of my boys, young as they are, are

acquainted with it, having had an occasional sentence
of "ten days at the Island." Far away was a glimpse
of the dark sea line, and altogether it was a lovely
sight, as we left it with the sunset lights streaming
over from the west.

We went back in a Cambridge car that took us to
Park Square, and it was crowded with children who
had come early in the afternoon all the way from
Cambridge. They told us that they came free; that
is, any children who went to the City Hall in Cambridge and asked for car-tickets were given them to
go all the distance from Cambridge, over the pretty
bridge, then through Park Square to South Boston
and to the Pier, where these children had passed the
afternoon. They had had a jolly time and would get
home a little after sunset.

We often walk up to the edge of the park here, at
sunset, to get the beautiful changes of life, — the park
that I began my letter with; and I did not finish
then about the book I was reading, so intensely exciting, the life of Laurence Oliphant. I do hope you
have got hold of it and are reading it. It is interesting as a history of our last half-century; for Laurence
Oliphant was " in " the very height of all its motion.
There was not a war nor a revolution nor an insurrection but what he sniffed it afar, or else he was in
the midst of it,—before it began, as you might say,—
in the Crimea before that war, in Japan among the
first, in the Polish insurrection. How many wars,
indeed, our half-century has seen, and this man was
in the midst of them all. Then his own private life
and thoughts were so intensely interesting. I do
hope you will read it, only my telling you to is like
the English woman, who told an American friend she
met at a *pension* that she hoped that her husband,
who was on his way to Rome, would go and see

St. Peter's. " He would find it quite worth his while ! " For " everybody " is reading and talking about the life of Laurence Oliphant, and doubtless you are, among the rest. And I, who do so little reading, who am I, to advise you ? You ought to tell me not to write so much to you.

And I have not written you about my going to the celebration of Jennie Collins's birthday. She it was, you know, who founded " Boffin's Bower " and gave dinners to the working-girls. One of the rooms at the " Helping-Hand Home " — of which you shall hear more — is named for her, and her picture hangs upon the wall. It is the sitting-room, and there, too, are some of her favorite articles of furniture. Before she died she asked " that her memory should be kept green," and so her birthday was celebrated in this room. The room was fragrant with flowers and there was lovely music, and reminiscences of all she had done were related. It was all intensely interesting. " More in our next."

CHAPTER NINTH.

XI.

HARRY TO HIS MOTHER.

Boston (at the office), July 24, 1891.

My dear Mother, — We are in for it this time, I can tell you. And if this letter stops in the next line, and these old newspaper people have to fill up with the third book of Chronicles — indeed I do not know. But it is all now settled that the concern will move here. Our temporary engagements are extended. We take five-years' leases of the sheds and houses and of our nice office here. And notices were given Monday for the whole staff to report at this office next Monday morning.

Of course they have all known, more or less, that something was in the wind. But nobody could know certainly, because the chief and the directors did not know themselves. But now they have had the great meeting in New York. The "proxies" were all as they should be, and there was no turn-out of our old board; only Mr. Gunn became vice-president, and then, as you know of course, the treasurer's office almost had to be here, and everything else had to follow.

You can see what a break-up this makes at Leeds. All told, the pay roll is for forty-eight men, and I suppose thirty-five of them are married. Leeds will be in tears for the loss of so many of its people. I am afraid Boston will not know that they arrive.

But I know; for I have a sheaf of letters under my
hand here from the different fellows, who want me to
hunt up rooms or tenements or houses for them, so
that they can send their furniture right on and find
it here when they arrive with their families. I am
slamming round in a cab, every minute the chief will
give me, looking at houses and deciding the fates
of these poor women who have to be dumped into the
rooms I choose for them, without the luxury of house-
hunting for themselves. As for the men, they only
sleep at home, and they bring their old bedsteads with
them.

I tell you one thing, dear Mother. I do not put
any of them into tenement houses. I hate that whole
business. I write and advise, and advise and write,
that everybody must have his own house. Or perhaps
I do give one house to two families, and make one set
go up one flight. But beyond one flight, none of my
clients go. This means that I take most of them five
or ten miles out of what Mr. Champernoon calls the
"city proper," into some Boylston or Brighton or
Allston or Roslindale. I am becoming very learned
in suburban time-tables. I have placed two or three
families on the high lands in South Boston. And
this will make you understand what our Rapid Transit problems are, which I dare say you have skipped
when you read your Journal. The company allows
two days for moving. That is, the office at Leeds
closes Thursday night and all these gentlemen report
to us Monday morning. The mail begins to come to
us Friday. What we are to do with them, the chief
and I and the Russian Bear and two or three temporary copying-clerks, on Friday and Saturday, remains
to be seen.

Is not this emigration of a whole community queer?
I suppose such things happen all the time. If the

emigration was from Boston to Leeds, the Leeds newspaper would have told of it, and the Boston papers would have copied the paragraph, and as much fuss would have been made about us all as if we were Pilgrim Fathers and Mothers — which we are not. As it is, nobody in Boston except me knows they are coming.

Do you not remember that picture at the Hartford Athenæum of the procession of the first settlers from Cambridge to Hartford, when it took them seventeen days to go ? I remember there is a white horse in it, which used to seem to me to be our old Sally. I could not help thinking of that, as I made these arrangements for twice that number of people — twice the number of the Pilgrims indeed — when we gave them a week's warning for their change of home and gave them two days to make it in. But I think I am wiser than the Pilgrims. I have not put all my people together. They had better not talk "shop" all the time; so I have put two or three families at South Boston, some at Roxbury, two at Dorchester, three at Boylston, two at Jamaica Plain, two at Roslindale, and one at Central, four at Allston, two at Melrose, and three in Cambridgeport. I always let everybody have an old neighbor from Leeds. But for more than that, they must make new friends. It does not make much difference what I do for them; for at the end of six months they will all move.

I had to decide about their houses in very quick metre sometimes. There was one nice house I went to twice, and I was more pleased the second time than the first. But just as I came downstairs, I saw a large girl — I supposed a servant girl — thrashing a poor little boy awfully in the front garden. I interfered, which was dangerous. To which she said, "Mind your own business, and I will mind mine. I

am his mother. And if I cannot slap him who can?"
I fled confounded. But I told the agent that I did not
want the half-house where she ruled supreme in the
other half.

How they will all like their new homes I cannot
pretend to say. But they will all arrive, bag and baggage, Friday night or Saturday morning. I have been
coaching the Russian Bear and the office errand boy,
as well as I can, about the difference between Melrose
and Roslindale, and I hope that I shall not get many
bad mixtures. If we can keep the right babies with
the right mothers we shall do well. And as for
trunks and carpet-bags, they must take their chances.
Really, I feel quite proud of myself as an organizer of
emigration.

.   .   .   .

CAMBRIDGE, July 30.

You must thank Nahum for his nice letter. Tell
him I wish I could write him a separate letter now.
But as soon as the moving is all over, I will write him
a letter all for himself. I understand very well what
the children say about my letters being grown-up
letters and not funny letters. This shows you, dear
Mother, how the cares of life are gathering on my
head. But Nahum and Florence will both like to
hear about the Fall of Pompeii. I so wished they had
been with me when I went around there.

When we came into the grounds we found them arranged as follows. The grounds were oval. In the
middle was an oval artificial pond, one hundred yards
long and fifty yards wide. Around this pond was a
race track like that at the circus. Along one of the
long stretches of the track were the seats, not stretch-
ing around the track as they do at a circus, but ex-
tending in a straight line with many tiers, so that

they might accommodate perhaps ten thousand persons. The lowest seats were about fifteen yards from the track.

On the other side of the pond, across the farther part of the track, stretched the buildings of Pompeii in a line. The scene represented, I suppose, a street running alongside the water. There were a number of temples, but nothing that looked much like a dwelling-house. Between the track and the buildings the street was some thirty yards wide, giving room for processions and athletic feats. Directly to the right of the extreme right-hand building was a gigantic sign painted white on a black fence, "Read the Daily Traveller." One of the young men suggested that it ought to say, "*Lege Viatorem Cotidianum.*" Perhaps Nahum's Latin is up to that. If not, he must ask Mr. Walsingham to explain it to him.

The first part of the show began at about eight o'clock. It was a procession of the citizens of Pompeii. Usually there are programmes to tell what is going on; but on this night the programmes did not come. The citizens of Pompeii consisted largely of dancing girls with very short skirts. The very first one who appeared danced very well; then they gradually deteriorated till the last girls, who were frequently out of time and not at all graceful. Before and after the dancing there was a little pantomime acting. It was supposed to represent some well-known scene in Bulwer's "Last Days of Pompeii." But no one paid much attention to this part of the performance; for one could not make out much of what was happening, even if one wished to know.

Two gymnasts now appeared with a clown. They came running round the track till they were directly between the spectators and the water. In the space between us and the track were three horizontal bars, parallel, on the same level, about eight feet apart from each other and about twenty feet from the ground, with their ends toward us. The athletes were very agile and really did their part well; and the clown was extremely laughable. There was a net stretched underneath the bars, so that there was no danger. This is really necessary; for the other day a man broke his leg there. The two gymnasts ended up by getting hold of the same bar and doing the "giant's swing" at the same time, going round and round, with great clouds coming from red fire behind them. It was very effective. Tell Nahum to ask Will Babcock to try this with him.

Then there was a galloping race between horses, a race between a man and a horse, and a two-horse and a four-horse chariot race, — all just like the races at a circus. Then there was a bicycle performance, the interesting thing about which was a little bit of a girl who was the chief performer. She seemed about six years old, with a short white frock and long slender black legs. The bicycling was on the other side of the lake and race course, just in front of the buildings. The citizens of Pompeii were standing about to watch it, with no apparent surprise at the sight of an invention two thousand years after their day. Two men rode round on a bicycle; then another mounted to their shoulders; then the little girl climbed up till she sat on his shoulders. Then she gave an exhibition ride alone. She did a number of pretty tricks, sat side-saddle running the machine with one leg, jumped off and on again while the bicycle was running at full speed, and finally rode up to a man who lifted her, machine and all, up into the air, where she still continued to ply her little pedals vigorously, much to the amusement of the spectators.

Soon after this it was half-past nine, and observant

spectators noticed a flame coming out of Vesuvius, which was well represented (in pasteboard, I suppose) directly behind the ill-fated city. A moment later Roman candles began to shoot out of the crater, and at the same time the buildings of Pompeii began to burn and fall to the ground. The inhabitants, who were, as I understand, about to make a human sacrifice of some Christians, were much dismayed and rushed away. But we paid them no attention; for we were looking at the fireworks, all of which were startling and some beautiful. The prettiest were the rockets which exploded and gave out splendid showers of colored stars. Then there were pin-wheels which shot to and fro above the surface of the pond, and some strange things were thrown into the water that kept spitting out fire. A great elephant was exhibited, made in outline with fireworks, and moved by some arrangement so that he seemed to walk along the side of the track as far as the turn, where he slowly burnt out.

The night happened to be "Newspaper Night," so that there were two ridiculous "set" pieces in honor of the newspapers, one representing a prominent editor. After this a few more rockets, and then the great crowd filed out. I have since noticed in the newspapers that almost every night seems to be somebody's night, either " Newspaper," "Cadet," or something of that kind. I cannot but hope they will have a night for our company and send us all "dead head" tickets. Ask Nahum if he knows what a "dead head" is. I am afraid it will not do for him to read this on the conversation day at the High School, for they will think his brother is engaged in very frivolous amusements.

CAMBRIDGE, 11.30 P.M.

I still live, and that is a wonder. We have had a field-day of it indeed. At one time I thought it would have been better had I taken the whole party of my emigrants and encamped on Boston Common with them. Then the Boston people would have found out that they had the arrival of a new colony here. But at this moment all my people are in bed somewhere, though I will not swear that Mrs. Smith has not Mrs. Brown's baby without knowing it, and Mrs. Brown Mrs. Smith's. It has been the hardest work I ever did; but, at the same time, it has been the funniest day. If I ever write a farce, it shall turn on the adventures of such a transmigration. The incidents shall be the loss and recoveries of babies and baggage by the emigrants.

And the difficulty mostly came from a piece of over-caution, — as, I believe, usually happens. Of course the Company wanted to do everything to make it easy, and as here were more than two hundred people to move, — more than half of them children, — it occurred to the president, but only at the last moment, to ask to have a special train made up at Leeds. Of course this was easily done, and in the separate train they came. But the railroad people rated it only as a separate block of what they call the "Thunder Express." Nobody told us at the new office that there was any separate block or special express. Only we were told to be ready at the station at 11.30 prompt to meet the whole party and to tell them, men, women, and children, where they were to go. So we were. The regular train came — and not one of our people !

Nobody at the station seemed to know or care where our people were. I supposed they had had a change of heart of some sort, and so, leaving the rest with my lists at the station, I slammed back in a cab to the office to telephone on our own wire to Leeds. They said at once that the people had all started. I slammed back to the station, and sure enough, there they all were, dividing themselves as they could to their different homes. John was standing on a trunk with my list. We had engaged thirty-five cabs and hacks, and the cabmen were waiting to be told where to drive. Sometimes it was to other stations, and sometimes it was direct to the houses which had been hired. It would have been a deal easier had our company built thirty-five houses for them and been done with it. But you know they would not like that near so well.

Here it was that the change of babies undoubtedly took place. The novels of twenty years hence will turn on these changes. You see we had thirty-five mothers, thirty-five fathers, and more than a hundred children. Now it is impossible, you know, that those mothers could have known all their babies, they looked so exactly alike. Anyway, the great row of the day, which has taken more telephoning and cab-hire and scolding, not to say swearing, and in the end rejoicing, belonged to this baby business. I was mystified for a few hours, but now I understand it all. And I will relieve you at once by telling you that Mrs. Outlake is all right, and, I suppose, has her baby in her arms. It would have been better had he been in her arms at noon to-day. But he was not. He was in the arms of a certain Bridget, a nice, plump young Irishwoman, just over. My Russian Bear met them as they got out of the car. He was most anxious to be of use. "Name!" says he to her. "Vot ish your name?" "Bridget," said the girl, courtesying. Then he thought aloud, in Russian, I suppose, for he always does. He looked on the printed alphabetical list which the cabman had. He spelled B-r-i-g — satisfied himself that that this spelt "Bridge" — h-t, said that this would do for "et," and took her in triumph at

once, before anybody saw him, to the cab — such fun
— of our Mr. Bright, the first cashier, who had out of
grandeur and courtesy and pure kindness come down
to see the thing. He had gone up into the superin-
tendent's office, and had handed the Bear two or three
of his cards, if he wanted to send any one to inquire
for him.

My dear Mother, I cannot make you see the fun of
this! This Mr. Bright is the one swell man in our
office. He is very much of a bachelor. He has the
most elegant rooms in the Romeo, which is the most
swell bachelors' hotel in Boston. With his card, my
friend the Bear and Bridget go out to the street, and
Bear shows the card to the policeman who directed
our thirty-five carriages. He calls Mr. Bright's cab,
which was not one of them. The cabman takes the
card, takes Bridget, takes the baby, and carries them
to the Romeo.

I meanwhile return to the station, as I tell you.
As it happens, I send the Bear to South Boston
Heights at once with a party. Soon I hear that Mrs.
Outlake's baby is lost, and Bridget is lost. Soon all
the women think all their babies are lost or will be.
The excitement spreads. The emigrants are greatly
discouraged, Mrs. Outlake with reason. Mr. Bright
comes downstairs, finds his cab has gone, and goes
back to the office. Rumors of the row at the station
do not ascend into the sacred private room of our
chief cashier. It is not till six in the evening, when
he returns to the quiet of the Romeo to dress for an
evening party, that the poor man finds to his dismay
Bridget and her baby sitting in his finest easy chair,
looking out on the baby-wagons in Arbella Square!

Imagine his dismay. Imagine my relief when I
get a telephone from the office, at the Providence
Railroad station, where I am taking a hasty plate of

soup and wondering where in thunder that Outlake
baby can be.   Imagine the relief of the station
masters of the different police stations, and the satisfaction of our thirty-five hack-drivers and cabmen,
each one of whom had been charged with eating the
baby.   You see it all came from Mr. Bright's being
so grand as to hire a cab to go down there.   If he
had gone, as I did, on a street car there would have
been no baby lost and none found.

.   .   .   .

Saturday Afternoon.

Now that the babies are most of them in their
right homes, I can go on with what I was saying to
Nahum.   If he wants to read this at the High School,
so that they shall think that I am gaining the advantages of a great city, I should like to tell about the
afternoon I spent at the Natural History Rooms.
There was really nothing at the office; it was a sultry
afternoon, and out of pure pity the chief sent us
youngsters off at three o'clock.   He said that he had
a long letter to write, and it was nonsense for us to
sit kicking our heels there.   Walter seized his tennis
racket at once and went out to Longwood, to take his
chances as a substitute in a match there, where he knew
some of the fellows.   But I had no chances in any
match, and indeed my racket was at Cambridge.   So
I tried the fortunes of a "child of the public," which
is what I call myself, and went up to the Natural
History Museum.

It is just beyond the Public Garden, which I know
you remember, where I am going to make you come
down some day and see what they call the floral
effects with me.   It seemed funny enough to be going
to such a place merely to kill time, and I could not
but wish that some of the children had been with me.

You always see a good many nice children there.
And in winter they have a guide there, a gentlemanly
looking fellow, who has a badge on to show that he is
a public guide, and it is his business to take you about,
particularly if you are a woman or a child, and to
tell what he thinks you had better know about the
collection. He does not take you if you do not want
to have him, but after you have seen what a nice
fellow he is, you do want him. I always find I drift
into the bird room. I am wretched about natural
history, as you know; but I can tell the difference
between blue and black, and the humming-birds and
the other bright-colored birds please me, if merely
as so many bits of color. I wish I could make all
womankind understand that the birds are a great deal
prettier here than they are when they have them on
their bonnets. But I am afraid that the wave of public
opinion is going a little backward in that business.

Nahum would delight in the mammoth, and I am
not sure that I could not get him a special permit to
ride on the mammoth's back. In each of the large
rooms there are one or more of these gigantic skeletons,
— I do not mean of mammoths, for sometimes they
are of other creatures, — but they are the solid centres
of the concern. I met Mr. Woodford, a gentleman
whom we sometimes see at the office, who is half a
man of science and half a man of business and half a
man of leisure, like a good many of these Boston men,
and he told me what is a pet idea of his for the Frog
Pond. I cannot help hoping that they may carry it
out. He wants to have, not a bronze statue of a frog
in the middle of the Frog Pond, but a real cast from
one of the antediluvian monsters, one of those nice old
creatures, half snake, half alligator, and half griffin, of
which you see dreadful pictures in the natural history
books. You know you could have him right in the

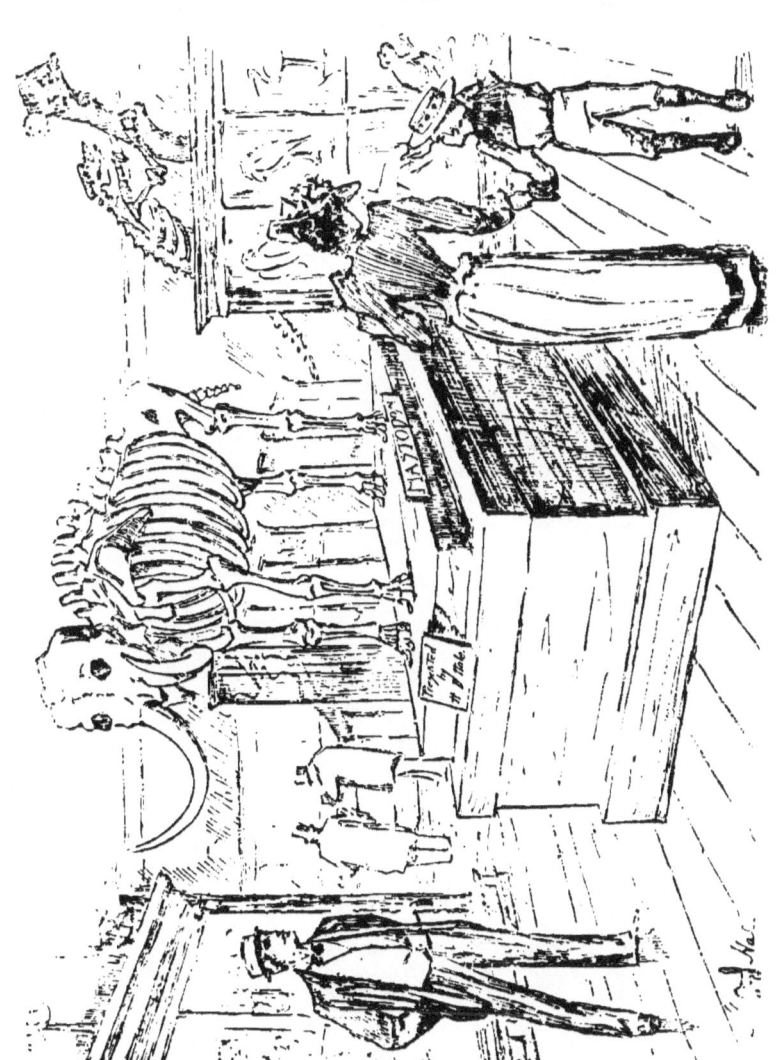

"The mammoths are the solid centres of the concern." — PAGE 114.

middle of the Frog Pond, with his horrid old neck towering up seventy or eighty feet into the air and bending over there, as if he were going to catch any naughty boy or girl whom he saw disporting in an irregular manner upon the bank. I suppose that will be the way in which the twentieth century will teach natural history to children.

When you go in at the door of the Natural History Museum, if somebody has told you where to look, you turn to the right and walk across the room, and there you see a gilt orange, or something about the size of a gilt orange. This represents the sun. Then you walk back to the extreme left of the great hall, and there is a little bit of a speck which represents the earth. And these two are to give you a sort of measure-staff, as the Germans say, by which you can know how big is the solar system and how big the earth on which you live. You see it is for fear you should be too grand. This little speck holds the same proportion to the orange that the earth does to the sun, and the long walk from the right to the left of the hall represents the ninety-two millions of miles, more or less, between us and the sun. After you have gained this measuring-staff, by which you are to compare humming-birds and mammoths, you go in. This is one of those places, I should like to say also, where you can sit down and rest yourself, if you are tired. Nobody molests you nor makes you afraid, and if you have seen all the beasts and birds and fishes and insects and snakes and polyps and mollusks that you want to, you sit down in a comfortable chair, and I will not say that I have not seen people go to sleep there.

Just as I came out, while I was hesitating whether to go to Cambridge or to the Public Library, my Miss Sandford passed by. I thought she was coming in;

but she turned, and, as if she were afraid of rain,
went off again; and I was a little too shy to join her
and walk home with her. If I had done so, I should
have known where she lives. I meet her in such odd
places and always just without speaking to her that I
really should like to have an opportunity to call in
form and leave a card. But nothing happened that
day.

* * * * * * * *

WINDSOR HOTEL, WINDSOR, N. B. Aug. 4, '91.

What happened the next day was very curious.
For the next morning — all this is last week — I had
in the afternoon to go up to the State House to see
about the certificate of our corporation. No matter
what it was, but it was supposed that they had made
some mistake about our taxable property. I went in,
and with a nice lady I found there, overhauled the
whole concern and was coming out with my documents, when I met a wild little boy, who might have
been a hoodlum, but who seemed to be in great distress. He rushed right up to me and said, "Mister,
do you belong here?" I said no, I didn't belong
here; but what was the matter? "Why," said he,
"they've locked her up!" "Whom have they locked
up?" "The teacher! She's locked upstairs and I
can't get the key." "Who's the teacher?" said I.
"The teacher?" said he, "she's Jamaica Ginger —
no, she isn't Jamaica Ginger, she's Miss Sandford."
This name startled me, because, as I said, I met my
Miss Sandford the day before and had been wondering
where she lived, and I did not suppose she lived at
the State House. It seemed to me so queer that this
boy should have another Miss Sandford, and that he
should be at a loss to get her out from the place she
was in. However, I soothed him down and made him

tell me about it. It seemed that he had been up in
the top of the State House with his teacher, and by
some accident she was locked in, in the cupola, he
said, and I supposed it was so.

I went and found the sergeant-at-arms, and he sent
me, with the proper janitor, to see what was the
matter. The boy explained again that they had been
up to the cupola to see the view; he had come running down first and had missed his teacher. When
he went back the door was locked. He could hear his
teacher on the other side of the door, and she had
told him to go and find some one to unlock the door.
But when he came down, he had lost his way among
the staircases and so ran against me first of all. As
we were on our way up to relieve her, I wondered
very much whether she would prove to be my Miss
Sandford. The janitor went up, not overwillingly, to
tell you the truth, and went to the door and opened
it, and there was no one there, not even a cat or a rat.
The boy was very anxious to go on up into the cupola,
but that seemed to be nonsense. His teacher would
never have retired there. The janitor gave him an
awful blowing-up for taking us up all those stairs for
nothing, and that was the end of it. I inquired of
the boy where his teacher lived, and he did not know.
He only knew that she was a teacher in one of the
vacation schools, of which you have heard in the
newspapers. I was very curious, of course, to know
whether she had flown out of the window as she
would have done in a fairy story, or indeed whether
she were not dying or faint in that great dome, which
is all empty — so much lost space. If there had been
a bell in the State House she could have rung it, as
Goody Two Shoes did; but there is no bell.

I made the boy tell me where the school is and was
going there the next morning. But the next morning

they sent me down here to New Brunswick again on that business about the cherry wood, and I am writing this letter now in the Windsor Hotel, as you see. So I do not know what has become of the girl. She may be dead and she may be alive. And I do not know at all whether she is my Miss Sandford.

CHAPTER TENTH.

XII.

LUCY TO KATE.

Boston, August 10, 1891.

My dear Kate, — I believe I have a little adventure to tell you; at least it seemed like one while it was going on, though you may say it did not amount to anything. But for a few minutes I did have a little fright, with a touch of that fear of having been left all alone in the world that, I suppose, makes up a great part of the terrors of children. This was how it came about. Anna and I had been planning to go to the cupola of the State House some afternoon, to see the view from the very top of the building, and I decided to ask one of the boys in my class to go with us. I happened one day to have quite a talk about it with a harum-scarum little youth — of course named Mike — and he declared he knew all about it and would show us the way, and that he had been up and down two or three times in one afternoon. So we met him by agreement on the steps of the State House one day, not much expecting to find him there at the appointed time. But there he was, and he really knew the names of the statues that stand in front of the building. We did not need his introduction much after we were inside, for we were shown about with great distinction, actually seeing the celebrated codfish in the House of Representatives, and being shown the outside of the Governor's room and the other offices, besides being taken up and down in elevators.

Finally we mounted the stairs into the "gilded dome," and were truly repaid for the climb by the glorious view. I ought to stop and tell you all about it; and I will say that it satisfied my heart's desires in its pictures of the harbor and the gay scene of ships and boats and of the Charles River and the numerous bridges that seem to make "mainland" of a greater part of it, with Bunker Hill not far away, that we must climb sometime. Well, we suddenly found that the time was slipping away, and Anna wanted to go somewhere for an errand on Winter Street and left first, I agreeing to meet her on the Common at an appointed place. What would she have done if I had not met her!

For I lingered after she left; and even after Mike and I had decided to go down, I stopped to see if it were possible that there was an ocean steamer visible far away in the offing. Mike went scampering down in front of me, half a dozen steps at a time, and I, at last, followed him, hearing his footsteps echoing far below.

What was my horror, when I reached the foot of the cupola stairway, to find a door shut across at the bottom, and when I tried to open it, I found it was locked! Still I was not much frightened at first, as I supposed Mike would come back for me, and I waited a few minutes, shaking the door, however, and trying to open it. Presently I thought that I heard steps outside, so then I pounded on the door with my parasol, and shook the handle again — with success; for some one put a key in the door outside and opened it. There was a pleasant-looking gentleman who, it seemed, had been coming out of one of the offices below and had heard my knocking, and happily he had a key to the door. He might have been one of the clerks or the governor of Massachusetts, for his politeness; for he showed me downstairs, after inquiring if any one else was left in the cupola, before he locked the door again. I think he took me down some short way, and I lingered awhile in the entrance hall below, looking for Mike, but could see nothing of him. Nor did he appear as I wandered slowly down the steps. I was just turning away to cross the Common, when I looked back once more, to see a figure of a small boy flying to meet me and waving his arms in the air. It was my Mike, who came up to me breathless, not at all sure that it was I, but stammering out a succession of questions, and wondering how I came down from the cupola. And had I seen "the gentleman," and should he go back and tell him?

It was sometime before I could find out that "the gentleman" was somebody he had fallen upon when he discovered I was probably locked in the cupola. As I supposed, he had run down, quick as a shot, from the cupola to the lower front hall of the building, where he waited for me when he found I had not followed him. He flew back to find that the door was locked, and then hurried away to look for me below, meeting a gentleman whom he interested in his search for the janitor, whom they found at last and when they had mounted the stairs and opened the door, of course I was gone, and the janitor very mad apparently. Then Mike went on to tell how "the gentleman" said he knew Miss Sandford, and how his name was Merton, because he heard another "gent" call him so, and how Mr. Merton said he should call the next day at the school to find out if Miss Sandford had flown out of the window; for Mike had told him Miss Sandford was the teacher. So I was in a flutter the next morning at the school, but no Mr. Merton appeared, and I can't find out how much of Mike's story is correct, and it all seems odd.

This incident made me a little provoked at my stupidity the day before it happened. I was passing by the Natural History Museum and had determined to look in for a few moments, but was hesitating whether I would go then or wait for Anna some day, when I saw this very Mr. Merton standing on the upper step. I had a sudden foolish feeling of not wishing to seem to go and meet him, and I turned away, much disgusted with myself afterwards, when I began to think about it; for I should like to have asked him many questions, — how he recovered himself that afternoon when his boat upset in the harbor, and about the white bandage on his head; and it was so stupid of me to have avoided him in this way.

For meanwhile I have learned something about him. Don't you remember a Harry Merton that came over to the base-ball match at Astney last summer? I was to have gone, but it turned up we had a house full of friends, and I sent off the Whitney girls in our wagon instead of going myself. And Jack and the other boys went, and I stayed at home lamenting. When they came back Caroline had a great deal to say about this Harry Merton — for I am very sure it was he — and my mother knew all about his family, and we had a great talk about him; and there was a plan of having him over to visit us. It seems to have been the beginning of the series of adventures that prevents us from meeting. I am most provoked with myself.

All of which reminds me of last summer, and I will answer some of your questions about the dear old home at Astney. Yes, it is let for the summer, and

my father and mother have moved away. It makes
me melancholy to think of it, so I have managed to
avoid the subject. But this spring, in the family
councils, it was decided we must economize and earn
money as well as save it. Why not let the house?
everybody asked. It was soon found that we could
let it to some New York artists and very favorably,
and that my mother and father could go to my grandmother's down in the village. Uncle Enos and his
wife are there, to be sure, but they have no children,
and there is a large house, much unoccupied, and I
might have gone there too. But I had planned, you
know, coming to Boston for university education; and
I decided I might as well start a little earlier, if I
could do it economically; and Aunt Martha's kindness
in inviting me here has helped me in this.

It is hardest for my mother; for Uncle Enos and
his wife are regular workers and they leave her nothing to do, and she has always been used to being at
the head of things, with a house and a large farm to
oversee; and I am very sure it is hard for her to have
anybody else in our dear old house on the slope of the
hills. I wish that Uncle Silas, who has managed to
lose all my father's little property in his speculations
— I wish that he could have had half the head for
economizing that Uncle Enos has. They write me
that the New York artists admire the dear old house,
and that maybe they will want to buy it. But I have
wild ideas of earning a great deal of money, with the
help of my brother Jack and the younger boys; for I
can't bear to think of its passing out of the family.

Yet, I can't say that I am low-spirited on the subject. I think the change of coming here has been
good for me. I am gaining some idea of how different
people live, the rich people away from their large
deserted houses, enjoying themselves in the deserted

farmhouses on the hillsides, while down in the narrow streets are crowded, alas! men, women, and children. But there are compensations for all of it; so I try to console myself, and I am learning what a great city can do in the way of teaching and education, as well as in its care for the sick and poor.

I have really begun on my French lessons, and every afternoon — with few exceptions — I go with Anna to the Berlitz School on Tremont Street, in some large, airy rooms near the top of the building. We begin by talking French directly, if you can believe this of your friend. But there are great advantages in this summer school; for, as the class is not large, we have the more benefit of the professor's instructions. He is very painstaking, and he will not let a single error pass in pronunciation or grammatical construction; and he takes a personal interest in each of us. The method is very systematic and practical and not a word of English is spoken in the class. We are taught from little text-books, where the exercises are very bright and really interesting. The professor brings pictures or objects to represent the things spoken of in the lesson, and he talked with us about them in the very first lesson, avoiding the difficult things, so that at the very beginning we were quite surprised how many every-day sentences we could make. The teacher leads us, indeed, into a variety of conversation which is really agreeable. We propose keeping this up through the winter, and we find it now a delightful occupation for an afternoon.

We have found a rival to our delight in these lessons, and that is in the Old South Lectures. They are given Wednesday afternoons at the Old South Meeting-House, so that I have enjoyed the pleasure of seeing a "truly" old meeting-house. I found Miss Dexter was feeling rather envious of its distinction,

which she would like to have claimed for her beloved
Brattle Street Church. Anna and I went early one
afternoon, thinking we could go about the church and
see some of the "antiquities" that are exhibited there.
But we found already a crowd gathering for the seats.
The subject, you will see, takes up just the period of
history that you know I am most interested in. It
was the beloved Dr. Hedge who gave the suggestion to
me, a year or two ago, when I was planning a study
of history, that I should begin at the time of the Cru-
sades, as being the "New Birth of the World," when
the great nations of Europe were just dividing into
separate existence. So imagine my pleasure to find
that this was to be the subject of the Old South course
of lectures. A friend has given us some tickets, and
the first lecture we heard was exceedingly interesting,
given by Professor Marshall S. Snow of St. Louis, on
"The Builders of the Cathedrals." The lecturer was
very brilliant and the story admirably told, beginning
with a picturesque description of the great towers of
the Cologne Cathedral. It was exactly what we
wanted to hear and know, and the whole lecture gave
a splendid picture of the time; and you somehow felt
as if you were starting at the beginning of all modern
history and could already begin to understand what
came afterwards. Why, Anna and I were so inspired
by it that we went directly to the Public Library, my
first visit.

I remember that summer in Astney, when we were
talking over a winter of study, Caroline and the other
girls all said that it was not so easy to find time in
Boston for all the study I was planning, and they
quite envied me my long, uninterrupted winter evenings at home. I tried to explain that we were not so
terribly uninterrupted at home, and that we do have
our evening entertainments, our teas out, occasional

dances at the hall, and famous lecturers from Boston
and elsewhere, and music now and then.   Still, I had
to confess that we also have quiet hours for study and
reading, only we do not, alas ! have the books to read;
and what sort of use to us is all this time, if we can't
find our books and have no libraries even, to suggest
to us what to read.

But now I have been in Boston all this time, and I
am ashamed to say that I had not even been into the
Public Library.   I have seen the outside of the beautiful new library building, that is to be finished sometime or other, and I have seen the outside of the
Boston Athenæum; but I have not done one thing yet
about " visiting the public institutions," and I therefore learned only the other day what a delight it is
to be able to go up to the quiet rooms of the Public
Library, with the consciousness that you can ask for
any book you please and your wants will be gratified.
Anna, with the advantages of an old inhabitant, knew
how to take me into one of the retired rooms at the
back of the building.   She showed me the reading-
rooms below, and she took me through the library upstairs, without waiting to explain to me the methods
of getting a card for taking out books, and then seated
me at a large table.   Here, after some inquiries, large
volumes of prints and engravings were brought, and
we could look up exactly the things we wanted and
study up the difference in the architectural styles that
Professor Snow had been explaining to us, all while it
was fresh in our minds.   It seemed really as if we
were sitting in some friend's library; only here the
shelves of books were inexhaustible, and we had such
kindly help and suggestions of new volumes that we
had known nothing of, that the afternoon was quite
too short, and, indeed, I wished now I could bring the
leisure of our quiet country days to fill in with the

treasures of all these books. So you can imagine us crowding in these delightful literary afternoons, with our French lessons and so many other things.

We have had some delightful outings. I have gratified a longing of mine to visit an island in the harbor — actually. But that needs quite a preface, and I must go back to my visit to Miss Dexter, when I went down to carry some flowers to the poor woman who lives in the rooms below. I did find such a sad, sick-looking woman, who was indeed delighted with my flowers, especially for the sake of the sick little girl she held in her arms ; for the sick little thing did look up and smile at a gay red nasturtium. The picture of her quite haunted me, so I went down to see her again, and found, this time, that the poor little girl was struggling with a severe illness. I directly thought of the good place I had been told of, where sick children could be carried, on an island in the harbor of this hospitable Boston. I did not venture to speak of it to the mother till I had inquired more about the matter ; but I hurried directly to the West End Nursery in Blossom Street, where I met such a pleasant friend, Miss A., whom I had learned to know at the Flower Mission.

She was directly and most kindly interested and told me of the " Children's Island." Does it not sound something like a fairy tale ? And it is what I used to dream about, an island where children could go and do just what they please and break their toys if they wanted to ; only I don't remember ever really wanting to break my toys. I was very sorry when my doll broke her arm, but I loved her just as much after her arm was broken, especially as she did not seem to mind it and got on very well with the one arm.

But this " Children's Island " is devoted to the in-

valid children, from the close, warm streets of Boston,
who often need only the fresh invigorating air of the
sea to restore them.   Is it not a most kindly charity ?
My friend was quickly interested and went with me to
see the sick child and her mother, and made arrangements to take them both down to the island directly.
They are very glad at the island to have visitors, so Anna
and I decided to go down and spend the day.   We were
all to meet at the Eastern station to go on together to
Marblehead.   Anna and I found we were making an
early start, so we went round by Faneuil Hall Market,
which I had never before visited, and so tempting
and picturesque with the fruit stalls outside.

As Anna was wandering on in front of me, I
could not help stopping at one, most especially picturesque.   Here was a great basket of melons outside,
and peaches and plums, every fruit you could think
of, most artistically arranged, so that I stopped to exclaim at them.   The man who was selling them
looked as picturesque as the rest.   Somehow I fancied
he must be a Greek from the "beautiful isles," and,
almost involuntarily, I ventured an effort upon a sort
of greeting in Greek.   "*Kal' heméra*," I said, for a
good-morning.   Whereupon my Greek friend started
from his languid position and, beaming with smiles,
he poured forth a flow of unknown language, out of
which I could pick out a word or two.   "How could
he serve me ? "   " Did I understand Greek ? " — I
hardly know what.   But I had to buy a few peaches,
and he insisted upon thrusting a bunch of grapes and
some flowers into my brown-paper bag, the finest specimens before him.   And I had to hurry away from
his ardent expressions of delight at hearing his native
tongue.   Anna was coming back to see what had happened to me.

At the station we found the poor mother, holding

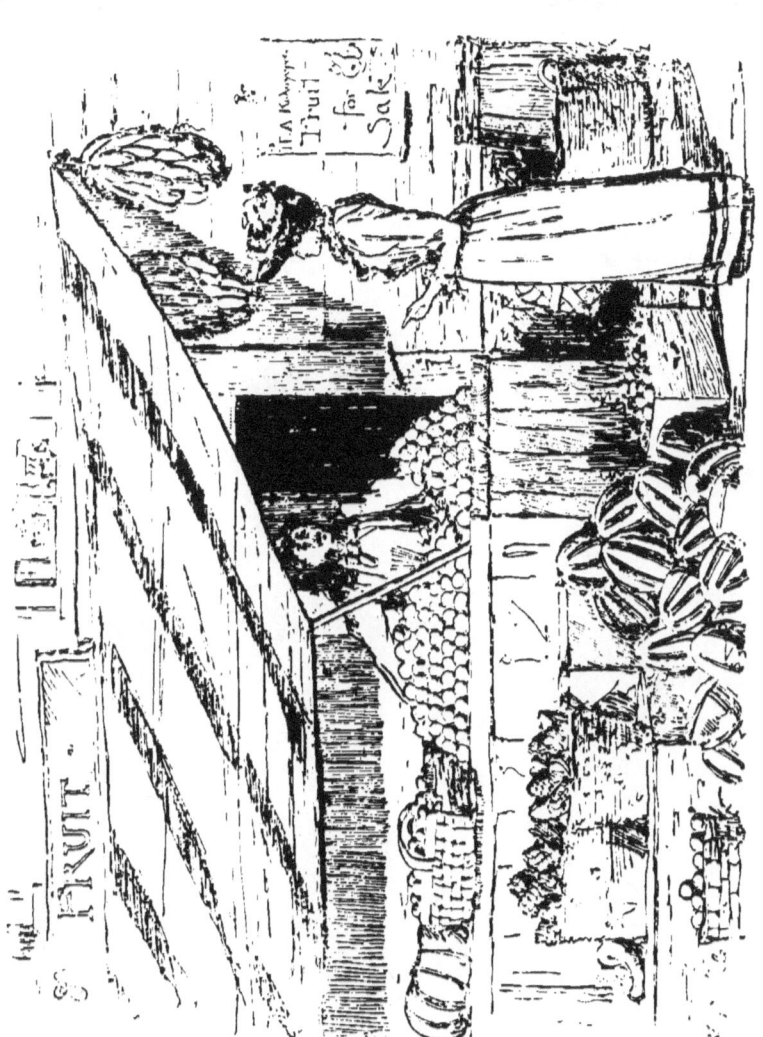

" So tempting and picturesque with the fruit stalls outside." — PAGE 128.

her little girl in her arms, both so wan and sick that it seemed almost hopeless to take them further. But it was wonderful how the fresh air revived them, as we went on in the train, catching the sea breezes as it passed along the shore. So by the time we reached Marblehead, we could pass through its quaint old streets without trouble, reaching the wharf, where a real sailboat was to take us over to the island. This used to be called Lowell Island, as there was a large hotel there to which the Lowell people loved to come for the summer. But of late years the island has been taken for a hospital for sick children, Mr. Frederick H. Rindge having bought the whole place, with its hotel, for a summer home for such invalids, with the sole condition that no question of race, creed, or color shall ever be raised in admission to its privileges. The sisters of Saint Margaret take charge of the institution, which can accommodate fifty children. A change is made every week, when twenty-five children are sent back to their homes or institutions and twenty-five more children are received.

Two other children were being taken over in the boat with us, and, with our little girl, they began to look better in the fresh breeze of our little voyage across to the island. One of the older girls had never seen a boat or the sea before, and, as we landed, she flew out and up the rocks with the delight of a bird let loose from a cage, or of a horse turned out into the fields.

Indeed it did not look anywhere like a hospital. There are one hundred and seventy-five rooms in the large house, which stands on the edge of the sea, so that from the back you look directly down upon the rocks and the waves dashing below. On the lower floor are parlors and a large dining-room and play-

rooms for the children; and above are the sleeping-
rooms, and on this floor a toy-room, where every variety of plaything can be found. Besides the sick
children, some boarders are allowed on the island,
girls and women who cannot afford to pay the high
board of a seaside watering-place, and who are accom-
modated here at three dollars a week.

We wandered over the island, which is a lovely
place, with charming views in every direction. Far
away is the lighthouse at Gloucester with which
Miss Elizabeth Stuart Phelps has made us acquainted.
Then they pointed out to us the Baker's Island lighthouse, Nursery and Gooseberry islands, etc. Anna
and I thought we could pass the summer there with
pleasure. And we were invited to come again to see our
little invalid and her mother, and both of them seemed
already improving before we left. Is it not a valuable
institution? And anybody visiting it would be glad
to contribute liberally towards keeping it. The winter storms have injured the old house, and much could
be done to improve it. Just a sight of the poor sick
children, cared for in the airy rooms, makes one feel
happy that such a place can be found for them; and
then one passes to the cheering sight of the children
who are getting better and need not be kept in their
beds, but who are having a delightful time plashing
in the pools among the rocks, fishing and bathing,
throwing pebbles into the sea, or wading about on the
beach. As we sat upon the rocks talking with the
sisters, Anna and I talked over the numerous friends
we knew who would surely like to contribute something to that delightful work of making all these children well and so happy. Much is needed in repairing
the old house and all the daily necessities of the
home are dependent upon public charity.

I have not time to tell you more of the lovely trip back to Marblehead in the sailboat, and of the few moments we had to walk about the picturesque streets of Marblehead, before taking the train to return. Anna and I are planning more excursions in the harbor.

CHAPTER ELEVENTH.

XIII.

HARRY MERTON TO NAHUM MERTON.

CAMBRIDGE, August 16, 1891.

MY DEAR NAHUM, — You must let mother read this letter. But it is your letter, all the same, and it is in answer to your nice letter to me about the huckleberry party. You managed famously when the boat was upset, and I am glad you all came out safe. The way you dried your clothes was very clever. Now I will tell you how we take our boating parties here, when we do not go out in the harbor. For I went yesterday afternoon.

There are three sets of street cars, not to say four, by which you can go out of town toward the south, and one of them, which goes among houses rather more than shops after you leave the Common, — which is the middle of the town, just as the Common is at Atherton, — is called the Columbus Avenue line. I think they will put a statue of Sir William Pepperell there some day; for I notice that they have a statue of Columbus in Louisburg Square to celebrate Pepperell's great victory. So it would be only fair to give Pepperell a statue here. Well, one great merit of the Columbus Avenue cars is that they go to the Providence station and the Albany station both. And so when we want to go to Riverside to row or to sail on the Charles River, you go to the Columbus Avenue station of the Albany train. And among other trains there, they have one which keeps going round in what

they call a "circle." What they call a "square" here
has three corners or seven or five, and what they call
a "circle" is not round. But it is called a "circle"
for short, because it goes no farther than Riverside,
and then, while it keeps on, it comes back to Boston.
This is what delights the real "Bostoneer," because
he can start on his journey and be sure that he will
not be carried too far from his dear home.

Now, really, it is first-rate fun going to Riverside
and getting a boat there. It takes us maybe fifteen
minutes from the office, and then it is, perhaps,
twenty minutes more to Riverside. It is a pretty
ride, through nice towns where people live who come
in to Boston to do their work every day. And the
railroad people have so much more money than the
stockholders can have, or than the people of the State
want, that they plant pretty rose-gardens up and down
the tracks, each way from the stations. You have
everything to make you comfortable except hornets'
nests, as it says in the story. When you come to
Riverside, if it is Saturday afternoon, fifty or a hundred people get out and tramp right down to the
water to choose their boats. Other days there are not
so many, but Saturday is a sort of holiday. There are
so many of us in our building who like to be sure of a
boat that we give a standing order that the "Rose Stan-
dish" shall be kept for us at Partelow's Saturdays.
Then in the morning, if it proves that more fellows want
to go than will use the "Rose," why, Mr. Stroak tele-
phones up to Riverside. Yesterday we were two parties
— my party and another — and both boats were ready.

Do you not remember a little red book, "Red and
White," which I had at Christmas in the T. T. T.
Club ? And it tells about some Indians on the
Charles River ? Well, this is that same river at
that same place, and I believe that the man that

wrote the story comes to Partelow's to row. I keep
saying Partelow, because he is the man I know.
There is another man who lets boats, and they look
like good boats. But Partelow's are as good as they
can be, and the best is good enough for me.

You can go up the river or down the river. You
may say this is always true, but it is not. For instance, if you launch your canoe at the foot of Niagara
Falls, you would find it rather hard to paddle up,
even if you were a salmon with a very stiff tail.
Here, there is a little fall, four or five miles below
Partelow's, at Waltham, and there are other falls
above, which are called Newton Lower Falls and
Newton Upper Falls. Between these falls — I do not
know how many miles, but I should think seven or
eight — is the long, winding stretch of Charles River,
which is the pleasure ground of sensible Boston during the days from April, till it is frozen up in winter.
And it is here that the Indians, as I have said just
now, came down in the expedition which is described
in " Red and White." Sometimes we go up and
sometimes we go down. I will tell you another time
about our going up to hear the great echo where the
aqueduct crosses the river, but not now.

Our party was myself and James and Mr. Stroak.
I let them row the first half of the time, while I had
the helm. Both sides of the river are well wooded.
I believe there are gentlemen's places behind, the
woods of which run down to the river. But it all
seems as wild as if nobody had been there since it
was made, excepting that, every now and then, there
is a nice little boathouse running out. But the birds
seem to feel at home, the wild flowers are abundant,
and you do not have a feeling that you are within ten
miles of a great city.

James had never seen the monument to the North-

men, so we went there first. That is just where the
river makes a sharp corner, which is on the edge, I
believe, of the town of Waltham ; and here a Cambridge gentleman found some entrenchments, some
years ago, which he thinks are the walls and fortifi-
cations of the city of Norumbega. So he has put up
a great tower, fifty or sixty feet high, where you can
climb up and see all the kingdoms of the world.
And there is a great granite tablet, as big as the
front door of our house, with a great deal of history
carved upon it, which will remain there . for some
hundred years to tell the world what he thought
about this first discovery. We went into a little
creek, which is so narrow we had to ship our oars to
get in, and this, I believe, is the harbor where the
Northmen's ships are supposed to have entered and
traded with the Indians. Exactly how they got up
above the waterfalls at Watertown and Waltham, I
do not know, but all the same the tower is there, and
it gives you a splendid view of the country, and one
learns a great deal more about the geography of Boston than he can from any other convenient place that
I know. Stroak said he was there last spring when
the apple-trees were in blossom all through this
valley, and it was one of the most beautiful gardens
you can see in the world. I can well believe it.

We did not want to waste our afternoon studying
geography at the tops of towers ; so, as soon as
James had seen what there was to see, so that he
could come again alone, we pulled down towards
Waltham. One of the nice features about the expedition, which I had taken before, is that while at one minute you are all alone and imagine yourself in a lake
at the head waters of the Mississippi, the next moment you meet a party of people whom, perhaps, you
have been talking with half the morning. Just as

we came out into the river and went down towards
Waltham, we fell in with what Stroak said were two
Waltham boats, and in these were half a dozen people
whom I knew quite well. Mother will remember my
writing about going to Class Day, and the pretty Miss
Sandford that I danced with there, and some of the
Cambridge fellows who were having their "spreads"
as they left college. There were three or four of
these in this boat, and Miss Sandford, who is the same
I last heard of shut up in the cupola of the State
House, was one of the party. So I know that she is
not a prisoner there still.

It is queer enough ; it is nearly two months since
I saw all these people first. I am all the time running against one or another of them, but with hardly
any chance to talk to them, though one night I did
meet Miss Osborne and her brother at a party. But
this time I was glad to see that Miss Sandford, who
seems to be a very nice girl, had got out of her im-
prisonment. For I have found out certainly that
Mike Flanigan's "Jamaica Ginger" is the same as
my Miss Sandford of Class Day. I believe the last
time she saw me was when I came out of the water,
like a drowned rat, at the side of the "Newark." She
did not know, when I made my elegant bow to her,
that I had called at her schoolhouse in the morning
and found it shut up.

This is the way you go and come on the river. We
went down till we lost ourselves in a tangle of islands,
and none of us had any map to show how to get back
again. But the tangle was not such that we spent
thirty years of our life there, as Robinson Crusoe did,
and by some pretty stiff rowing we got back in time.
Not in time for our train ; you never get your own
train. But there is always another train going in
about twenty minutes, when you are late for your

own. You can see what a nice way this is to spend Saturday afternoon.

Now, dear Nahum, I have written you what grandmamma calls "a nice, long letter." Take care that you write as long a one to me. Tell me about all the fellows and how the club gets on, and particularly if you get overboard again in " Bombazine."

Always your affectionate brother,

HARRY MERTON.

XIV.

HARRY TO HIS MOTHER.
Sunday evening.

My dear Mother, — I have been writing a separate letter to Nahum, and you must take that as a part of my letter to you. I like to keep up the dear boy's interest in correspondence, and I think he writes a capital letter. All the same, I am glad you do not ask him to show them to you. It is the freshness of the thing which gives it half its charm. One of these days he will be coming here himself, and I think he will enjoy Boston all the more because he has an older brother here to show him its ways.

You need not be anxious about my eating and drinking. By virtue of being in the Summer School I have a card at the Foxcroft Club, and that is rather a pleasant thing, because it brings me in with nice fellows whom I am glad to know. "Foxcroft Club" means this: The college Memorial Hall is crowded and overcrowded all through term time. They can't receive half the fellows who want to take their meals there. They are trying to mend this now by throwing open half the tables as they would be at a hotel, so that a man can go just as he chooses and when he chooses, and they hope thus to accommodate at those tables twice as many as they had before. How that will work we cannot tell now, but it is the best they can do.

But somebody — I believe Professor Shaler — observed that this made the other boarding-houses costly, and that there was quite room for some other arrangement for students who did not want to eat ice-cream and plum-cake all the time. And he or some-body else organized this Foxcroft Club. It means that you have a sufficiently good breakfast, dinner, or supper, and do not have to pay for it any more than it costs. I believe there was an old minister named Foxcroft for whom it was named. And, by the way, somebody told me he was a sort of relation of Ralph Waldo Emerson. And, do you know, they say that Emerson, theorist and idealist as people think him, was one of the most practical men about these affairs of the direction of every-day life whom you could stumble on. I wonder if it is not that which gives a certain Yankee raciness to everything which he wrote. You used to be surprised that I swore by Emerson so entirely; but I tell you all the young men I know, who are worth knowing, are quoting Emerson all the time, and, as like as not, have some little Emerson handbook in their pockets. And in all my Sunday adventures, I am bound to hear something of Emerson's pushed into every sermon, no matter whether I am in a Baptist church, or in a high Epis-copal church, or at some place which your friend the deacon would think awfully heretical.

I am glad I came out to Cambridge. There are excellent loafing-places here. The Botanical Garden seems to be open to anybody. I have asked no ques-tions there and nobody has hindered me, but I can go about and read the names on the little tags and im-prove my botany after my own fashion. This is a thing you cannot do in the new park in Boston. Whether they know the names of their plants or not, I do not know. They have a lot of loafing policemen there, whose business, somebody told me, was to insult the people who come there, under pretence of seeing that they do not pick the flowers. But none

of them know what any of the plants are, so there is
no good asking them. And there are no notices of
any sort. When you walk on the Common, you have
a notice to tell you that the elm-tree is an *Ulmus
Americana ;* but not in the new park. However, I
suppose they will come in time. Perhaps the things
will develop, if they water the flowers long enough.
But at the Botanic Garden there is no difficulty. You
can really pick up a good deal there, as the season
goes by. You have a chance of seeing what are the
steps in what Mr. Higginson called " the Procession
of the Flowers," all over New England ; for they
have almost everything here. Somebody told me
they got a pink pond-lily from Cape Cod, though I
have not seen it.

I went down on an errand last week to Kingston,
Rhode Island, where the agricultural experiment station of the State is, and I wished ever so much you
had been with me there. They have a man named
Cushman there, who is very learned about bees and
honey. He was very good to me and showed me the
whole process of honey-making and wax-making, and,
I have a right to say, of bee-making. I was wishing
all the time that you were there. You remember the
old story in Hood about the boy who told the other
boy that, if he would come to see him, he had got a
hornets' nest ready for him and everything else to
make him comfortable. I was quoting that to Nahum
just now. Well, Mr. Cushman had five-and-twenty
swarms of bees ready for me, and made me perfectly
comfortable at the same time. He put on me a sort
of helmet of gauze, which screened my face, and took
in his own hands a " smoker," which seems to be a
sort of pocket pistol which you have ready to suggest
to any bee that he must not sting you, and we went
around. I saw the operations of the little fellows

face to face, not to say hand to hand. The whole science of honey-making has changed in the last fifteen or twenty years, and the product, for all practical purposes, is very much more plentiful, and the process, so to speak, is very much improved. It seems queer to say that the bee can improve his process; but every bee makes now about five times as much honey as any bee did thirty years ago. Mr. Cushman asked me if I preferred the flavor of clover honey, or of buckwheat honey, or of aster honey. He had, I do not know how many flavors of honey boxed up there, according as it was made in one season or another. All of which you would have understood a great deal better than I. The whole place is a capital place for a boy to get enthusiastic about gardening and farming, and I shall want to talk to father and you about sending Nahum down there for a winter.

You said you were surprised that I had taken no chance to hear our new Bishop, Phillips Brooks. You have brought me up so well that I do not care much to tramp round in search of my religious instructions. And, as I told you, the People's Church and Dr. Haynes are good enough for me. What am I but a child of the public? and I believe the name interested me. And another thing, which I suppose Dr. Haynes knows nothing about, and which I believe I never told to you. Years and years ago, that time when I made my famous visit here on Aunt Jane, one Sunday when I was at the Sunday School, the children had a chance given them to give one brick each for the building of that church. Lulu and I agreed to unite. I believe I gave nine cents and she gave eleven. Any way, we were told we had contributed a brick between us, and, from the moment I came to Boston, I felt the grandeur of a proprietor, and I have been very glad I did.

But yesterday I wanted to obey your orders and show the town to our neighbor, Miss Clara Fenton, and, like all other strangers, she wanted to hear Phillips Brooks. We knew he was at Mr. Lowell's funeral Friday, and we thought he might be at Trinity. He was not, but we were well repaid for going. The whole service was interesting, the sermon was admirable, and she thanked me heartily for showing her the way.

I did not know who the preacher was. But as soon as he gave out the text, we knew that he was going to speak of Mr. Lowell. And, all the time, dear mother, I was thinking of you and the time when you first read " Sir Launfal " to me. This gentleman almost took it for granted that " Sir Launfal " was Lowell's greatest and most remarkable poem. He read from it some of the lines you know by heart and are so fond of. And what it was very good to hear, and what, in that place, seemed to me very brave, he said squarely that the divinity of humanity is the special religious lesson of this time. He said Lowell showed himself a poet of his time by teaching that " he who does it unto one of the least of these my brethren, does it unto me." He said this was the special lesson, or the enforcement of it the special business of the " men of this neighborhood, the men of Boston and Concord and Cambridge; " and that he would ask nothing more of them than to own that their ancestors were moved and quickened by the death of Christ as they are moved and quickened by his life. The life of Christ and the divine life in each of God's children — these made the sermon ; and this is your doctrine so perfectly that I wished you had been there to hear.

There is talk of making this Trinity Church into a cathedral. That is, they propose to throw it open to anybody who will come in — well, much as the

People's Church is thrown open. If it is a cathedral, it will be Phillips Brooks's cathedral, and he will preach here when he can. Naturally, of course, the people would like to hear him when they can. I could not help thinking to-day that the attendance justified this idea.

For this is what the Transcript, last night, called "the dead day of the year" in Boston. That means that everybody is away that can be away. And, indeed, in that neighborhood we could see that three houses out of four were shut up, and you might say sealed up, for the summer. Still, here was a large congregation, clearly of strangers like ourselves. You cannot say that they came to hear a preacher who had been announced beforehand. There had been no announcement; the chances were five out of six against Dr. Brooks, for instance, being there, or any other particular person whom these people wanted. They came, certain that there would be a good service, well rendered. And they were rewarded by having more than they came for. You see everybody took any seat he could find. There was no need of ushers, because the whole body of the church is thrown open in July and August.

The church is as beautiful as you described it. There is nothing gaudy about the colored glass. I am sorry to say there is at our church and in most of the churches where I see it. But here the man has controlled himself — or the men. I believe it is the New York glass you were telling me about. Good-night, dear Mother. Thank you always for your nice letters.

. . . .

Monday evening.

If they will let me have a few lines more, I will tell you about our drive this afternoon. I had succeeded

so well with Miss Fenton that we made a little party
this afternoon and I took her to drive.   After my success this time in showing the lions, you must not be
afraid to send me any one else.   Really, I think she
regards me as quite fine, and I cannot have betrayed
myself as a Vermont boy, only two months from
Leeds, more than a hundred and fifty times.   At all
events, she has been profuse in her thanks for my
little attentions, and I can see that for a perfect
stranger in Boston it must be convenient to have a
man about, even if he is a little green.

I forget what day I got your letter asking me to
look her up.   But Saturday I found where she was,
and Saturday evening I called.   It was a pretty forlorn, deserted, great boarding-house, stuffy and empty
as Mrs. Metcalf's was, before she and I marched out
of it with the honors of war.   And when Miss Fenton appeared and found out who I was, she certainly
was not at all ungracious, as you were afraid she
would be.   She said she was glad to see me, any way,
and I guess she was.   She had been "all sole alone"
all day and had found every living being away whom
she had called to see.   She had even been disappointed in her shopping in the afternoon, for half the
shops are shut up on Saturdays.   That is what people
mean when they call the fifteenth of August the dead
day and say the town is empty.   I can see it myself.

I told her how I had spent my afternoon on the
river, and she was not so "poky" but that her mouth
really seemed to water for such an expedition.   If I
had known in time, I could have got Mrs. Outlake or
some of our Leeds ladies for a chaperon, and, indeed,
I would have taken her, she seemed so forlorn.   As it
was, the minute she spoke of Trinity and Phillips
Brooks, I said I would gladly go there with her, and
that was how I came to be there.

As we came home from church, she told a pretty story, which she never would have told me but for the sermon. She was almost betrayed into it. It seems that they were belated as they came into town and that she was alone after dark at the station. However, as she said laughing, "I am no chicken and can manage my own canoe," and I do not think she was at all frightened at being alone. She simply took the first hackman, gave him her checks, and sat in the carriage waiting for him and the trunks. As she sat, a poor girl came along sobbing, with an enormous bundle in checked cloth. Miss Fenton had seen her in the car and had speculated about her. When she saw the girl sobbing, she spoke to her and asked what was the matter. The girl was frightened and still sobbed, but I assure you Miss Fenton can be kind, if she is stiff and "poky." And, in a minute, it appeared that the poor girl had come from Fredricton or Annapolis or heaven knows where among the Bluenoses, and was to meet her sister at the station. No sister! I suppose she had managed to come to the Boston and Maine instead of the Eastern. You see there are four Northern Stations, as we call them, where there should be but one.

Miss Fenton said to me that she would willingly enough have taken the girl with her, bag, baggage, and bundles. But she did not know these "swell" people where she was going, and they did not know her, and she did not know what they would say. The Bluenose girl had, of course, lost her sister's "direction card," as she called it, or thought she had lost it — which was just the same thing. Just at this juncture came the hackman with the trunk. Instantly he took in the case. "They always lose their tickets," he said. But he meant, of course, that when they lost them he heard of it, and that he never heard of

the successful ones, what you may call the upper-class
adventurers, who do not lose them.   Then he looked
around wildly.   "Where is Miss Blodgett?" he
asked; "she was here just now."   And he rushed off
into parts unknown.

In a little, he appeared without Miss Blodgett.   He
said she had been and gone with some other women.
And it appeared that Miss Blodgett is the wonderful
woman who makes it her business to attend these
eastern boats and trains to see to just such lost
women.   Is not that the twenty-fifth chapter of
Matthew?   "But there!" said he, "it don't make any
difference, mum; if you don't mind going round by
Warrenton Street, mum, we shall get there before she
will."   And it appeared that at Warrenton Street is
the Young Women's Christian Association, where are
Miss Blodgett's headquarters.   So Miss Fenton said it
was all right; the Bluenose woman was bundled into
the carriage ; her checked bale was put on the seat;
and this good fellow went off with her check for her
trunk.   He made no row, though Miss Fenton said it
was awfully large.   They got it on the back of the
carriage among them, with the other trunks, and all
jumbled off to Warrenton Street, a strong mile out of
their way.

And all was as this stout fairy with a whip had
said.   As they drove up to the door, Miss Blodgett
appeared with three other women.   She heard the
story and was delighted.   "It was as if Jenny Lind
or Florence Nightingale had happened along," Miss
Fenton said.   And the trunk and the bale were left,
and Miss Blodgett said she would find the place, and
Saturday night Miss Fenton had a card to say they
did so.

Now hear the end of the story.   When Miss Fenton
paid for her hack, she expected to pay an extra fare of

course, but the man would not take it. "No, mum," he said resolutely, "we don't take pay for such as them." Now you may jeer as much as you choose about cabmen who read Browning. I think they have read "Sir Launfal" to some purpose, when you can tell such stories as that of them.

All this story Miss Fenton told me as we walked home from church. In the evening I made our nice Mrs. Seabright call on her with me, at her forlorn old boarding-house. Mrs. Seabright very pleasantly asked her to go to ride this afternoon, and then sent a note down to the office to beg me from Mr. Bright, so that I might go. There is not, alas! a stroke of work in the office, and he was glad to be gracious. He sent me to the Seabrights', where I lunched, and then I drove this afternoon. The two ladies and I were all the party.

You know the joke on Boston people is that when they want to entertain their friends they take them out of town. Well they may, for the drives are beautiful. We drove through a part of Franklin Park and admired the view of the Blue Hills, seen through that vista which makes you feel as if you were in a wild forest country, and not in the suburbs at all. It is really wonderful to see how they have made the most of their space there. Not many people were there to enjoy it that day. There was a little "carriage company" besides ourselves, and I saw some children and numbers of bicyclists, men and girls both. But there was nobody on horseback and few walkers, and I wondered why there were not more. Sunday is the great day here, of course, when lots of people come who can't at any other time. But I can't help thinking that if the more leisurely people were to take the horse-car ride out here oftener than they do, they would find it paid.

I was glad that Miss Fenton enjoyed it as much as she did. As she was just from the country, she enjoyed it more even than the Arnold Arboretum, which is not very far away, where we drove next. You will wonder why her being just from the country should have taken off the edge of her pleasure at the Arboretum. But, you see, it could not give her the intense pleasure it gave me, who am now something of a "town mouse," to see great banks planted thick with sumac and golden-rod and bayberry and no end of other wild things, looking as if nobody but the birds and the winds and all the rest of Nature's workmen had ever planted them at all. There were fine trees, too, of course, and I know I should have enjoyed wandering about and seeing what they had. But we stuck to the carriage road, and that took us through these wild hillsides I have been speaking of, up to a high, fine view at the top of all, though it was too hazy to quite make out the sea.

But as for views, the finest we had that day was in a place we went to afterward over in Brookline; for Mrs. Seabright had a call to pay over there, and while she was with her friends we drove up on what they call Aspinwall Hill. I believe it was all a fine old estate once, with a fine old house on it, which I didn't make out. I think it was on the other side of the hill from that we drove up. The hill has now been covered with nice new houses, some of them very pretty indeed in their yards and gardens; and in one place there are what they call terraces, in the English fashion, — not what you and I would call terraces, but a number of very attractive houses built together in blocks; not, however, like city blocks, but with a very pleasant air of their own. Well, you pass all these nice houses — I wish I had placed some of my people here — and you drive higher and higher up, and after

a while there is a sign saying, " Dangerous Passing."
But you go straight on and don't find it dangerous at
all. There are scattered apple-trees there and golden-
rod, planted by those workmen of Nature I was speaking of, and away up on top of the hill you look off,
and there is a view that is a view! I'm not much,
you know, at description; and you probably won't
care to hear how we saw Bunker Hill Monument and
the State House and the Back Bay buildings and the
rest of it all; but the stableman, after we got home,
said it was the best view near Boston, and I don't
think he was far out. I don't think people go up
there much.

I like Brookline, everything looks so finished and
so complete, and as if people had their own way there.
You know it's a town and takes care of itself, and
won't join this great city of ours.

As we drove out of the Arboretum, turning a sharp
corner, we met a fine carriage; and as we passed, I
noticed that one of the ladies bowed to me. I had
my whip in one hand and my reins in the other, but I
was just able to "bob" in reply. I write this only
to amuse you. For it was Miss Sandford, I think, the
" Jamaica Ginger " of the cupola, whom I meet so
mysteriously.

Always yours,

HARRY.

CHAPTER TWELFTH.

XV.

LUCY TO KATE.

Boston, August 25, 1891.

My dear Kate, — I ought to be able to send you a more satisfactory letter than I have yet written you; for the Vacation School is over and our vacation has begun. But I foresee that I am not likely yet to reach that "summer leisure," of which I have dreamed, even though my daily occupation is over.

Our school closed last week and is considered a great success. It was, indeed, a delight to see the interest that all the children took in it day after day. I am very much surprised myself to see how much they have learned in so many different ways, and yet without "book lessons." I can believe that the influence of the kindergartens is already showing how much more children can be taught by " observation," by looking at things and seeing how they are made, than by cramming and being forced to study and commit to memory things that they cannot understand.

I have an idea that this might be carried too far, and I think it would be a pity not to cultivate the memory of children, while it is easy for them to learn things "by heart," as we say. Perhaps, after all, that is the true phrase, and what they truly learn "by heart" may always stay by them, while what they really learn "by rote " is only a stumbling-block to them. I am sure I am grateful for having been taught many things "by heart" that continue to stay by me and help me, and that I learned, I can't remember how and when, — a list of dates, for instance, on which I find myself hanging a great many valuable things.

Many valuable things these children had to carry home with them from their summer schooling, and though they did little with books, I can see that they saw that in this study of many things they were discovering the real use of books, and learning why they were made to study them, and what a pleasure they might find in reading them. I know many of the boys in my class are planning to go to the Public Library in the days of the vacation remaining to them before school, and I gave many of them lists of books that they are to find there, on subjects that I have talked about to them.

Among other things, I have told them of the World's Fair and the great Centennial, and they are going to read all about Columbus. Of course I told them of the new life of Columbus, published by J. Stillman Smith and Company. Then, I am going with a party to visit Bunker Hill, and they have promised to read an account of the battle of Bunker Hill before we go.

I wish you could see some of the things these scholars have made. Hetty, the old housekeeper here, is much delighted because I succeeded in getting two favorite old chairs reseated for her by some of "the class" who were putting fresh straw seats into old chairs. She is quite proud of them because they used to be in Aunt Martha's grandmother's parlor, and she has held on to them as relics of great elegance; but the seats were all worn out.

I went with Mike to his own home, and he was equally pleased at showing me his grandmother, sitting in an old "cane-bottom" chair that he had reseated; and she beamed over with pleasure as she rose to show me how fine it looked. "And we were just going to cut it [up for firewood," she exclaimed, "when Mike took it off and brought it back as good as new. And it kept him out of mischief at the same time, too," she added. I can't help feeling that these Vacation Schools are among the best things that Boston provides for her children.

We had a delightful "doorstep" talk on this subject the other day. I went out to Arlington to spend a day and night after the close of my school, and it was on the pleasant doorsteps at the Brands', looking out from their porch into the moonlight on the lawn, that we sat talking till a late hour. We fell to telling, each of us, what we could remember best, the Latin verbs, the French verbs, the lists of the Latin prepositions; and we presently found there was one thing we could all of us remember, and it was that delightful string of nonsense that we all of us had learned from Miss Edgeworth : "So she went into the garden to cut a cabbage leaf to make an apple pie of, when a great she-bear popped his head into the shop. 'What! no soap?' So he died! And she very imprudently married the barber, and there were present at the wedding, the Joblilies, and the Garyulies and the Piccaninies, and the grand Panjandrum himself with the little round button on top. And they all fell to playing catch-as-catch-can, till the gunpowder ran out at the heels of their boots."

I write it all out for you; for I am really afraid your education was neglected at this point and that you never heard it. But I shall have to add that we decided that it might be considered a mark of our high education that we were all able to repeat it, — some of us a little mixed on the subject of the Garyulies and the Piccaninies, but well up on the rest. For its history I must refer you to the second part of Miss

Edgeworth's " Harry and Lucy," for I have too much else to write about.

Among other things, I ventured to speak of something that has been on my mind since I have been teaching these boys. I notice that they all read much easier from their primers than from any other books. Now it is true that in some of these primers can be found very interesting stories, and I know very well that children like to read over and over the same stories that they are familiar with ; but I know that they do like to read something new, and I have formed the idea that they find the large print of the primers easier. Now, why need the primers, even for the youngest child, be put in such large print ? Their eyes are as fresh as ours, and what use is there in enlarging the letters for them ? It might be a good plan to put books into large print for elderly people, but a child ought not to read a large letter more easily than a small one, if it is sufficiently plain. As it is, the children all have to learn over again how to read in common type, having been taught to read in large letters.

Some of the others exclaimed against this, and Mr. Jones said that the reason the children liked large type was because it made less to read, and they could get through quicker. I did not agree with him, and said that children certainly liked long stories, and always wanted "more," if a story stopped off soon. Godfrey Brand agreed with me in this, and said he remembered how he hated the first Latin book he learned to translate, his *Liber Primus*, because the sentences were so short; and there were little, short fables and anecdotes that were very tiresome, and he only got on when he had something long, to read. His father gave him, for instance, " Robinson Crusoe " in Latin, and he learned a quantity of new

words and more of the language than in months'
study of the primers.

They were all of them joking me about our last
meeting with our friend, Harry Merton — my "distant" friend, as they call him. But I am going to
write about more serious things first, lest I should be
interrupted and they should be left out; and I long to
tell you of last week's lecture at the Old South. Before we went to it, Anna and I had found a chance to
go to the old meeting-house to study the numerous
articles on exhibition there at our leisure. Here are
many most interesting things. There is so much to
throw a light on the old colonial history, — old his-
toric implements of the Stone Age, with tomahawks,
arrows, and spears, and many things that told of the
terrible Indian warfare, which I described to one of
my Vacation School boys whom I had invited to go
with us. We looked at Eliot's Indian Bible, and I
asked my boy how he would like to have such words
in his spelling-book. For there was a placard giving
the longest word, "Wutappesittukgussunnookwehtunk-
quoh." Sammy was much staggered by it. It means
"Kneeling down to him." Our language surely looks
a little simpler.

Here was a skillet made from the bell of the Old
South, an older Old South than this. It was taken
down in 1729 to give place to the present building.
The skillet was presented by Mrs. Hannah Dilla-
way, of Somerville, the granddaughter of the original
owner. We saw an autograph letter of General Washington, written in December, 1798, and a remnant of
the flag that hung from the Liberty Tree on Washington Street in 1775. Here was a silver thimble marked
T. H. How little did the Thankful Holden who
owned it in 1765 imagine that it would be so preserved! I must tell you of another thing that amused

us very much. This was a printed notice of an entertainment or "sociable" that took place here in Revolutionary times. At the end this information was
given: "Nabor Zodiga Turner will be there to see
that nobodye yields to levitye more than is becominge
and to see that nobodye takes more Baked Beans than
is consistent withe these fashionable times." Is not
this delightful? I think I shall have this printed for
use in our Sewing Circle. The truth is that we are
apt to be too solemn on such occasions at home, and
Caroline and I have to turn ourselves into a sort of
minstrel show to keep up the spirits of our Sewing
Circle old ladies, who sit doggedly sewing their seams,
as if there was nothing amusing in life. But perhaps
the notice itself may excite a little "levitye," — not
more "than is becominge." Our old housekeeper,
Hetty, furnishes us Sunday mornings with "truly"
Boston baked beans and brown bread. We propose
now not to take more "than is consistent withe these
fashionable times."

Besides all these and many other older relics, we
saw a cup made from wood from the log cabin of
President Lincoln. The first afternoon that we went
we had read the inscription on the pulpit window:
"Through this window Warren entered to deliver his
famous oration on the Boston Massacre." The old
pulpit is no longer there. There is a platform below
and a reading-desk for the speakers, and the window
with its inscription is far above. Over a door opposite, which was probably the principal entrance, is
another inscription: "Here Washington entered after
the evacuation of Boston. Looking down upon the
havoc caused by the British riding-school, he said
reverently that he should have thought that the English, who had so much respect for their own churches,
would have respected those of others." Above a large

gallery there is another, still higher, which we were told was intended for the colored people. And I remembered that Miss Dexter, in describing the inside of the old Brattle Street Church, told me that there was such a gallery, placed high up over the organ, for the colored people there.

But after this description, I must tell you of the lecture here, a week ago last Wednesday. It was an intensely hot day, yet Anna and I persevered in our plan of going to the lecture, taking a car to the head of School Street. Hardly any one was in the car; but as we walked down the street we passed through a little crowd gathered around the Parker House door. We looked at each other with sad questioning whether we could believe the sorrowful news we heard spoken of, — that the poet Lowell was dead. This was our first intelligence of it, and we walked on silently into the old church. We were scarcely there and had found some seats in the large, quiet assembly, when a sudden thunder storm came up and the whole place was darkened. It seemed as if it were the beginning of a grand, solemn service in memory of the dead, in this old building that might, in a certain way, serve for a Westminster Abbey of our later time. And Mr. Mead, who was to introduce the lecturer, passed on to announce the death of Lowell and to speak of his character and his writings. There could not have been a more magnificent service in such a place. Professor Hart was to lecture on "The Revival of Learning," and he began with a quotation from Dante and paid a tribute to the poet who had been such a student of Dante. All of his lecture seemed, somehow, appropriate to this subject; for he gave a history of the universities established about the year 1200, and he told how the students flocked to these universities, some of them having as many as fifteen thousand students. Was not this interesting? You cannot think what a consecration came to the service from the magnificent peals of thunder above us.

The sun had come out as we went home. We passed up through Winter Street and around the Common, and, sitting down on a deserted bench in a quiet place, we recalled our favorite passages from Lowell. I repeated to Anna the poem I like best of all, " The Beggar : " —

> " A beggar through the world am I, —
> From place to place I wander by,
> Fill up my pilgrim's scrip for me,
> For Christ's sweet sake and charity !

> " A little of thy steadfastness,
> Rounded with leafy gracefulness,
> Old oak, give me, —
> That the world's blasts may round me blow,
> And I yield gently to and fro,
> While my stout-hearted trunk below
> And firm-set roots unshaken be.

> " Some of thy stern, unyielding might,
> Enduring still through day and night
> Rude tempest-shock and withering blight, —
> That I may keep at bay
> The changeful April sky of chance
> And the strong tide of circumstance, —
> Give me, old granite gray.

> " Some of thy pensiveness serene,
> Some of thy never-dying green,
> Put in this scrip of mine, —
> That griefs may fall like snow-flakes light,
> And deck me in a robe of white,
> Ready to be an angel bright, —
> O sweetly mournful pine.

> " A little of thy merriment,
> Of thy sparkling, light content,

Give me, my cheerful brook, —
That I may still be full of glee
And gladsomeness, where'er I be,
Though fickle fate hath prisoned me
In some neglected nook.

" Ye have been very kind and good
To me, since I 've been in the wood,
Ye have gone nigh to fill my heart;
But, good-by, kind friends, every one
I 've far to go ere set of sun;
Of all good things I would have part.
The day was high ere I could start
And so my journey 's scarce begun.

" Heaven help me ! how could I forget
To beg of thee, dear violet ?
Some of thy modesty,
That blossoms here as well, unseen,
As if before the world thou 'dst been,
O, give, to strengthen me."

The next lecture was also very interesting, on " The
Changes which Gunpowder Made." It was given by
Mr. Frank A. Hill, Principal of the Cambridge High
School. About two thirds of the audience were children, apparently from the High Schools, and they listened most attentively ; for they were much interested
in his description of the suits of armor. He described
the baron of that day and showed how all the pieces
of armor were made and fitted, explaining the reason
for each piece and telling the children how they could
see specimens of the complete armor at the Art Museum. He showed us, too, how helpless the people
were, who could get their rights only by conquering
these iron men, so that we really felt glad to hear of
the discovery of gunpowder, and that in consequence,
because cannon were invented and later the musket,
the common people were free. He quoted Carlyle as
saying that gunpowder makes all men alike tall, or

something to that effect. It was a new thing to me to look upon cannon and muskets as civilizers. We had a beautiful, bright afternoon, and the children were out in great numbers. The girls looked very bright and fresh in their summer gowns and hats.

And this reminds me of the "sand gardens" again, where I saw the younger children made so happy. I believe they are closed now with the Vacation Schools, but they have been going on every afternoon in seventeen places and perhaps more this year. The "gardens" are like three immense cigar-boxes, twenty feet by twenty, and half full of sand. Each child has a trowel furnished to dig with, and such fun as they do have. Children of all ages, from babies who can hardly sit up to girls of twelve or thirteen, are there, having a most happy and quiet time, filling boxes, kettles, little wheelbarrows, wooden tubs and divers other things with the sand, and then emptying it out in little heaps. It is too funny to see the serious way in which they roll round their little wheelbarrows and tip out the sand, as though they were doing some great work. Some of them build houses or roads, but the greater part just fill and empty their barrows in a most business-like way. There are a great many of the mothers with them, who seem to take solid enjoyment in just looking on. I have wished, whenever I have seen them, that I had time and a trowel, as I would like to have joined the party.

I have been again to the Charlesbank Park, of which I wrote, where I first saw some of the "sand gardens." There were probably fifty children in the three sand beds and many others standing outside, filling their pails from the beds and making most delicious pies on the benches. These little cooks, I noticed, dug the sand rather deep; for, as one little girl told me, "When it was wet, it baked better."

The children were all coming and going at their own free will; as soon as they got tired of the sand, they quietly left and went to the gymnasium or to the other yard to enjoy the delightful swings. The teacher of the gymnasium was walking about, helping and directing the children. When some of the children were tired of exercising they came again to the fascinating "sand gardens," before taking off their gymnasium suits. Afterwards I saw the same girls, who had put their suits in the lockers, reading "Our Little Ones," "Babyland" and other magazines for children, which the "locker lady" handed to them. There was a most delightful breeze, and everything looked so bright and pleasant that I could not help thinking what a blessing this park is to these children. For, from their faces and dress and general appearance, I should say they were from the very poorest families. The reports of the "sand gardens" of last year show how perfectly successful they have been. Not only are children amused all summer, but they are kept out of dark and dirty tenement houses; many of them are taken from brutal parents; and they are taught, besides, habits of cleanliness and how to obey, and — even in play-time — how to consider each other. Quiet and orderly games take the place of a mere noisy good time, and the children are pleased, when visitors come in, to exhibit the new songs and marches they have learned.

I have not told you of a lovely visit to Cambridge that I made with the Brands, when I was staying with them. We went, one afternoon, to see some friends of the Brands who took us to the Agassiz Museum; and I was perfectly delighted at the lovely botanical collection of flowers, — that is, my dear, it is a collection made for botanical purposes, where you can study carefully all the parts of the flower. For, instead of having to work with the fading stamens or seed-vessels, you have them all perfect, because they are made of glass. I think one shudders at the idea of glass flowers, as being something artificial and conventional; but just one glance at these beautiful specimens made me perfectly in love with them. They are surely the most wonderful and beautiful things I ever saw, and I found it hard to take their word for it when Rosamond and the others told me they were really made of glass. No one would ever guess it. You seem to see the branches of the real plants placed in the glass cases, the flower and stalk and leaves; then all the parts of the flowers, with here and there a magnified section of some one part of the flower. This exquisite work was done, I believe, in Switzerland, by some descendants of the famous Venetian workers in glass, a father and son, who seem to have a peculiar artistic power in creating these exquisite specimens. I think the family name of the artists — for surely they ought to be so called — is Blaschka. The flowers are not yet arranged. The coloring and texture is wonderful. I cannot describe them or give you any idea of them. They were presented to the museum by Mrs. E. C. Ware and Miss Mary L. Ware in memory of Dr. C. E. Ware. These ladies found them in Switzerland.

I had another delightful excursion with the Brands. We drove over to Waltham and to the Charles River, where we took a boat to row up the river. It was a peaceful, lovely afternoon, and we had quite a gay party together, three or four of us. And then came our little adventure. We turned a corner suddenly and met a boat going down the river, far away on the other side. It gave us a little start, for Godfrey Brand was pointing out something to us on the shore on our side. I turned suddenly, to find a young gentleman bowing to me, just as he was passing beyond us. It was Harry Merton, my "distant" friend, or the "mute, yet glorious" Merton, as Mr. Jones insists upon calling him — though I declare that he can talk very well if he ever has a chance. For I remember how agreeable he was on that famous Class Day. It was he who told me about the crowds in the streets in Boston, and how two or three women a week are killed by being run over at Park Square, and how the policemen have to be constantly renewed at the corner of School Street, as so many are killed there. And they all laughed much at his way of putting it.

But the thing grows more and more amusing. For the afternoon we were at Cambridge, a friend of the Brands went about with us, and he said he had just been showing the flowers to Mr. Merton, "whom I think you know," he went on to say, " as I remember seeing him with you Class Day. I wonder you did not meet him as you came in; but perhaps he took the short cut across the grass." We all looked at each other and laughed. We had seen a youth striding off in the other direction. Then, another day we went again to the Arnold Arboretum. In turning a corner near the entrance we came suddenly upon an open carriage, a gentleman on the front seat driving two ladies. He turned his head suddenly and in time for me to bow to him. Again, it was Mr. Harry Merton!

CHAPTER THIRTEENTH.

XVI.

HARRY TO HIS MOTHER.

CAMBRIDGE, August 31, 1891.

My DEAR MOTHER, — Just think that summer ends
this rainy day!

In a little note which Fanfan sends with the parcel
of stockings, she begs me to send her a little line all
to herself. She says she hates to read a letter which
she shares with all the other people in the world. I
believe the COMMONWEALTH people would be well
pleased if she did. You know the Ten Times One
Club thinks there are more than a thousand million
people in the world. If there were ten in a family
— and there are not — this would make at least a
hundred million families, and that would require a
hundred million COMMONWEALTHS every week. I can
see how that would be fine; for all the people would
be so intelligent then, and sensible and manly and
agreeable, that there would be no Balmacedas and no
rebellions; no houses would crash down without
cause; no sailboats would be overloaded. There would
be no lies in newspapers, no drought on prairies. Let
us indeed hope that this will happen.

When I got this letter of Fanfan's it set me thinking. So when I took my last round to the office I
asked them how many they did print. They said the
number varied — less or more, according as they had
one of my letters in or did not; and they said so little
that I could not find out, without asking directly,

which was less and which was more. They are print-
ing the woman's letters on the "off" weeks, but I
never see them. They did say, however, that they
were glad when they printed three hundred thousand
copies a week. Well, I asked a pressman, a good
fellow whom I meet at Thompson's Spa, how many
they could run off in one hour. He said he did not
know what presses they use, but that four or five
thousand an hour was enough, if they had handsome
cuts. And I said they had. So you see, at eight
hours a day — and Fanfan does not want any one to
work more, I am sure — the letters would have to be
electrotyped twenty-five hundred times, and twenty-
five hundred pressmen kept at work with twenty-five
hundred presses, so that the shepherd boy in Arabia
Felix and the seal hunters on Oonalaska might have
their COMMONWEALTHS.

What an interesting community this would make,
would it not? These twenty-five hundred pressmen
and their wives and children would make one ward in
Boston. They would have the proud consciousness
of supplying a world with its better reading! That
would be a little paradise in the tenderness of its
affections and the sweetness and light of its surroundings. But I forbear, dear Mother! These are only
a few of the reflections which Fanfan's letter has
opened before me. But I ought not to inflict them
on you.

I will say, however, that I believe I know, what
Fanfan means. For I know how much more I was
pleased by her dear little note than I should have
been by all the narrative she could have sent of the
ups and downs of Atherton, how Mrs. Knox's coach-
man had sprained his ankle, or what had become of
Ceylon Ross. In an old magazine article I was reading
yesterday, it said that facts are not the material of

conversation any more than an earthen plate is the material from which one makes a pie. And I suppose that the same is true of letter-writing. So I beg you to thank Fanfan for her nice note, and say that I believe what this unknown writer says of conversation is true also of the " eloquence of letters."

All the same, I suppose you, dear mother, do want to know of a few such vulgar facts as (1) whether I am alive or dead; (2) whether I have enough to eat, and of what quality; (3) whether I spend my time in those haunts of revelry and debauchery against which dear Dr. Primrose warned me, or in those higher regions of elevated culture and of the true humanities to which he bade me mount. So I must mention some facts, while I know dear Fanfan is dying to have me — I do not say tell some lies, but — embroider on the canvas of these facts, or, as the unknown writer says, make a pie, which he would have gladly spelled " pye," in the shaping of these plates.

Firstly, then, as dear Dr. Primrose would have said, and as I see the very best of them still say sometimes, — firstly, there is not business enough done in the office to occupy four flies. I suppose that is the reason why we were moved here in summer. I do not see that the chief worries. In fact he is not here much to worry. He has a lovely place at Manchester, which is fifteen or twenty miles northeast of us, a place where your south wind is off the water, which, they say, happens in the kingdom of heaven. Any way, it happens so in the Narragansett country, in Beverly, and in Manchester. The way I know it is a lovely place is that George, who is the chief's special clerk, has to go down there with parcels, and sometimes to write the chief's shorthand for him, and he says it is just perfect. As for the chief himself, he only shows up on Monday morning and perhaps Thursday. George and Mr. Out-

lake open the letters, and the rest of us "fool" round.
We file old letters, alter the boxes of 1879, 1883, 1885,
and so on, and pretend we are of use. The cashier is
as clever as he can be, so if there is any decent excuse,
and if you have not asked for leave the very day before, you can get off to go anywhere. Indeed, we close
the office now at three-thirty, except that we take turns
to see who shall stay after that.

For all this we shall have to pay when the busy season comes round. I am not afraid that the market for
clothes-pins has become glutted, as the books say. Do
you know what that chair-maker up in Worcester
county said to our Mrs. Outlake? She had been all
through his factory and was having some lemonade and
a biscuit in one of the great store-rooms, when she
said civilly, "I do not see where all these chairs go
to."

"Well!" said the manufacturer, well pleased, "I
guess settin'-down ain't gone out of fashion yet." I
have like views as to our clothes-pins.

, So you see I have more time for loafing than I shall
have by and by. Only it was desperately hot last week.
The summer climate of Boston involves three days out
of five when you breathe a sort of thin paste, which is
called air, made up of a good deal of nitrogen, a great
deal of hot water, more or less carbonic acid, something sticky, — I do not know what, — no ozone, and
just enough oxygen to keep you alive. Ask Fanfan to
look in her book and find how much that is.

The thermometer has not much to do with it. I
mean it is not much worse at 93° than it is at 82°.
It is this pasty, sticky sort of feeling which makes
you uncomfortable. You do not want to eat much.
You do not want to do much. If you have just a little
to do, say a good book to read, or, best of all, if
you are on the extension of South Boston, sitting with

two or three thousand other people on the benches there, with a book in your hand or the last Common- wealth, so that you could read if you wanted, why, it all goes well enough. Nobody does anything of any account in any other office more than we do in ours. And the nights, out at our place any way, are suffi- ciently comfortable. The best time of the day is from five to nine in the morning. But it is not one person in fifty who knows that it is light after half-past four. The milkmen do, and the icemen.

You ask about my lunch. Sometimes I take some- thing in from Cambridge to the office and eat it there with a cup of coffee. We are high there and overlook all the bay and have a good breeze if there is one any- where; so that of a deadly hot day you are as well off there as anywhere. We have facilities for a cup of hot tea or coffee, have a few table things, and the young ladies attend to such things so well that you must not think I am starving because I do not go to a restaurant. We are not far, you know, from Parker's and Young's, and there are clubs, like the Press Club and other clubs of gentlemen, where, as like as not, somebody asks you to go in. As yet we have not formed any club of clothes-pin makers. Really the place which would interest you most is this Thomp- son's Spa I spoke of. I believe there is really no Thompson now, and a gentleman named Eaton carries it on. It is as often called "The Temperance Bar" as anything else, and I heard somebody say, the other day, that it was the most attractive, and, he said, the most hospitable liquor saloon in Boston. But it is a liquor saloon where all the drinks are "temperance" drinks. Somebody told me that they had more than fifty drinks on their bill of fare.

When your Miss Clara Fenton asked me what was "the most curious thing in the social institutions of

Boston," and she did put it in that high and mighty
way, I told her — not to fail of an answer — that "The
Temperance Bar" was.   She asked if she could see it.
I said yes, if she would go at the right time; but that
in the middle of the day it was so crowded that nobody could get in without waiting, and then you could
hardly pass through.   So I took her one day last week
in the quiet time in the afternoon.

It is what you would call a little store, even in Atherton.   Good Miss Percy's candy shop is bigger.   But
this is elegance itself from one end to the other.   I saw
opposite me a handsome, well-dressed, fine-looking
young fellow escorting a dried-up, prim, and rather
over-dressed lady, and I was just going to say to Miss
Fenton, "See, there is another lady, just as I told
you," when I saw that the two were reflections of me
and of her in an immense mirror.   Then I saw a third
couple, who were also ourselves, on another side.   Here
are high counters and, I believe, one or two tables, and
behind, almost as many clerks, men or women, as can
stand there, ready to give you what you want, from
coffee round to egg phosphate, — which, I believe, you
have seen at Atherton.

Mr. Outlake says that the orders are that no one is
to leave the place dissatisfied, and I should think so.
The young men are nice-looking fellows, very neatly
dressed in white coats, always with a *boutonnière* of
flowers; and whatever they have is of superexcellent
niceness.   This is the reason why we all like to go
there, if we only have a minute, and if, as I say, it is
not in their crowded time.   In the middle of the day .
you can hardly wait to have your turn.

You will be amazed to hear that I still speak of
Miss Clara Fenton; for I know you did not mean that
I should attach myself to her for life.   But you must
understand at once that she is no longer "your" Miss

Clara Fenton. So to speak, she belongs to our firm, or
company. For it seems that her brother-in-law took
some of our stock for her when our stock was at seventy-five, and now that nobody thinks of selling our
stock nor dreams of calling it less than 450, of course
she holds it still. What is more is this, that she holds
so much of it that Mr. Outlake, not to say all of them,
desires to be awfully civil to her, as who would not ?
She always sends her "proxies" virtuously to Mr. Outlake, and of course, she would continue to.

But poor Mr. Outlake said to me frankly that he
thought he should die before his last interview with
her was over. He says she talked to him about Wagner and Paracelsus and the unearned increment and
Mahatmas and Cheelas — if that is the right way to
spell them. I believe all this is an exaggeration.
Poor man ! He says : "Merton, I want to keep well
with the rich stockholders, but I had rather make a
million pins than talk high art or philosophy for one
hour." All this is his nonsense, of course. But he
was very much pleased when he heard that I had
taken her to Trinity, and he tells me to render her any
service the office can render, so long as we do not have
to go to a Buddhist conference. So when she sent me
a note asking me to lunch with Colonel Higginson and
Mr. Howells and Dr. Holmes and Whittier at the
Thorndike, and afterward to drive again if the day
was pleasant, I showed it to him, and he gladly gave
me leave for the afternoon.

Well, when I came there it proved that Dr. Holmes
was not there, because it was his birthday; Whittier
declines all invitations; Mr. Howells was in the country; and Colonel Higginson could not come; so I had
to share the elegant lunch with Miss Clara and a Mr.
Whortleclaff, who was greatly interested in Michael
Kelly's change of base, and a Miss Welsh who had

been at Wellesley with Miss Clara. So far as I could
find, there had never been the least reason for thinking that any of these lights of letters would come, excepting that Miss Clara, who did not know one of them,
had written to invite them.

Well, we had a first-rate lunch, as you would take
for granted if you knew about the Thorndike. Miss
Welsh turned up her nose very much at Mr. Whortleclaff, — is it not a funny name? — and a little at me.
You have no idea how the regular old-time Boston
woman can turn up her nose when she tries. But
they are very easily frightened, and it is not hard
to take them down. I gave her as good as she sent,
any way. After the coffee she went off to a meeting
of "The Society for the Improvement of the Upper
Classes," or something of that sort. The base-ball
man went to see the match between Boston and Mil-
waukee, and Miss Clara Fenton and I were left to see
how we would pass the afternoon. Was not that
great? Well, I told her it would be a good time to
see Thompson's Spa, and that that was an institution
really, though there was no board of managers and no
anniversary and no charter. And then — dear Mother,
you will think I was crazy — then I said : " Would
you not like to take a Charlestown car and see Bunker
Hill Monument?" You see she is "immense" on
history, and had wept over the loss of the Paddock
elms, and asked a policeman on the Common where
were the traces of Percy's encampment, and what
were the lines of the redoubt on Fox Hill ! The man
thought she was crazy ; and I do not wonder.

Well, this is a very long story. But the excellent
Miss Clara said she would. You see she had, to my
wonder, excused herself from Miss Welsh's meeting
on the ground that she had made an appointment
with me. Heaven forgive her ! So it was that we

went to Thompson's Spa, and I initiated her into the
mysteries of egg phosphate. Then she really wanted
to take an open carriage that we might drive out to
Charlestown. But I said no, that we were children of
the public, and it was a great deal better to take a
public carriage. So we went to Charlestown in a car.

Our dear old Mr. Cradock says that the upper part
of Charlestown looks just as Boston did sixty years
ago, when your mother lived here; so I told the
excellent Miss Clara that, and she made a note of it
in her little note book. I tell you we got on grandly,
and she thinks I am fine.

My first blunder was about the elevator. There
used to be an elevator there, and a steam engine to
pump you up. Mr. Outlake told me there was, and I
told Miss Clara so. But when we came to the monument, there was no elevator at all and no steam
engine. I believe they thought it was *infra dig.;* any
way, it is all gone. But Miss Clara did not flinch.
To tell the truth, she took it very bravely. I found
out that there are two hundred and ninety-five steps
and I told her so. "Oh! nothing to Milan!" she
said. "One gets used to such things in Europe."
Who was I to shirk when she led the way? There
was an excellent fellow-citizen from Pittsburgh, who,
when he heard of the two hundred and ninety-five
steps, turned aside like a Leave-ite. What he expected
of a monument two hundred and twenty feet high I
do not know, unless the steps in Pittsburgh are two
feet high. Who knows?

There is a statue of Warren in the entrance room,
and on the outside one of Prescott in the linen frock,
only it is in bronze, which he fought in. Do you not
remember?

Well, I told Miss Fenton "to rest on her feet," as
the White Mountain guides say, and up we went.

You walk round and round a circular shaft which makes the middle of the monument. Miss Fenton had with her quite a large rolled-up map, which they had lent her at the hotel. "Hales's Map," it said, "of Boston and Vicinity." Of course I carried it and I knew what it was for. To tell you the truth, we did not have a very grand view after all our climbing. But I do not think Miss Fenton cared for that. I think she wanted to say in her journal that she had been there, or in her book, when she writes it.

The chestnut is that when an Englishman was told that Warren fell there, he said with horror: "What? fell? Did it not kill him?" As in fact it did. But the embrasures of the windows in the top room are so deep that you are not tempted to climb out, and, in fact, they cut off the view a little. Still, I think the loss of the distant prospect helped us a little in making out the neighborhood. You see perfectly, for instance, the shape of the peninsula of Boston, the great Ames Building, as high as the monument practically, and the State House so strangely near. You see at once how impossible it was for the English to keep their ships there, if we had a fort on the hill.

All this Miss Fenton made out on her old map with interest, and I helped her as well as I could with my two months' knowledge of Boston. The only other people there were two wide-awake Irish boys, determined to see everything there was to be seen, and a young lady who seemed to have brought them. We were at one window when they were at another, and, of course, I only saw her back. But as we changed places, who should it prove to be but my mysterious dancing partner of Class Day, the lady of the White Fleet and the cupola of the State House, Miss Sandford, better known to her many charges as "Jamaica Ginger."

Really, my dear Mother, we had just seen each other so often, and I had been so mystified by her disappearance that I fairly laughed. I should have been mortified by this but that she laughed too. Miss Clara, I think, was both mortified and surprised at such bearing, but I could not help that. I touched my hat and said : "I am glad to see you, Miss Sandford, when I am not nine-tenths under water." She said, "If we are locked up this time, we are both on the same side of the door." Then we laughed again. I asked Miss Clara if I might present my friend. She bowed a little more stiffly than was worth while, and then we all three fell to talking, while the two little "Micks" ran round and looked out at the windows.

I had to tell Miss Fenton the story of my sudden ducking. Miss Sandford helped occasionally with a detail, and between us we quite warmed Miss Clara up to take some interest. Then Miss Sandford said : "But I heard of you, Mr. Merton, and indeed I saw you, after you had broken your head." So I had to tell Miss Clara that story too. But I added : "I am not the only unfortunate person in the world. Miss Sandford herself is a sort of Goody Two-Shoes. So I told my half of the State House story. "How she got out," I said, "I did not know, and I do not know now."

She did not take this up, however, as gayly as she had taken up the other story. And then I saw that she looked pale. She only said that a gentleman who heard her let her out, and she stopped rather suddenly. She did ask Miss Fenton if she did not find the walk up very tiresome. Now Miss Fenton is as strong as a horse, and nothing so delights her as to have to show that she is prepared for what they call "emergencies." So she opened a great *chatelaine* bag she had been lugging round, which I had thought held twenty sawhorses of gold, and she produced three different smelling bottles, for three sorts of "emergencies." I was terribly afraid that one of them would be Jamaica Ginger. But fortunately it was not. To give the bottles their due, I think one of them, at least, did some good.

. . . .

September 2.

I was writing this at the office, and though, as I say, there is nothing doing there, I was interrupted. So I will finish my long story to-night here at Cambridge. All the same you may not see it, for those COMMON-WEALTH people may cut me off again in short metre.

For me, my chief service was sending one of the boys downstairs to bring up a mug or glass of water, with charges that he should not hurry so as to spill it. In a moment Miss Sandford rallied and said she should feel better as soon as she had rested. She should have sat down as soon as she had finished the stair work, and I think she had not acted on the guide's rule, "Rest upon your feet." In an incredibly short time the little hoodlum — who was not a hoodlum at all — returned with a mug really half full of water. Miss Fenton dipped her handkerchief in first, as one who was used to "emergencies," and "bathed her brow," as they do in books. Quite as much to the purpose was the drinking of what there was left, I believe. Any way, Miss Sandford fairly laughed, said she had made fuss enough, and would go downstairs. I could not offer my arm, for the passage is not wide enough. But I went a step in advance, and begged her to balance herself on my shoulder. This, however, she hardly did. Going down was a great deal easier than going up, and she had a good flush on her face and seemed all right when we came to the bottom.

Then Miss Clara, who really came up to the mark like a "trump," made her sit down again in the arm-chair. Miss Clara fussed round a great deal more than I thought worth while, buying guides and photographs and other memorials. But again it proved I was too hasty in my judgment. The good soul had sent off the other boy, and had made him bring a carriage to the gate where you go in to what is left of the battle-ground. In five minutes, which she had filled up with her "pottering," the carriage came. As soon as she saw it she closed her bargaining and insisted that Miss Sandford should get in.

So she did, after protesting that she could go home as she came. I took the third seat, as Miss Sandford, from the carriage, was giving her two attendants money for their car fare. But then Miss Clara, who is a "trump" after all, said they had better come with us. She bade the bigger boy ride with the driver, and he did, nothing loath as you may imagine, and the little one, Terry, as it proved his name was, sat by me on the front seat. Miss Fenton asked Miss Sandford where she should go, and to my surprise, she named a number, not very high, on Commonwealth Avenue. I say to my surprise, because, as I have told you, three houses out of five on Commonwealth Avenue are closed, and I do not suppose that the Commonwealth Avenue people generally spend the summer in keeping schools. Since this I have heard of another who does.

She did not seem at all out of order as we rode home, and she and Miss Clara talked very pleasantly and sometimes merrily. She is quite a stranger in Boston, as we two were, and one reason why I have met her at these different show places, I suppose, is that we have both been doing the lions, as strangers do. But Miss Fenton said at once that she knew nothing of the sights as Miss Sandford did; and without any of her "poky," high-cultured air, said she hoped she would feel well enough to be her guide on some other expeditions, "which do not involve such high climbing." I said that at the Ames Building they have an elevator, and told Miss Sandford how I had deceived Miss Fenton by promising her an elevator at Bunker Hill.

We rode by the old West Church, I remember, through Lynde Street. Miss Sandford said that if we would promise not to lie awake nights, she would tell us what an old lady told her. Then she said to me that this old lady was our friend, Miss Tryphena Dexter. Miss Tryphena Dexter told her that her mother saw the carts come through Lynde Street after the battle of Bunker Hill, with the wounded soldiers, and that you could see great drops of blood fall from the wagon from freshly opening wounds! Is not that ghastly? And was it not a story to end a visit to the battle-field with?

Well, nothing much happened as we rode home. We drove up to the right door on Commonwealth Avenue; the door was open, and a nice, pleasing young lady was sitting there, in the hall, beside her easel, at work on a water-color drawing. She came running down when she saw it was Miss Sandford, and took in enough of the situation to ask us all to come in. I do not believe Terry was ever asked in from a barouche to a Commonwealth Avenue palace before. We declined, but I took care to say I would call to inquire after Miss Sandford. Miss Fenton said the same thing, and we went off to her hotel rejoicing. We sent off the boys triumphant, and I went up to her parlor.

Then, I can tell you, I had to go through a course of inquiries as to my acquaintance with the lady, and

who she was, and who her father was, and all the rest.
As to which I knew very little. She said it must be of
the firm of Merton and Sandford, but I said I had
never heard of any such firm. All I knew was that
she danced well and talked well and had been the
keeper of a Vacation School. And she said: "There
are Vermont Sandfords at Astney." So there are. Do
you not remember Dr. Sandford?

I know, dear mother, what a broken letter this is.
But is not life all made up of breaks and new begin-
nings? All that I am afraid of is that when the clothes-
pin season begins, there will be no time for writing.
For there is a season for clothes-pins as there is for
peaches and oysters and marbles and operas and sym-
phonies. Does it not say something to that effect in
the Bible? And where have I heard that there is
a season even for letter-writing?

Truly yours,

HARRY.

CHAPTER FOURTEENTH.

XVII.

LUCY TO KATE.

BOSTON, September 8, 1891.

. MY DEAR KATE, — I cannot help writing to you directly about something that has just happened, though it is hard to say whether I am most pleased or provoked — with myself, I mean. I am, indeed, so amused and entertained by the adventure that I am not sure but that the whole thing is very delightful, and I do not know that I would have it otherwise. All this must confuse you. And does it not sound very mysterious? I have half a mind to leave it all to your imagination and content myself with an every-day account.

Are you prepared for a guide-book description of Bunker Hill Monument? — because that is what this letter was planned for yesterday. I had agreed to go to Charlestown some day with two of "my boys," when one of them appeared unexpectedly here, asking if I could not go that very day. I will not stop to describe how we went, and the intricacies of finding the right cars, and the absurdities of my boys. I do believe they inspired me to great activity in going up all the steps of the monument, when we finally reached it; for, though I began by taking the two hundred and fifty steps leisurely, they were running far ahead of me, and I went on and on, without stopping to take breath. I did sit a moment on the upper step, but I saw my boys leaning out of the window, now and then

looking back to ask me a question; so I had to lift
myself up and went to the window to look out with
them. I have never had before that dizzy feeling that
people tell of experiencing at such a height, but suddenly I found my head whirling round, and in the
midst of it came a voice that I half recognized, for
it was that of Harry Merton!

I fancied I was in a dream, but I do believe I recovered myself enough to answer intelligently and to
question him in my turn. Yet I fancy we had the
wildest kind of a talk imaginable; for I saw suddenly
a lady standing behind Mr. Merton, who was glaring
on us as if aghast. She wore spectacles that somehow
made her eyes seem wider and larger, as if she were
trying to open them to take in something remarkable.
This started me off in one of my laughing fits, that,
you know, I can't easily control, which seemed to
wake Mr. Merton to the remembrance of his companion, whom he introduced to me as a Miss Fenton. I
began to grow sober, but much terrified at my impolite
fit of laughter, when I grew more and more dizzy, and
I am sure I do not know what would have become of
me if it had not been for Miss Fenton's kindness and
for a large bag she had, which contained things I had
never heard of before. And I believe it was smelling
in one of her bottles that restored my consciousness;
for I did lose it a minute and did not know what was
happening to me, except that somehow or other we
were getting downstairs and presently into a carriage,
with my two boys going along with us.

I have been wondering ever since what would have
become of me, if Mr. Merton and his friend had not
been there; for I do not know how I could ever have
found my way down the stairs even, with only the
help of my harum-scarum boys, and I know we should
have been lost among the horse-cars. For it was a

regular attack of faintness that came over me for in-
sanely running up all those steps; so do not pretend
to think that it was caused by excitement at meeting
my "distant" friend, Harry Merton.

I can't help thinking that drive home one of the
pleasantest experiences I ever had. I began to gather
my courage as soon as we were in the fresh air again,
and Miss Fenton was so cordially kind that I felt as if
I were with old friends whom I had always known,
and I was almost sorry when the carriage stopped at
the door.   Anna happened to be in the hall, with the
door wide open, and came down to greet us, full
of wonder at seeing me thus escorted by strangers;
and Miss Fenton insisted upon coming up the steps
with me and has promised to call again.   So has Mr.
Merton.

I do wish I could give you some idea of the talk in
the carriage; for Miss Fenton seemed entirely different from anybody I ever met before, and fell to talking
about most recondite subjects; and when she perceived
that I had, apparently, never heard of them before,
she would look at Harry Merton with an anxious, inquiring question. I think I caught her touching her
head in a significant way, as if she thought I were
still a little out of my mind, because I could not
converse upon the high topics she brought up.   This
seemed to amuse Mr. Merton exceedingly, which is
why I called him "Harry" Merton just now; for we
seemed to become very intimate at once, as he perceived I was not out of my mind, but frightened by
his remarkable friend.

All this I wrote the other day, and that very evening Mr. Merton appeared, with Godfrey and Rosamond
Brand, and joined our party on the doorsteps. Anna's
brother, Mr. Davis, and his wife were there, as they
come every evening, either to go somewhere with us or

to sit with us; and you can't think with what com-
placency I look at Mrs. Davis sitting on the upper
step matronizing us; for I think even Aunt Martha
and Maria would be perfectly satisfied with the dignity and refinement of our chaperone. Mrs. Davis is
very bright and amusing too, and enters into the fun
of our talk with the rest of us. Mr. Davis is here on
some business matters, so they are staying on at the
Vendome. Harry Merton told us more about Miss
Fenton and how he came to know her,—all very interesting. Then it turned out that Mrs. Davis knew
about her, and she decided that she ought to call
upon her with Mr. Davis. I believe she is now at
the Thorndike, not far away. She is to come and see
me, and, as Mr. Merton declares, she was very much
pleased with me.

A great many excursions were planned and talked
of. We are all going to Nahant together, to Mount
Auburn — I can't tell where — and there was great
joking about my having lost the grandeur of the view
from Bunker Hill Monument; and Mr. Brand insisted
that we all ought to go and see the view from the top
of the new Ames Building, because they have an elevator there, and there will be no danger of my disgracing myself again by fainting. Mr. Merton did say
that we must surely ask Miss Fenton to go with us,
and he should insist upon her carrying her huge hand-
bag with its different kinds of smelling-bottles, which,
indeed, she always has for "emergencies."

He declares that I did really bear myself very well
in the carriage on my way home, only he could not
help being amused at my bewildered look when Miss
Fenton began to talk about "Mahatmas." It seems
she is a great enthusiast about Buddhism and also
about Browning; so I am looking forward to much
pleasant sympathy on that subject from her.

As we were planning our expeditions, Harry Merton
said that there was one trouble, — that Miss Fenton
always insisted upon taking a carriage. He went on
to say that he preferred considering himself one of the
"children of the public," as he called them, and he
liked to use the advantages provided for the public,
and preferred street cars to carriages. Whereat we all
exclaimed, — for that has always been our method this
summer; and when we went on to tell about our South
Boston and other expeditions, which we had been able
to take at small expense, it appeared that he had been
doing the same things, and it was only a wonder that
we had not met more often. I agreed to bring Miss
Fenton round to our opinion, and I even promised that
it should not be long before I should take her about in
my favorite excursion in the West End car, going all
round and through Boston and coming back to the
starting-point, all for five cents! In the midst of our
talk I never discovered who Miss Fenton is or where
she comes from.

.   .   .   .

You must not imagine that this intercourse has filled
up all our time. As I take up my letter again, I
can see I am not doing my duty as to my daily history.
You must picture to yourself that Anna and I still
cling to our afternoon French lessons, that we still
spend our hours in our beautiful park, not far away.
I must not forget to tell you that we had a very amusing talk with Harry Merton about the party that I
wrote you of, when Godfrey Brand and I saw him
through the window as we went down Commonwealth
Avenue one evening. Even that house is now shut up.
It seems it was only opened for that especial occasion,
and Mr. Merton declares if he had only seen us he
would have come down to invite me in for a dance;
for there were not many young ladies, and he is

sure that his hostess would have been delighted to see me.

I must not forget the lovely exhibition of plants last week by the Horticultural Society. I did wish my uncle could have come all the way from Vermont to see the ornamental-leaved plants and palms. It all looked very tropical. Besides, there were some exquisite white water-lilies in tanks, and lotus-plants, and two beautiful Victoria Regia, which I have never seen before, the blossom a foot in diameter, the leaf nearly six feet. Think how it has saved us a voyage to the Amazon; we only needed to walk to it one afternoon, after our French lesson, to see this wonder of the world.

I am glad that I have left a space to tell you of our expedition to Nahant, which has just come off. A perfect day it turned out to be, after some days of rain. We planned a large party, Mr. and Mrs. Davis and Anna, the Brands, and some friends of theirs. Miss Fenton decided not to go. We think she was a little afraid of being sea-sick; and perhaps it was as well that we were all a young party, as we did a good deal of walking and climbing.

The Davises and I were on board the Nahant boat in great season, at Battery Wharf, reaching it by the East Boston cars. We found none of our friends there, and began to fear they were not coming, as it grew later and later. Harry Merton was to come with the Brands and some other friends of theirs. We stood near the plank, watching the various passengers as they came, and had half a mind to try to exchange our tickets for another day, when at the last moment they appeared and hurried on board, breathless. They had been detained by a stoppage or a break-down of the street car and came near missing the boat.

Then such a lovely voyage! The sun was veiled by

clouds, but there were exquisite colors on sea and shore. We sat all together at first, watching the motions of the boat in leaving the pier. Then all the interesting places were pointed out to us; we saw old Fort Winthrop, Fort Independence, Thompson's Island, and Deer Island. I could see everything more distinctly than on our shorter "White Squadron" voyage; and as we passed on we saw all the settlements along the shore, Revere Beach in the distance, till almost too soon we reached the outer point of the peninsula of Nahant, where we landed. Then came up the question whether we would take one of the "barges," which would take us round Nahant. But we all preferred to walk, and it proved that Godfrey Brand was familiar with the whole place.

So, at the very beginning he took us down to the edge of the water to see a picturesque "Swallows' Cave." We had 'great fun in scrambling over the rocks, and I was sorry enough to leave the beautiful place. We kept along a little on the shore, then mounted to the path along the cliffs, and what a perfect view there was before us! All the wide ocean seemed spread far away in the wide horizon. We had to stop often and admire, finding comfortable nooks in the rocks for talks with one and another. And when the time came Mr. Davis and Mr. Brand opened some mysterious baskets they had brought along, and in a rocky nook shaded from the sun we had a most refreshing luncheon; and here we rested a long time, chatting on every subject under the sun and laughing at everything, till somebody looked at somebody's watch and declared that if we wanted to see Nahant it was time for our walk round the peninsula.

We were enchanted with everything. I never saw such luxurious ivies, covering the picturesque houses, that looked as comfortable as they did artistic, and

"On the trip home I had a talk with Harry Merton." — PAGE 185.

brilliant geraniums all in blossom, and such inviting-looking porches. There is a picturesque old billiard-room on a cliff, and Godfrey Brand had much to tell me about the delightful people who for many years have come to Nahant for the summer. The cliff walk is just perfect, and as the afternoon went on the sun came out, and we came home in a glorious sunset.

On the trip home the party separated; Anna walked about with Godfrey Brand, Rosamond was with some friends, and I had a talk with Harry Merton. I was going to say a "long" talk, but it seemed all too short as we neared the shore. We seemed to talk about everything under the sun, — very serious things, I should be inclined to say, except that you cannot always tell with Harry Merton; you think he has said something just to make you laugh, and it turns out that he has led you into really a serious strain.

On the rocks we had quite a discussion about the life of Laurence Oliphant, and it proved everybody had read it. I could not quite tell if Mr. Merton had read it or only the notices of it. Everybody had something different to say about it. Anna Davis said that she could understand the temptation that Alice Oliphant felt to join such a community, that she had often herself been made very gloomy to think how hard so many people were working only in daily drudgery, and that it seemed as if we ought to do our share. Rosamond Brand agreed to this and said she did not wonder that Alice Oliphant felt that her merely gay and social life at home was useless and without object; and then perhaps, after all, she was happier teaching the miners' children in California than spending tiresome evenings with the rest of the aristocracy and nobility of England. I could not help saying that might be, but that by coming in this way to America, she only added one more to the "drudges"

we had here, and if all the ladies of the aristocracy
and nobility followed her example, we should only
have so many more immigrants to take care of. Mr.
Davis considered this a very practical view of the
subject, and they all laughed. But we all agreed that
the Oliphants must have had a happy ending of their
life at the colony of Haifa, where they did not have to
forsake each other.

In our afternoon talk we went back a little to this
subject, and I could not help saying that perhaps one
reason that the idea of a "small-community" life did
not attract me was because I lived in a small place at
home, and that I had been much wearied with the
little things that people talked about, and had longed
to get out into a larger space, where you could seem
to be doing something with a great many people and
sharing in the larger life of a city. This set Harry
Merton to asking a little about my life and to telling
me about his present life and plans, and I found that
his home was also in Vermont and not far away from
Astney, and we knew many of the same people; and
the steamer reached the pier long before we had
come near finishing our conversation.

CHAPTER FIFTEENTH.

XVIII.

HARRY TO HIS MOTHER.

CAMBRIDGE, September 8, 1891.

MY DEAR MOTHER, — I have Fan's nice little note, and yours. I attended to your commission at once, as I hope I know.

Really, I think dear Dr. Primrose would be satisfied better than he is if he saw what Sunday is here, and what church attendance is. I cut out of the newspaper and sent to him a scrap which the Congregationalist people got up about the attendance in church in Boston on that sixteenth of August, of which I remember writing to you that it was called the most dead, or perhaps the deadest day in the year. If he showed it to you you will see that a very large proportion of the people between ten years of age and sixty must have gone to church that morning, if you allow for the very large number who are certainly out of town. I think I spoke of that in that letter.

Well now, last Sunday night, one would have said, was almost as dead a night. It was a rainy night, there had been no particular effort made to secure a congregation, Dr. Haynes was going to preach in the regular order at our church, and yet there was certainly a respectable, I should say a good, congregation. I could not help wishing all the time that you had been with me. Do you remember giving me Hughes's little book on "The Manliness of Christ," when I was quite a boy ? I have never forgotten the book, and it lies on my table now. That was really what Dr. Haynes preached about. The text was; "Howbeit in vain do they worship me, teaching for doctrines the commandments of men." And he illustrated the Saviour's real manliness by the heroic indignation with which he spoke to the hypocrites who say, "If a man say to his father or mother, It is Corban by whatsoever thou mightest be profited by me, he shall be free."

I am always wishing, when I hear Dr. Haynes, that I could write shorthand. I did take out the envelope of your letter, and wrote down two or three scraps. "No churches, no hospitals, no foreign missions, no this that and the other, until that mother is cared for on the Vermont hills !" I could not help thinking of you when he spoke of Vermont hills. "That is what Christ says. Not the heretic Professor Briggs, not Tom Paine, not this, that, and another, — not one of them is so much a heretic as are the two church-member brothers who go to law over a lot of pots and kettles, . . . who scowl at each other at the funeral, and only come together when the will is read."

"Two men are going up to the judgment gate. The first, a poor, bent philosopher, had spent his life in studying the doctrine; the second, a poor workman, only knew how to follow Christ. The philosopher questioned the workman, 'Do you understand this matter, that matter, and so on ?' 'No,' the workman answered; 'no, I only know how to do as Jesus did. I don't know how I'll get in. That's all I know.' The gate opened for the old workman as soon as for the philosopher."

I was glad I was there, and glad I made George go round with me. I am quite satisfied that I made no mistake in choosing my Sunday home.

September 15.

We are still having some warm days, but one can no longer complain of the languor and disinclination to go about which I have growled about so often as the summer went by. And we begin to find some business in the office. The orders come in from all parts of the country, and we are satisfied that hanging out clothes is not going out of fashion, as my Worcester County man said about the chairs. The order of business, you know, is this in the summer: The Western men let their wives and children take them to the seashore. This is what fills up our seashore. This is what fills up our Rye Beach, our Hampton, our Narragansett, and all other seashore places. But the first week in September comes a northeast storm, and they find the seashore hotels are very uncomfortable. What is much more to the purpose is that "the crop begins to move," and the Western men, who have had money enough to spend, must go home to move it. So all the railways running westward are piled up with baggage, all the seashore hotels are emptied, and the very pleasantest month for the seashore — indeed for the open air anywhere — is lost by that sort of pleasure-hunters.

But, on the other hand, the people who have their own houses in the country, who have gone from Boston for instance, stay in those houses till the first of October. Mr. Outlake told me that the private schools generally do not open till the first of October, and there is a proposal made every year to set the opening of the public schools later and later. I met a friend of mine who is a teacher in the Girls' High School, and she told me they had three hundred and twenty-four new girls present on their first day, and that they should not see the whole of their new class until the beginning of next month. That seems to show that fitting girls to be teachers is not going out of fashion yet, any more than the making of chairs or clothes-pins is.

I told Brand that I was going to call on Miss Sandford to make my proper inquiries, and he said he would go with me. When I went round for him just before it was quite dark, his sister was easily enough persuaded to join us, and we had a very jolly call. It was one of those warm evenings when for a little we sat on the top of the broad steps and watched the fading out of the sunlight and the coming in of the stars. There seemed quite a party on the ground, but the only two I talked with were Miss Sandford herself and her friend Miss Davis, — a nice bright girl. They are holding the fort, that is to say, living in the house while the regular people are away somewhere; I was told where, I believe, but I have forgotten.

They told about listening to the music and even watching the dancing through the windows, when poor Mr. Champernoon gave his summer party which frightened him so terribly. I told her how short we were of partners there, and that if we had known they were so near as the other side of the street we should have gone over, like the people in the twentieth century, and compelled them to come in.

We could not sit on the steps after it grew cold, and we went in. It is a beautiful house, with some fine pictures which I hope I may see again. We had some music. Miss Davis plays — Rosamond Brand proved to play wonderfully well — and Brand sang some college songs. So it was a very pleasant evening.

Out of all this, and from dear Miss Fenton's determination to see all that could be seen, there grew up a party to Nahant. You see, since it has proved that she is our Miss Fenton, who holds so much of our stock, I may be off duty any day to attend to her. So I was in for a trip to Nahant, and Brand and his sister were to show us the way — and the Sandford-Davis duo were two more. (Did it ever occur to you that *duo* and *two* are the same word ?)

After all, poor Miss Fenton had a sick headache, and we almost lost the boat waiting for her to make up her mind to stay at home. But I did not have Quixotism enough, or virtue enough, to go back to the office; and I went all the same as if she had been with us. For which may I be forgiven! When I went before I went to Lynn by rail, and so over Nahant Beach in a bus. But it is much nicer to go by the boat.

You may have seen all this. But I know the children have not. First of all, there is the "embarkation," which is always somewhat exciting. There stands at the gangway a policeman, to make sure that the boat does not receive more than its proper number of passengers. This number is determined by its size, and there is always a notice on any of these boats which shows how many they may take. Such things make me creep a little, as do the sight of the life-preservers and the instructions how you are to put them on. It seems a little like the old Egyptian feasts, but I suppose that the gentlefolk who go up and down every day take them all as a matter of course, as you might pass by a cemetery.

We were there almost at the last minute, for, as I say, we had to go for Miss Fenton, and she had to make up her mind whether she could go or not. Now, making up her mind takes a great deal of time. But when we came there we found our other young ladies waiting for us, and off we went.

The view of the city, as you recede from it, is very

fine. It is the imagined view of Boston rising from the sea, with the State House ruling the whole of it. Then you go by East Boston, which you remember as Noddle's Island; I have heard you tell about picnics there in the old days. There is a little island which they call Apple Island, that I think I should like to live on, though I do not know how I should get there. And then you come to what is known as Shirley Gut. Point Shirley is named for the famous war-governor of a hundred odd years ago, and this gut or channel is a channel between it and Deer Island, where the city has the poor-houses and other such establishments. There is a story always told, and I hope it is true, that the Constitution once ran through the Gut when she was pursued, and that the English vessels did not dare to follow. I say I hope it is true; I do not believe it is, and I rather think the story, properly told, would go back to Manly's days, when he was picking off English cruisers in Washington's time.

After you pass the Gut you have a run of two or three miles in the open sea, and it is here that very delicate people are a little seasick. I was glad, on the whole, that Miss Clara did not come. Nahant rises higher and higher as you advance, and as you come up to the wharf you see what a mass of rocks it is.

Our Mr. Outlake showed me some old sketches of Nat P. Willis, — whom he seemed to think everybody would know, but whom I had never heard of before, — in which he makes much of the Nahant of his day. He says it is as if the devil had been knocked down and was nearly covered with water, but his arm and hand were stretched out, so that Nahant Beach is his arm and Nahant itself is his hand. I do not know that you know how the devil's hand and arm would

look if he had been upset by Michael, so that simile
may not help you. More simply, here are say four
hundred acres of rocks, piled in together; and what
the joke calls "cold roast Boston" has gone down and
taken possession. There are I do not know how many
beautiful houses, built wherever there is a chance to
get in a house. There are the most elaborate asphalt
roads and sidewalks laid from one to another, and the
wind — north, south, east, and west — is off the sea.
It cannot be hot there, you might say; certainly it
was not, the day we were there.

It was a good deal nicer going with the Brands, who
had friends there, so that we could cross their grounds
without trespassing, and they knew just where you
had and where you had not rights. But everybody
has rights on the sea-beach; that is one of the inalien-
able privileges of a citizen of Massachusetts; so that
you can walk all around Nahant without trespassing.
The most extraordinary thing we did was to go through
Swallows' Cave. This has no bottom and has no top,
you might say, though they have made a sort of path
where you can walk through. The tide fills it at high
tide, so it is always wet and always covered with sea-
weed. In old times I believe there used to be swallows there, but we saw no swallows. Of course it was
rather an adventure, carrying the ladies through. I
should think it was seventy feet long. The entrance
is so low that you have to stoop, but after you are
once in the cave is fairly twenty feet high.

You know everybody jokes about the sea serpent at
Nahant. But I found, in the face of the joking about
it, that the sea serpent, by a regular old Boston man,
is regarded as being a real creature, quite as much as a
sperm whale is. It is more than sixty years ago that
the original appearance of the sea serpent off Nahant
was made. Then he was seen by some of these grand

people who lived there, and they were old ship-masters who had made their fortunes in the Northwest Coast, and never permitted anybody to laugh at their story. And Mr. Outlake says that when Mr. Wood, who was no fool of a naturalist, was here, he was willing to accept the scientific basis of the story. Indeed, I think Agassiz himself gave way. He lived at Nahant a good deal, and saw all the people who held the old traditions.

So much for the outside facts of Nahant, as Fanfan would say. Now, as to our particular expedition. It was really a party of pleasure from the beginning to the end; and do you know, dear Mother, my experience of parties of pleasure is that they generally turn out to be parties of pleasure, notwithstanding the warning which the Sunday-school books all give, that they will certainly turn out parties of pain. For my own part, I had a right good time, going down and coming back again. Among other things, I had two nice, steady talks with the mysterious Miss Sandford, who on this occasion materialized, and was not behind an oak door, and was not faint, and was just like any other sensible Vermont girl. For it proves that she is a Vermont girl; she is one of those Astney Sandfords, whom you must remember. She is a cousin of that tearing beauty, Ethel Sandford, who bewitched the professor, and whom he carried off to his shingle college at the West. I think you must remember the story. Don't you remember Mrs. Brown told you they didn't know at Longfield whether he was going to honor with his preference Miss Ethel Sandford, or that nice Carrie Swift, who was at the Christmas party, until the engagement was actually announced? My Miss Sandford — Miss Lucy Sandford, it seems, her name is — did not seem to know much about her handsome cousin, but she did know that she was now

Mrs. Bainbridge. She knew Carrie, and spoke of her
in the very pleasantest terms.

We talked about all sorts of things. Of course,
there was a great deal of fun about her disappearance
from time to time. But after the joking about that
had been pretty much exhausted, I made her tell
about her summer experience, and compared it with
mine. For we came here within a fortnight of each
other, and have been knocking around the town, each
of us as a stranger, in a good deal the same way. She
was a good deal interested in Miss Tryphena Dexter,
whom she had really seen to more purpose than I had,
and she told me a good many funny stories about the
old lady. Miss Dexter is a regular cockney, as I have
found out before, and Miss Sandford says she knows
a great many of the old Boston stories. She had observed, as I had, the droll habit she has in the street
of turning round at the end of every four steps to see
who is behind her. She noticed the supreme contempt
with which Miss Dexter speaks of every person of
foreign lineage; and it is wonderful that we two,
who came from Vermont, are not classed with " them
Irish" or "them Eyetalians" or "them Canajyans." I
told her of my effort to make Miss Dexter go into the
country and spend a fortnight at Atherton. She
laughed very heartily at this, and said she had tried
the same experiment, but that she never would be
happy under any trees but her dear trees on the
Common. She and Miss Tryphena had been on
the Common one Sunday afternoon, somewhat after
the fashion of which I wrote you when I was first
here.

Then we drifted into talk about books. She was
reading this funny "Tourmalin," just as I am. But
she was very enthusiastic about Laurence Oliphant,
and I think you must try to get that book for the

club. I hope I did not disgrace myself. For I did
know who Laurence Oliphant was, I had read THE
COMMONWEALTH's notice of him, on the back of
one of my letters to you. But she went a good deal
into detail about it, about the community life that
they all had together, and so on; and it was this
that led up to all the talk that we had about Vermont
and Ethel Sandford and Carrie Swift.

All of us walked home together, and this gave a
chance for us to show the ladies some of the queer
places down near the wharves, where they are not in
the habit of going. There is one eating house that I
am very fond of, which is up high enough for you to
sit at an open window looking all over the bay, while
eating your clam chowder or oysters, — for oysters
have come again.

Nahum would have liked all of these lion-hunting
expeditions, because he would have seen medals and
pictures and old swords and pitchers to his heart's
content. He would have seen the famous Ben Franklin suit, of which the story is told. It came about by
Mr. Outlake's thinking he must do something himself
for "poor dear Miss Fenton." He got himself up one
evening, and made Mrs. Outlake go to the Thorndike
and call. She was very funny about it when I saw
her the next day. There is this standing joke about
"Mahatmas" and "chottas" or "chattas," — and they
pretended great fear that Miss Clara would put them
through their Buddhist catechism. But she was very
merciful, and only talked about the Concord School,
and Sir Launfal, and Mr. Smith's sermon, and the
mystical articles in THE COMMONWEALTH. Mrs. Outlake asked her to dinner, and so on; and Mr. Outlake, in a fit of enthusiasm, asked Miss Fenton if she
had seen the Historical Library, and she said "No," —
to his great delight. For it is one of his fads, and is

really, in the line of shows, about the nicest thing
in Boston.

You see, to belong to the Historical Society is about
the only order of nobility there is left here. I mean
it is the only thing left where a good many people
wish they were in who are not in. You have to be
a hundred and fifty years old to belong, in the first
place; and you have to know everything, in the
second place. And, granting that, there can only be,
say, a hundred and twenty. So it is quite a " select
thing," as an old lady said to me of a parish sociable.
They are good as gold about letting people in to see
the library and collection, and really anybody may go.
But practically you feel easier, when a top-sawyer,
who came over with Endicott and whose grandfather
was a founder of the society, asks you.

Well, I think Mr. Outlake wanted to reward me for
my attentions to Miss Fenton, so he asked me to join
the party with my friends, and I took Miss Sandford
and Miss Davis. We all met at Parker's and lunched
in one of the private parlors. Then it is only a short
walk to the Society's Library. First you have to climb
three flights of stairs. So Dr. Holmes called it the
"High-Story-Call Society," the day after they moved
into these new rooms. Was not that just like him?
The rooms are not many and not very large, but there
is everything curious in them.

Between the proper work-room of the Library and
the elegant Dowse collection, on the door, is the frame-
work with two swords, of which Dr. Primrose told us.
One is the sword of Prescott who built the redoubt on
Bunker Hill, and the other is that of Linzee, the English Commander who fired the first shot at the redoubt
in the gray of the morning. Prescott's grandson married Linzee's grand-daughter; so their children united
both lines. The grandson was the historian. He used

to have the swords crossed in his library, and when he died he gave them to these people.

The Dowse Library seemed to me the most attractive room I ever saw; lined with books, on three sides, and those books selected for something, in every case, — not bought by a drag net, I mean, — by a man who was thoroughly interested in English literature and meant to get the best. He had money and good taste and information, and he had the best editions of all English standards, not to say of English historians, and he had them bound in the most elegant manner. Mrs. Outlake told us his history. She remembered seeing him when he was an old man. He was the typical apprentice in Boston. He had been born in Charlestown, and could just recollect the burning of his father's home the day of the battle. He tried one and another thing, but finally became a leather dresser, making the more elegant kinds, such as book-binders use. Something started him on collecting books, and when he died he had this collection, by far the most valuable collection of English books in New England at that time.

It would be such fun to nestle down here to read; and, so far as I saw, any decent loafer in Boston might do so. There is an awful warning story which Mr. Outlake told us. When he was fifty years old his English agent sent him an advertisement that an English collection of pictures would be sold by raffle. He persuaded a neighbor to join him in buying three tickets, and he won two of the three best prizes. The neighbor had backed out, so he had all the tickets. Part of the prize was a collection made, most of them, in the old fashioned English water-colors. I have seen it at the Art Museum, where it is now. They seemed to think that this fixed his taste; and till he died, he was perfecting this library.

But is it not interesting? For now I suppose he and the other man who bought the ticket could be sent to jail for corresponding with a lottery agent! The story is that it was proposed that Harvard College should give him some honorary degree, as heaven knows they have given them to many men who had much less hold on literature or science. Then some joker said it should be LL. D., Learned Leather Dresser. And it is said that this joke made him angry so that he left his library to the Historical and not the College. I do not know if this is true. I should say it was quite as useful here as there. Perhaps " Mr. Ward knew his own business."

. . . .

You have no idea of the variety of commissions which come to us in the office. It seems the bankers have the same experience. If the president of a bank in Cranberry Centre has a good strong account here, he will think he may trouble them to match a ribbon for his wife, or to send an autograph of Phillips Brooks for his daughter. So our correspondents, and that not our largest correspondents, will put in a postscript into an order for clothes-pins, asking us to attend to this or that errand for them. And this time a man we have at Roaring River, who sends us cedar, wanted to know if we could not make special rates for Baker's chocolate for him. He had a fad, that it would be better for the men in camp than the strong coffee they drink. And he stuck to the national motto, as Mr. Outlake calls it, and was bound to "get the best."

So the chief gave me the letters, and told me to "go out and see the people at Baker's. There are no Bakers now; I believe they are Pierces now; but the reputation is so great that it must not be lost. I crammed up first, in a cyclopædia, that I need not be quite a fool. Do you know that while now "chocolate" and "cocoa" have meanings wholly different in the trade, this is merely arbitrary? It seems the *latl* was the Mexican word for water, so that choco-latl only means cocoa, or choco, and water. But now cocoa and chocolate are quite different.

Well, there is a street railway out to Milton Falls where the mills are, and this afternoon I have been out there. I gave my letters to the people, who are very civil, and they gave me their bottom prices for our Aroostook County man. But I thought I would follow my hand; and I asked them, a little bashfully, if I could not see the work of the mills.

With perfect courtesy the gentleman I dealt with called a clerk and told him to take me over the factory. He had a great book, which he put down on the table and asked me to register; and so I did. He showed me first several glass jars in the office. One large jar contained in alcohol one of the large brown pods which hold the cocoa beans. The pod is about the size of a moderately large musk-melon. It looks much like the outside leathery substance around a butternut. Then we began in the basement. There he showed me the large engine, three hundred horse power. We got on a freight elevator and went up to the fifth story, which is the top story. Here was the storeroom where the bags of cocoa beans are received. The beans look much like good-sized brown kidney beans. These beans are put in large perforated cylinders. As they whirl around in these cylinders, dirt, small pieces of refuse, and small stones drop out through the holes. After that the beans are picked over by men. They were picking them over just as I remember, when six or seven years old, picking over beans for Sunday breakfast baked beans. A good many beans stick together in pairs. These have to be separated. After this the beans go into what we should call large "bakers." Each of these roasters holds a long ton, 2,240 lbs. The roasters look like large tin portable ovens. The next process is the mixing, and cracking off the shell, and winnowing. Winnowing I call the process which blows off the lighter shell from the nut and leaves them separate. This, before this machine was used, had to be done three times in order to do it well. This new machine does it better, and the beans only need to go through once.

After this cracking and fanning, the beans go pretty directly down into the great grinder, made of steel rollers, which does the work that used to require fifteen ordinary machines. There are only three of these large "grinders" in use in the world. The rollers are warm and the chocolate pours out like paste and rolls down into pans.

The next room is very noisy. You can't hear a man's voice. Here is what I call the kicking process. The chocolate is put into the little tin moulds in which it is sold. About a hundred of these moulds are put on an iron about three by four feet. From below a machine keeps bouncing the iron plate up and down. As the chocolate is ladled out into these moulds, the jouncing makes it fit down beautifully smoothly. It is the kicking process that makes the great noise. Then these little tin moulds of chocolate are taken into the cold room in the basement. Here it gets solid and hard, and is then shipped. This cold room is very cold, although to-day is one of the hottest days of September. The cellar is kept cold by brine running through pipes around the cellar, just as rooms are made warm by steam going through pipes around them.

The man who showed me about said he was sorry

he couldn't show me the factory when they were running in full. During this next month and half of the next they make repairs. This is the annual vacation during which they do little.

P. S. You will be as glad as we all are that Dr. Haynes is not going to Chicago.

Always yours,

H.

CHAPTER SIXTEENTH.

XIX.

LUCY TO KATE.

BOSTON, September 24, 1891.

MY DEAR KATE, — I have never told you about the expedition that Anna and I made to Mount Auburn a week or two ago. We went as "children of the public," starting first from Park Square. We had to wait about half an hour for the electric car that was to take us to Cambridge, but it was not one of the hottest days we have had lately, so we did not mind. And we were fully rewarded for our delay by the beautiful ride in the open car over the lovely Charles River, which seemed most enchanting that afternoon, with the blue sky and the bluer water, and the red brick houses of Beacon Street across the water. I imparted to Anna my plan of turning these houses round, so that they might face the lovely sunset view and that they might add to the picturesqueness of this excursion over the bridge. She was rather uncertain whether the owners of the houses would sympathize with my æsthetic ideas of improving the view from the bridge, but we formed our plans all the same, and decided that when we owned a house on the "waterside" of Beacon Street we would build it to face towards the sunset, with a picturesque boat-house, and a lovely row-boat, in which we should row ourselves when we went to make calls. Or if we drove out of town we would look back over

our bridge, to the picturesque part of our house
which should be a joy to all beholders.

We were so occupied with our plans and imaginings
that we were quite surprised when the conductor
shouted out, " Change cars for Mount Auburn." We
had to stop in a little hot station which seemed filled
with flies and pickled limes and crying babies. After
a painful waiting of ten minutes our car came along,
and the delightful ride that followed was a balm to
our souls. We went on through the loveliest part of
Cambridge, by the beautiful college grounds with its
fine buildings, and reached the magnificent Washington elm, and could see Elmwood, where Lowell lived
and died, and passed Longfellow's beautiful house,
and came at last to Mount Auburn.

Happily we had a long afternoon before us, for indeed as it was we could not do all we wanted to in
wandering over the beautiful grounds. We did visit
the burial-places of Longfellow, of Agassiz, and could
see many of the famous monuments of which we had
read; but we had to hurry away to an electric car, at
sunset, to make our way home, declaring, however,
that we would come again as soon as we could have
a whole day for exploring the beautiful grounds.

. That was many weeks ago, and we have never been
since till last week, when I had an invitation from
Miss Fenton to drive there with her one morning. It
was one of the lovely September days we have been
having that she called for me in a most inviting looking victoria. Anna and I have been much amused at
the contrast of the two expeditions. No waiting at
Park Square, no struggle with flies at the little station! Anna could not go, and Miss Fenton and I
leaned back upon the luxurious seats, going whither
we would, without delays, or noise of crowds.

I suggested our going across the new Harvard

Bridge, as we drove out through the Commonwealth Avenue park, — "my" park, as I am inclined to call it, — and Miss Fenton was willing to admire all its rural charms, the picturesqueness of its arched bridge, and the figures of gay autumn flowers along its roads. Then we crossed the bridge and admired the views up and down the river. I did not venture to impart to Miss Fenton my plans for the Beacon Street houses, for I found her very enthusiastic about Boston just as it is. Indeed, I think she admired the institutions and public buildings more than the rural charms of its public parks, as I displayed them to her. And is it not remarkable? I find that she, too, comes from Vermont, and she knew all about Astney and my father and mother, though she has not seen them or Astney for years. I think one reason she did not admire more enthusiastically the "Joe Pye" weed and golden-rod along the drives in the park was because "she had always seen them in Vermont," and there was "nothing so very new about them."

So we saw lovely Mount Auburn again, and I could take her to some of the famous places, and we went to the burial-place of Charlotte Cushman. Did you know that she loved Boston so much that she selected this spot in Mount Auburn that could overlook the town where she was born? For she was born in a narrow street of the "North End" and the "Cushman School" stands in memory of her in that very street; for she left to the city a bequest for the use of the school children.

Miss Fenton was much interested in all this, for she had seen Miss Cushman on the stage, and gave really a brilliant account of her appearance as she saw her in the part of "Lady Macbeth;" and she knew friends of Charlotte Cushman, when she lived in Rome, and had much that was interesting to tell.

I was not sure but I enjoyed Miss Fenton more in such reminiscences than when she began to talk about books, for then I cannot quite keep along with her; and as we came home I was really sorry to lose some of the beautiful sunset views, in trying to understand all she was telling of one of her late readings.

But this is not telling you what a delightful time Anna and I had at the Art Museum last Saturday. For the Museum is open to the public Saturdays and Sundays, and we went as "children of the public," as Harry Merton would say. Anna is to enter one of the classes this autumn, and she is very familiar with all the delights of the whole building. She wanted to see some especial pictures that are exhibited here just for this summer, so we were merely to make a tour through the different rooms to give me an idea of their geography, passing only through those on our way to the picture galleries. So she ruthlessly bore me on through the different apartments.

We turned to the right on entering, passed along the lower floor, then turned a corner, going on to the back of the building, where we went up some stairs. I did insist upon stopping a moment to exclaim and admire here and there, — in the Parthenon Room, for instance, where I plan to go for a long study some day, and then in the corridor I had to make her stop for me to delight in the Japanese pottery and screens, and I did go back to look into the Japanese room and I could not bear to leave it; but she absolutely tore me away and bore me off with her to the entrance of the fifth picture gallery at the other end of the corridor.

She condescended to let me put my head into the water-color gallery, that I might know where to find it another time; but she would not let me look at a single picture, and she herself would not stop at a single thing till we were fairly planted in front of some of the pictures she had been longing to see. First, she wished to see the Corots, and I was delighted to find that I could thoroughly delight in them. I am always afraid, after I have heard so much of a great painter like Corot, that I shall find I do not know enough to enjoy his pictures. But, oh, I was so glad to find that I need not "know;" for they are so lovely, so exquisite, — to have in one's own room of a winter day, for instance, like a window let out upon a summer scene. I envied much the happy owners and was glad indeed that Anna had hurried me about, so that we could have leisure for all the treasures in this room.

The name of Daubigny was another that I was rejoiced to grow familiar with; such a beautiful picture by Jacques of sheep resting under a tree. And then how we were arrested when we came in front of the splendid picture of the horses of Achilles by Henri Regnault. That was the way with us; we had to stop suddenly; for the whole group is so spirited and wonderful, with Automedon standing between the heads of the horses, all so full of life and animation. You feel as if he were holding back the horses away from you. As we admired the energy of the figure of Automedon, Anna told me of a story of the picture that she had read; how Regnault had been honored with an appointment to the "Prix de Rome," which made him a student there for many years. And in return he was bound to send at a certain time (or times) the painting of a nude figure, and he sent this "Automedon." Thus it was not a mere figure in pose for an artist, but one part of a significant group that perhaps struck me more than anything else in the room. Of course, when we went home, we hunted up our Homer, and decided that Regnault had really carried us to the plains of

Troy; and we questioned if he had not seen the wonderful horses of Achilles in just such a vision.

I am sure that one ought to see no more than one picture at a time to enjoy it thoroughly, but thanks to Anna's persistency in dragging me to this room, in spite of other enchantments we did have time to admire many others. Such a lovely mother and child by John S. Sargent! I was delighted to have a chance to see this picture, giving such a charming idea of the work of a favorite artist, and an American too. Then there are some lovely Millets, whom we all know by the "Angelus" and these have the same charms, especially "*La Bergère Assise*" so full of expression too; and here were many of William Hunt's pictures, some of which I had never seen, though I am familiar with so many. Of course I could feel a fresh pride that he was born in my native state of Vermont. Then there was a lovely picture by Lerolle in the southern corridor, a real out-door picture, and so breezy, some women walking by a river. Then, in another room were Vedder's pictures, — the wonderful one of the Arab listening at the mouth of the Sphinx. And here was a very striking and beautiful picture by Sprague Pearce, "The Widow," her cloak covering her head and falling over the child who rests in her arms. I was charmed by a beautiful snow storm by Claude Monet, and a lovely "Shore and Sea" with graceful ships on the water. And here was Millet's "Trumpeter," — the American Millet's. The picture represents an old-fashioned Dutch scene, the interior view of a house where two men and five women are seated. The Trumpeter is surrounded by the women, while the other men smoke in the fireplace; the light from the fire, reflected on his face, is wonderfully done. It is a fine picture.

I was interested in two of Dennis Bunker's pictures, — the artist who has lately died so young in the beginning of his career; and I liked a spirited picture by Gaugengigl, of Mr. Outram Bangs as a matador, also a delightful picture by Abbott Thayer. And we did have a little time for the Dutch room and some real Van Dycks; one of them, "The Senator," a very self-composed senator, I admired for his dignity. I must not stop now to tell you more of them, for I shall go again soon. Only I must speak of a lovely pastel Anna and I saw one day on exhibition at Williams and Everett's. It is a pastel — some hollyhocks against a stone wall, and in front a little colored girl carrying a black kitten. It has such a sunny, bright look that it charmed me, especially, perhaps, because its hollyhocks reminded me of those against the stone wall at home. It is by Miss Ellen D. Hale.

I inspired Miss Fenton with a desire to visit the Art Museum, and we are to go there together soon. I told her how Anna and I looked up the story of Automedon. You may like to find it yourself in Bryant's translation of the Iliad, the 17th Book. She was much amused when she found that we had also studied it up in the Greek, — as much surprised, perhaps, as I am at her Buddhist talk and account of Madame Blavatsky!

I had another excursion with Miss Fenton, when I persuaded her to go with me to Franklin Park by way of the street cars. We took a Grove Hall electric, which frightened Miss Fenton a good deal, and she amused me by planting her boot-heel on the floor of the car, thinking she should thus escape an overflow of electricity! But she forgot her terror as we went on. We reached the Park, and Miss Fenton was pleased to find that there were "barges" running, which we could take, and could be conveniently

14

carried about the Park for the small sum of twenty-
five cents! So we had a delightful tour and were
shown all the principal points of interest, passing on
through lovely avenues of trees, and returning to our
car in time to be home before sunset.

I have not had much else to do with Miss Fenton,
for in this lovely September weather I went to make
a visit to the Brands, and I was with them some days.
They are close upon some lovely woods, where we
could walk every day; and then they took me some
charming drives, and I could learn all about the
beautiful environs of Boston, without the long drive
from its centre through close streets lined with
brick houses. We saw a wonderful illumination at
Waltham, over the river, one evening.

Anna and I wasted time one day in a feeble effort
to secure some seats for the afternoon rehearsals of
the Symphony Orchestra. I call it "feeble" because
we could have found out by inquiry that there was no
use in trying for them; but when we saw $7.50 seats
advertised for the winter course of rehearsals, we
formed the brilliant plan of buying a ticket, and
securing one seat, and taking turns in making use of
it to hear the music, thus sharing the expense. But
anybody might have told us that we could not practise economy this way, and that even the afternoon
rehearsals are an aristocratic treat and that one has
to pay high for the privilege of buying them. However, we followed a little crowd Tuesday morning
into the Music Hall, and found our way to some
front seats. It was not for some time that we discovered what was really going on, and I came near
making a bid for a ticket that seemed to come within
our means, but Anna pulled my arm and pointed out
the placard announcing that the bids were for the
"premium" of each seat, to be added to its price of

$7.50. And we soon found that there was nothing likely to come within our reach that day nor the next, and we left, feeling, however, that we had been in distinguished company.

We do not lose hope of hearing the rehearsals, however, for the upper balcony will be reserved for twenty-five cent tickets, and if we can only go early enough we shall stand as good a chance as some thousand or two others for a seat in the upper balcony, or a favorable "stand" somewhere. But we had hoped to own a seat between us, which we could share each afternoon, taking turns in sitting.

One afternoon lately we went to the "matinee" at the Boston Theatre to see the play of "The Old Homestead," and really it was great fun. The Brands told me I ought to see it as presenting a true picture of Vermont life, and we did enjoy it immensely. I laughed and I cried, for the scenery and effect of it all is indeed charming.

There is a scene representing the old house, and a well, with the well-sweep and old oaken bucket, — even a log lying partly chopped with a pile of chips, and a churn, with pails and bee-hives ; perhaps one would not see them really all together in this way, but surely it is a homely scene. And would you believe it ? — in comes a yoke of oxen, drawing a regular load of hay ! this did upset me, and I fell to laughing and crying, I believe. I can't tell you whether the New York drawing-room is as true to life. It was all so very well acted, too. I do not know that I shall find myself dropping in often to renew my remembrances of my country home, but this surely was a delightful afternoon's entertainment, and it is a pleasure to see how those quiet things of home out-door life can be shown in so picturesque and dramatic a way.

We have had our visit to the Ames Building that we have been planning lately. Godfrey Brand succeeded in getting us a "permit" to go; for it seems there was such an unruly crowd pressing in to go up to the top of the building that "they" have had to limit the number of visitors.

Perhaps you have heard about this building, which rises up, fourteen stories high, at the corner of Court and Washington streets! Happily a great many elevators make it possible to reach all the different numerous apartments of this building, and there is · besides an express elevator, that takes one straight up to the top, without stopping at any offices, or "stations," below. We did not have Miss Fenton with us, and her smelling-bottles, but I almost felt as if I needed one of them as we flew up to the top with bewildering quickness. Yet I did not disgrace myself by another fainting fit, for the air was very refreshing as we got out upon the roof.

Here, indeed, was the whole broad roof of the building for us to walk out upon, and such a magnificent view on every side! It was one of these beautiful September days we have had, with an east wind bringing in just a delicate mist of a fog to give a soft light to everything; and the practical part of my mind was much delighted by having all the numerous points of view explained to me. My old friends, Bunker Hill Monument and the cupola of the State House, were easily seen, and the islands in the harbor came most picturesquely into the view. It was, indeed, all a charming sight. If I am ever a lawyer, I shall surely have an office in the top of this building, and then if I have no clients I can solace myself with this view.

Do not be afraid, my dear Kate! I am not turning my mind to any of the learned professions. Indeed,

you will think I have forgotten about my University
plans. No, they are still seething, but I have not yet
decided about the courses I am to pursue. I have not
yet decided, either, about my boarding place for the
winter. I would like much to be able to go to the
pleasant home of the "Helping Hand" Society on
Charles Street, and I have been allowed to see one of
its comfortable rooms overlooking the Charles River,
and the sunset view beyond the bridge ; but if I find
I can afford to pay more than the low price needed
for board and lodging there, I feel that I ought to
leave the space for some one else. There are many
comfortable houses open to such students as myself,
who come to Boston for their education. I went to
see one of these boarding-houses the other day on
Berkeley Street, where perhaps I may decide to go.

I wish much, however, that I could join some such
arrangement as is offered by the University Settlement in New York. You know that is placed in one
of the poorest and most hopeless districts in New
York, and the workers there make of their own home
a central place to bring in the children, the women
and the families of the poorest class about them, not
only for entertainment, but for improvement in
health and cleanliness.

I would like very much, in my winter life here, to
be able to do something for somebody besides myself,
and if I had a home among a poorer class of people in
this way, where I could visit and help sometimes, I
should be consoled in thinking I was spending my
winter not merely in improving myself, but in being
of use to other people. I have come out from my
own home life, and have not any of its duties to
occupy my time, and surely I ought to be able to find
some leisure time to give to others. I have felt it the
last week or two, when I have been going round

vaguely amusing myself, and to one entertainment after another. To be sure, we have been having a back-ground of study, with our French lessons and with my University preparation. But I am quite longing for my course of study to begin, when I shall have my regular hours for going to recitations and lectures, leaving me certain allotted hours for other interests.

If I cannot find any boarding place on the University Settlement plan, I think to ask permission to give my services to the Associated Charities institution. These charities are carried on on so liberal a principle that I am sure I shall be glad to work with them. The different visitors take charge of certain families, for whom they become responsible. They are not to provide for their needs, but they are to find out when they need sympathy and are ready with advice. They help the heads of the families to put aside their money in savings, and I do not see why they cannot work to encourage the Neighborhood Guilds, of which I am reading and which I am much interested in. These are intended to keep up the home and social life of a neighborhood; clubs can be formed of members of a family, of young women, or young men; but, besides, social meetings are proposed, so that a small community can feel that it is working together, and that its members are not mere beneficiaries helped by other people and mere objects of charity, but as if they contributed to the life of all.

I have had a chance to talk with many of the devoted workers for the "Associated Charities." One advantage of this work is that it is "associated." They know of all other work going on in the same direction. They keep record of all applications made to other societies, so that they become acquainted with the regular "mendicants" that go from one benevo-

lent society to another for mere temporary relief.
When I talk with one of the workers in this society,
I wish I were five or six young women, instead of
being only one, that I might offer a dozen more hands
and half a dozen more heads instead of my little one
for their service.

I have been reading an interesting article by Miss
Octavia Hill in the "Nineteenth Century," on "Dealing with the Poor," where she speaks earnestly of the
advantage of co-operation in all the numerous schemes
for improving the condition of the poor. In the
same magazine we found the account given by
Francis Galton of "Identification by Finger-tips."
You have probably read the notices of his statements
of this "visible token of identity" which he describes,
finding it in the marks on the tips of the fingers, and
as persisting throughout the whole of a man's life.

We were much amused at his suggestions of its
utility; but how convenient it will be, if they can
only carry out the discoveries a little further! Galton gives a description of a convenient apparatus to
use in recording the impressions taken from the
finger-tips, in what he calls "finger-printing." But
will they not in time invent some kind of sealing-wax
that can be used without burning the fingers? And
then we can make our own impressions from our
fingers in sealing our letters! Think of the value of
such an impression! It will be truly a signet, not of
any fanciful family coat-of-arms, but our own personal signet, — an impression of my own fingers, that
cannot be forged or mistaken! You must imagine
such a signature to this letter!

CHAPTER SEVENTEENTH.

XX.

HARRY TO HIS MOTHER.

Boston, Sept. 27, 1891.

My dear Mother, — We have had a lovely day, and I know how you have enjoyed it at home. I wish I could see your maples and chestnuts as they begin to take on their fiery colors. You see I am back in good Mrs. Metcalf's. I broke camp at Cambridge on Wednesday for two excellent reasons.

First, the college term begins next Thursday, so that they wanted my room there, unless I wanted to enter as a special student in making clothes-pins or some other art or science. Second, that I had told Mrs. Metcalf that when the "family" came back from Swampscott with her, I would come too. We thought then that this would be cool weather. In truth, it is as hot as blazes. The "family" would be happier at Swampscott, and I at Cambridge. But we cannot all have what we want to have. So here I am, — mosquitoes, thermometer at ninety, and everything else to make one comfortable.

The weather is still so like summer that we keep up our out-of-town excursions. Saturday afternoon, you know, we have free; and I had ventured to ask Miss Brand and Miss Sandford if they would not like to go and see the Middlesex Fells. The Middlesex Fells are, or is, a bit of forest, rock and wilderness, which has not been broken into in two hundred and fifty years, since old Governor Winthrop ate some

bread and cheese there. A gentleman named Wright
made a vigorous effort to have it retained as a sort of
State park. He is dead, and I believe nobody cares
anything about it now. But all the same, it has not
yet been cut into building lots.

Saturday was a charming day. It was very hot in
the morning, but in the afternoon we got an east
wind, or what the newspapers call an " anti-cyclonic
reaction from the Atlantic Ocean." As a matter of
practice, I am rather glad I do not have to say this
every time I want to say "east wind."

We met by agreement opposite Winthrop's statue in
Scollay Square and took one of the street cars. There
was a Malden car just ahead of us, and our first
adventure was in Charlestown, when one of the
horses on that car fell down, almost dead. I suppose
that is what happens on these hot days, with these
relentless loads ; but that poor dying horse, which, in
a way, had died that people like us might have a
pleasant afternoon, was a sad sight as we passed by.
It made me long for the time when cars worked by
steam power, cable cars, or electric cars, might take
the place of these horse cars. Our car was terribly
overloaded; we stopped on Winter Hill, which I
remember reading about in the Revolutionary books,
and when the horses started again it was really
terrible to see their struggles before the thing would
go.

You pass near enough to the Tufts College buildings to see what a nice establishment that is. I
hardly knew the name of the place before. There is
a beautiful chapel, which perhaps is the finest building of them all. One of the antiquities of Medford is
the old Cradock house, but that we did not see. We
did pass the old Royall house, which has nothing to
do with royalty, but with a certain Colonel Royall.

He built the house, copying the house of a nobleman of Antigua, but he was so far true to his name that he went off to Halifax at the beginning of the Revolution and afterwards sailed to England. Tory or not, he said in a letter which we found in the history of Medford, " I shall leave North America with great reluctance, but my health and business require it, and I hope, through the goodness of God, if my life is spared, to be able to return soon." All the same, the State confiscated his property as the property of a Tory, and he never did return. But when he died he left twenty thousand acres of land to Harvard College for a professorship of law, and out of this the Harvard Law School was born.

At Medford Square we left the car, as I had been instructed by Mr. Outlake, and walked right over to the Fells. It is not a long walk, and both my young ladies were country-bred, so that they were not afraid of it. For the first time this year I was tempted by hard apples lying along in the lane. You know they say that evolutionists call the longing for green apples atavism, or a retrogression to the appetite of our ancestors, when they all ate vegetables.

When we got fairly into the wild region, first of all we climbed a little hill, which had a fine view south and east. The "gilded dome" shone out bright and clear. Then we had a regular ramble through the woods, and I might have fancied myself in Atherton. Miss Sandford said it was "Astney again." It seemed so like home to be walking over the light soil of pine needles and leaves. There is nothing in the Fells which compares with one of our mountain climbs, but still the whole region is rocky and picturesque. A part of it has been taken for some sort of water-works, so that you stumble on a gate house when you suppose you are in the midst of a

swamp. But they have not spoiled it, and it would be
pretty hard for them to spoil it. Spot Pond, which is
almost wholly surrounded by the woody region that
we call Middlesex Fells, is one of the really beautiful
ponds. I believe it comes in, somehow or other, into
the system of the water-works, and Mr. Outlake told
me that it was regarded, at the time when the water-
works were built as having the very purest water of
any pond in eastern Massachusetts. It has proved
since, he says, that this purity or non-purity of the
water depends on certain general laws; and that,
as you approach the sea, it is more and more affected, no one knows exactly why; so that a pond
on the top of your hills at Atherton is necessarily
purer than a pond here. But the great point is to keep
them free from surface drainage, and one of the
great advantages of making a State park of Middlesex Fells would be that the water in Spot Pond
would be preserved uncontaminated.

But I need not say to you that Miss Brand and Miss
Sandford and I did not discuss questions of hygiene
nor the chemical composition of water. We had a
regular old-fashioned Vermont time. We made Miss
Brand confess that the way to spend every day of
September and October was to spend it in the open
air. I told them that Boston was as good a place for
country life as Astney was, if you would only think '
so. They were ready enough to assent to this somewhat bold proposal; but I should think that, like all
other Boston girls, they were laying out for themselves this winter enough work for fourteen strong
women to carry through. At any rate, there was
great talk about Associated Charities and University
Settlements and other things which made me hold my
breath. I understood some of them and did not understand some of them; I only saw that they were quite

eager to put the whole world in apple-pie order. Do you remember your old story of the lady who looked so unhappy because she could not make everybody happy? I should say that her sin was rather the sin of the general run of the conscientious women who make up the feminine life of Boston, so far as it shows itself to an outsider.

I note what my dear Nahum says about leaving school. When I was at his age I told our dear father the same thing; and he said to me that I must stay at the High School two years. I was wild to go off, as Nahum is, and try my fortune at Burlington or at St. John. Father said to me, in substance, that there are two sorts of men in the world, — those who tell other people what to do, and those who do what they are told to do. He told me that I was to stay at the High School, because he did not want me to belong through my life to class number two. He did not so much as ask me whether I wished to stay or not; but I stayed.

That is the reason why Nahum must stay. And I tell him to stay the more readily because of a talk I had in the street car, the other day, with one of our directors who has been kind to me, and, I think, likes me. He asked how the office liked being moved from Leeds to Boston, and then told how he came himself. He said: "I am the regular mill-boy of the story books, only I never was in a mill. I am the boy who walks to Boston with a quarter in his pocket when he comes in."

Here I pricked up my ears, for I was thinking of Nahum. Mr. Welsh went on with his story and said that his mother wanted him to stay at school, but he thought he knew better. So he started to find his fortunes. Well, he found they were very small fortunes. Glad to get three dollars a week and to

spend it all for his board, he was. The truth was
there was nothing he could do that other people could
not do better. He was, however,• too proud to go
home. And the upshot of it was that he had to put
himself night after night at evening schools here, so
that he could make any show at all. " Four winters,
Mr. Merton," he said, "I slaved at the evening
schools, three hours a night, counting my study at
home. I could not go to the theatre or to a concert.
I made all my visits Saturday and Sunday evenings,
so that I might make up what my mother had wanted
me to do at home." And he said he was much obliged
for the evening-school system ; but if he had not been
a fool of the first order, he should not have needed ·to
resort to it. And I should think that after a boy had
done what he had to do all day, handling casks and
barrels and boxes with his own hands, running freight
elevators, standing over stevedores with the thermometer at fifteen below zero, he would not have had
much heart for his algebra or his French.

I found Mr. Welsh was curious about Mr. Price
Hughes, the English preacher. So I asked him to
come to church with me to-day, and he did. The
church was crowded. People said it began to look
like regular work again. I was glad to help the
ushers, who were hard-worked, and so I got Mr. Welsh
a good seat. As for me, I was glad to stand.

Mr. Hughes does not look as I supposed he was
going to. He is a very efficient working minister in
London, but he looks more like a college man, — a sort
of scholarly look, — wears his beard, with a small
moustache, and spectacles. But you very soon forget
how he looks. He is very wide-awake and strong.
His sermon was "Thy will be done ; as in heaven, so
on earth." And it was just the sort of sermon that
you would like.

"We are not under any obligation to wear sandals because Jesus Christ wore them." There was that, sort of "horse sense" in the whole thing, enough to show that he was used to dealing with men and women right in the midst of life, and was not satisfied with any studies of the Dark Ages or any other ages. I was particularly taken by the point that God's will must be done among men on earth, and not in any cloister or hermit's cell, as we think Catholics believe, and for that matter not to be done in Paradise, as, perhaps, Protestants believe. It has got to be done here — I suppose in the making of clothes-pins or the washing of clothes — precisely as it is done in heaven.

It was very clear that he interested the people, and Mr. Welsh was very glad he went. I shall try to go Tuesday night to hear him again. I was glad to see so many sensible people there, who, I think, will give him a good welcome here.

.   .   .   .

I wrote all this before going to church in the evening. I have been round again, and our own Dr. Haynes preached. As the Western man said, for a steady drink he is good enough for me; and I should not have minded even if we had not had the evangelist in the morning. But I suppose I am old-fashioned and do not care for variations on Sunday. He talked about publicans and sinners. I suppose the sermon was not meant for me, because he said directly that he was not talking to boys or girls or to women, but to hard-headed men, men of middle age. He had plenty of them there to hear him. Indeed, I was rather surprised when an English gentleman, who came into the office the other day and was talking with Mr. Welsh, said that a great many more men came to church in America, he thought, than were in the habit of coming in England. He said also, what I should not have believed from hearing Mr. Hughes, that the English preacher cóndescends in speaking to his audience. He laughed and said that in a high-and-dry church you would hear a man in a very white surplice say in a patronizing way to the congregation: "You may not be aware, my dear friends, that many centuries ago the wickedness of the world was such that the great God was obliged to wash it out by a universal deluge. It will be of interest to you to know that He preserved one chosen family of those who had not bowed the knee to false idols, and who were to be the seed of His true church, by the remarkable expedient of placing them in an ark, together with all the animals the lives of which he wished to preserve. The history of the ark is very curious and interesting," — and so on and so on.

Certainly that is not the way that Dr. Haynes talks to us, nor was it the way that Mr. Hughes talked, and I do not hear much preaching in that line. Dr. Haynes described Jesus' supping with the publicans and talking with Matthew. "If Jesus should come to-day, he would surely be found down in the Stock Exchange and in State Street." "The Whitechapel of society in America is not at the lower end; it is at the upper end." "Men like to see how a theory works. If you object to creeds, come to the example of how the creeds work; come to the life of Jesus itself."

But I am afraid you have found out before this, dear Mother, that I am sleepy; and I shall follow your great gospel of going to bed when I am sleepy, and preach my own sermon from the text, "If he sleep he shall do well."

. . . .

I meant to have written you, dear Mother, last night; but I was "dead beat," and following up the gospel with which I closed Sunday night, I went to bed as soon as Mrs. Metcalf would let me; and I am much more fit to write to you now, before breakfast, than I should have been if I had tried before.

You see we had — or we thought we had — on the Pavonia, which came in yesterday, some friends of the Outlakes, a Mr. and Mrs. Fordyce whom they met in Switzerland. Mr. Outlake, by way of hospitality, wanted to have some one meet them, and I was sent over, which was good luck for me; for it was a good place to spend some hours of a deadly hot day. I do not dare tell you how hot it was on the sunny side of our office.

It is a very curious business, and, as dear Dr. Primrose would say, " very instructive." You see she had — the Pavonia, I mean — nearly a thousand passengers. It was a town afloat, and a bigger town than Atherton at that. More than half of these people were steerage passengers, which means people from every country in the world, who have come over to become Americans. Of course, I knew the Fordyces were not there. Between first and second-class cabin passengers I did not pretend to discriminate.

But there is a handy printed list of first-class passengers; and it was easy enough to find that among the F's there were no Fordyces. I found the purser, and he said that at the last moment, almost, they changed their tickets. So I had nothing to do but to watch the others. And just as I was crowding around some people who spoke a language I could not speak nor understand, and which no one else could speak or understand, who should I run against but my nice, pretty Miss Lucy Sandford, who had come across a Swedish woman who wanted to meet her brother and her sister. We found them easily enough, and a very pretty scene it was, the hugging and kissing and

general joy as they met, after I do not know how
long. While they were occupied in their caresses,
and while we were waiting for the Custom House
people to be sure whether they had or had not brought
any brandy or diamonds, — or tin plate, I suppose, —
Miss Sandford and I had a chance to study other
romances of which there were a plenty.

For, really, a great many of these people land as if
they were in a wilderness. I saw a man with a gun
and a shot-belt, who really thought, I believe, that he
was going to kill his own rabbits and partridges as he
walked up to the State House. Poor fellow! I am
afraid he saw nothing but sparrows, and the policemen
would not let him shoot them.

The whole scene is chaotic enough. But there
were over nine hundred and fifty intelligent people —
or people of more or less intelligence — who were trying to bring out order enough for their own purposes.
There were fifty or sixty officers and as many teamsters and as many hack-drivers — who are glorified
teamsters — trying to do the same thing, and among
us all we succeeded after a fashion. The Swedish
friends bade us good-by with many broad grins and
expressions of gratitude, and Miss Sanford and I
were left to find our way over to the city together.

You see all this happened at East Boston, which
is your old Noddle's Island, where you went on the
lobster picnic of your famous stay.

. . . .

I finish this broken letter after coming home from
Worcester. Perhaps you saw that the Democratic
convention met there. Do not think I went. No
constituency is, as yet, so far advanced as to invite
me to go. And though I had so manly a look, which
generally savored of good-will to man, that the ticket-
man offered me a cheap return ticket, I was obliged

to confess that no such honor belonged to me. By the way, is it not a little curious that, seeing there is such a row about free passes when they are given to men in the legislature, every convention of every party should insist on having what is virtually a free pass — that is to say, half rates — when people meet annually for partisan purposes. The legislator is sworn to be impartial. These delegates are not sworn. In fact, they go because they are not impartial, because they are partisans. But they must have free tickets all round, while the poor senator or representative must not touch one with one of his fingers.

But I do not often write politics to you. No, I did not go near the convention, having more attractive temptations. I knew that Miss Sandford and her friend, Miss Brand, were going to Worcester, if it were pleasant, to the Commencement of the new college, Clark University. And when I found in the morning that there was really nothing to do on our side of the office, I asked for an afternoon off, thinking I would go to the Commencement too. It is the college where William Stevens thought he might get the professorship of English Literature. Perhaps he would; but they have not yet appointed any such professor. Well, Mr. Outlake said "of course," and I slipped off. I had just time to slam over to Kneeland Street in a herdic, and took the train just as it started. I found my ladies, without Godfrey as it happened, so that I had the pleasure of being of some use as escort. The day was splendid, though hot like all the week so far. It is an interesting ride and the outlook is pretty. I tried to show them my pet lions. The soldier was not visible, however. About six miles out from Boston, you see the only soldier the United States maintains on the mainland of Massachusetts — if you look sharp enough.

He is the sentinel at the Watertown Arsenal. And every day he has to put on his white cotton gloves and take his empty musket and walk up and down outside the gate there because — in the days of chivalry it was necessary to keep a lookout at Tamworth Castle! At least, I do not know any other reason. Sometimes he is tired of walking and stands still. Then I call him our standing army. Tuesday we did not see him at all. Perhaps in the freedom of opinion, he asked for a day off, as I did, and went to the Democratic convention.

The Clark University is an enormous building, with lecture rooms, laboratory, and all that, I should think a mile south of Worcester Common. I got the ladies out from the crush of people who surrounded a very gorgeous brass band, with blue and white uniforms and a magnificent drum major; and we worked our way without difficulty to the right place. But it proved we were two hours too early for the ceremony, so we had a chance to see the Worcester lions, and Miss Brand led the way at once quite to the other end of the town, to Antiquarian Hall.

You never know where to find things; but Mr. Outlake had told me, if I went to Worcester, to see Michael Angelo's Moses and his Jesus Christ. He said the only copies in America were here; and these not at any art museum or church, but at Antiquarian Hall. I thought that would please Dr. Primrose, and, indeed, anybody who thought seriously. It seems to say in such a straightforward way that American history is born from the laws of Moses and the life of Christ. But they have a thousand other things to interest you at "The Antiquarian" and are awfully good to visitors. They have the largest collection of newspaper volumes in America, and some of the very earliest. They have wonderful illustrations of Central America, and are, indeed, the people who carry on explorations there. We were sorry we had taken so much time for our lunch and that we could not stay there longer.

But at three we had to be at the other end of the town, at Clark University. There is an electric car, "the spinner," all along the street from one end to the other. Here we climbed to the top of another high-story-call building and found four or five hundred people assembled for the Commencement. It is the only college I know of where the Commencement is at the beginning of the term and not at the end. Dr. Hall, the president, is the "Education" man, — Dr. Stanley Hall. Don't you remember his lovely articles in Scribner's about the sand town with wooden inhabitants that those boys established civil government in?

Well, the Commencement also differed from other Commencements in other respects. Instead of having a lot of boys tell you, in periods of eleven minutes, seven minutes, or thirteen, according to their rank, a lot of things about which they knew nothing, you had here a lot of men to tell you what they did know. First and chiefly, their wide-awake president. He startled everybody, I think, by saying and showing that this is the most remarkable year ever known in the history of organized education. "Ever known!" Think of that! He proved it too.

After him Colonel Hopkins spoke on Governor Davis, and after him our Boston man, Doctor Hale, on Doctor Sargent. Those are two of the trustees who have died. Then Doctor Carter, president of Williams College, made a very interesting address. What pleased me was that one of the Catholic priests offered the opening prayer, and the whole congregation joined him in the Lord's Prayer. That did seem

/

catholic. I had never heard a Catholic priest offer prayer in our language before.

Well, you see it was a very good time. The young ladies met their friend at the college; they showed us round a little; and at half-past eight I was at home, and now am going to bed.

Dear Mother, I am always yours,

HARRY.

CHAPTER EIGHTEENTH.

XXI.

LUCY TO KATE.

BOSTON, Oct. 7, 1891.

MY DEAR KATE, — I have been so occupied in these beautiful September days that I hardly find time to write you my history; yet I feel that I must send it to you, even if for nothing more than to see how much I can remember of the impressions I have taken as the days go by, and because I have promised to write you of what I am seeing in Boston. I almost feel as if I might persuade even you that this is the place for you to come and live in.

We had a most enjoyable time the other day at the Old State House, built, as you remember, in 1748, on the spot where the first Town House stood. Every Bostonian ought to go there; for here are collected many valuable relics of the olden time, hundreds of things of interest that we stopped to look at and talk about. We saw some very interesting portraits; in particular one of stern old Cotton Mather, and we were surprised to see what a genial man he seemed. We thought him almost worldly looking, with a fine, curly wig, and a generally stylish look. We wondered if some of these imposing-looking worthies would not, indeed, be disappointed if they had to come back to the present day and show themselves to their friends without their majestic wigs. It is no wonder, perhaps, that the youthful generation no longer look up to their elders with the same awe that the young people must have felt in the older days, when they had to come into the presence of these dignified beings.

There was also a picture of Edward Bromfield, who was born and died in the first house built on Beacon Street. Could he have been aware of what a distinction it was to give him? — glory enough for one man. There is also a portrait of a most "fetching" girl, if you can imagine such a thing in these olden days. Only she did not belong quite as far back as the days of Cotton Mather, or she might have been counted among the "witches." But she is dressed very stylishly, and looks as if she were used to being admired. We were not surprised to read under it this title: "A noted Boston Beauty, Anne Black, who married a Blake in 1800." She has a most coquettish, yet rather winsome face. There is a handsome painting of Josiah Quincy by Gilbert Stuart, — a refined, delicate face, — and a striking picture of Edward Everett.

In the large front room is a full-length portrait, also of later days, of that most magnificent lady, Mrs. Harrison Gray Otis, by Healy. A stranger can see that she was a woman of a very strong personality, and one does not wonder that she presided over a *salon* and held position in society, where she was fond of displaying a wide hospitality. And she showed her influence not merely in society; for in the days of the Civil War she was active in helping to promote the gatherings of women assembled to work for the soldiers. She is represented with one shapely hand resting on a book and the other hanging gracefully. Her dress is very elegant, with lace stripes. If I had been told this was the picture of an imperial or royal lady, I should not have been surprised.

Then there were many older things of interest; a fac-simile of an invitation to attend the funeral of Sir William Phipps, — a most gruesome affair, surrounded by death's heads and solemn mottoes, one of which was, "Remember to Die." Here was the Liberty Tree lantern, used at the repeal of the Stamp Act, and a fine old eight-day clock that belonged to Matthew Byles, of whom my father used to tell entertaining stories. This bore the date of 1750. There was also a heavy old chair that looks as if it would never wear out, made of wood from the ship "Resolute." Another old chair belonged to Elbridge Gerry. There is, too, a very old picture of the battle of Bunker Hill. One reads, printed under the picture, the words, "The late battle : 700 Provincials against 11 regular regiments." Besides all these, there was a queer old cannon, that we were told was fired by Lafayette, when he visited Boston in 1824.

Then it was exciting to see a fan belonging to Agnes Surriage, and to have the feeling suddenly that she is a real person and did not live merely in the book where we read about her. It was just a simple-looking, little paper fan, such as we might buy for a small sum at Houghton and Dutton's; but how valuable it seemed to our eyes, because it had been carried by a regular heroine of romance !

There were many pictures of old buildings in Boston that are now destroyed. We saw some beautiful tiles taken from the John Hancock house. I have been told much of the regret that this house no longer exists. It was very picturesque, and a most interesting memento of the olden times. It stood on Beacon Street, a little below the State House, standing back from the street, and you went up to it from a series of green terraces. It was of gray stone with white facings, and it would have been indeed an ornament in these present days, in place of the modern row of brick houses that takes its place.

The room called Curtis Hall contained many inter-

esting engravings. One colored print was very striking, representing Washington in Trenton after the
Revolution. Washington was riding down the street
on a white horse, and hundreds of people, blacks,
whites and Indians, were evidently hurrying along,
with crowds of ladies throwing flowers in front of
him. This picture was greatly admired by some
schoolboys who gazed at it for a long time ; and I felt
as if I ought to look up some of my Vacation School
boys to interest them in these bits of history and give
them some idea of the lives of these heroes.

In the same hall was Benjamin Franklin's printing-
press, — a queer old affair, now brown with age, —
with fac-similes of the papers he printed. And here,
as a bit of later history, was a fine print showing the
opening of the Cochituate water-works, and I remembered how my father has told me that he was present
at this great celebration, — for such indeed it was, —
when an immense crowd collected, filling the Common,
to see the white column of water rise slowly up,
higher and higher, from the Frog Pond below, in the
midst of the shouts and admiration and wonder of the
people below, who could now really believe that Lake
Cochituate had come to Boston.

There were a number of people in the rooms, men,
women and children, all going about and deeply interested. I have only picked out a few of the hundred
things to tell you about. The building itself has been
restored to as near its original condition as it was possible to make it. Even the carved figures of the lion and
unicorn that originally decorated it have been replaced
there. The Boston Massacre occurred in front of its
doors. In it Samuel Adams said Independence was
born. In October, 1789, Washington received the
greetings of the people from a balcony at the west
end. In 1776 the Declaration of Independence was

read from its balcony.   I think it ought to be repeated
from that place every Fourth of July nowadays.

I have given you all this account because looking
into the past is so much in contrast with the other
life that I am having here, in the world outside of
Boston and in its present history.   We have still continued to take delightful excursions into the beautiful
suburbs ; and if I could tell you all that we have done
in these wanderings you would not believe that I
have really begun my university life and rank myself
again a schoolgirl.

Admitted ?   Yes; but I feel that I must do a deal
of studying to keep myself along in the ranks.   My
hours are not yet absolutely arranged, so I am taking
advantage still of these wonderful summer-autumn
days to continue our outings.   But I cannot take time
to tell of our delightful day at Middlesex Fells, north
of Boston, where we could really believe we were
miles away from a city and from universities and from
old histories of the past.   I do not know but Mr. Merton and I tired out our companion, Rosamond Brand,
in talking about Vermont and its woods and hills, and
in comparing our life here with the home life there.
I really think the excursion was a very great help to
me, as I was worrying a little about my university
work, and it was delightful to fling all my thoughts
and doubts to the winds and have a day out of town.
This I owe to Mr. Merton ; for he insisted upon it
that we ought to take this day for an excursion, and
he quite jeered at us for plodding on at work.

And I don't know but he likes to jeer at me for my
desire to mingle all kinds of life with my student life
in Boston.   He says we are all trying to do too much
here.   I have ventured to speak but little to him of
my plans for doing something to help the many, who
are struggling here to live, just to live a little more

happily, by working with the Associated Charities. As soon as I begin to talk about it I feel as if it were very conceited of me to think that I can accomplish anything. Still, I cannot content myself with the idea of giving myself up merely to a student's life, and of shutting myself up with books for my own personal education.

Even with all this explanation I am afraid you will think my life just now is, in truth, a " gadding " one; but we do find so much to think about in our visits to the interesting places here that I must write you about them. For example, we had a delightful day in the Egyptian Room at the beautiful Art Museum. I told you that I had inspired Miss Fenton with a desire to go there with me some day ; and I find that she is deeply interested in Egyptian things. She heard all of Miss Edwards's lectures about Egypt, and reads everything she can get hold of on the subject of its antiquities. This is all delightful to me, although I am very much behind her in knowledge of Egypt. We had such a delightful morning together that she is very excited about it all and is really beginning to plan for a winter, when she " will take me up the Nile with her ! " Do not be frightened; for I am sure I am not yet done with Boston and its present and its past.

I took to Miss Fenton the catalogue of the Museum of Fine Arts, and after looking at it, she immediately decided what she wanted to do. It is really a bit of education to be with her in this way. For she not only knew, but she could explain to me what we had better do and why it was a good thing to do it. She pointed out to me that we should get a real bit of history if we went directly to the Egyptian Room, containing the Egyptian casts. This would give us the connected history of Egyptian portraiture. The cata-

logue shows admirably how thoroughly Egyptian this
study of portraiture is, and how important it is to understand it. The Egyptian was not satisfied with
embalming his body, which might be easily destroyed;
he had buried with him a statue of wood or stone,
evidently a portrait of himself. In this way are preserved these lifelike representations.

Just think of going into this room to find arranged
in order a series of casts of their statues and portraits,
with photographs of those that could not be repro-
duced! Here was the statue of King Chephren, who
lived about 3660 b. c.; and yet, only the other day, I
was filled with wonder at the portraits of men of
scarcely two hundred years ago. Here he stands in
full vigor, with head erect, and by his side another
king, Hosi. The face in all these portraits is given in
profile, the eye in full front; the chest and shoulders
are in front view, while the legs and feet are in
profile; for this is the Egyptian fashion. Hosi, too,
lived between 4000 and 3500 b. c. And then come
reliefs from the tomb of Ti. He was an Egyptian
gentleman. I remember the interesting account that
Miss Edwards gives of him in her book of Nile
travels. Here are pictures of farm life, even of
milking the cows, with the calves tied to tufts of
grass, all reminding me of the homely scenes I wrote
you of, that we saw at the theatre, on the stage, in
the representation of "The Old Homestead." Old
and new scenes, so far apart in time, yet so alike!
Here is the driving home of the cattle, with the ante-
lopes, asses, storks, and geese drawn like life, the
herdsman bearing the calf on his shoulders. I think
I must send you the catalogue itself; for it gives such
an interesting description and explanation of it all.

And you will see how this valuable record is kept
up chronologically; for next we came farther down

to 2430 B. C. to a funeral stele, representing a long
funeral procession. It records the name of the de-
ceased, with a prayer to some god that he would
supply provisions and all things necessary for the
support of the *Ka*, or soul, of the dead, — his spirit, for
which he is so anxious always to provide. But I
cannot give you a list of the busts and statues. Miss
Fenton is intensely interested in all that explains the
religion of the Egyptians, and she likes to study up
everything that tells of this wonderful care that
every Egyptian showed in providing for the suste-
nance of this *Ka*, or spirit.

But I must speak of a row of queens who are
shown by their busts; among them the queen Taia,
wife of Amenophis III., who was a Syrian princess,
and was painted with light hair and blue eyes. If I
was thrilled, as I told you, by seeing actually the
picture of Anne Black, who lived as lately as the
beginning of this century, you can imagine how I
felt in looking at the portrait of a queen who lived
over three thousand years ago! She was one of the
most brilliant monarchs who sat upon the Egyptian
throne. Women had great power in Egypt; and
Miss Fenton told me how, in one of her lectures,
Miss Edwards read some documents to show that, at
one period in the earliest times, when a woman was
married the property was settled upon her, and out of
it she fixed a pension to be granted to her husband
during his life. This shows that a woman's housekeeping talent was recognized then in its widest
sense.

We stopped a long time to study the long relief
that shows the wars of King Seti, about 1350 B. C.
These are found on the walls of Karnak. The figure
of the king is distinguished by his great size, far
above the other men or his enemies; the artist has

also elongated the bodies and legs of the horses as well as of the human figures.   After this comes the bust of the great King Rameses, the famous conqueror, whose portraits appear on monuments in every part of Egypt; and he is the hero of the great figure, I remember, of which Miss Edwards gives such an interesting account in her book of Nile travels.   Then we passed on to later dates, 666 or 358 B. C., that seem quite modern in comparison with those older ones till we remember the Old State House and our respect for these younger dates of Boston; and then one begins to touch Greek art and Roman emperors, and there is a whole history between.   The way is to read Miss Edwards's Nile travels before going to this room, and then to take it up afterwards and to study the catalogue carefully while examining the portraits, not overlooking the photographs, which give copies of the very earliest figures.   And after all this study we can comprehend a little the list of the kings that Miss Edwards gives at the end of her book; so that, with just this study of these portraits, one can begin to understand something of Egyptian history.   For this is just the beginning, Miss Fenton and I have agreed. She has more leisure to give to this work than Anna has, so I am charmed at the idea of having her as a companion some day again.

To all of which I must add an interesting episode. Our old housekeeper here has lately been training a Swedish girl as chambermaid, and I have been interested in talking with Lina, who understands English enough to tell me more or less of her history.   But one day Hetty came into my room much disturbed. She said that Lina insisted upon it she must go over to East Boston to meet her brother and sister, who were to arrive in the English steamer.   Hetty was sure that Lina could never find her way there and

back, and she was sure Rebecca, her daughter, could
not give the time to go over with her, because her
dressmaking work was just coming in. She wished I
would speak to Lina and tell her it would be just as
well to wait till they landed, and that it was their
business to hunt up Lina, and not Lina's business to
be losing herself in the Boston streets. So what I
did, when Lina came to me, was to tell her I would
go over to East Boston with her and take her to the
" Pavonia; " for that was the name of the steamer.
Hetty was doubtful about the whole matter, and
evidently thought I was as likely to lose my way as
Lina, but she agreed that I had a tongue in my head
which might be more easily understood than Lina's.
So we started off.

It was one of the fine days we have been having,
and I took Lina across in an East Boston car, and we
had a pleasant excursion. I am always delighted at
an excuse to cross in one of the ferry-boats ; and the
tongue in my head helped me to find my way and to
take the right direction to get to our steamer. It was
amusing, however, that it was one of Lina's Swedish
friends who helped us at the last, by showing us
where to go, so that we should not hunt up our
steerage friends among the first-class passengers.
Then I had a surprise in suddenly meeting in the
crowd our friend, Harry Merton. His friends were
among the first-class passengers; but there was a
great crowd, nearly a thousand passengers, and he
was looking everywhere for his friends, while I was
trying to induce my happy Lina to bring along her
brother and sister and come away from the pier.
They were so happy at meeting that I do believe they
would have stayed there all day. Lina, however, has
a clear head, and she had made her plans as to where
they were to go to meet other friends. So after Mr.

Merton learned that his people had not arrived after all, we made our way together, reaching the ferry-boat, where the Swedish party huddled together jabbering in their delight, and Mr. Merton escorted me home.

I have written home the account of our day in Worcester. Anna was invited to the Commencement at Clark University there, and I went with her. Much to our surprise, just as we were leaving the station, Mr. Merton appeared, also bound for Worcester and the University; for I had told him of our plan of going. But I can't repeat the whole story. You must only imagine it to have been a delightful day.

It was on the beautiful October Saturday of last week that we went to Milton, Miss Fenton and I taking the cars there and afterwards a carriage·to the Blue Hills, through lovely lanes still luxuriant and green. Then up and up, till we finally climbed to the top of the Blue Hills, where there is an observatory, and where the view is really like a mountain view. Here again was the glorious harbor spread before us, and Boston and its suburbs below, far away. But I was much surprised at the country view on the other side, and to see how much is left of really forest land and uninhabited region, — great cultivated fields and wide spaces still not yet settled upon. It was as wonderful and exciting as is the view of the great city, and it gives one a certain repose to think that beyond all the seething turmoil of those narrow streets there is still this wide extent of field and country so near and not yet crowded. I am told that these Blue Hills were called by the Indians "Massachusetts," meaning The Great Mountains, and that this was the origin of the name of the State.

This week we are busy visiting, when we find time,

the "Health Food Show" at Mechanics Hall, the
large building devoted to such exhibitions. I am
again reminded of my country home, for here can be
seen a herd of cattle. They are Holstein-Frisian
cattle. Then you must not be surprised if you hear
that Anna and I introduce Mr. Edward Atkinson's
"Aladdin's oven" into our household plans; and we
are getting many ideas about scientific cooking. But
I have no doubt that you are deciding with Harry
Merton that we are doing too many things. I have
not told you, either, how I am going to hear Mr.
Herford preach every Sunday; for, alas! Arlington
Street Church is to lose him very soon, and he will be
sorely missed.

From yours,

Lucy.

16

CHAPTER NINETEENTH.

XXII.

HARRY TO HIS MOTHER.

Boston, Oct. 9, 1891.

My dear Mother, — I am well aware that Nahum regards our life here as very dull, and that when he runs away from home, with a bundle on a stick over his shoulder, we must look for him at Burlington or St. John, and not in the effete civilization of this provincial village. Now, as one of my special desires is that he shall come down to the office into a capital place, which I will have ready for him when he can write a decent French letter to our correspondents in the island of Madagascar, I do want to present Boston in its most attractive lights. So I hope you will not consider this letter too frivolous.

We have a great many correspondents among the retail grocers. If you will think of it, although clothespins do not come under the ordinary definition which you or I would apply to the word "groceries," they are sold by the gross, or by the "groce," as Dr. Johnson would have spelled it. And, not to be too learned, if you sent Nahum down to the village, before breakfast Monday morning, for a couple of dozen new clothes-pins, he would go to old Mr. Pepper's store. So it is that the exhibition of food products here, which has been set on foot by the grocers of Boston, brings lots and lots of our customers down to town from all New England. I have very little to do with the buying and selling, you know. But I can see that the chief and Mr. Outlake and all the other gentlemen are pleased, and that the orders every day are very, very large.

Yesterday a nice old gentleman from Aroostook County came in and had a long talk with Mr. Outlake about "Jim" Blaine and "Tom" Reed and I do not know what else. When he went away he said he was going to the Food Exhibition, which we, of course, knew perfectly well before. But he had not told us that his wife was with him and waiting for him at the American House. It was clear he could never find her and then find the exhibition without help. So I was detailed to escort them, and to inquire at the same time if it was too late for us to make an exhibit of clothes-pins. We have two very handsome cases in which the clothes-pins are arranged in imitation of plate armor, and I believe most of the boys in the office think that Ivanhoe and Richard were really dressed in clothes-pins when they went to tournaments. These cases are on purpose for exhibitions, and it is with them that we get our gold medals and crosses of different legions. But our Mr. Snale, who has charge of them, is an Englishman and rather slow. He did not "catch on" in time to the idea that clothes-pins, because they are groceries, belong in a food exhibition; so our knights in armor are still at the County Show in Knox County, where they do not do us as much good as they would here.

Well, we found up the excellent Mrs. Fosdick, who is perfectly lovely. She is a sort of cross between Miss Tryphena Dexter and our dear grandmother, and looks like your picture of Miss Hannah More. I got them both safely to the exhibition, bought their tickets, and got them by the turnstile. Then, I am ashamed to say, I waited for Miss Brand and some other ladies to pass, then went in myself, and, dear Mother, you will laugh at me, I had lost Mr. and Mrs.

Fosdick! And I have never seen hide nor hair of
them from that moment to this. Now I was to take
care of them in the intervals of arranging for our exhibit; so this is an awful disgrace to me, and you must
never mention it.

Well, while I was looking for them, naturally I saw
a good deal of the show. And I ran against twenty of
our customers and placed I do not know how many
hundred "groce" of pins; so that I guess there was
no harm that the Fosdicks saw the show for themselves. They and I were such early birds that most
of the things were not ready when we arrived.

On this account I went downstairs first to look at
the Holstein cattle. The first thing I came across
down there was a great English shire horse, with a
neck about twice as big as he needed. As Aunt
Agatha used to say about me, he must have an
enormous "swaller." The cattle did not look very
remarkable; but they were, all the same. The boy who
kept them said that one of his cows, like those here,
had given fifty-six to fifty-eight quarts of milk a day,
which seems enough to feed a small army. When I
asked about the quality of the milk, he said that this
same cow had made thirty-nine pounds of butter in
a week. To say that the cow "made" the butter
seemed to me somewhat exaggerated.

When I got back in the hall things were well
started. What first attracted my attention was a
Smith Premier Typewriter. I do not know whether
this comes in under the "Food" or the "Health"
part of the exhibition. I told the man who had
charge of it that I was interested in typewriting, and
he explained the whole thing. The one he showed
me had a key-board like the Remington; but they
make them with key-boards like the caligraph. The
work it did and the action of the machine seemed to
me excellent.

Cobb, Bates, and Yerxa had the whole end of one of the large halls filled with their groceries. There was some Pettijohn's Breakfast Food there, with a courteous young lady to serve it to all comers. It was very nice, and I thanked her for helping me so generously. She said something about being able to distinguish possible purchasers and dealing generously by them. I did n't buy any, although it was only six cents a pound. She said that it would make thin people " fleshy " in a short time ; whereupon I asked its effect on "fleshy" people, and she said that it strengthened the muscular tissues.

There was a man who had a self-calculating set of scales on exhibition. I asked him to show it to me; but he answered by asking me if I had any interest in the grocery business. I told him that I had not just at present ; but that I might at some future period. He said that he supposed that, at any rate, I wanted to see everything new, and then he showed me the scales, which so far as I could see, was, as he said, really a machine with brains.

I made a rule of eating and drinking everything that was free, and thus managed to take in a good deal of varied nutriment. I tried Huyler's cocoa, which, I was informed, came straight from the cocoa bean. There were some cocoa beans there, but no way of telling whether the prepared cocoa came right from them or not. On the whole, the effect of the generosity of the people who gave away their food was that you regarded exhibitors as stingy who did not give anything away. S. S. Pierce, for example, had a nice-looking department; but as he had no gifts to offer, I did not dally long about his stand. On every hand there were buckwheat cakes being made and distributed to any one that wanted them. They were all good, so that I do not wish to discriminate as to which were the best. They were served with syrup at the Fleischmann's Yeast counter. There was a man there cooking some peculiar style of bread. I asked him what it was, and he replied that it was something to eat.

Upstairs in the Art Gallery was Mr. Atkinson's Aladdin Cooker on exhibition. I was able to state to those who were looking at the cooker that things cooked in it tasted very well; for I have had several opportunities of trying them. There was a large department, near the cooker, reserved for Van Houten's cocoa. A polite young woman invited me to partake, but I was obliged to pass on, because I thought my stomach could not stand too great a variety.

Downstairs they had some " health " coffee on trial. This makes a fairly good drink, but it seems to me that it rather fails of its purpose. For if people are in the habit of drinking too much real coffee, they probably are very fond of its flavor and would not be satisfied with something that tastes entirely different. Thus the only ones who could be brought to drink " health " coffee would be those who never cared especially for Mocha and Java.

Among the favorite things to exhibit were flavoring extracts. These I did not sample. A number of other exhibits seemed to be far removed from " Food and Health." Thus the Kroeger piano could hardly be eaten or contribute to a man's physical welfare. Carriages could, I suppose, carry a patient to the White Mountains for his health, while market wagons could bring him food.

Bovinine was advertised as having been General Grant's food for three months. They might have added, " at the end of which time he died." From the top of one of the great halls was suspended a trade

mark of Welcome Soap, one of those pictures of a pair
of hands clasping each other, you know. Every one
who desired was given a guess as to how far apart
were two red crosses, one on each of the two coat
sleeves. The distance was obviously somewhere
between five and ten feet. I judged a good deal from
the windows behind the picture, and guessed seven
feet, three and three-eighths inches. The polite man
who received the guesses then gave me another try,
and I said seven feet, ten inches. The smallest
estimate made was by a lady, who modestly pronounced the crosses eleven inches apart. The prize
for the best guess is a silver tea-service. I also have
a confused remembrance of a gold watch and some
other things, second prizes, I suppose. I expect to
get something splendid. I hope you don't look on it
as gambling.

There was a man selling microscopes, who let
people look at a drop of water and other small things.
It was very unpleasant to see the water, for there
were a number of disagreeable-looking snakes disporting in it. To afford me a pleasant change, he gave me
an opportunity to see the dust from a cheese. This
was an awful sight. The dust was filled with
creatures abounding in legs, who wandered about in an
aimless way and filled me with horror. If we have
got to eat animals involuntarily, I do wish we could
have more prepossessing ones.

The two great halls are filled with exhibits, and even
the upstairs part is put in requisition. When you go
out you are so confused that you can scarcely remember a thing that you have seen; but afterwards
things keep occurring to you. I wound up by going to
the restaurant, which was fairly good. Old Miss
.Tryphena, whom I met prowling round, complained
that it was too expensive, and that as to the things

that were given away, there was too much to drink
and too little to eat, the only thing that she had had
to eat being "malted" milk, and I don't exactly
see how she managed to eat that. At the restaurant
I had some sausages and mashed potatoes, both of
which proved excellent.

On the way home I had a chance to see some paving
being done on West Newton Street with this kind of
artificial stone which they use nowadays. It is fine to
see how they level off the earth before they begin to
pave. They have two wooden frames running across
the street; and they take a long sort of board and
draw it over these frames, which are about ten feet
apart, thus making the earth between them beautifully
rounded, like the frames themselves. It seems to me
as if they ought to have some of the stone made just
half the common size at the quarries. As it is, when
they want half-pieces, as they frequently do, they
have to cut a big one in two, which is no end of
bother.

．　．　．　．　．　．　．　．　．

October 12.

You may skip all this. It is specially for Nahum's
eye, because he is so curious about all quarry work.
If he had been here last Wednesday night I should
have taken him with me to see "The County Fair."
I wonder if the fame of Mr. Neil Burgess and "The
County Fair" has gone as far as Atherton. I observe
the "swell" gentlemen in the counting-room here
turn up their noses at it — and then go, on the sly, to
see it, just as they go to the circus because the
children waut to go. I went last Wednesday night
although it rained guns ; indeed, I thought I should
have a better show on a rainy evening, for, of course,
I went on a "standee." The play is going to run for
a whole year ; just think how tiresome that must

make it for the actors. Other people certainly
have n't got tired of it yet, for in spite of the weather,
every available seat was taken, and I had to stand up
all through the evening.

I reached the theatre at just about the right time,
so that I could stand up behind the central back seats
and lean on the kind of elbow-rest that seems made
for the purpose. I suppose I looked like one of
Raphael's cherubs. Lots of people were coming in,
and, among others, a man at my right pointed out
Police Commissioner Osborne. I looked as quickly as
I could, but could only see the back of a respectable-
looking gentleman in a silk hat. I stared at every
one in the boxes, and tried to recognize the bonnets
of the ladies who sat in front of me, but bonnets and
hair are not very characteristic. I did not see a
single person in the audience that I knew. I have
heard that most of those who come to this play are
country people, like myself. Strangely enough we
seem to like to see our own life represented on
the stage. After the band had given us a variegated
edition of "The Star Spangled Banner," the curtain
went up.

The principal character in the play is a New England spinster, called *Miss Abby*, whose home is at
Rock Bottom Farm. Mr. Neil Burgess acts this part,
and he is very funny, although the other actors
are nothing remarkable. What brings down the
house in the first act is where every one has gone
to bed except *Miss Abby*, and just before she retires
she goes to the door at the back of the stage, with a
candle, opens it and calls out, " Kitty, kitty, kitty."
Every one laughs, because, I suppose, every one has
seen some old lady do the same thing. Certainly you
and I have.

Miss Abby, though no longer young, has two wooers,

one nice and one horrid, as the children say. The nice one has been "courtin'" her for fourteen years, but has never screwed up his courage to the point of asking her to be his, though she is always ready to say yes, when he does. As for the villain, when he finds he has no chance, he warns her that he is going to foreclose a mortgage of $1,600 on her farm. The mortgage comes due on the day of the County Fair, with ten more days of grace. Now *Miss Abby* has taken in a homeless young fellow called *Tim*, who can't do much but ride on horseback. He makes up his mind that her horse, Cold Molasses, is the fastest in the country round, and finding out that the running race at the County Fair is for a prize of $2,000, he forms his own schemes for paying off the mortgage. He manages to practise up the horse on the sly; for *Miss Abby* has no idea of what is going on.

At the end of the third act *Miss Abby* is in the barn, very disconsolate. She feels that every one has gone back on her, even *Otis Tucker*, the man who has been "courtin'" her for fourteen years. She sits down in her rocking-chair, close to where the horse's head is sticking out of the stall. "No one cares for me at all," says *Miss Abby*, "not one." And then the horse puts out his great head and licks her face, while the curtain goes down. It is ludicrous and pathetic at the same time.

The last act represents the Fair. It begins with one of those shallow scenes which they have when something interesting is going on behind. *Miss Abby* appears and is astonished to see *Tim* in his jockey clothes, leading Cold Molasses. *Tim* is dressed up grandly in a green shirt and white trousers, with top boots. But even now *Miss Abby* does n't know what is going to happen. Lots of people are going to and fro, when suddenly there is a shout and a scurry, and every one runs off the stage. Then the back scene rolls away, and through a kind of veil you can see five horses with jockeys on them, apparently galloping at full speed. Behind them is one of those fences that they have around race courses, and that is made to move like lightning the other way from the way the horses are going. The illusion is complete; but oh, horrors! *Tim* is behind them all. Two horses are bunched for first place; two more behind; and *Tim* and Cold Molasses in the rear. But in a moment you can see Cold Molasses begin to crawl up. Nearer and nearer he comes and finally passes the two horses next him. Every one was shouting like mad, with that long "Hey-ey-ey!" that you always hear at a race. I was screaming "Cold Molasses!" at the top of my lungs. *Tim* began to beat his horse with a vengeance, and the noble animal responded, so that he came slowly, slowly, up with the leaders; got even with them; his head came out beyond them; and then—all was dark. The yelling and excitement of the audience beggars description. I never heard such a noise at a play.

Then we saw the County Fair scene again. When it was told *Miss Abby* that her horse and *Tim* had won her $2,000 you can imagine how delighted she was. She and *Otis* decided to get married immediately; but when he brought the marriage certificate, she tore it up, thinking it was one of the programmes of the fair. Poor *Otis* ran to get another; but this time, as he was coming back, holding it in his outstretched hand, Cold Molasses, who had come in with *Tim* on his back, seized it and ate it up; at least I think he was meant to, but that night he dropped it after he had chewed it for a while. Then the curtain went down and every one went away.

Coming home, the electrics were crowded, and I was almost pushed backwards over the edge of the plat-

form. Every one was good-natured, except a very fat
man, who exclaimed that he had a right to get on and
off as much as he wanted to, because the rest of us
expressed our agony while he pressed by us. We all
uttered ribald shouts at him, which attained their purpose in enraging him; but which, I fear, could not be
ranked as the most refined style of wit. And so, with
a good deal of rain and some swearing and a great deal
of good temper, we all got home at last. But I tell
you that race was perfectly fine.

.   .   .   .

If I had not spent so much time upon Nahum's
amusement I should have been able to tell you about
my pleasant visit to Peacedale last week. There was
a great festival there in honor of the dedication of a
memorial hall to the memory of Mr. Hazard, who died
a few years ago, a very old man. He was connected
with the creation of the woollen manufacture in this
country, and the works at Peacedale are very remarkable. The Hazard family has always lived there, in
the midst of their work people, — as somebody said, so
that the whirr of the machinery could be heard from
the parlor windows. And the whole place shows the
charm of the common interest of the work people,
from the top to the bottom of the establishment. The
present Mr. Hazards have now built, in memory of
their father, a beautiful hall, which is everything that
you would like to have in Atherton, for the central
comfort and convenience of the village. There is a
great hall for audiences, a capital public-library room,
— and, what is more, they have got a good library to
put in it, — and rooms for the meetings of the King's
Daughters and other societies of the place.

They have a Choral Association, too, and I wish you
might have one in Atherton. It is made up actually
of five or six hundred of the young people of the town.

The singing is really magnificent. We do not get anything better here, as far as I hear it, and I found that the connoisseurs were disposed to say the same thing. If you ever thought of it, music is the active agency which brings together a lot of people who succeed in quarrelling about everything else. For instance, in this Choral Association, all the young people of the town can meet together, no matter what they believe in, no matter what country they come from, no matter whether they went to a high school or to an academy or to a Friends' school. I should think that was a good deal the character of Rhode Island, where, on account of their extreme independency in old times, one man is as good as another, and people seem to meet with great friendliness. Any way, I was very glad that it came to be my business to go down to Peacedale. I went there, not to "tout" for custom, which is what I generally have to do when I go away from Boston, but because Mr. Outlake had not been well, and Mrs. Outlake was afraid to have him go alone. He made a great deal of fun of this, and, in point of fact, he no more needed to have somebody to take care of him than I did. But I suppose, if he had had a fit in the cars or had broken his neck in getting off the train, I should have had to telegraph home to his wife to say so. Any way, I got out of the thing a charming expedition and was out of the office for a day. I believe you think the principal business of the office is that I may go "a-gadding" and have good times. And I am sure that anybody who reads these letters would suppose it was for that end that the Boston establishment had been created.

> Tuesday, Oct. 13.

POSTSCRIPT. You will be amazed when I tell you that this is written in Philadelphia. You are not more amazed than I am. It happens thus : —

Our nice Mr. Outlake, who is always so good to me, is very much interested in the plàns for the congress of nations, or at least of republics, which is to be held next year or the next. He is, like a good many of the old Abolitionists, a man much respected in the committee; and he determined, rather suddenly, to go on to a preliminary meeting which is in progress here to-day. Now, he has been troubled for some time past with sudden attacks of vertigo, and Mrs. Outlake — the same who took Miss Fenton to the high-story-call lions — would gladly have come with him. But something at home prevented this. So she surreptitiously asked our chief if I might not be spared, to be in Philadelphia at the same time with Mr. Outlake, all "unbeknownst" to him, and so to speak, to keep an eye on him. Of course, I was only too glad to come, and here I am. He was much surprised when he saw me at the Broad Street station, eating my oysters by his side. He little supposed that I had come three hundred and more miles that I might have that pleasure.

I told him, what was the truth, that I had a message to our agents, Line and Reel. He said he should not be able to see them, and told me that if I could get an hour, I had better come round to the Academy of Music and hear some of the papers. As this was exactly what I had been sent to do, I consented, of course; and so I have been behind the scenes of a theatre for the first time in my life. Do you not remember, in "Joe" Jefferson's life, how good a time those children had in playing in the daytime behind the scenes?

The meeting, you see, of all sorts of governors and secretaries and presidents and things was in the large green-room. Is it not exciting to be in a green-room, and have hundreds of portraits of actors and actresses, some horribly faded and some preternaturally bright,

smiling or frowning down upon the governors and
secretaries, from Charlotte Cushman round to Ole
Bull and Minnie Hauek? The dons, like Mr. Outlake
and the committees, sat round the tables and in the
seats provided. But the attendant loafers, like me,
crowded together on the dark stage, which, in this
theatre at least, is directly accessible from the green-
room. We could see and hear there. Nahum will be
glad to know the walls of a green-room are really
green.

Mr. Outlake did not speak himself, but a great
many interesting people did. Judge Arnoux interested
me; he is a New York lawyer. There was a very intelligent governor there from Wyoming, Governor
Hoyt, and a doctor of philosophy, who spoke English
with as little accent as I, but who is a native China-
man. A black man offered prayer, and a Chippewa
Indian spoke, so we had four races represented. In
fact, I should think it was all a good deal like one of
the best of the old Anti-slavery meetings you like to
tell us of. Nobody was afraid to say anything, and
everybody had some special fad which he was very
much in earnest about.

As for Mr. Outlake, it was all nonsense my taking
care of him. There was much more likelihood of his
taking care of me. I say nothing about the wonders
of the city itself, because I remember how well you
know it. Love to all, from your son

HARRY.

CHAPTER TWENTIETH.

XXIII.

LUCY TO KATE.

BOSTON, Oct. 21, 1891.

MY DEAR KATE, — I have been making such intimate acquaintance with the street cars lately that I
feel as if I ought to turn into a walking guide-book
and make my information useful to the world. It may
not be of advantage to you in Colorado, but it will
show you how I pass some of my time.

I have described to you the Miss Dexter whom I
have visited several times, and who used to be a
dependent in my mother's mother's family long ago.
She is a thrifty little body, who has carefully laid by
some savings, and has been living years and years in
the same place. She tells me that, when she first
went into this room the windows looked out upon a
little yard with a pear-tree in it, and she has told me
how Boston used to be famous for the pears it raised.
Now it is all built in, and a tenement house has its
dark windows overlooking her room at scarcely ten
feet distance. Apparently, the character of her neighbors has changed greatly too.

"I used to know everybody in the house," she said
one day, "but now the tenants of the rooms above and
below me change so fast that I can't keep the run of
them." She has always had some kindly people about
her, however, who have taken a care and oversight of
her, and she seems such a conservative old body that I
never should have ventured to propose to her to move

away from such surroundings. But my mother has been turning over some plans for getting her away from this crowded part of the town, and she remembered a Mrs. Travers, who knew about Miss Dexter and all the old traditions of my mother's family. She had a letter from Mrs. Travers, telling how she had taken a house lately in Roxbury, and that she would be glad to let one or more of the rooms to some quiet body. So I had a letter from my mother, asking me if I could not persuade Miss Dexter to make the change into a pleasanter neighborhood, — the more easily as Miss Dexter knew Mrs. Travers and might feel as if she were living among old friends.

As I have said, I should as soon have thought of proposing to Bunker Hill Monument to move. So I was much relieved to have Mr. Merton, the other day, say that he would suggest it to her. You may remember that I found to my surprise that he, too, knew Miss Dexter. He talked it over the day we were at the Middlesex Fells; and since then the whole thing has been managed in the most diplomatic manner, with a series of visits and consultations that I won't bother you with. Finally, we gained her consent to moving. I don't believe we should have succeeded if there had not been a threat that a street was to be cut through the little court she lived in, and that the inhabitants were likely to be turned out any day. So at last Miss Dexter said with a sigh: "Well, Brattle Street church was moved, so I suppose I can go."

I made a succession of visits upon Mrs. Travers in Roxbury, looked at her rooms and measured them for carpets and furniture, previously studying up all the varieties of street cars that might connect with the place, and then reported them to Miss Dexter. Mr. Merton has been splendid about the whole affair and has really done all the difficult work. We were sur-

prised to find, when we came to the point, that after
Miss Dexter knew that she must move, she was really
very amenable to the plan of going so far.   It proved,
indeed, that she was highly satisfied with the idea of
living in Roxbury, if she could not live in Boston
proper.   It was not one of the new-fashioned suburbs
that have grown up in a day, and Mrs. Travers's house
is in a respectable old quarter of the town.   Miss
Dexter remembered going out in an omnibus, that used
in old times to go over the "Neck," as the upper part
of Washington Street was called.

   She says that a great-great-grandfather of mine, or
some such aged ancestor, used to live at the North
End; and she remembers hearing how, when they had
occasion to visit some of their cousins at the South
End, who lived as far away as Essex Street, they
used to have an early dinner so that they might have
plenty of time to drive there with their horse and
chaise, — very different from nowadays, when to the
true "South Ender" Essex Street seems very far
down town.

   Miss Dexter only stipulated that we should not
expect her to go out in one of the electric cars.   She
declared she was not afraid of them.   "It was quite
likely they wouldn't take fire while she was in
them, she went so seldom."   But the step was very
high, and she did not think an old lady ought to try
to get in.   Happily, we found that the Norfolk House
car, which passes near her old residence, would take
her not far from the house of Mrs. Travers.

   But I had previously made this close acquaintance
with the various street-car lines that I have explained
to you.   I had a most wearisome adventure the first
afternoon that I visited Mrs. Travers.   She wrote to
me to come and see her at the end of the day, as she
was to be busy all day long, and she invited me to

dine with her at six o'clock, promising that some one
should escort me home. This suited me very well,
as it was one of my busy days too. Among other
things, I went for a short visit upon Miss Fenton at
the Thorndike, whom I had quite neglected the last
ten days. Now, a short call is very impossible upon
Miss Fenton, as she always involves me in some long
and really interesting discussion. Then, too, I had
been delayed before going to her by my efforts in
hunting up some one else on Boylston Street, not far
from her; but whether above or below the Thorndike,
it took me a long time to discover; and I had to go
up and down the street in a muddle whether it was
my head that was idiotic or whether the numbers
were.

I was relieved when I discovered that I was not
so much of an idiot as I feared. It seems that each
house represents four numbers, between Tremont
Street and Arlington Street, and you have to calculate accordingly. I could not understand the reason
for this Boston peculiarity, but Mr. Merton has explained to me that it is a new arrangement of numbers. For these houses were originally stately
dwelling-houses, most of them with broad fronts on
the street. Now they have been seized upon for
business purposes, offices or shops. Each house,
therefore, requires a number for its shop and another
for the entrance to its stairway and rooms above.
This accounts for two numbers on each house. Then,
in Boston, the numbers are carried from one side of
the street to the other, the odd numbers on one side,
the even numbers opposite. But between Tremont
Street and Arlington Street there are no opposite
houses; the space is occupied by the Common as far
as Charles Street, and by the Public Garden farther
on to Arlington Street.

Now, according to law, not only are there no houses but there never can be any, in these spaces; so the innocent observer in counting up the houses, as he passes up Boylston Street, finds it difficult to allow for an odd number in the opposite row of houses, where there is none and never ought to be. You may think it stupid of the innocent observer not to notice each number, as he or she passes along, instead of going through the difficult sum of adding up four for each house. But some of the numbers have been changed and some have not; and some houses have both the old and the new numbers. Some are so conservative as to cling to the old numbers by which their friends have always known them, who are bothered to find that the house that was numbered a little over one hundred has now jumped to three hundred and something. I don't mean that you find four numbers on each house; for most of the houses have already their shops and entrance doors plainly marked; but those that have not these modern improvements have to be so numbered, because they may have them sometime. So you are bewildered by finding yourself, as it were, four doors higher up the street, when you have passed only one house. The house in which Williams and Everett's store is placed is numbered 190, and the one before it 186, which looks puzzling!

Forgive this long story; but I wanted to explain how I reached the corner of Boylston and Berkeley streets, to find that already it was a quarter past five. These short autumn days shut down on one fast enough any way, and by five o'clock the sun is disappearing behind the houses, and darkness and electric lights begin. And alas! as I reached the corner, it began to rain and the wind to blow. Happily, I had my umbrella, which I had not been needing all these pleasant days ; for I had to wait twenty minutes, tossed by the wind and wet by the rain, before the West End car appeared. This was to take me to the Northampton Street corner, where I was to find a Norfolk House car. But here I had another period of waiting. Every other kind of car came along but the one I wanted. I dashed out into the middle of the street in all the wind to each one, to see if it were for the Norfolk House. I grew so tired of the Bartlett Street cars, there were so many of them. Anna and I have thought previously it might be well to move to Bartlett Street, as it seemed to be easier to get there than anywhere else. But we concluded it must be too populous for us, if it requires so many cars. Somebody calls them "Bartlett Pears," because two are apt to appear together.

I thought of my great-great-grandfather, and envied him his quiet, early dinner and peaceful horse-and-chaise journey to tea with his friends in Essex Street. But I, his great-great-granddaughter, had fallen into the hurried tide of the times ; I had been filling up my day with a succession of occupations that would have made his hair stand on end, — if he had not worn a wig, — and now I was finishing the day by reaching Mrs. Travers's late to dinner and in a drenched state. All things come to an end, however, and so came the Norfolk House car ; and at its end, much to my surprise, I found Mr. Merton.

In this affair I have taken the responsibility of arranging with Mrs. Travers in Roxbury, while Mr. Merton has been struggling with Miss Dexter ; so I was much astonished to find him awaiting me at the door of the car at the Norfolk House. It appeared that Mrs. Travers had invited him also to dinner, as matters might thus be more easily arranged, and he had arrived in good season. Both were much disturbed when the heavy rain came on and I did not appear; so Mr. Merton kindly set out to meet me at the Norfolk House. He declared he was really very anxious, and, indeed, I was thankful to see him; for by this time it was half-past six and "pitch dark." He insisted on carrying my umbrella, and I don't know how I should have found my way to the house without him. I was quite ashamed to arrive so late and in such a condition; but they were all so kind that we were soon laughing over the whole affair, though they were full of pity for all my sufferings.

I saw the rooms then for the first time, and they are charming. I have been there since on a bright, sunny day, and I was pleased to find that the windows look out upon a little garden and a pear-tree, so that Miss Dexter can seem to be renewing her old life.

Mrs. Travers had many old stories to tell that evening; of former days in Boston and Roxbury; and Mr. Merton was "the escort" into town whom she had promised me. We had again another delay on our return; for there had been a blockade far down by the Tremont House. As the rain had stopped, Mr. Merton proposed our walking down to the Jamaica Plain "electric," as it would take us in quicker. But everything was delayed forty minutes, so it was late when I reached home. Yet we had a most amusing time, and we agreed that, though the ancestral days of horse and chaise might have had their charms, yet we were glad to live in these later times, when one could growl at the street cars, if they did not take us in five minutes from one end of the town to the other, and when our lives were certainly more varied than if we had lived then.

The final excursion, when we really bore Miss Tryphena Dexter away from her old home to her new abode, was a most entertaining one. I went down in

the morning to find her. Mr. Merton was already in
her room; the expressman had been to carry off some
of her effects; and everything else was packed and in
good order to follow her. Mr. Merton seems to have
an especial managing talent for conducting such things.
I have not needed to do a single thing about the boxes
and furniture, and evidently it has all been made very
easy for Miss Dexter.

She seemed a little dazed as she followed us downstairs through the court, on our way to the Norfolk
House car, which we were to await on the corner of
the street. She came behind us, — for she walked so
slowly, — and begged us not to wait for her. She had
a singular whim of turning all the way round now and
then to look behind her, stopping in the middle of
the sidewalk. I told Mr. Merton that I thought she
was sorrowfully looking back upon her past and re-
gretting to leave it. But he said he had heard that
she had always had this peculiarity of locomotion
even in her earlier days, — if locomotion it could be
called to stop deliberately now and then to look
backwards. I suppose in her younger days the sidewalks were not so crowded, and it could be more easily
performed; and perhaps nowadays it may be some
advantage for an old person to look round frequently
to see if there is an electric car coming up behind or
a herdic in sight. Mr. Merton had insisted on taking
all her bags except one small and precious one that I
conveyed. She herself carried two shawls and a large
green umbrella that had lost the ring that once held it
together. In this comical manner we reached the corner of the street, where we awaited the horse car,
Miss Dexter bringing up just in time.

Happily, there was plenty of room at this early
stage of the journey, though the car filled up as we
went on. I was fain to give up my seat; but Mr.

Merton would not allow me, though I am always willing to stand, and do not object at all to being asked to
" move forward," as I can then rest myself against the
front door of the car. Miss Dexter recovered her tone
as we went on, so that, as we passed along the length
of Washington Street, she could give me a history of
its numerous changes, — how a part of it was called at
one time Marlborough Street, and another part Newbury Street, and so on. A little beyond Dover Street,
she said, were some buildings called " The Green
Stores," — I believe they are still standing, — and it
seems this was considered a distant limit of Boston
proper. To walk to " The Green Stores " was considered a good stretch for a constitutional walk for one
day, and some young ladies managed to take it before
breakfast every day. But Miss Dexter was inclined
to think this was not healthful. Mrs. Travers assisted
in testifying to some of these facts, after we reached
her house, which we did at last. There was the same
comical method of walking performed by Miss Dexter,
as we went up the street leading to Mrs. Travers's
house. For we insisted upon her going in front of us
this time, as I was afraid she might really be lost or
drop out into some of the streets that we passed.

I think she was truly pleased with her room when
she came to see it. Mr. Merton had managed to have
some of her furniture there before we arrived; and
she looked with evident pleasure upon her old ward-
robe and tables and her old bedstead in a recess; and
she was really touched when she looked out of the
window and saw the pear-tree below, now laden with
pears. So we left her for the day, and we hear she is
very comfortable and likely to take up her life in her
new home with, perhaps, a little more cheerfulness
than in her old one.

It is astonishing how much Mr. Merton accom-

plished in all this affair; for he is very busy in other
ways. He has been away from town once or twice in
these last weeks, and he went to Philadelphia for a
meeting of the committee on the Congress of Nations,
that must have been immensely interesting. So I
think it was amazingly kind of him to give so much
time to making this old friend of his mother comfortable, and to do everything in so thoughtful a way.

. . . .

Meanwhile people are returning to Boston. We
see the children playing again upon the sidewalks
along our street, and the youngest members of society
are being dragged about in their wicker wagons by the
nursemaids. The shops are filling up with visitors,
and the street corners are more than ever crowded. I
have done a little shopping myself. I am discouraged to see that the fashion of birds' wings and
feathers for hats and bonnets is filling the shop windows with all kinds of gay plumage, that gives me a
sigh. I tried to get some flowers the other day, — artificial ones, — and I had to go from shop to shop.
Mrs. Davis, Anna's sister, groans about this. She has
just come from Paris and she wishes she could have
brought more of the exquisite roses and every variety
of flowers that make the Paris shops so charming.

The making of flowers is a fine art there, and nobody can resist trimming their hats and bonnets with
them, whatever the fashion may be. But she declares
that Boston has a craze, now and then, for feathers
and such trimming, and that the shops are not willing
that one should wear anything else. It amuses me,
since I have come from the country and am fancying
Boston to be a large city, to hear her call it very provincial in this respect, in that it does not allow more
variety in such matters of taste. She declares the
shop windows are all alike, and that there is the

same thing in all. I have to agree with her with regard to this feather business. But I must say that I enjoy going through the large shops with my un- sophisticated eyes, which find much to admire and much to suggest.

My people have not got back yet to Boston. Aunt Martha is still at Bar Harbor, and Maria has gone with some friends to the White Mountains to find the bright leaves — if there are any. Cousin Rupert has gone off, nobody knows where. Meantime, Aunt Martha is anxious to have me stay here till her return, and I am very glad not to be hunting up my boarding- place in these busy days.

Anna and I have had some delightful "rehearsal" afternoons. It is lucky that we have strength and spirits to go through it all. The concerts do not be- gin till half-past two in the afternoon, but we present ourselves at Music Hall long before the doors are open, to stand our chance of getting in for a seat. Before the winter is over we may learn how those "some- bodies" manage who do get a front seat in the upper balcony. We are always among the first at the doors, and we have some speed of motion; but one afternoon we had to content ourselves with seats on the steps of the stage, which we considered a great success, and the other afternoon, we took turns for a seat in one of the side rows of the upper balcony. But for all our struggles and standing and waiting we are fully repaid, and we enjoy more and more the delights of the music. I consider it a liberal education to hear it, and it makes one only long for more.

Anna and I have amused ourselves by getting out an old book from the library here, "Sandford and Merton." I don't believe even you have been suffi- ciently educated to be familiar with it. But it was a famous book for children in its day. My father and

LUCY AND ANNA. — PAGE 267.

mother used to think a great deal of it and tried to make me read it; but I remember I did not get on with it very well. But we are quite entertained by it now and we wonder that the youthful generation are not made acquainted with it. To be sure, there is ever so much of it, and the volume we have is in very fine print, and it looks as if it would take forever to read the whole. One opens upon such passages as this: Harry says to Mr. Barlow: "Pray, dear sir, read to Master Tommy the story of Leonidas, which gave me so much pleasure. I am sure he will like to hear it." Mr. Barlow, accordingly, reads the history of Leonidas, king of Sparta, — in very large letters, — and the story follows, making four pages of close print. After it comes an admirable lesson in astronomy, and all is very instructive, you perceive. But this age of ours is instructive; and why not bring back "Sandford and Merton"?

The two names entertain Anna and me very much, and there is a Harry Sandford who is one of the heroes of the book. All of which reminds me that there used to be a tradition in our family that "Harry and Lucy," the brother and sister of Miss Edgeworth's story, were real characters; that Harry's family was named Merton, so he was a Harry Merton, and that his sister, Lucy, married a Sandford, from whom we are descended. It would be interesting to prove that our new friend Harry Merton is descended from this original Harry. But all this is nonsense; yet it seems to amuse us — when we find time.

I have just heard of a course of ten lectures to be given during this autumn and winter by General Francis A. Walker, the president of the Institute of Technology, beginning November 9, and continuing on Mondays at 11 A. M., on political economy. I am fondly hoping that I can go, and I feel it would be a sufficient reason for spending the winter in Boston, to hear these lectures.

I have been much surprised and interested, since I have been here, in learning how much has been done by liberal women in Boston, in individual ways, to assist the city in enlarging education in the public schools. The liberality of Mrs. Quincy Shaw has made the public kindergarten one of the possibilities in these schools. And earlier, Mrs. Mary Hemenway, beginning with liberal experiments of her own, succeeded in introducing into the public schools the teaching of sewing, and afterward, of cooking. Lately, in the same way, she has called attention to the Swedish system of educational gymnastics, which is now introduced in the schools. Through her munificence, the Swedish system, under the instruction of Baron Posse, was a little while ago offered to a class consisting of public school teachers, who were also given a course in anatomy by Dr. Emma Call.

Mrs. Hemenway has now inaugurated a Normal School of Gymnastics, to instruct teachers in the Swedish or "Ling" system. This is established at the Paine Memorial Hall, Appleton Street, under the charge of Claes J. Enebuske, the Swedish teacher and lecturer. I have been reading with interest his address given to the masters of the public schools. He shows how important such physical training is for the pupils of our schools, who spend so much time in a cramped, sitting position, and he carefully explains the advantages of the Swedish exercises and gymnastic games.

I am much interested in the account he gives of the Swedish love of such games and gymnastic dances. He says: "It may give you an idea of some of these dances, when I tell you that it is but about twenty-five years since, in certain provinces of Sweden, a girl looked upon that man as inferior who could not kick twice his own height, and in the dance lift her over his head while, on his toes, he moved his feet in time with the quick rhythm of the music."

I can't help thinking what an admirable bit of education it would be, if it were possible that, along with the solid instruction we are requiring nowadays, we might also bring in a love and pleasure in such a healthy use of the muscles of the body. How I should like to stir up some of our good neighbors at home with a Swedish dance, which need not be quite so muscular as the one described by the Swedish teacher, but which they could not object to, as they would have been taught it as a school exercise among the other courses of instruction!

CHAPTER TWENTY-FIRST. .

XXIV.

HARRY TO HIS MOTHER.

Boston, Oçt. 27, 1891.

My dear Mother, — This time, at least, Nahum shall not say that my letter is uneventful. Was it he or one of the others who said I might as well be at Astney? Faithless Nahum! who shall say what may yet come out of Astney? Indeed, dear Mother, you may receive this by parts; for the writing is hurried, and I know it will take more than one stamp. But if I see any notice with names in the newspapers, I shall mail it to you; for I know you will be frightened then, and I shall want you to know at once that all's well that ends well.

It all happened just before dark last night. There had been some trouble about the delivery of some of our boxes. And on inquiry it proved that the particular man who drove the particular express wagon which the shipping-clerk thought or guessed took them lived at South Boston. So I was told to clear up my work early at the desk and go over to South Boston, see this driver, and get out of him, if I could, what he did with the boxes and what he did not do. This was how I came to be in Gold Street at all. For I had never heard of Gold Street myself any more than you have. And how should you ever have heard of it, seeing it was all under water when you lived here.

Well, I was poking along through Something-else Street and had not turned into Gold Street, when I saw

that half a dozen or more little "muckers" in front
of me ran hastily forward with yells and disappeared.
The thing is so common that I never should have
thought of it again but for what followed. If I thought
of it at all then, I supposed that there was a grinding
organ or a monkey or a cart of apples. But when I
came into Gold Street I saw as large a crowd as if
"The Cornet Man" were there. Yet there was no
sound of a cornet, but rather the real presence of
battle.

I am so tall that I saw at once what the matter was.
Three Salvation Army girls, in their uniform, had undertaken some errand down there. I know enough of
these people now to know that it was some errand of
mercy. But nobody in their dress was to pass these
hoodlums. Observe, they had no band of music, nor
were they singing or shouting, not even speaking, except to each other. But so soon as these little black-
guards saw them, they began crying out with impudent
cries, and then closed up round them so as to frighten
the girls. Then somebody flung a cabbage stalk, heavy
with its root and the dirt on it, at one, and it struck
her full in the face.

The poor child screamed out with the sudden pain.
This was, so far as I could learn, the first cry or
spoken word that any one of them had uttered, except to each other. But it was enough and more than
enough to precipitate what became the battle I speak
of. Instantly boys and girls began to pelt them with
such missiles as they could most easily pick up. A
lady who came into the street at the moment rushed
up to protect them. More sticks and stones on all
four. The scream was what had called the party I
saw.

I myself had not noticed it. The crowd constantly
increased. Oh! there must have been more than a

hundred of these little wretches round those four poor
ladies when I turned into Gold Street. By this time
they were pulling at their clothes and hats, while the
four were huddled together in a group, trying to crowd
against the wall, so as to have their enemies only on
one side. They were on the sidewalk and on the steps
of a door, which lifted them rather above most of the
mob, for mob it was, but made them a better mark for
the missiles.

Of course, the minute I saw this, for it was quite
light enough to see, though the sun must have gone
down, I rushed across to the rescue. Boys and girls
gave way to the right and left, and until I came there
I did not use nor wish to use my stick. I remember
thinking I was sorry it was not heavier. It was the
stick Nahum cut on Ascutney and trimmed for me so
nicely. But it proved better as it was.

I stumbled on the edge of the sidewalk as I rushed
on. I should have fallen flat, but there were quite too
many of these hoodlums, male and female. I only
fell, so to speak, on them. I had the stick by the
middle now and I did not distress myself by any questions as to where it struck. I had no time to read any
Riot Act. I was not dissatisfied when I heard a good,
loud yell of pain, which did not come from one of the
beleaguered ladies.

But at the same moment I was conscious of a stout
pull at my left arm, which I could not at the instant
throw off. I recovered my footing securely, however,
and brought up my stick so people could see it and
know at once that we were all free men here. I felt a
smart tug at my coat behind. But I closed against the
wall so suddenly that that little pirate found his head
was softer than the bricks. I heard his mumbling
threats as he retired. I watched another boy and
brought down the stick just heavily enough not to

break on his head. But by this time there was no pressure on us. They were scattering like pigeons, right and left, scattering faster than I could think even my prowess deserved. I dared turn my head to look, and three good fellows, who proved to be policemen in citizen's dress, were coming up on the other side. The battle was over, and nothing was left but to rescue the women and get them out from further danger.

Actually, my dear Mother, each one of those three girls was bleeding from the blows of the sticks or stones. I did not understand that any of the cowards had struck them, but they had thrown these things from a distance. Their hats were crushed; their clothes were torn; and the dirt and blood on their faces were fearful to see. Poor things! they had been crying, as well they might, and now they hardly knew what they said. I gave one my arm, and each of the policemen took one of the others and the fourth woman, who had come down from the house. We walked along to Dorchester Street or Dorchester Avenue, whichever it is, as quick as we could without appearing to be in flight. I was trying to encourage my companion and get the story of the affray from her. And it is from her and what I saw and what Lucy told me afterward that I have made the account I have given you.

For, dear Mother, strange to say, when we came to Dorchester Avenue it proved that the fourth lady in the party was Lucy Sandford. She had been on one of her charity visits, and came down, as I said, just before I saw the affair. When I came up, the poor child was actually bending down to protect one of the " Salvation " girls, who was fairly sitting on the steps. So I did not then see her, nor she me. When the policemen appeared she turned to speak to them, and I was talking and threatening and shaking my stick at the

18

last of the fugitives. And it was not till we began our rapid retreat, for retreat it was, that she knew who was in front of her. For me, I did not know at all who was behind me until we came to Dorchester Avenue, where, of course, we had to wait before any car came. If I had known, you may guess whether I would not have asked the policeman who had given her his arm to exchange with me.

I cannot, dear Mother, send the rest of this letter in print. It is really only for your eyes. I sent them yesterday the beginning of this story. But only you must have the end.

[NOTE BY THE EDITORS. — We find this remark made by Mr. Merton at the beginning of page nine of his MS. It places us in rather an embarrassing position. All we can say is that the office boy of the C. D. I. D. C. P. Co. brought round the envelope containing the following sheets, as he always does. The compositors are waiting for two columns and a half of copy, the space reserved for Mr. Merton. We shall therefore put this in type. If he countermands it, why, he can. If not, we must suppose he has changed his mind.]

.   .   .   .

I told the policemen I would see the young people home, and at last the Dorchester Avenue car came the right way. There had been a plenty going the other way, as I need not say. I am afraid I must confess that I let the "Salvation Lasses" comfort each other, while I asked Miss Sandford a hundred questions as to the fate which brought her into Gold Street and her share in the battle royal.

It was all, I believe, as I have said. She had some poor person whom she had gone to see, or to try to see; for she had the wrong number, or the poor person was a fraud. After inquiring from room to room in vain, she had come downstairs disappointed, when, stepping out on the stoop, she found herself in the midst almost of the fray. "Of course, I could not

think of going back then," she said, "though for a
minute I did ask myself whether I could not get the
poor girls into the house. But, to tell you the
truth," she continued, "I was not much more sure of
the house than I was of the street. Perhaps, you
know, the fathers and mothers might have taken part
with the children."

Then I tried to make her say that she would not go
to such places alone again. I did not think it was
any fit venture for her. I said I would go with her, if
she were willing to go after five in the afternoon.
But of course, she parried this. She said she thought
she had better go by daylight than in the dark, and, of
course she was right there. She said it was nowhere
written that such enterprises should be agreeable.
Indeed, she dropped her voice a little and said that
she had never been taught to shun any duty, because
it was disagreeable. She said she had never had so
much respect for these young women with us as she
had to-day. They had not spoken an unkind word in
the midst of it all. They had undertaken to do this
thing, wisely or not, and, because they thought it
was their duty, they were going to carry it through.

Thus we had a very interesting talk all the way.
We "transferred" to a Broadway car into town, and
this brings you close to the "Salvation" headquarters.
There we got out with the poor martyrs, as I shall
always call them, and Lucy went upstairs with them,
I following. You see all the officers of this division,
or company, live in part of the building, close by the
hall; or at least, if they do not live there, they have
to report there. So the young ladies, for ladies they
are, thanked us very prettily, and I explained to
the officer I found our share in the business, and then
leaving the "Salvationers," we two went our way.

I wanted to find a cab to take Miss Sandford home;

but this she would not hear of. It was quite dark by this time; but when she found I meant to go home with her she said that she would walk. I made her take my arm, and we went through Pleasant Street and crossed through the Providence station to Boylston Street, and so to her home.

I knew, of course, dear Mother, that I had no right, then or yet, to take the tone of a protector or of an adviser. But I did feel that somebody ought to, and that so sweet a girl, or if it is better to say so, so noble a woman, ought not to put herself in the way of a stray "brickbat" from any hoodlum boys who might have been drinking more beer than was good for them. This time I said that, — rather more cautiously than I had said it in the horse-car. I knew I must not go too far, you see, or she would cut me off very short. I had tried that once before.

But I did say that, granting all she had said, — that we must bear each other's burdens, and that no one had ever promised that the burdens should be light, — still there is method in everything, I said, and there is a right way and wrong way. And that such work as this seemed to me to be fairly the work of men, and that this afternoon had proved it so. I said that the whole presumption of the Associated Charities people, to whom she had joined herself, is that they are going to make "friendly" visits in Gold Street and the other places. "Not alms, but a friend," is their motto.

Now, I said, it was almost absurd to pretend that she was making a "friendly" visit, when she did not even know where her "friends" lived and when she was not sure their "friends" would not throw a rotten egg at her. But she would not laugh. She only said that, if society were divided in such fashion that she could not have friends in Gold Street, so much the worse for society; that, for her part, she would have nothing to do with it, except to put it on a higher and better plane. And this she said, not in any heroic vein, but as a woman of sense, who had thought the thing out, and was not talking at random.

I need not say that I wished the walk was half an hour longer. Only then it would have been, not a walk, but a jumbling ride in a cab, and would have been over in half the time. But we were both of us very serious. I was not thinking of myself, whether I should please her; I was only thinking of her, and how to save her from real danger. Only too soon we came out at the steps of the house in the avenue. I rang the bell and said good-by.

Then the dear girl said no, that we must not part so; that I must come in and have my dinner with them. "And then," she said, "I will repeat to them what you say, and they shall decide whether I shall go to Gold Street itself or to any other Gold Street again. I have no wish to be heroic," she went on, "but I do want to be of use. I am not satisfied with finding out how other people live." This is a favorite phrase of mine, which she had heard me use. "I want, if I can, to live with all sorts and conditions of men and women and children, and to be of use to them — if I can. I have had experience enough already to know that they will be of use to me."

Dear Mother, I wish you could have seen her sweet, sad smile as she said this. We were in the house now and were just turning into that elegant drawing-room, with its flowers and books and pictures. As for her, she looked like an angel, as the light from the chandelier fell upon her face. As I say, there was just a smile, but a sad smile. For I think we both felt the contrast between the elegance of these surround-

ings and the plain board partitions of the Salvation
Army quarters which we had just left, — yes, and the
squalor and grime and dirt and blood of the flight of
steps in Gold Street.

Without saying a word, I had accepted her invitation. Indeed, it seemed a matter of course now. I
felt I must stay as near her as I could, even if the
next hour I was told that I should never see her again.
But at the moment I had no chance to answer. Miss
Davis came in with a cousin who was visiting them,
and very naturally they were excited and nervous;
for Lucy was a great deal later than usual. They
knew she had been going over to South Boston
and they were almost as anxious as I should have
been. As luck would have it, Lucy had laid her
handkerchief on the table, and it was all red with
blood that she had wiped from the face of one of
those poor girls.

"Where have you been? What has happened?"
cried Miss Davis. And do you know, I found out
afterward that there was a great yellow smooch from
an egg on my shirt front, and that my face was well
blackened by a lump of mud which had hit me in the
fight. Of course, between us, we made such explanations as in a few words we could. Lucy explained
that I was to stay to dinner, and then I was hurried
to a dressing-room to make myself comfortable, as
Miss Davis said. She was too civil to say to make
myself look decently. Really, till I looked in the
glass I had no idea how battle-stained I was. I made
myself as decent as I could, and joined the party at
dinner.

I need not say every one was excited. We fought
our little battle over and over again; Lucy from the
point of view of a person assailed, and I from the
point of view of a spectator. Both of us did full

justice to the policemen, who were excellent fellows, and without whom I am sure I do not know where I should be now. Lucy would not let me be too modest, and acknowledged that her first sense of relief was when she heard my first battle-cry, though she did not know who I was; and she confessed to a certain satisfaction when my stick descended on the hard hat of the boy whom I hit hardest. The ladies cannot be said to have listened a great deal. I observe that nobody ever listens a great deal to anything. They were full of ejaculations and suggestions of what they had thought and said, and what they had heard other people think and say, and protests about how badly the city was governed, and so on. I do not myself think that we had much to say about that, because the policemen were the people who rescued us. If anybody wants to talk about how badly the children in the streets are educated, and what is the condition of things in which there can be such a troop of banditti ready to fall on three unoffending young women, I shall be glad to discuss that matter with him. But of this nothing now, dear Mother.

I was not even hungry, and I know it bored me to have that well-trained servant bring round the things that I was expected to eat and to attend to. I suppose it was a very good dinner, but for my part I wished it was over. I did not know why I wished it was over; only I knew it was all very irrational and unnatural for us to be discussing the government of Boston and political economy and the social condition of the world in general, when I wanted to be alone with Lucy Sandford. I did not catch her eye once through the dinner, although I sat on the opposite side of the table from her. I need not say that they all made her talk, but, as I said, I think I was the only person who really listened.

[At this point Mr. Merton's letter really stops, and the editors are compelled to believe that the pages which have been published since the editorial note above were sent by mistake to this office, instead of being put into the cover which probably inclosed the remainder of his narrative. But it seemed so evident to us that our readers were entitled to the rest of this incident that we have availed ourselves of the general resources of a newspaper, and of that omniscience which is fortunately one of the attributes of our profession, to complete the narrative which Mr. Merton has left broken. — EDS. COMMONWEALTH.]

Of course, Harry Merton could have bowed himself out of the house as soon as coffee had been served in the drawing-room. But it must be hoped that we have some readers, courageous enough and determined to see this exciting enterprise to its real end, who will say that of course he did not bow himself out. Those readers are quite right. He did not. He waited bravely to see if there might not be one chance more to speak with Lucy Sandford alone. If he were taught in no other way that he must speak to her alone, the mere choking in his throat, when he made absolute efforts to swallow a piece of potato or of cauliflower, would have told him that he could never pass that night, without solving that question of infinite importance which their walk had not been long enough to solve.

"You will hardly feel like going to the Dorcas, Lucy?" This was Miss Davis's inquiry as the last coffee-cup was carried away. No, Lucy did not think she would go out again, though she again asseverated that she was not tired; only she thought she had better not take the chances of being wet. With great resolution she did say, and that in an unconcerned voice, — as unaffected as her voice always is, — that she hoped her absence would not keep them at home. She knew Anna had to report for her committee and that she would be missed. Indeed, she said firmly that if Anna would not go without her, she should put on her hat and coat and overshoes again and go with them. Miss Davis made no motion to stay. She said that Lucy had better go to bed early, and she and Miss Wentworth excused themselves to her and to Mr. Merton, while they made themselves ready. A carriage was called by telephone, and Harry and Lucy found themselves again alone.

But Harry did not yet seize his opportunity. He was not yet wholly sure that it was an opportunity. He did not mean to be interrupted by the ladies as they came in hatted and shod, not to say booted and spurred, for the Circle. He did, however, lead back directly to the conversation in their walk. "Miss Davis," he began, "takes my side, you see, in our discussion." "Did she? Does she?" said Lucy, less at ease now than she had been at any moment. "Do you know, I hardly knew what she said or did not say. Not that I am faint again, — I am not so foolish; but perhaps I was thinking of myself more highly or more carefully than I ought to think."

Harry almost bit his tongue out. He would have been so glad to say that nobody could think highly enough of her, or to take that chance to say that he thought of no one else. But still the terror of the reappearance of Miss Davis and her friend subdued him. He even affected not to hear what Lucy Sandford said, and asked, as if he cared, how often the Circle met, and if Miss Davis's friend was a member. To which questions Lucy replied, accurately or inaccurately. And then he asked what the Circle was for. And as Lucy was replying, the servant announced the carriage, and Anna Davis and the friend appeared. "You must excuse our running away, Mr. Merton; but, in truth, we shall be late as it is, and Emily has a paper to read."

Harry did or did not say that the sooner they were gone the better. He tried to be civil, and probably was. If Lucy had any hope, thought, or fear that he would take the occasion to bid her good-evening, she was disappointed. He came back into the parlor and fairly took her hand and led her to the sofa.

"My dear Miss Lucy, I am so glad they are gone. I have waited bravely, because, before I sleep this night, I must know whether I am a fool or not. Or let me put it better, my dear Miss Lucy. I spoke as we came home as if I had a right to advise you, to warn you, to beg you not to risk your life. I know and knew that you must think I have no such right. But if I say that no minute of my life passes in which I do not think of you and pray for you; if I say I was overjoyed to see you to-day, even though such a risk had brought us together; then I shall earn my right, or shall make my excuse for putting myself into your concerns. I cannot help it. That is, all my life will not be worth living, if you say I must not say such things."

There had been just so much eagerness in his tone before they had reached the house that Miss Sandford was not wholly unprepared for this sudden declaration. But she was not prepared with a word of answer. Harry had had the long-drawn hour of dinner to know that he would speak, and to ask himself what he would say. The man had his rights, however. He had respected hers, and she would not fail in respecting his. So she tried to speak.

She looked up at him, — sadly was it, or eagerly? The boy did not know. She tried to speak. "I — You — It is —" She bit her lip and grew pale. "I do not think — I did not think — " and then her head fell for a minute. Then she looked him full in the face. "Really, Mr. Merton —" And she put both her hands in his, and smiled with a face alive with sympathy and glad with joy.

He did not trouble himself for any more reply to what she had said. He flung his arms around her and kissed her again and again.

CHAPTER TWENTY-SECOND.

XXV.

LUCY TO KATE.

BOSTON, Nov. 2, 1891.

MY DEAR KATE, — I have to write you about some
very mixed-up days, because, as the season changes, I
find I must arrange my winter plans, and so many
different views come up before me and so many things
have to be considered that I grow quite bewildered.
I feel more and more thankful to Aunt Martha that
she arranged this pleasant home for me here, which
gives me time and opportunity to study this great city
and to try to decide what I want to do. You know
my mother has always said that her principal advice
to her children has been, " Find out what you want to
do, and then do that." We have always declared that,
indeed, this first decision of "what we want to do" is
the most difficult. Yet I do have a firm conviction of
what I want to do, but I am moving hither and thither
to find out how I had better do it.

I have told you how interested I am in the Swedish
system of gymnastics, and I had an opportunity to go
one afternoon to one of the classes at the Posse Gymnasium. This is in the Harcourt Building in Irving-
ton Street, where many prominent artists have their
studios. I did not find Miss Knowlton at home, so I
have not yet seen her summer work, which is always
interesting. In the hall of the gymnasium rooms I
found a large class of children from the Boston public
schools, who receive free instruction at the gymnasium.

This is especially a normal school of gymnastics, in the truest sense of this term, and the teachers who are gaining their education at this school are assistants in conducting this class, which meets twice a week. Here were two hundred and fifty children, filling the hall with life and animation; but when the signal was given they fell into line, ready for the exercises. The hall is large, well-lighted and ventilated, and fitted up with all the Swedish apparatus, and also with chest weights, dumb bells, Indian clubs and the like.

It was most interesting to see the method of the general exercises, marching and military drill forming a part, besides the especial Swedish exercises for every part of the body, all carried out under the direction of Baron Posse himself. The student-teachers, meanwhile, were taking charge of the several squads of children that formed the whole band, the children being grouped according to physical proficiency, and each squad having two or more normal pupils as leaders. This gives these students admirable practical experience as teachers, and they are, besides, called upon from time to time to take charge of the normal class. They have also the advantage of a special course of lectures by prominent lecturers, in which the various gymnastic systems are discussed, examinations are held, and lectures and recitations are given by Baron Posse, introducing the study of medical gymnastics, all making a complete ·education for a teacher, and especially needed in the public schools, where the system is widely introduced. I heard that some of the teachers take their pupils into the school yard at the time of such exercises, when the weather permits. It was cheerful to see the bright and happy faces of the children as they went through it all, and as they rushed from the general exercises to the special exercises in

the spacious hall, where each little squad could be
watched over by its teacher in trying the different apparatus so temptingly placed.

In a great city one sees so many different kinds of
life. Only the other day I had a kind invitation from
a friend to go to see one of the peculiar Jewish ceremonies. It was a most interesting occasion, and I was
very grateful for the opportunity. We went to the
private house of one of the well-known and esteemed
Jewish families of Boston for the celebration of the
Feast of the Tabernacles, which takes place in October and continues for eight days. We received a most
kindly and hospitable invitation to go to see how the
occasion was celebrated. It is the harvest festival,
not unlike what we might meet with at one of our
Thanksgivings in the country. We were ushered in
through the magnificently furnished house to the open
garden beyond, which had been shut in as a tabernacle
with boughs of trees for a roof. These were all hung.
with fruits of every description, making a gorgeous
display. Here was every variety of fruit and vegetables imaginable, apples, pears, oranges, bananas, glow-
ing squashes and pumpkins, ears of corn, masses of
grapes drooping everywhere in the midst of the green,
and great sheaves of palms shutting all in, and everything gay with color, making the whole place brilliant,
and pictures here and there in the midst of all the
glow.

And crowds of friends were thronging in and out;
for the family had sent invitations to everybody, rich
and poor. And these last came with petitions for help
to the liberal host, who was willing to stop and listen
to their petitions and complaints in the midst of all
the coming and going. Everybody, indeed, was received with a cordial hospitality; the delicious fruit
was served in exquisite china to every comer; and

we were asked to go over the house and admire the
choice pictures and the beautiful adornments. It was
an occasion, surely, to be remembered and to be grateful for.

1 could not but contrast it with our occupation the
next evening, when, by invitation of Miss Fenton, I
went with her and Mr. Merton to a lecture before the
Theosophic Society on the "Astral Body." It seemed
as if I were suddenly called upon to consider the two
oldest religions in the world in two days, one after the
other, as I went into this hall and saw a Hindu image
placed before me. But I cannot stop to tell you of
this, for other things come up.

. . . .

You will have read the peaceful part of the beginning of this letter, wondering, I imagine, that I could
begin so calmly without entering upon more exciting
events. But perhaps it is as well that the journal of
those days was written earlier; for I am sure it would
be hard to remember what happened a week before,
when so many eventful things have since been going on.

In the first place, I will and must speak of the
wonderful news that Cousin Rupert brought to me of
your engagement. It was the very evening before my
South Boston expedition, of which you will have
learned, because it has become now so great a part
of my history. Cousin Rupert declares that it is in
the newspapers, but I cannot believe him. Indeed, I
could hardly believe him when he told me, the day
before that expedition, that he was going to marry
you!— and that you are the "friend in the West" to
whom he was engaged! 1 confess to some indignation at first that you should both have kept all this
in secrecy from me so long; but I can understand
that, if you were afraid to tell your mother of the

matter in her illness, you could easily be unwilling
to write of it even to me.

Now I am glad that all is going to be so happy with
you, your mother better, and you, indeed, to come to
Boston. Rupert has been talking with me about all
your plans, and I am astonished at them all. It seems
he is not going to content himself with apartments in
the house here with his mother; but he has absolutely
persuaded you to consent to a house on the water side
of Beacon Street, — one of the beautiful row of houses I
have often looked at with admiration as I walked over
Cambridge Bridge and back. I approve of the plan
very much, my dear, and I am quite sure that you
and Rupert will make a happy home there, and that
it will be just the place for the true hospitality and
the liberal kind of home life that I am sure Bostonians
love.

I believe I am amusing myself with writing upon
your affairs because I am not used to talking of my
own, and I scarcely know how to write of them. I do
not wonder now that you found it hard to write to me
of your engagement, since I find it so difficult to speak
of my own or even to think of it; and, indeed, I hardly
know whether to believe it myself. Rupert will have
written to you and will talk to you about it, as he goes
to you this week, and I have promised to send by him
a special note to tell you more than my giddy head can
say now.

And it was Harry that wrote the whole thing first
to my mother; for I could not quite understand it myself or make out what it all was. In fact, it seems
long ages ago since that evening when Rupert confided
to me all your interests and plans, and his, too; for
that was the very evening before my eventful day.

Since then Cousin Rupert and Harry have learned
to know each other and to like and respect each other

much. With both of them I have already had much to say about that fateful visit to South Boston. We have talked over and over the events of that expedition, and we have wondered how it would have been if it had been different, and how it would have been the same if it had been different, and how we had rather have it the same, but perhaps it had better have been different! Did you ever know anything so incoherent?

But, you see, I did go over to South Boston all alone, and to a rough part of the town, and it was in connection with my Associated Charities duties; only that is not my district, — South Boston, I mean, — but I had promised somebody I would look up a case there. One reason I wanted to go is, that Anna and I have not, or had not, quite given up the idea of creating, as it were, a "University Settlement" of ourselves. For we have talked of establishing ourselves somewhere in one of these destitute parts of the town, where we might make a happy and a useful home centre for our neighbors about us. So I thought I would combine this "Charities" expedition with one of inquiry into that neighborhood. And, finally, Anna could not go with me that afternoon, so I set forth alone.

Cousin Rupert declares that I must have been satisfied that the neighborhood was destitute and forlorn enough to lead me to desire to plant myself directly in the middle of its delightful inhabitants. And why not? I answer. Surely it is time to teach these little hoodlums — for so he called them — better manners. And for my part, I am thankful I was there to help those three Salvation Army girls in any way I could. Of course, my little help might have availed nothing if Harry Merton had not appeared, and if he had not been there, strong, brave man that he is.

But I can't help saying that if it had not been

Harry Merton it would have been some one, — some one to help us. For there were those brave policemen; and one who took charge of me. But that strong cry of Harry's it was that gave me a sense of relief, though I did not then know who it was. I am not sure but what I felt less brave myself when I found that he was there to protect me. Before then I held my courage up and thought with pity of those poor boys who knew no better than to attack us. They somehow reminded me of my Vacation School boys.

I really did not mean to go over the whole story with you, since Cousin Rupert will tell you all; only you will want to know my view. You will have heard, too, how Harry came home with me, and how Anna had her friend Emily Wentworth staying with us; for there was to be a meeting of a society they are interested in, and I was to have gone to hear Emily read a paper. But they insisted I had better not go out again, and so they went off together. I was glad Anna was there, for she is more at home than Emily, who was frightened out of her wits. And I was almost sorry I had not followed them, when they went away and I found Mr. Merton was to stay.

But I must tell you another story, — that Anna is to marry Godfrey Brand. She had been off to spend the evening and night before with Mr. and Mrs. Davis, for they were to take her to the theatre to see Modjeska, and Mr. Brand joined them there. I believe their matters were not settled till the next day; but one cannot tell about these things. You can imagine, however, how much Cousin Rupert has to ask about what has become of Anna's and my plans for establishing a "settlement;" and he wants to know if Godfrey Brand and Harry Merton belong to the poorer classes, and if we are proposing to elevate them and give them high-toned amusements.

But I will leave you to his railleries, and I will reserve many other things for that private note I have promised Cousin Rupert he shall carry to you; for he says that my letters are public property, that you read them to your mother, and that everybody knows about them.

Aunt Martha is very kind to me. She is to arrive in a day or two, and meanwhile she has written me most cordial messages. I believe that Harry in his letters to her and to my mother won their good graces directly. Before this, in her letter telling of Rupert's engagement, she explained how the rooms intended for Rupert and "his bride" would now be vacant, and she should insist upon my staying with her for the winter. How it will be, I cannot yet tell. My mother is to come for a visit after Aunt Martha's return — and then?

Meanwhile everybody is very kind. Miss Fenton, who is deeply interested in this matter, came one day, when she knew Harry was away, to take me to drive, actually bringing me an "engagement" present of a cup and saucer. It was one of those lovely afternoons we have been having lately, and we had an exquisite drive. Miss Fenton, though a great talker, knows, as the morning birds do in spring, how to manage her silences. We went out through *my* park, at the end of Commonwealth Avenue, and then to Chestnut Hill and took the drive round the Reservoir.

The next day, when Harry came, looking all worn out, — I think they do work him too hard at his office, for he seems to have to do some of everybody's work, — I inspired him so with the account of our drive that I made him start with me in the electric car, which took us to Chestnut Hill. Here Harry was seized with a fit of elegance and insisted upon taking a carriage to drive round the Reservoir — and how we talked and admired the gorgeous colors of the leaves!

I am going to send to you by Rupert the book called "Cecilia de Noël" that has excited us all so much. I do not know that he will let you have any time for reading it, but you will like to read it to your mother. I wish you could put it all through at one sitting; for it is the final chapter that gives the key-note to the whole. Yet all the way through, it is most wonderfully and wittily written, and the gospel of the closing chapter is most inspiring and elevating. I believe it is the only thing I could have read just at this time, when the whole purpose of my life seems suddenly to be changing, — only not really changing, because I can see that every aim is still to be the same. Only, instead of *my* aim, it is to be *our* aim.

It seems indeed strange to have somebody else taking up my work with me so intimately. And yet I did not know of that somebody's existence a few months ago. I had been thinking I was quite an independent sort of person, and I flattered myself that I could take care of myself, and I was looking forward to a winter when, for the first time in my life, I should have to attend to my own concerns and make my own decisions.

But only the other day I had a letter from home, telling how John Jones, a nice young fellow there, was planning to go to San Francisco. He had decided to go, but he felt rather homesick about it, as he does not know a single person in California. I was talking to Harry about it, and I said I thought it would be as hard for a young man who had never been away from his country home as it was for a young woman, to find himself among strangers.

Harry immediately said, " Let me go to the ' Lend-a-Hand ' office and see if they can't send word for somebody to meet him when he arrives." But I did n't want Harry to do my work, and then I remembered that John used to be connected with the "Look-up Legion," which did good temperance work among the children in our town, and I asked why I should not go too.

Harry was surprised to find I had never been to the "Lend-a-Hand" office here, and declared he must take me there directly. So the other morning we went together, and were so fortunate as to find both the president and the secretary there. Of course, the moment I told the story they knew exactly what club to write to, and were much interested in John Jones; and, in fact, the secretary wrote a letter at once. And now, when he arrives in San Francisco he will find some one waiting at the dock to meet him, and, in an hour's time, I venture to say, he will be quite reconciled to having to go so far away from his home. I speak confidently, for if you could see the enthusiasm of that office, you would feel as we did when we came away, — that the world is very small, and that all its inhabitants are brothers and sisters.

We went to the "Lend-a-Hand" office about half-past eleven. The president said, "At noon we have our monthly business meeting, and if you would like to know something of our work you had better stay." Of course, we felt at first as if we might be in the way, but the delightful informality and hospitality of that office overcame all scruples, and I stayed while Harry went to speak to one of the gentlemen in the outer office.

About fifteen ladies were present. Some were strangers to the others, but interest in the same sort of work made them friends from the start. There was evidently no time to lose, and it was amusing to see the earnestness with which each one would make an inquiry with regard to some work of charity, reform, or education in which she was especially interested. " What is the news from the infirmary in Alabama ? " "Has money enough come in to supply a trained nurse ? " "Have you read what the Ogontz Club is doing in Chicago ? " "Have the rooms been secured for the 'Noon Rest' in Boston ? " "There is another letter from Kansas asking for relief." "Has any letter come from Florida offering a home to the invalid ? " And here was I with my axe out in California. You won't wonder that I was a little dazed for a moment; but all these people seemed so accustomed to jumping from one of these places to another that I soon began to see that the distances were not so great.

After transacting a little necessary business — these clubs have the least machinery of any clubs I ever knew — a young lady came in from Montgomery, Alabama. It seems she and a friend opened an industrial school for colored women and children there a few years ago. When the pupils can afford to pay they do so; but many of them cannot, and some of these clubs have taken scholarships in the school. The price of the scholarships is but eight dollars per year, a small sum for the amount of good accomplished. The club which takes the scholarship is put in communication with the pupil for whom it pays, and some of the letters received from the little colored girls were exceedingly interesting.

Miss Beard told all about the school and the work that it is doing. Last year there were one hundred and ten pupils, from seven to fifty years of age, and among them were five married women. After Miss Beard had finished her talk about the industrial school, the secretary asked the ladies if they knew of positions for a stenographer, a kindergartner, a journalist, a German teacher, an industrial teacher at the South, and others which I have forgotten. Dr. Hale, the president of the " Lend-a-Hand " Clubs, said laughingly, "Because this is the ' Lend-a-Hand ' office, people think we know everything ; " and he told some funny stories which I will not repeat here. But this thing is true, that the " Lend-a-Hand " Clubs, established some twenty-one years ago, do a great deal of work. I wonder that I had never been to these rooms before, and that I had not appreciated the workings of these clubs. They seem to be an organization that minds its own business and seeks little publicity.

These rooms are at 3 Hamilton Place, far up in one of the higher stories. We looked out from the windows, down over the trees of the Common, into the busy street filled with street cars and throngs of people, and down even upon the telegraph and telephone wires that are uniting all the great cities of the world, and we could feel how the whole world may be united as one.

CHAPTER TWENTY-THIRD.

XXVI.

HARRY TO HIS MOTHER.

Boston, Nov. 10, 1891.

My dear Mother, — The long letter I wrote you last week, with dear Lucy's in the same cover, has told you so much that I need go back upon the history of those happy days only to say that every day is happier and happier, as we see life open before us and know for the first time how much better a cart goes on two wheels than it does on one. She, dear child, is constantly saying that it is a comfort and pleasure to her to have some one to rest upon; and for my part, it seems as if I had not known how to think, when I had no one to whom I could tell my thoughts as they arose. But if I begin in this strain I shall never be done, and you and the children will want to know something of my journal.

Only let me say that I do not believe in long engagements. I do not think you do. I frighten Lucy when I tell her how little I believe in them. And for one, I am already looking — I do not say for a flat; for I hate flats. I call them all tenement houses, though they be Charlesgate or the Hotel Agassiz. I am looking for a little five-room house, like those they have in Chicago, where Lucy and I may grind one axe, cook one slice of liver, and, as Chancellor Kent said, have two cups, two saucers, and one teaspoon. You must not be surprised if I tell you, or if you hear, that I have one.

I thought I was seeing something of the social life of Boston, or what I believe the newspapers call its organized life, before. But these girls know everything of which we men know nothing. Lucy has been living in a sort of university life. She talks to me about education in athletics and æsthetics and ethics and philology and geology and biology, about concerts and recitals and rehearsals, while poor I had been satisfying the cravings of an undisciplined mind by going to see Neil Burgess and his horses. I wonder if you have read Anstey's last novel, "Tourmalin's Time Cheques." The hero marries a girl who puts him through his paces, I tell you. She makes him read Buckle, even to the third volume, if there is any. I tell Lucy that she is improving my mind in the same way. But somehow she does it so agreeably that I am quite willing to be improved. Any way, there is a great deal of satisfaction in going to one of these places and coming back with her, instead of sitting in the gallery and looking over the house to see if possibly she is present. I really think that I shall get a great deal more good out of this winter than I possibly could have got without a guide so sympathetic; and, indeed, what she does not know, dear Mother, is not worth knowing.

And now I do not have to ask any Miss Fenton or Miss Brand or Miss Davis or Miss Brown or Miss Jones or Miss Smith to go with us. We are our own chaperons, and I do not think anybody looks at us in the street, or that anybody knows we are engaged.

You are so enthusiastic about "The Light of Asia" and "The Light of the World" that you will want to know, and the girls will want to know, about Sir Edwin Arnold's readings. That was really the first time that Lucy and I went together anywhere in form. For she had been very much occupied with different friends who, before the engagement was even announced to the public, came round with their congratulations. And, indeed, she and I were too much occupied in sitting and talking together in the dark parlor to want much to go to public occasions. But she roused up last Friday and said it would be a shame, as Sir Edwin Arnold was to be here for two days only, for us not to hear him, and she was not willing to be responsible to you if I missed him. So I got tickets and we went. I forget whether I have told you about the Music Hall. The reading was there. I suppose they knew the audience would be large, and so they had nearly the largest hall in Boston. I think it was too large. I should think Sir Edwin would a great deal rather read twice in a smaller room than once in such a great cavern as that is. However, his voice is strong and I had no difficulty in hearing. Some people who sat farther back complained that they lost some of the low tones. This would be a pity; for with a great deal of action and energy, he still kept a good deal of the conversational tone which gives all the value to narrative.

His pictures do not by any means do him justice. They give you an idea more than his face does, I think, of an old soldier, or, perhaps, a hard-worn statesman; but the impression of his face is very pleasing. Still, it is all marked with care. I wonder whether that has anything to do with his having lived in a tropical country, and, I suppose, having had very critical work thrown on him in young life. Because, you know, he was in the English East India service, and that is the way that he knows all these awful languages and about all these different religions. He is a man who did not have to study them out of books merely, but learned them from the people he was with; and to him a Sudra or a pariah is just as much a matter of course as old Aunt Dinah is to you, or any tramp who comes along and asks for break-fast. There was something about the naturalness with which he spoke in his little explanations of East Indian things that made us feel as if we were almost " Easterners " ourselves.

Somebody told me that he had Italian blood. I think if I had not been told so I should have guessed it from the vividness and energy of his gesture, and indeed of all his " delivery." Don't you remember what Mrs. Butler was telling us about the Italian *improvisatori*, — how they made the story real by their action even if you did not understand a word of the language ? It is by just such action, which is intense in its quickness and vivacity all the way through, that Sir Edwin Arnold makes the ballads or narratives so entertaining. The first thing he read was the address of Buddha at the end of " The Light of Asia." I don't think I should have chosen it for a beginning; but I can see that it is immensely valuable as a key to the whole system. But Lucy and I liked more the ballads and narrative pieces, which are wonderfully bright and strong.

Then Saturday afternoon is always a half-holiday with us, — the people at the office are very good about that, — and we took a train out of town to see some cousins or something of Lucy to whom she wanted to announce our great news in person. They are two sick ladies, who never go out and to whom for some reason or other she thought it was not best to write. So we had that lovely day — I wonder if it were as lovely with you — in the country, and as there was no cab at the station we had a long walk together. I am glad she is as good a walker as she is. When we came back we got out at the Huntington Avenue

station, as, by the way, almost all the passengers do
now, — they will have to make their great station
there, — just as the sun was going down. I am beginning to understand now why the real old Boston
man insists that there are no sunsets like those over
his beloved Back Bay. There is no longer any bay,
but the sunsets still linger.

Each of us gave up our own church on Sunday to
go to hear Father Hall speak. I had met Father
Hall more than once. He was at the office once
about some clothes-pins he wanted for some of his
charities, and I was detailed to talk with him. He
always wears what you or I would call a nightgown,
though it is not a nightgown, — I mean a long, black,
clerical robe, — and I think this prejudices you against
him at first. But he is that straightforward sort of
person that calls a spade a spade, and does not think
of himself more highly than he ought to think, and
thus attracts you at once. What he does not know
about poverty in Boston is not worth knowing, and
his relationship with all sorts of people, rich and
poor, is frank and unaffected and interesting. The
sermon was after your own heart. There was no
nonsense about an authoritative church or form or
formula about it; it was simply a sermon about our
being sons of God. I have noticed that some ritual-
ists are a little shy about using that particular phrase,
but Father Hall was not. And another thing I liked
was that he said nothing about the circumstances
under which he is called away from Boston. It
seemed as if he wanted to have his last words words
which should always be remembered, and I am sure
they always will be.

In the afternoon we were at quite another place.
It was an audience of what you would have called
"Jerusalem wild-cats," I think; and Mr. Champer-

noon, who was there, said it was quite like one of the old-fashioned antislavery audiences of fifty years ago. It seems, for I am telling you all this at second hand from Lucy's information, that they have organized what they call a social institute or some such thing for the systematic study of such social problems as Mr. Bellamy and Henry George and the people who have abolished the poll tax and, indeed, all the more serious politicians are discussing. I never should have heard of this in the world if it had not been for Lucy. But she was quite indignant that I should live in a city like this and be satisfied to eat its bread and butter, as she said, without knowing what its word for the present or the future is. I do not mean to say that she used any such grand phrase as this, but after hearing these people talk I feel as if I ought to get into the swing of the dialect. It did not seem to me that it promised very well for the new civilization that we waited fifteen minutes before anything began. But it seems that half the speakers who were announced had either forgotten it or had not put in an appearance at all, and they asked plaintively from the platform from time to time if Miss Conway had come in. Who Miss Conway is, I am sure I do not know; only that she was not at the place where she was announced.

However, I did not care what happened so long as I was sitting with Lucy with a good chance to talk to her; and, as Miss Tryphena Dexter said of the lecture on the Correlation of Forces, it was warm there and the seats were comfortable, and she would as lief be in one place as another, she said, and particularly liked a place where she did not have to pay for her fuel and her light. Lucy and I had not come to this pass in our housekeeping, but we sat out at the end of a settee, where we could talk to each other without

being heard, and by and by the officers and speakers
came upon the platform. Your old hero, Colonel Higginson, spoke first, and he speaks wonderfully well.
In the first place, he is a gentleman through and
through; you can see that. In the second place, he
knows what he is going to say. And in the third
place, he says it. I should say that the people who
go to such places merely to see high and lofty tumbling
would be at the beginning displeased by the quietness
of his manner; but even those people must be interested in the simplicity and frankness of the man's
talk. They had given out as a subject " Literature and
Reform." I rather think that was because they wanted
three or four people connected with literature to speak,
and they thought this would be, as we say at the
office, a good enough peg to string the line from. But
Colonel Higginson took it in a very unaffected way as
an opportunity to speak of the relations between the
literature of the United States and reform, particularly in connection with antislavery matters.

He said something about Theodore Parker which will
interest you. He said that if there had been no anti-
slavery or any great cause for him to take up, he
would have been a most extraordinary literary man.
He said his memory was so absolutely accurate that
he would take·down a book that he had not seen for
twenty years and turn directly to the page on which
there was a particular passage which he wanted to
show you; that he had that gift of reading books
rapidly and possessing himself of their contents and
remembering just what the contents were to a degree
which startled everybody who talked with him, and
which made him a living authority on subjects of the
first interest. I had myself once or twice taken out
from the Public Library a book which belonged to the
Parker collection there, and I had noticed how you oc-

casionally met a word in his own handwriting, which showed the thoroughness of his reading. It was very interesting to hear Colonel Higginson's account of the method in which he worked.

Colonel Higginson's speech closed with a sort of parallel or, if you please, contrast of Henry George and Bellamy. I never could read Henry George myself, and I have tried it a good many times; but Colonel Higginson says that his style is perfect, and that no one can escape the clearness of his logic. It seems that his views and Bellamy's are not the same; and Colonel Higginson was very funny as he spoke of his own difficulty in reconciling the opinions of two writers for both of whom he had so much esteem. Every way the speech was an interesting, and, as dear old Dr. Primrose would have said, a valuable one, and I was glad that Lucy had taken me there.

Then Dr. Hale spoke. You know how much I have had to do with him, and how much I like him. It was clear he was interested in what he was saying, too, but his prophecy was not at all about this country, but about the general position of reformers in their connection with literature. That is to say, he began by stating that the people who were connected with organized institutions and wanted to have the carriage still run in the old ruts were not apt to be the people who made the proclamations of improvement. As he put it, the priests were a little apt to crucify the prophets when they got hold of them.

Beginning in this strain, he spoke, — well, I should think twenty minutes, perhaps more, in illustration of it in various lines. You would have been delighted to hear the eulogy which he pronounced on Howells at the end. He said that Howells had it perfectly in his power to keep on all his life making accurate and exquisite pictures of the things he saw, just as a schoolgirl who is pleased with the bright colors of a tulip gets a paint-box and puts those bright colors on paper and calls that a picture. But, he said, Howells had not been satisfied in the least with this mere presentation or re-presentation of the objects before him, and that now he never wrote a page which did not have a valuable lesson for the people who wanted to uplift humanity or, as Dr. Hale himself says so often, bring in the kingdom of God. He said that Howells did not seem to him to care whether people liked to read what he wrote or not, so he could bring in, by whatever means, something which would make the world a better world and a happier world. You know how much I like Howells; so I was very glad that Dr. Hale and I are at one in that, — as, to tell the truth, we have been in a good many other things.

That evening, in the wildness of what you used to call "Sunday dissipation," we went to the Second Church to their vesper service. ˙ We had to go early, because there is a crowd and you do not get a seat unless you go early, and I did not want to make Lucy stand. It is a devout, sympathetic service, and in this instance Dr. De Normandie, who is one of the newer men here, but a man whom everybody likes, conducted it, and conducted it with great sincerity. It is this sort of thing, dear Mother, which I think you and the children lose, and which makes me wish you would come down and spend the winter here another year.

Monday night we went to the Lowell Institute. I told Lucy it must be very different from what it was in your time. The hall is the large hall of the Institute of Technology. It is called Huntington Hall, from a rich broker who gave them a lot of money. Lucy had got two tickets by sending some of her admirers to stand for her. She says that I shall have to do this for her in the future. If you are real "children

of the public " and have no tickets, you go and wait
outside, as if you were Peris at the gate of Paradise.
Then, two minutes before the lecture begins, the men
who take the tickets retire and you rush in without
any. At the same time those ticket people who had
seats rush for the empty seats which are better than
theirs, so that it is a sort of game of Puss-in-the-
Corner.

You know well enough that I should never have
gone had not Lucy been going. But all the same, I
was interested and glad I went. The lecture was
about meteorites; that is, on the substances they are
made of, largely iron by the way, and on the internal
structure of the mass, which is very curious. The last
fifteen minutes were given to stereopticon pictures,
which gave several curious points of structure better,
I think, than if you had had the meteorites in your
hand. Lucy had been to all the other lectures, so she
was able to "coach" me. I need n't say it was a very
pleasant evening.

But, really, my dear Mother, I will not try to go on
in this talk about outside things for which you and I
just now care so little. Really, I am living in a new
life all the time. I see out of different eyes, and whatever I hear has a different sound. I do not want to
write about lectures and concerts, and I do not believe
that you want to have me; and I do not want to write
about Lucy either. I want to talk about her, or to talk
with her, or, better than either, to have you see her
and know her and love her, as I am sure you will.
Did she not write you a pretty letter? And she was
so pleased, dear Mother, with the nice answer you
wrote to her.

Now do you not see that the best way of all will be
for you to come down here now? I am sure that the
girls and Nahum can run the machine, and I am sure

that they will urge you to come. You were coming any way as soon as the first of March came in, and it will be a great deal better for you to come now. Lucy thinks so as well as I. She does, seriously. There are ever so many things that she wants to consult you about in her plans for the winter, or our plans for the winter, and really, she will not be half satisfied unless she has you at hand. Then you can tell her lots of things that she ought to know, and can keep an eye on her, so that she shall not work too hard at her old schools, and so that her feet and all shall be right in wet weather, and lots of other things that nobody else will understand half as well as you will.

Mrs. Metcalf has a large room with an alcove, the same that Mrs. Ireson had and that was left suddenly unoccupied when Mrs. Ireson went to Sitka. It has a south sun, looks out on a little court that was made when people played croquet, and, for a Boston room, is very cheerful. You can bring down as many of your own things as you like. Then every evening I will take you round with Lucy to any of the shows or sights or improving assemblies where you would like to go. And daytimes I know Lucy will come in and spend half her time with you, while I am selling clothes-pins for the common cause.

There! I have not told you how good they have been to me at the office since they heard of the engagement. Every one of the gentlemen has spoken to me, even the president, and I am to have a rise at New Year. By way of special courtesy, I have been told that I need not carry any letters to the post-office, and a special boy is detailed to do my typewriting for me. I do not get quite used to having a "slavey," but I dare say I shall. Any way, if you will only come down, dear old Mother, you will see that we have plenty of time to put you through and to show you everything. As for Lucy, she is going all through the Temperance Convention, and I tell her she will get so intimate with marchionesses and duchesses that she will have nothing to say to me. But really, the only duchess is Lady Henry Somerset. Lucy will tell you all about her in her letter.

Dear Mother, I am

Always yours,

HARRY.

CHAPTER TWENTY-FOURTH.

XXVII.

LUCY TO KATE.

Boston, Nov. 12, 1891.

My dear Kate, — I find it difficult to write you any kind of a letter, for I have so many different things to tell you of that I hardly know how to choose among them, and I cannot yet write you of my own affairs because they are still so unsettled. But you tell me that my letters are of great interest to your mother who, being an old Bostonian, likes to hear of Boston things even from so new a Bostonian as I am. I feel as if just now there was a little pause in affairs before my mother comes for a promised visit to Aunt Martha. And Mrs. Merton is also coming to Boston, and after that every moment will be filled in. I shrink from seeing Mrs. Merton, though, indeed, I ought not to, for she has written me such kindly letters, and I know I shall feel happier after I have seen her.

Meanwhile the time is very busily filled in. We go to everything together, Harry and I, but of course we cannot really go to " everything " that is going on in Boston; yet it does make a chance for being with each other in the midst of all we see, and we look upon everything in a new light together. I wish I could have written you a journal of all we have done, as you would be astonished to learn how much there is to do.

We went again, the other day, to see Miss Tryphena Dexter. She amuses us very much with her remarks about the newspapers. She says that after reading the deaths and marriages in each day's paper, she looks at the accidents. " I am almost sure," she says, "that I shall find my name some day, as an old lady knocked down by a herdic at the corner of Park Square." And she also reads the Court Calendar carefully to see what damages the old people get that are knocked down. She wonders very much at seeing so often a statement of "jury out," because she thinks they ought to be attending to their business more steadily and that after they are sworn in, they ought not to be allowed to go out.

Aunt Martha, meanwhile, is at home, and Cousin Maria, and both of them most kind and cordial in their care and interest for me. Cousin Maria says she never knew so much about Boston as I have managed to find out; but then it is the " summer " Boston and not the " winter " one, which has hardly begun yet. But they are very busy already with wedding receptions, marriage occasions at church, etc.

Some muddy days came just before this lovely weather, and I avoided the street cars. In walking, I can manage to pick my way on the sidewalks and crossings so that I can reach a friend's house with even my boots clean and my skirts quite free from mud. But it is hopeless to be free from mud, if I trust to the tender mercies of the street car, — that is, of its driver. I think he has some impulse to improve upon the Aldermen's rule, printed in street cars, "to stop at the further crossing; " for he always goes "further" and regularly leaves one in a mud-puddle. I have heard that the Philadelphia street-car drivers are very careful to stop just on the crossing. I wish the drivers here could go to Philadelphia for their education, and learn how to "bring up" at least within leaping distance of the crossing. I counted up the other day, when I took the street cars frequently in my hurry, that out of six times descending from the cars, I was left five times in a mud-puddle and only once within stepping distance of the crossing-stones. These crossings, indeed, are perilous places, with an electric car, perhaps, approaching in either direction. I usually select passing between two horse cars, trusting to the supposed humanity of a horse, which prefers not to step on a human being, and might spare one from being crushed.

Perhaps you may detect from the handwriting that I did not write the paragraph above enclosed. Cousin Maria came in to summon me away — "Mr. Merton below" — and when she saw my paper on my desk she perfidiously added the above, declaring she had heard me say just such things.

I was not, however, summoned to Mr. Merton, but to two small boys who proved to be Vacation School boys that happened to have a half-holiday out, from a broken furnace in their school or something of the sort. Aunt Martha kindly suggested I should take them to the Art Museum to see the pictures by Walter Crane exhibited there, and furnished me with tickets for them and for myself. So I deserted my letter, and a long time has elapsed before I could return to it. The exhibition of the Walter Crane pictures is delightful for the children as well as for everybody. At first I was afraid it might be above the heads of my small boys, but I was pleased to find how many of the old stories that are illustrated by the pictures they knew about. I went round with them, making them read the whole of the story where we could, and they were delighted. I was enchanted myself to see the original drawings of the

"Cousin Maria came in to summon me away." — Page 310.

beloved "Toy Book," on which I was brought up, with its Cinderella and Forty Thieves and the Noah's Ark, A, B, C, etc. Here were the original sketches of "My Mother" and of "Blue Beard," too; and I was delighted with some drawings for a new book that has just appeared, "Queen Summer," with such exquisite figures of all the different flowers personified. My boys, of course, were delighted with Ali Baba and the Forty Thieves, though they had not been before acquainted with Puss in Boots. So I went through it all with them, and the story of the Marquis of Carabas delighted them; and after they had begun to find out how they could trace along the different stories, they rushed from one to the other case with delight, and at the same time behaved themselves very nicely and quietly.

Before we left, Harry himself appeared. He had been to the house for me, and Aunt Martha informed him where he would find me. So he could help me with the boys, and in getting them away, which we found a difficult task; for, of course, they wanted to go wandering all over the Art Museum. I could only get them off by promising that I would come with them some Saturday and take them all over the Museum. But Harry added a crowning touch to their pleasure, after we came out, by taking us all to see the finished part of the new Public Library building. There has been an exhibition there, which I did not get a chance to go to, so I was very glad when Harry found some one to let us in and I could see the inside of this beautiful building. We went up into the magnificent hall that looks out from the front of the building, and we quite longed to have it all finished and occupied. It will be a bit of education almost, without its books.

We looked out from its front windows into the

handsome square below, and decided that this Copley Square is perhaps now the most beautiful part of Boston. There is, indeed, the magnificent view from below the State House at the head of Park Street and Beacon Street, where one can look down the Beacon Street Mall under its splendid arch of elms. We have always admired our wide street of elms at Astney, but it cannot quite compare with this beautiful row of trees that forms a leafy arch down Beacon Street to Charles Street. And yet this wonderful archway of trees is threatened by "Rapid Transit" and plans for a Beacon Street railway! One cannot at Copley Square look down upon so beautiful a view as the Beacon Street houses command; still we admired it all over again as we came down from the Public Library out upon its front steps. We dismissed our boys, who hurried home, after thanking us for their afternoon's enjoyment, and we remained a while to look at the buildings about us, which represent fairly so many of the wonderful advantages that Boston possesses. You remember that the library stands on the upper side of a triangle, and that Huntington Avenue and Boylston Street shut in this triangle on the right and left, meeting in a point below to continue as Boylston Street. On our right was the beautiful building of the Museum of Fine Arts, rich in coloring and filling in the space till you come to the picturesque Trinity Church, which faced us. Then, at our left, was the ivy-covered front of the Second Church, where we have been on Sunday evenings to hear the vespers, and where I went often for the Sunday services in summer. Higher up, just at our left, is the New Old South, with its picturesque tower, at the corner of Dartmouth Street.

A little farther away, on Exeter Street, is the South

Congregational Church, with its Sunday services, and in its week days, too, doing much Sunday work with its "South Friendly Society" and numerous helping clubs that meet in its vestry rooms. Behind this church, on Newbury Street, is the new school for the deaf and dumb, the Horace Mann School, one of the public schools where the dumb are taught to talk though they have no voices, and to hear with closed ears. Opposite is the Prince School, and the Normal Art School is there also. Just below Copley Square stands the Institute of Technology building and that of the Natural History Society. This very afternoon there was a meeting of the Associated Charities going on in the Technology building that we had meant to go to if Harry could have come for me earlier. We heard afterwards that Robert Treat Paine addressed the meeting, and that Rev. Brooke Herford also spoke.

And I learned, too, that the Young Travellers' Aid Society was holding its meeting that very afternoon at Trinity Chapel just opposite us. We met one of its members coming away, who told us of its interesting work and how one of its matrons had reported that in the past year she had directed over eleven hundred young women to suitable homes who had arrived at the railway stations without any idea of where they were going, and some of them with hopelessly little knowledge of the place they had come to, or of their own object in coming.

But as we stood there, looking down upon all the possibilities that Boston offers in this Copley Square, we decided it would be a beautiful place to live in. So we imagined ourselves taking an apartment in its neighborhood, perhaps where we could look out upon one of its picturesque buildings, and we imagined the happy life we would lead there. We could go to every one of the courses at the Lowell Institute; we could follow up our study of the languages at some of the Technology classes; we could have our days for taking some of the boys to the rooms of the Public Library to help them about taking out books and to show them the treasures of the library; and besides making ourselves acquainted, too, with the treasures of the Art Museum, we could help others to know them; and on Sundays we should be in reach of the sound of the chimes on the Arlington Street Church, although we could not for long hear the voice of its pastor, Rev. Brooke Herford. As we walked away the setting sun streamed down Boylston Street and lighted up the beautiful tower of the New Old South, and the sky was clear with promise and beauty.

.   .   .   .

November 18.

Since writing the above I have had the meeting, which I did a little dread, with Harry's mother. I went to arrange the rooms that she occupies at Harry's present home at Mrs. Metcalf's. The rooms are very pleasant, and I took some chrysanthemums and bright flowers to make it all look gay, and I was there when she arrived, and received from her a most hearty greeting. And this was the day before my own mother arrived; so we have since had very exciting and confused times, which came in all this busy week in Boston. Harry and I found it hard to hold on to our Lowell Institute evenings and to our regular occupations; but Mrs. Merton and my mother were equally interested in the temperance meetings and in the receptions to Lady Henry Somerset and the foreign delegations.

Everybody, indeed, is enchanted with the courteous grace of Lady Henry Somerset, and I wondered if we Americans are behind in "courtesy" because we have no "court" to study it in; and then I remembered that on this point I was once reminded that we Americans consider that every woman is a princess in her own right, and therefore every woman ought to know what courtesy is, and show it always in every place she is in, which, indeed, she can make her own "court."

Mrs. Merton and my mother have been very much interested in the meetings, and they think the day at Faneuil Hall was indeed something to have come to Boston for. The meetings are so crowded that it is difficult to make any personal acquaintance with the speakers, but it is a pleasure to see how great their influence is. I was very glad to have a chance to see Miss Frances Willard preside, and to admire her readiness and the quickness with which she grasps an occasion. And then I have had one or two chances to hear Lady Henry Somerset speak, and to feel the graceful charm in all she says.

Think of it! We were present when Frances Willard made her splendid speech welcoming Lady Henry and the English delegates, at the end of which she bent down so prettily and kissed Lady Henry's hand. Everybody in the house was waving handkerchiefs, and for me I was crying my eyes out. Lady Henry made a beautiful speech, and, indeed, she is a charming person in every way.

By great luck, just at the last moment Harry got some tickets for the balcony, and we went to the banquet. The banquet, you must know, was in the Music Hall, and I do not know how many people were there. It was great fun looking down from the balconies and seeing the marchionesses and duchesses, as Harry calls them, from our superior position. Lady Henry spoke again charmingly; Miss Willard made a very good speech; Governor Long made a funny speech; and all in all it was a very nice occasion.

But here, indeed, I have some news to tell you so

wonderful and important that I do not know how I am
going to write it; I will only try to explain to you
how it has all come about. For this is, indeed, my
last letter to you, and so it must tell you everything.

All matters are now arranged, my matters, I mean.
We are to be married, Harry and I, in Christmas week!
You will have the cards. So, you see, it will be just
two weeks after your marriage; and perhaps you and
Rupert will shorten your wedding journey so that you
can be present at my occasion. If you feel in as much
of a flurry as I do now, you will hardly find the time
to read this letter or to understand it if you do. But,
indeed, I am not all the time in a flurry; I find myself in a state of great composure most of the time, for
it all seems right, and everything only too happily arranged. It is only when I stop to think of what you
will say, and my other dear friends who are not prepared for such changes, that I put myself in a flurry.
I will, however, try to send you a coherent account.

One day, in the midst of all the going and coming
of which I have been writing to you, Cousin Maria
and I were sitting in a pretty upstairs room, where
she has her embroidery work and where we come for
all our morning confabulations and plans, and I was
planning to go out to lunch with Mrs. Merton, when
we were interrupted by a summons from Aunt Martha
to go downstairs for some visitors. Something in the
glance of the eye of our little Swedish maid made me
suddenly suspect that Harry was one of the visitors,
and, indeed, she said it was Mr. Merton, but he had
not inquired for me. Cousin Maria began to laugh at
me for my apparent anxiety, and we were presently
both of us summoned down.

There, in the large front drawing-room, I found assembled quite a party; Mrs. Merton was there, and
Aunt Martha, and my own mother, and, besides, some

gentlemen I had never seen. Suddenly it seemed as if
I were on the stage, and as if there were an important
scene going on in front of the footlights, and as if I
were one of the principal characters. Only I did not
feel so frightened as I ought to; for there was Harry,
restraining himself from coming to meet me, because
"his vice-president" came forward directly to shake
hands with me. I had seen Mr. Outlake before, so he
introduced me to Mr. Champernoon, one of the directors of Harry's concern, and both of them rather stiffly
asked me how I was.

But then Mr. Outlake hurried on to what he wanted
to say, and I believe he began at the wrong end and
said first what he had meant to say last. He explained that he and the directors were planning to
establish soon a branch of their concern, which they
wanted to place in South Boston; and they especially
wished to put Mr. Harry Merton at the head of it as
overseer. They wanted somebody who would not
only direct the business there, but who would also
really oversee the men and their families and live in
South Boston, where he could watch over them in
their homes. It was quite important, he said, that
all this matter should be arranged this winter, so that
they could begin work by the first of next year.
Then he looked at me and then he looked at Harry,
and finally blundered on to say that he had himself
suggested that it would be a good plan if I would consent to Mr. Merton's making his home in South Boston. Besides this, he hurried on, it was very important to send Mr. Harry Merton to Washington in the
latter part of December to arrange about some patent
business before he should establish himself and the
concern in South Boston.

Now Harry and I have discovered that we have a
terrible way, in the midst of most serious matters, of

seeing the comic side of them; and during all this statement, which indeed was stammered out so as to seem very long, I looked round under my eyes to see the faces of all my friends looking so sober that it seemed as if the last end of all were approaching. Then I looked up at Harry opposite me, and there he was almost laughing as he came towards me, and yet very serious, too, as he said, " The thing is, Lucy, will you marry me Christmas week ? "

I don't know how it was that I could answer so quickly, but it all seemed like a play and as if it were my part to give him my hand and to say that if he wanted it I would. And Harry has since declared that he had to come forward then; for he was very much afraid that the vice-president was going to make his offer of marriage for him!

So we all stood up in a row, and everybody shook hands, and it might have been the marriage itself, it was all so solemn. While Mr. Outlake was talking about South Boston I stole a glance at Aunt Martha, and she looked very grim; for she was disgusted at the idea of our living there. But when the question of a marriage in Christmas week came up, her face changed entirely; for the idea of a wedding delights her heart. She has all along been disappointed that your wedding and Rupert's is not to take place here in Boston, and she insists, therefore, that we shall be married here at her house, though I confess I should like to go back to our dear Astney. And so this wondrous scene closed; the gentlemen would not stay to lunch, but everybody else did.

Harry has since taken occasion to insist that I shall not decide to live in South Boston ‑unless I really want to and my friends are willing. He is sure that he can arrange to be there when he is needed, wher-ever we may decide to live. So he has been taking me to look at apartments in the neighborhood of Copley Square, because that was our vision of happiness that afternoon of which I have written you. And we have had most amusing times answering advertisements and looking up houses and trying to determine the delicate line that divides the apartment from the tenement, as we scorn the word "flat," that combines the two.

We have seen all sorts of funny things. One man told us, when we looked at his house, that we should not need any fires, as the sun shone there all day, and none of his people ever complained of the cold. And Harry and his mother have been exploring also in South Boston, and they, too, bring amusing accounts of their adventures. Finally, we decided that we had better find our house and get it in order, so that we can occupy it as soon as we return from Washington.

This visit to Washington and the plan of the wedding seem to reconcile Aunt Martha to the whole affair. She has already written a pile of letters of introduction for us to influential friends of hers in Washington, and I think she has written a number to precede us. And she plans with my mother to put the finishing touches to our house while we are gone. She even consented to go with Harry and me to South Boston, and the other day along we went with my mother, to see the results of his investigations.

We drove there in Aunt Martha's carriage, and indeed it was as good as a play to see how her nose went up as we passed through the close streets of the South Cove and all in among the railroad tracks beyond. Even my mother's face wore a somewhat anxious expression. But presently, when we came out into wider streets between rows of handsome, new brick houses, Aunt Martha began to look much surprised. "I had no idea there was anything of this sort here," she exclaimed.

So we went on and stopped before a house, where an elevator carried us to the upper story, and the doors opened for us upon a suite of large, airy, sunny rooms. Harry and I have had a discussion over small and large rooms. I have been fascinated with an apartment with tiny little rooms, all most comfortably arranged with every convenience, but which might have been all put into one of the large rooms we were now looking at. But Harry has always objected to the little rooms: they might look cosey, he agreed, and one could fit them up charmingly; but he has always represented the large size of certain family bookcases he depends upon bringing into his own apartments. "And then," he would say, "what will you do with your parties of Vacation School pupils that you propose to have, and how are you going to accommodate all the men and their families who are to come and see us from the factory?"

So I saw directly that these large rooms were after Harry's own heart. And, indeed, I saw at the same time that they must needs be after my own heart. For opposite me were some broad windows, and when Harry took me up to them we looked out upon a glorious view, — the ideal view that, you know, I had always supposed we should see from every house in Boston! Here we could see spread before us the beautiful harbor, all dotted with islands, and between them, far beyond, the horizon of the sea.

You know how I have longed for this, and how I growled a little when I first came, and complained that I supposed that Boston was a seaport, but that I could see this water view only when I drove with Aunt Martha far away to the lovely hill at the Arnold Arboretum. And Harry declares that I was hunting for this from the cupola of the State House and from the top of Bunker Hill Monument and from the Ames

Building elevator, etc. And here I was to have it in our own home; for so I directly determined it must be.

I turned back to look into the room to see Aunt Martha and mamma pacing it to calculate about the carpets. I fancied Harry's bookcases there, filled with the companions of our future evenings. Here we shall find Harry's ancestral edition of "Sandford and Merton" and mine of Miss Edgeworth's "Harry and Lucy." And both of us fell to imagining how we would invite the boys and girls and the men and women in our neighborhood to help us enjoy our happy evenings there; and how first we would begin by making it a happy home, a home of our own enjoyment in its highest sense, in the full life of which we could have the best, and then begin to impart it to others.

I took Aunt Martha to the windows, and she exclaimed, "Lucy, your view is really superior to what Kate's will be!" Harry and I looked at each other smiling; even Aunt Martha was forced to acknowledge that our view was equal to that from the "water side" of Beacon Street!

We lingered before the windows with more serious thoughts. Whatever might be our life within those rooms, here we could find inspiration always in looking out upon that horizon line. And yet, wherever we were, we said, and however full our life might be with its little crowding duties, we could always keep before us the idea of a horizon line, — of something beyond.

From the Boston Daily Argus.

MARRIED at Astney, Vermont, by Rev. Dr. Primrose, of Atherton, Mr. HARRY MERTON, of Boston, and Miss LUCY SANDFORD, of Astney.